RON RICHARD

GROUP SIX AND THE IMPERIUM

LET THE GAMES BEGIN

CHRISTOPHER MATTHEWS PUBLISHING

GROUP SIX SERIES

GROUP SIX AND THE RIVER
Of Water and Brimstone

GROUP SIX AND THE CRATER
Magic is Born

GROUP SIX AND THE IMPERIUM
Let the Games Begin

RON RICHARD

GROUP SIX AND THE IMPERIUM

LET THE GAMES BEGIN

Group Six and the Imperium, *Let the Games Begin*
by Ron Richard

First Edition May 2024

Christopher Matthews Publishing
Gleneden Beach, Oregon
ChristopherMatthewsPub.com

ISBN:
978-1-945146-56-5 (hc)
978-1-944072-99-5 (pb)
978-1-944072-98-8 (epub)

Library of Congress Control Number: 2024905828
Genre: *magic, fantasy, adventure, humorous, mythical creatures*

Cover design and formatting by Suzanne Fyhrie Parrott
Cover art by Gaurav Srivastava (@hephaestusart, Fiverr.com), © Ron Richard

Please provide feedback

10 9 8 7 6 5 4 3 2 1

Printed in U.S.A.

For Martha - The Victor

TABLE OF CONTENTS

N
W
E
S
OORIA
THE NORTHLANDS
AMORAN SEA
OCEAN
AXENON ESCAPRMENT
OSTICA
CRYSTAL PALACE
TALUS RIVER
PRAKIN'S PASS
BREEOS
ABAKAAR
WITCHHEART CRATER
SERIN SEA
ERIM RIVER
TRESK
NOXUS RIVER
SYLVAS
TRESKAN IMPERIUM
LEAGUES
0
100
200
300
400
500

MAJOR CHARACTERS

GROUP SIX

SERENA

A 27-year-old Macai Northlands Warrior. A fierce fighter, she values honor in battle above all else.

ORCHID

A 30-year-old Macai. Raised by Eryndi foster parents, she practices the nature based Worldly Magic, which is unusual for a Macai.

FOXX

A 33-year-old self-taught Macai Magician, inventor of the Knowing Spell, which allows him to read moods and influence others.

TRESADO (trĕ-'sä-dō)

A 45-year-old Eryndi Magician who practices the more powerful Absolute Magic.

THE TRESKAN IMPERIUM

1332 years ago

ELDER TRESKA
Eryndi founder of Tresk

FARINNIA
Aide to Elder Treska

ZAROSEN
Eryndi shipping coordinator; son of Jarayan

1301 years ago

ELDER YURZAN
Successor to Elder Treska

PARRALON and **QUEROKAN**
Young Government Magicians

1287 years ago

PARMONERA and **JERRAICA**
Explorers from Tresk

QUEROKAN
Senior expedition leader

1232 years ago

CHIEF PRESIDER CONSTANZIA
Head of the fledgling Coalition

1014 years ago

ONDERAST
Magician in the city of Yessua

GENERAL KOROVEL
Commander of Yessuan military forces

TERSIAN
Young dirk fisherman just starting out

849 years ago

TERSIAN
Wealthy businessman – owner of a large fishing/shipping fleet on the Serin Sea

BORA
Tersian's servant

SENATOR BALATINE
Influential Treskan politician

DEXOS
Co-commander of Tersian's expedition

BURTENAL
Researcher

PRAXAN
Researcher

107 years ago

IMPERATRIX ALYTHYA OF TRESK (ă-'lēth-ē-ə)
Ruler of the Treskan Coalition

OCTAVIA
Twin sister of Imperatrix Alythya

DEMENTUS, THE MAD TRESKAN
Noted traveler of the world – considered semi-mythical

MERAK
Strange visitor to Tresk

Present Day

IMPERATOR MERAK (mə-'răk)
Ruler of the Treskan Imperium

GENERAL PRIXUS SCAPULUS
Commander of the Treskan 12th Legion

PRIMUS BARRIA
Adjutant to General Scapulus

PRIMUS LUCILLIA MANGINUS
Commander of the Third Cohort of the 38th Forward Legion

STICKITUS OWTUS
Aide to Imperator Merak

VARYUS
Young Treskan officer

ROCKUS
Treskan Legionnaire

DANIKAN PRISSILLIA TYRE
Revolutionary or terrorist, depending on who you ask

FEELIA EFFICIOUS
Hospitality coordinator at the Imperial Residence

SEQUIOUS FINNIK
Propriety Monitor at the Imperial Residence

KARTIA SCINTILLUS
Imperial jeweler

TERNKEUS
Head jailer at Stadium

PHAROX
Centurian in charge of Stadium prisoners

SPIKY
Stadium prisoner

SEVERUS
Stadium prisoner

PUGGNAYSHUS
Stadium prisoner

RUGLUM
Stadium guard

SUTURUS
Stadium healer

LITTLE OLD ERYNDI LADY
Stadium visitor

VOCALUS PROJECTIVUS
Stadium Emcee

PRIMUS KAPATIUS AMPOL
Head of the Imperial Guard

BUMPUS
Civilian yard worker

MAGISTER PETRARUS
Weekly Honor Day religion teacher

TEENIA
Student

DORFUS
Student

GLADIATORS:

SIXTUS MANLIUS - THE MERAKIAN MAULER
HUMFREY OF TORD - THE ISLAND MENACE
MARCELLYA OF TRESK - GUNBOAT MARCY
MAN MOUNTAIN NEMOSTHENES
SCREAMIN' SAMMY SOULTAKER
MEGANA THE ICE QUEEN
PYROXEMUS THE TOASTER (WITH THE MOSTER)
SQUIRE BUCKMINSTER GOLD

MISCELLANEOUS

PROFESSOR ABADIAH GENERAX
Owner/Operator of Professor Generax's Traveling World of Wonders – mentor to Foxx

JAKUNDARANA SLIVERSHKANENT TRYSTELLIAR
Steward of the Crystal Palace –also known as Jakki.

MISHANNA and REVINAL
Eryndi foster-parents of Orchid

ELDER KAZOREL
Director of the Melosian Academy of Worldly Arts

PROFESSOR JENNICK
Professor of Life Empathy

HALFKLAM THE NAVIGATOR
God of Raiding in Northlands mythology

KATRINA THE DEFIANT
Northlands Warrior and mentor to Serena

GUNNAR THE STEADFAST
Northlands Warrior and father of Serena Brimstone

VINGRID THE SHADOW
Northlands Warrior

TRIANNA OF SYLVAS
Poetess to the Glades

PROFESSOR HARIEL
Dean of Kadizio University

QUINTELL OF MERON
Apothecary, Soothsayer, Teller of Tales

HROLVAD THE BERSERKER ('rōl-väd)
A legendary hero and founder of Northlands culture

MARMOSEL
Adolescent friend of Tresado's

HEROIC HARE
A popular children's story character

PROLOGUE

1014 Years Ago – Mountain Kingdom of Yessua

The undeclared war had lasted over two years now. The Macai seemed inexhaustible. For every savage killed or captured, there were three to take their place. Their attacks on travelers were getting more frequent and simply could not be allowed to continue. The Eryndi caravans traveling the new tunnel and road through the mountains had proven to be a huge boon to commerce. Trade flowed back and forth between the city-states of the great plains to the east and the Treskan Coalition to the West. The mountain city of Yessua was right in between and served as a useful supply and recreation stop. The proprietors of gambling houses and taverns were making a fortune from traders with their profits burning holes in their pockets. But with these Macai raids becoming more frequent, merchants were hesitant to risk their goods and lives. Something had to be done for the sake of Yessua's economic future.

Commanding generals had come and gone. Every new battle plan looked great on paper, but somehow, the Macai always seemed to evade them. They knew the mountains too well. Every hidden cave and gulley served as an escape route or an ambush point. Now, a new plan was coming to fruition, but it didn't come from the mind of a military Eryndi. Specifically, it originated in the ninth tent from the north end of the third row, the tent of Onderast the Magician.

"It works! Gods' Woes, Bying, IT WORKS!"

Onderast grabbed his assistant by the shoulders and shook her until her head nearly fell off. Bying was used to these outbursts from her superior. They were always either ecstatic expressions of joy or howls of anguish. In his excitement, he tried to gather his papers, put on his jacket, slurp from his mug, and dig a finger into one of his cone-shaped ears to deal with an itch – all at the same time.

"Get me an appointment with the staff, Bying!" he said, nearly choking on his drink.

"Right away, sir," replied Bying in her usual calm, patient way.

She had already exited the tent when Onderast added to his order.

"And tell them I will need more Macai to demonstrate on – at least eight of them. Ten would be better! Yes, I will need ten savages, properly restrained, of course and . . . use of the command tent. Yes, I will definitely need the command tent and chairs for the staff. FOOD! Don't forget to get refreshments for everybody. All right, Bying, that's everything. Run and tell them that I have a way to win this war. That ought to impress those stonehead soldiers. Now on your way, hurry!"

Onderast, with his lack of attention span, did not even notice his assistant was long gone. His gaze returned to the captive Macai still tied to the chair. The man, whose murderous, wild-eyed manner had turned to calm, smiling submission, sat contemplating a bug crawling up the tent pole.

"Yes, my barbarian friend, you and your kind will make excellent servants. No, really! You'll be SO happy – not living like animals in the muck, eating filth and rats. You'll have warm beds, good food, and Eryndi masters that will treat you just as though you're members of the family."

It didn't take much convincing to authorize Onderast's plan. Several senior members of the Yessuan government were also wealthy merchants with considerable investments in the besieged caravan trade. Others, like commanding General Korovel, had a personal stake. His bondmate and adopted baby daughter had been killed last year in an attack upon the caravan they were traveling in. Everyone had their own motivation to stop the raids, whether it was to keep the wagons rolling, personal revenge, or to speed along the prospect of a rich supply of new laborers. King Prakin authorized raising an army of elite soldiers to deal with the Macai.

The statisticians had predicted that victory would occur between twelve to sixteen months. It was also predicted, however, that the Yessuans would suffer at least two thousand casualties during that time. More importantly, an expenditure of over eighty thousand gold coins would be necessary just to keep the army functioning. That, plus the incalculable loss of trade profits, made it imperative to try anything to end this costly conflict.

It was fortuitous for Onderast that this desperation came at this time. The development of his spell that he claimed would instantly tame the beasts into cooperative workers was quickly stamped with a seal of approval by all concerned. The lucky Magician and future zillionaire now proudly marched along the road behind General Korovel and his entourage. The young Eryndi was about to gain honor and fame for his role in stopping the Macai. He could feel it in his bones. He thought about working on his humble but triumphant victory speech yet decided it would be more prudent to prepare his mind for the task at hand.

The spell was complicated, even more so now that Onderast added the seeking element to the formula. To subjugate Macai prisoners one at a time, as he did in the demonstration, was one thing, but there were thousands of the savages out there somewhere. That was the beauty of his new spell, though. To affect a multitude, he would use their own numbers against them.

Magic is everywhere, in the air, the plants, the animals, the soil; but to shape and direct it takes a mind. His own psyche was the origin point. When the time came, Onderast would initiate the spell designed to seek out Macai minds and scramble their thoughts. Phase two of the spell would then reprogram their simple, animal brains with a desire for peace, contentment, and, of course, utter civility. The Macai would become so tame that they wouldn't need to be confined or even guarded. The beasts could be told to follow the army's tracks back to the city, where they would be introduced to their new homes and given their tasks to perform. The first target area was in the creek draw just ahead, where Intelligence reported that a group of about two hundred savages were camped. It would begin there. It would then be a simple matter to methodically move through the passes, subjugating every Macai band they encountered until all resistance ceased.

The enemy camp was less than half a league ahead, just below the ridge. General Korovel called a halt and summoned his aides. There was a quick, hushed conference, which Onderast was not privy to, but he had enough to think about.

The soldiers began a complicated dance as the archers went one way, the infantry another. The mounted cavalry took up position at the point. Not having military training beyond Basic, Onderast found the whole rigamarole rather tedious. He was a Magician, not a soldier. Korovel caught Onderast's eye and pointed a fat finger at him.

It was time. Onderast advanced to the head of the column. He took a deep breath and let it out slowly. His mind connected to the power surrounding him. When he was ready, the young Magician sent his spell formula into the ether. This version was much more powerful than the tests he had performed on the Macai prisoners. To affect two hundred of them at a distance would require more oomph. For that, the savages themselves would fill the need.

The processing power of Magic took hold. The invisible spell silently crawled its way through the fabric of Magic over the edge of the ridge and down into the camp of the Macai. Onderast was not where he could observe the effect of his spell, but in his Magical Eryndi way, he could feel that it worked. He turned around and nodded to his commanding officer. General Korovel himself walked up the hill to join his scouts, who were on their bellies, concealed by brush and observing the spectacle below.

There were two things that Onderast didn't know. Number one was the fact that there were not two hundred of the enemy ahead but more like seven thousand. The Macai had laid a cunning trap for the Eryndi. There were indeed two hundred of them intentionally out in the open where they could be seen by Korovel's scouts. The rest were concealed up among the high crags, waiting. The Eryndi army was surrounded and didn't know it. The second thing Onderast didn't know was that General Korovel had a plan of his own.

The spell definitely had the desired effect. The two hundred Macai were all grasping their heads as if hearing some high-pitched noise. Some of the savages fell to their knees as though exhausted. Others simply sat or reclined on the ground and made themselves comfortable. There were dropped weapons and blank stares all around.

The General clapped his hands in triumph. The Macai below were all incapacitated or uncaring. He pointed his all-authoritative finger at his aide, who knew what it meant and gave the order.

"Archers! Deploy to the ridge! Fix your targets!"

"Wait . . ."

Onderast was confused. This wasn't how it was supposed to go . . .

"LOOSE!"

A volley of over a hundred arrows angrily sped down upon the helpless Macai like a swarm of needle wasps. The weapons were most effective. Half the Macai were dead or dying, the wounded ones in distress but curiously uncaring. Another round or two from the archers would have finished the Macai, but that's no fun.

"Cavalry! Advance! Full charge!"

"Wait . . ."

The horse-mounted soldiers whooped with excitement as they spurred their equally eager mounts down the slope to the creek draw. Lances and long cavalry sabers took a frightful toll on the surviving Macai.

"Infantry! Advance! Mop 'em up!"

"NOOOOOO!!!"

The foot soldiers were not to be deprived of their fair share of the carnage. The few savages who were still alive did not remain so for long. A few minutes later, the triumphant Yessuan soldiers were gleefully engaged in collecting souvenirs – pelts and bone necklaces, daggers made of deer horn, and axes of stone. Nothing to compare to the steel weapons of the Eryndi, but stuff that would look great above the mantlepieces back home.

General Korovel smiled grimly as he looked upon his revenge. In his long-awaited gloating, he was oblivious to Onderast's pleas.

"General! General! This is not right! They weren't supposed to die! What about prisoners, sir?!"

The battalion of Eryndi was now becoming gradually aware of a strange sound, or more accurately, a vibration that started as a low hum. It was soon accompanied by the ominous rising of thousands of angry voices joined as one. From the surrounding crags, there was movement in all directions. Hosts of previously hidden Macai were descending the slopes and charging the scattered Eryndi. Korovel spun his horse around, looking for an escape route, but it was hopeless.

"SAVAGES! Reform your units! Reform your units!"

The soldiers scrambled to regroup, but with hostiles approaching from all sides, there was no place to form a line.

Onderast looked with terror at his approaching doom. He also heard that the vibration in the air was becoming more pronounced. It had grown to a loud buzz that vibrated his skull all the way into his teeth. He realized with confusion that he was the source.

"Wait . . . General, Sir . . . the spell is not yet finished!"

The Macai were almost upon them. The Eryndi archers got off a couple of volleys but didn't manage to hit much. The penetrating noise grew stronger and stronger. Before the two mismatched armies could actually come together and clash, soldiers on both sides began dropping in their tracks, holding their heads and screaming in pain.

Onderast felt his own consciousness slipping into darkness. Before he passed out, the young Eryndi Magician realized something. His spell, designed to seek out Macai minds and disable them, had spectacularly backfired.

Korovel's horse, which was also in apparent mental distress, bucked wildly and threw the General out of the saddle and into a bush. He stumbled over to Onderast and grabbed him by the tunic.

"Stop the spell . . . STOP THE SPELL!!!"

"I can't," slurred Onderast, almost incoherently. *"It's feeding on itself. It won't stop until . . . no more . . . minds."*

Korovel didn't hear him. No one on that field of battle ever heard anything again. Both armies, their horses, and even the flies that followed them were on the ground, their minds turned to mush.

The spell traveled from mind to mind, following its instructions. It was drawn to the processing power of a brain, whether it came from an evolved Eryndi or a dung beetle. The spell gained power exponentially with every mind it encountered. Birds, bugs, spiders, and snakes were affected as much as the Macai and Eryndi. It would have continued on forever and eventually destroyed every life on Lurra, but fortunately that didn't happen. The energy of Magic is quite plentiful but not inexhaustible.

The demand for power finally overwhelmed the ability of Magic to produce it. The fabric of the universe for twenty leagues in all directions, including up and down, imploded upon itself, taking the mountain peaks and valleys with it. In less than three beats, a great, bowl-shaped chasm of infinite nothingness appeared in this mountainous land. A terrible half-beat later, the implosion reversed itself. Chunks of rock strata the size of villages were hurled from the void to slowly crash back down, creating new mountains and destroying existing ones. The nearby city of Yessua and everything in a twenty-league radius was no more.

PART I:
THE MOUNTAINS

CHAPTER 1

Green vs Green, Sand Between;
Bricks to Sticks, and Candlewicks;
Heart and Heart, and Win and Loss;
Strife and Life Amongst the Moss;
The Rest Don't Rhyme . . .

- Travelogue of Dementus
the Mad Treskan

Today – Weekend Honor Day, Kondo 8-21876

The weather sucked. It really, *really* sucked. The craggy rocks along the narrow, tortuous trail occasionally deflected some of the wind, but mostly they created tricky, unexpected gusts that would reach into your mouth and pull the breath right out of your lungs. That wasn't so bad. Wind could be tolerated. Then it started to rain cold, pelting drops as big as silver paleens. The brave souls of Group Six hunched over in their saddles and pulled their ponchos tighter against the liquid assault.

Inexhaustible rivulets of water slithered across the narrow trail, soaking into the parched ground. Whatever mineral made up the fine dust in these mountains turned to oily slime when it got wet. It was the horses who had to deal with it. Their hooves sank deeper and deeper into the muck, making wet *shluck, shluck* sounds as they struggled along. One misstep and horse and rider could find themselves plunging down a hundred reaches of the gorge that yawned on their left. This also could be dealt with simply because there was nowhere else to go. It was when the rain turned into great balls of ice that even the nature-loving Orchid had to make a comment.

"Boy, the weather really *sucks!*"

"I don't know what we'd do without you, Orchid," quipped Foxx. "These up-to-date news alerts are what every stalwart adventurer needs."

"You wouldn't know *stalwart* if it bit you on your silk-wearin' ass!" hollered the blonde-maned Serena from the head of the trail. The way the wind was howling, they had to yell. "You think this is cold? In the Northlands, this is a spring day!"

"This trip sure would have been easier in the Queen's coach," said Tresado wistfully. He was the only Eryndi of the group. In general, an Eryndi is smaller and lighter than the more numerous Macai of this world of Lurra, but Tresado's swayback horse had to deal with his generous paunch and plentiful backside. Tresado had also gained a stone or two last month before leaving the Crystal Palace with its rich food.

"It was so bloody comfortable," he whined. "Smooth ride, Magical heater, sealed cabin . . . and it was worth a fortune. It probably belongs to some sod farmer now."

"You're pissed because you lost a bunch of money?" snarled Serena. "A good war horse like what Queen Minore gave me is worth a hell of a lot more than a bunch of loot!"

Orchid pulled her poncho tighter across her chest as a cold gust of wind snuck beneath her clothing like a cheap feel. "That's what we had! There were ten full casks of Abakaarian ale in that wagon!"

"Not to mention the seven stone of silver plate, plus the 3000 gold tormacs *each* and the chest of gems, which I appraised at 7250 tormacs by itself!" This was, at the very least, the 74th time Foxx had listed their losses.

"Did you count the copper gendrin I found in the cushion?" shot back Serena.

The bitch session continued on, getting louder and more vindictive with every drop in temperature and every gust of wind. Orchid was able to use her Worldly Magic skills to deflect some of the moisture and cold from the four horses and riders, but it was taxing and hard to maintain for great lengths of time. She shifted in her saddle to try to restore some circulation in her deadened butt and muttered to herself.

"Twigs, some birthday this turned out to be . . ."

Kondo 8, 21860 –
Exactly 16 Years ago – Orchid

Mishanna rapped gently on her adopted daughter's closed door.

"Orchid? This party is for you, you know."

Silence.

"May I come in?"

The answer would have been inaudible to all but Eryndi ears.

"If you wish."

Orchid sat cross-legged on her sleeping mat, hands clutching a wad of her party dress, which was being crushed into a wrinkled mass. Mishanna also noted the red swelling below the eyes.

"You know, I seem to remember feeling sad around my fourteenth birthday, too."

No response.

"If it's any consolation, those first couple weeks of school kept me so busy, the homesickness went away pretty quickly."

Mishanna studied her daughter's silent expression for a moment. As a Tintani District Judge, she had learned to read faces and intents. "But that's not the problem here, is it?"

Orchid looked up at the only mother she had ever known, and the tears began flowing again.

"How am I supposed to keep up? Eryndi are born to practice Worldly Magic! I know Father wants me to become a healer like him, but those few lessons he gave me showed me that I'm just not cut out for that. An Eryndi can learn to ease pain while still in First School! It took me weeks to master even that basic spell! I'm going to wash out, Mother . . . I'm going to wash out!"

"You know you're not the only Macai to attend the Melosion Academy."

"But I'm the only Macai enrolled *this* year!"

"Maybe, but some of those before you went on to become very skillful healers."

"Mother, I looked at the records. Some of *them* washed out!"

"And some Eryndi have also washed out. Success depends on how hard you work, not the shape of your ears."

Mishanna held her daughter tightly.

"Orchid, you know we can feel what others are feeling. Your Father and I both feel . . . no, we *know* that you have the talent and brains to achieve this."

"I thought that only worked between Eryndi," Orchid sobbed into her mother's sleeve.

"No, it also works with stubborn, thick-headed daughters. In fact, let me tell you this. You are right in one thing. Making it through four years of the Academy will be grueling. Being the only Macai this year won't help. All the students will be judged and graded on a comparative basis. But I'll tell you something else. Your best weapon to fight this is the fact that you *are* stubborn and thick-headed. You can stand up to your peers better than anyone I've ever seen. Remember that teasing episode when you were about nine or so? You were a head taller than any of those Eryndi girls who were ragging on you and could have flattened any of them. As I recall, you defended yourself with calm, logical arguments and they left you alone after that."

Orchid wiped her nose and snickered.

"I never told you this, Mother, but Basali and Tendra started up again the next day in the locker room . . . I flattened both of them."

"Oh," Mishanna shrugged. "Well, maybe that's what it will take at the Academy, too."

Orchid squeezed her mother hard. Mishanna pulled out a soft *mopa* leaf from her sleeve and wiped away the tears from both her daughter's face and her own.

"Now, let's get you back to your birthday party before all the cake is gone."

* * *

♪

May your birthday be swell;
Time to bid you farewell;
You're fourteen, Dear Orchid;
And your cake is caramel!

- TRADITIONAL ERYNDI BIRTHDAY SONG CELEBRATING OFFICIAL ADULTHOOD, SUNG WITH THE CUTTING OF THE TRADITIONAL CARAMEL CAKE.

Today – Western Perlan frontier

Other than sniping at each other, the only thing Group Six could do was to keep traveling. One plan had been to head north to the Amoran Sea and find adventure amongst the many traders and pirates that plied those waters. The other had been to head back toward Abakaar and get on the road to the Treskan Imperium that they had been on when they were "rescued."

Weeks before, the sentient Crystal Palace had accidentally teleported Group Six nearly a thousand leagues away to a danger-filled area near the canyon city of Abakaar. While there, they became involved in a violent incident and saved the life of the city's ruler, Queen Minore. In gratitude, she gifted them with her luxurious personal coach filled with an enormous pile of supplies and treasure. The Crystal Palace felt responsible for accidentally sending the group into a perceived danger. After finally locating them, it retrieved Group Six using the same spell. However, their coach and loot were left behind, and they were unceremoniously returned with hardly a copper coin among them.

They were not happy with Jakki and the Crystal Palace for rescuing them. The Steward of the Palace had offered an apology, saying things like, "I just wanted you to be safe!" and "I felt it was my responsibility!" Group Six's indignant attitude of '*But we were rich!*' wore rather thin on Jakki after a while. She allowed them to stay for a limited time, but what she saw as ungrateful, petulant whining led her to withhold any kind of compensation.

For two weeks, the impoverished quartet got by on whatever money they could scrape together or earn at the Palace. Foxx's gambling skills had contributed the majority of their slowly growing road stake. Eventually, they amassed enough money to purchase the four used-up mounts they rode and some meager trail food. The horse-trading had taken well into the aftermidday, and the original plan was to leave the next morning. As was usual with Group Six's original plans, it changed quickly and unexpectedly. Foxx didn't immediately tell them why.

The first day of travel away from the Palace could have been relatively comfortable. The switchback road leading down the slope of Mount Boronay was intentionally lined with fruit trees and grassy areas for animal grazing – all for the benefit of the Palace customers. Orchid, Serena, and Tresado would have been okay with a leisurely pace through this part of the trip had Foxx not been surreptitiously urging them on with his Knowing Spell. He seemed determined to break every speed record, putting distance between Group Six and the Crystal Palace and pushing his horse to the limit of its old, worn-out legs. It wasn't until they were a good three days away that he relented in his haste. Besides, his horse almost expired a couple of times, and he didn't want to walk. Still, Foxx looked back over his shoulder a lot.

Eventually, they reached a crossroads. Straight led to the eastern plains, right to the south toward Abakaar, and left to the north. Tresado and Serena were for heading left on the road to the distant Amoran Sea. At Orchid's urging, they had chosen the southern route toward the Perlan Mountains. Then they made the western detour into the wilderness, with the intent of reaching the Treskan Imperium, and Foxx seemed to finally relax.

That's when the nasty weather kicked up, and Group Six was miserable for days. The horses they were riding were nearly used up. The one that Serena rode farted constantly, and she was always in the lead.

"We're headed down!"

Serena didn't have to yell so loud now. The wind had calmed, and the hail had mostly stopped. The trail they followed rose and fell sharply as it snaked along the sheer south face of what was called Mount Blade. It twisted and turned so much that there was no looking back up the trail for more than a hundred reaches.

"You sure?" whined Foxx.

"She's sure," said Orchid, "cuz so am I."

"Me, too." Tresado really didn't need to remind them of that. They were all aware that, as an Eryndi, Tresado knew things . . . things like which way was north and what foods were unsafe to eat . . . and whether a trail was ascending or descending.

"Does that mean we found it?" asked Foxx.

"When we get past this mountain and to a valley, that's when we found it," replied Orchid.

In a way, their current predicament was Orchid's fault. A couple of weeks ago, a trader that she met at the Crystal Palace had told her a story . . .

A couple of weeks ago – The Crystal Palace

"You've never heard the story of Prakin's Pass?"

Orchid put on her best skeptical look.

"Should I have?"

"Probably not, if you've never spoken to me before, which is certainly my loss. Allow me to formally introduce myself. I am . . ."

"Quintell of Meron; Apothecary, Soothsayer, Teller of Tales," interrupted Orchid.

"Ah, so you do know me."

"I'm just reading what it says on your gaudy sign. I've . . . *noticed* you on the trading floor a few times."

"I am flattered beyond words." The Eryndi trader had a devilishly charming grin and breath that smelt pleasantly of griffleberries. His dark skin contrasted beautifully with his silvery hair and braided beard.

"Prakin's Pass, of which you ask, is a fabled lost road through the mountains connecting these eastern lands to the Treskan Imperium."

"I didn't ask, actually . . ."

"Construction of the road was begun by King Prakin the First of the Yessuan Mountain Kingdom more than a millennium ago. For generations, thousands of workers toiled to cut their way through the granite barriers . . . tunnels and channels and whole mountainsides carved out with sweat and blood and Magic. Prakin's hope was that in connecting the lands of the east and west, trade and goodwill would blossom."

"How interesting, but . . ."

"In those ancient times," continued Quintell without a pause, "the old king's wish was finally completed by his grandson over a century later. The new road through the mountains was soon heavily trodden with caravans and travelers from all surrounding countries. Commerce and friendly relations flourished!"

"I was told you deal in Treskan dermal gel . . ."

Quintell's handsome face turned foreboding. "Then . . . the dark times began!"

He would do well on the stage, thought Orchid.

"From out of the deep caves and hidden valleys of those mysterious mountains came hordes of savages . . . fearsome, painted Macai that preyed upon the peaceful caravans. Many of the Eryndi travelers and merchants were killed. Many others were taken, *but only the Macai workers.*"

"Dermal gel?"

"Finally, in retaliation, King Prakin the Third gathered an army of his finest warriors and Magicians to combat the savages. What subsequently occurred became known as *The Great Yessuan Cataclysm.* The army departed the city to hunt for the raiders. Soon after, a great quake shook the very foundations of Lurra. It is said the mountains themselves took revenge upon men for their violence and hatred and for the wounds inflicted upon the land in carving out the pass. The great city of Yessua and the road were buried forever 'neath rock and soil. To complete the cleansing, the gods unleashed torrential rains and floods to wash away any remaining trace of the sins of men. The pass through the mountains and the city have remained lost to mortal eyes ever since. All that remain are the ghosts of the devastated army. On a moonless night, their mournful songs drift upon the mountain winds."

At this point, Orchid was about to turn and leave. Quintell read her intent and gently took her hand. Orchid paused, finding his touch to be not all that repulsive.

"The location of this legendary passage to the Imperium could be worth an Emperor's ransom to the right people," said Quintell. "The closest existing pass is far to the south near Witchheart Crater. Why, the Treskans themselves have been searching for another way through the impenetrable mountains for a hundred years. Merak would see his Imperium expand even further into the interior!"

"Bully for him, but now . . ."

"Many have searched, many have claimed success, but none have ever proven it. Every explorer and adventurer from Efeegus of Linn to Dementus the Mad Treskan is rumored to have penetrated the mountains' secret. Many see the pass as a rocky shortcut to great riches and fame; others view it as disastrous if the Treskans could send their armies through to the east. Look here," said Quintell, pulling out a faded parchment. "This is the only known map of where Prakin's Pass once existed. This icon here represents a huge, upright boulder that marked the gates of Yessua."

"Could we get back to business, please?"

"But, My Lady, this *is* my business . . . teller of tales, purveyor of factual, historical events. A thrilling story, was it not? Well worthy of compensation. Now I propose that, in exchange for the tale and the priceless map, shall we say fifteen silver coins?"

"I don't have fifteen silver coins, and I didn't ask for the fairy tale."

"So," said Quintell, not to be deterred, "let us say the historical tale, the map, three fertipills, a half-case of dermal gel, and . . . AND, because you are such a beautiful and charming woman . . ."

Quintell the trader fiddled with his long, silver beard braids and looked about as though he were afraid of being overheard, then drew out an item from under a cloth.

"A piece of rotting wood?" inquired Orchid.

"A unique treasure, not to be found anywhere outside the ancient walls of Hashmenkis, itself . . . a genuine piece of the actual gallows that Anthamia of Salamanka died upon. It is said that this brownish stain here is from the witch's own intestinal discharge! It comes with a full certificate of authenticity. I propose all of the aforementioned items in exchange for that beautifully carved staff you carry."

In response, Orchid's staff rumbled ominously, spitting out angry white sparks that left little burn marks on Quintell's tabletop.

"Sorry, I don't need a shitty piece of wood and the staff is not for sale. All I'm interested in is the dermal gel. And all I have to trade for it is . . . skill."

Quintell's hypnotically beautiful brown eyes bored into Orchid's green ones.

"Such as?"

"Your aurora plant over there . . . quite valuable I should think."

"Aye, but alas, also not for sale. Anita, that's what she is called, has been with me for many years, since I first raised her from a single, tiny seed. I take tender care of her and, in exchange, she provides me with a small but regular supply of aurora berries."

"Which you sell as aphrodisiacs?"

"Quite potent ones, in fact. You . . . disapprove?"

"Not at all. In fact, what if I could . . . increase your yield?"

Quintell's left eyebrow twitched in the most adorable way.

"Hand me one of those fertipills, would you?" she said, hiding her smile.

Orchid took the small capsule over to the large potted shrubbery at the corner of Quintell's booth. She broke it open and sprinkled the powder over the soil. To it, she added a dash of some unknown pasty substance out of her own herb kit. A little water and she was ready for her spell. Orchid concentrated on the plant and on the ever-present Magic in the air. It was not a command but a request. Worldly Magic, such as Orchid practiced, was non-intrusive, passive, and self-sustaining. She opened her senses and perceived those of the plant. It had no intelligence or even a mind but, like all life, instinctively craved certain conditions and nutrients. Orchid's trained mind recognized them at once and fine-tuned itself for the task ahead. Pores opened in the buried roots. Water and the added nutrients were hungrily absorbed.

There were also toxins and other unwanted substances in the worn-out soil that needed to be filtered out, probably the remains of unfinished drinks and smoking ashes that had been poured and flicked into Anita's pot by passing customers. The fluidic movement within the roots and stems began an intricate internal dance of chemicals in the clogged circulatory system, sucking up the good and expelling the bad. Small twigs, nearly ready to dry up and break off, found themselves with a rushing supply of food and concentrated energy.

Orchid was not minutely aware of every tiny detail of what was happening. Her senses merely perceived the problem.

It was the natural processing and organizational tendencies of Magic that translated her desires into reality. Magic does not *obey.* It is not an entity and has no kind of cognizance. It is simply a powerful energy that permeates the air, water, and soil of Lurra. It is not alive, but it is said that Magic wants to be used.

The end result of Orchid's spell was a small but rapid growth and general greening up of the shrubbery. Fresh, young buds appeared on the tips of the branches, promising a fresh batch of ripe aurora berries within a few days.

"Ahh, glorious, glorious!" Quintell did a queer little jig and clapped his hands three times - a cultural idiosyncrasy, no doubt. "Many thanks, My Lady!"

Quintell eyed the tiny balls of potential profit hanging from the branches, turned back to Orchid, and grinned his best.

"Could you do that again?"

"Oh, I don't know," drawled Orchid. "That spell is hard on a girl . . . dries out the skin something awful." The batting of Orchid's eyelashes could have blown a moth off course.

"Perhaps a little dermal gel will alleviate the problem."

"Perhaps."

Quintell loved a good negotiation, and he knew a bargain when he saw one.

"Will half a case be sufficient?"

Orchid picked up the eight ampules of dermal gel, the map, and the remaining fertipills and packed them away in her bag. She passed on the scrap of wood.

"Adequate, Mister Quintell, adequate."

Another glance at the potted plant and a furious growth spurt burst forth. New branches thickened and extended.

Newly-born green leaves coiled upward and unrolled themselves. Tips of new roots poked out of the drain hole, threatening to break apart the ceramic pot. Ripe aurora berries were dropping off their stems like pearls from a broken necklace. Quintell carefully gathered them up into a small glass jar. He held one out to Orchid.

"Would you . . . care to try one?" There went that grin again.

Orchid sidled up to the trader and said in a low whisper, "I don't think I'll need one." Two sets of lips slowly started moving together. They were within a finger of colliding . . .

"ORCHID!"

The familiar aroma of Ostican Musk cologne accompanied the unwanted interruption. Her jaw protruded the way it always did when she was pissed off.

"This . . . is not . . . a good time!"

"No time like the present, I always say," said Foxx quickly.

Quintell cocked his head in the cutest way as he and Foxx evaluated each other. Orchid stepped between them, but being a head shorter than either one, she didn't block much. The trader broke eye contact first. He shifted his gaze back to Orchid and began delicately inhaling the aroma of his aurora berry in a meaningful way. Orchid slowly turned to Foxx, whom she was ready to kill.

"Are you in some sort of hurry?"

"Well," Foxx said. "Tresado and Serena are closing the deal for the horses right now. Come on, aren't you ready to get back on the road again?"

Foxx slowly eased into his Knowing Spell. He found it useful when he wanted to coerce his companions into something, but experience taught him to begin subtly. To cast the spell at full power right away would alert Orchid that he was influencing her. This time, for some reason, it took longer than usual to become effective.

"We gotta go . . . NOW!" he added, with another little boost to his spell.

"Well . . . all right," sighed Orchid. "If we gotta go, we gotta go. It was . . . *a pleasure* doing business with you, Quintell."

"Pleasure *is* my business. Please . . . visit my booth any time," said the trader wistfully.

Foxx took Orchid by the upper arm and quickly hustled her off the trading floor. They headed out of the Crystal Palace to the boat docks, where their companions waited.

"Just where are we going, anyway?" Orchid asked.

"We'll figure that out later . . . right now, let's just go!"

* * *

Inxa 13, 21862

Dear Mother and Father,

It's hard to believe I've been at school for almost two years. I guess I've been too busy to notice the time passing. I have a wonderful new teacher. His name is Jennick. Last month he started us working on botanic awareness. Like every new subject here at the Academy, it's hard at first. Every time, I swear that I'll never be able to grasp the basics, but somehow I always manage to squeak by. Well, this will have to be a short letter. The morning meditation gong just sounded. I should be able to come home next month on the 38th for break. It'll be great to see you again and to sleep on my own mat again. Love to you both.

- Orchid

CHAPTER 2

Today – Western Perlan frontier

Sensang was sinking lower in the western sky. Ahead they spotted a fairly flat area with a few patches of grass. It was as good a campsite as could be expected in this rugged terrain. All of Group Six was happy to call a halt to today's uncomfortable ride.

"Are you sure about this route?" asked Serena grumpily. "I don't see any marks of digging or building, or any sign that *anybody* has ever been in these stupid mountains!"

"That's what the map says," replied Orchid. "We passed around the north side of those twin spires, just like it shows."

"It also says these are called *The Haunted Mountains,"* said Serena, looking around at the surroundings. "They're probably full of ghosts!"

"Did you ever consider that your map might be a phony?" Foxx had just eased his aching butt out of the saddle. "In my time with the traveling show, I saw Professor Generax sell at least thirty treasure maps to customers. He had a whole drawer full of them."

"Well, it looks authentic to me," said Orchid, squinting at the yellowed document in the fading light.

"We can check it out later," said Tresado. He looked at the darkening sky, which was threatening another storm. "Let's get this camp set up before it starts raining again. Where's the tent?"

"See to your horses first!" snapped Serena.

Tresado, Foxx, and Orchid collectively sighed but obeyed the authoritative Northlands Warrior. The four nags were soon unsaddled, watered, and fed. Their equine entrees were sparse due to the lack of funds for such things as a large supply of horse grain. The rough grass that grew about supplemented. Only then did Serena allow them to make camp.

The *tent* was actually a worn piece of tarp scrounged by Serena before Group Six left the Palace. She pulled it off the back of her saddle, and they set to work draping it over a couple of dead tree branches. Orchid started a fire, and they sat staring into the flames and munching their dried, bland rations.

"Let's see that map again," said Tresado.

Orchid handed it over and pointed to a couple of spots.

"This is where we first entered the mountains from the road. Here's the spires that are about a day behind us, so this should be where we are now."

Tresado read the labels by the firelight. "This place is called the *Haunted Mountains?* Any reason you didn't mention that?"

"What's in a name?"

Tresado sighed. "This green line is supposed to be where the road was cut?"

"Yeah, we started by skirting the south face of Waxy Mountain after leaving the road."

"These mountains are pretty crudely drawn. How can we be sure that this figure is Waxy Mountain?"

"Well . . . it looks like it."

"It looks like it?" Serena leaned over Tresado's shoulder to scrutinize the map he held. His guy-ness involuntarily kicked in when confronted so closely by her imposing cleavage, and he couldn't help staring. Serena couldn't help smacking him.

"It looks like it?" she repeated with more emphasis. "It's two little squiggly lines that look more like a house than a mountain."

Tresado rubbed his sore cheek and turned back to the map.

"Wait a minute, you said we passed to the *north* of the twin spires?"

"Yeah, so?"

"But when we passed them, the spires were on our *right.* If we passed them to the north, they would have been our left!"

Long pause

"Oh."

Orchid held her neutral expression but couldn't hide the crimson blush that swept across her cheeks.

"I guess I . . . misread the map . . . so maybe we're . . . too far south?"

"Maybe you had the map upside down," suggested Tresado.

"I think our guide here was thinking too much about the dreamy trader that she bought this bogus map from," said Foxx. "We're on the wrong path, aren't we?"

Three unfriendly faces stared at Orchid.

"Look," she gulped, "all we have to do is to cut back to the north tomorrow. We should be back on the right trail in . . . two or three days."

"I don't think there *is* a right trail," said Serena, who usually sided with Orchid when Group Six got to bickering. "I think your trader was full of crap!"

"Hey, I might have trouble with my right and left, but I can read people," said Orchid. "Quintell was sincere! He told me that other people have been known to find this road in the past, *including Dementus!* Now we know that he was a real person. Why would there be a report of someone who didn't exist finding this road?"

"That doesn't make a lick of sense!" shouted Tresado, who was probably the most miserable of all of them. He was a city Eryndi, and all this wandering in the wilderness was not his pipe of jamba.

"So *Dementus* traveled this mythical road?" asked Foxx with a strange tone to his voice.

"Yeah . . ."

Foxx went over to the pile of gear by the horses. He reached into his saddle bag and pulled out a large, rectangular object wrapped in a rag. "Well, let's just see what the good Treskan had to say about that."

"Whoa!"

"How did you . . .?"

"Is that . . .?"

"Yes, it is."

A flash of lightning briefly illuminated the figure of Foxx standing there holding the Travelogue of Dementus the Mad Treskan.

* * *

This place is an anthropologist's dream. My collection has grown once again. Today I acquired an Eryndi icon representing the two spheres of so-called Magic and a monkeywood figurehead of a Macai sea goddess from a sunken Epponese galley. The icon is delicate and highly detailed with a beautiful symmetry of form. The figurehead looks like it was carved with an axe but is stout and sturdy and survived immersion in salt water for perhaps a hundred revolutions. How indicative of both species these artifacts are.

- *STARFISH* ARCHIVAL SPHERE 82

Today – Western Perlan frontier

"Dementus's diary?" asked Tresado incredulously. "What are you doing with that? Did Jakki give that to you?"

"As if," replied a smug Foxx.

"So you stole it?" accused Orchid.

"My Lady, so little you think of me. You talk as though I am some sort of criminal."

Three voices responded as one.

"But you are a criminal."

"There are several technical points to argue against that," replied Foxx defensively, "but we'll save the debate for another time."

"Are you saying you didn't steal it?" asked Serena.

"Yes."

"Did you buy it?"

"No."

"Trade for it?"

"No."

"Jakki wouldn't just give it to you."

"No."

"CRODAN'S CRAP! Would you just tell us before I have to cut your head off!?"

"That would be unfortunate . . . and also messy."

"Not the way *I'd* do it," replied Serena grimly.

"Okay, here's the story. I'll give you the short version," Foxx said, clearing his throat and adopting a histrionic pose.

"Jakki wasn't going to compensate us with cash or anything else. I may not always follow the law of the land to the letter, but I do have a personal code . . ."

Foxx stopped when he saw the looks on the faces of his three friends.

"I *do* . . . really! And it's this - if I think that someone owes me something, I'll acquire it on my own and not let some ordinance get in my way."

"Did you steal it or didn't you?" demanded Orchid.

Foxx had this performance ready, and he wasn't about to lose his audience by changing the subject. He had practiced the speech in his head a few times while on the road.

"So, there I was, ready to satisfy my honor with some righteous acquiring. I spent days casing the Crystal Palace, learning the staff's routines, the security, everything. Finally, I learned where the count room for the casino is. All the coin that comes in from the gambling tables, the percentages of floor sales, money spent on lodging and meals, it *all* goes into that room! I figured out a hundred different ways of getting in, but that wasn't the problem."

"Getting out was," offered Tresado.

"Exactly. Much of the coin is in small denominations. I made a few calculations and to carry out the equivalent of what was owed us would have required no less than eleven fully-laden wheelbarrows. I mean, there was all that gold and gems and the silver plate and . . ."

"We've already heard the inventory today – get on with it!" snapped Serena.

"Fine . . . all right. So, I tried for days to plan the perfect crime. I observed, I calculated, I learned the schedule of the money transporters, but nothing was working. Every scenario I tested would've gotten me caught within a few minutes. I decided I had to give up on the idea of the count room money. Then I got to thinking about Dementus's journal. Jakki seemed to place great value on the thing, even if we can't make head or tails of it. I figured it must be the historical significance or maybe there's some hidden clue or information in it that could prove to be profitable. *Something* about that book is very valuable. So, since acquiring coin wasn't feasible, I decided to switch targets. But even if I could get into her inner sanctum where it's kept, Jakki sees pretty much everything that goes on."

"Good thing we're getting the short version," muttered Orchid.

"So I took some of old Professor Generax's advice. He once said, 'If you can't do the deed legally, *make the deed legal.*' So I said to myself, 'Self,' I said, 'If I can't' . . . well, you know. What the Professor said."

"You tried to influence Jakki into giving you the book?" asked Tresado.

"No way. Jakki is a powerful Magician," said Foxx. "I'm good, but not that good. She would have detected any kind of influential manipulation. She was annoyed enough with us already. But Jakki isn't the only one with pull in that place."

"The Palace!" interjected Serena.

"Aw, you spoiled my denouement!"

Orchid, Serena, and Tresado all looked at each other and shrugged their shoulders simultaneously.

Foxx sighed. “The big finish to my story. Yes, the Crystal Palace itself. It is the keeper of the law around there. Serena, you told me that after it joined with your love spirit, it became a bit more understanding and forgiving. I got to thinking that maybe its sense of justice had evolved, too. So I had a talk with it.”

“Like the way Jakki communes with it from her inner sanctum?” asked Tresado, ever curious about new and different ways of practicing Magic.

“Exactly. My first thought after coming up with this idea was that I’d have to break into her office to do it. But a little experimenting showed me that I didn’t have to be in there. The Palace grew itself - the whole thing is one big sentient crystal. You could go into the janitor’s closet to talk if you wanted to. I did that one better and communed with it from the comfort of my room. I think Jakki likes to maintain the impression that only she can talk to it using some special trick or something. The truth is, anyone who can access Magic can chat with the Palace. It actually seems anxious to talk and make friends. I bet that’s also from the Love Spirit’s influence.”

“And what did you say?” inquired Orchid.

“Simple. I told the Palace the whole story of us finding ourselves in the middle of that desert . . . the weird monsters there, the bands of customers and players that weren’t really criminals, but made one mistake and were sent into that hellhole by the Palace itself! I told it about Abakaar and everything that happened to us there . . . about Tresado’s persecution and ordeal . . . me getting shot by Rastaban and the terrible battle that cost so many lives.”

“Trying to make it feel guilty?” harrumphed Serena. “That crap wouldn’t have worked on me.”

“No, not guilt,” answered Foxx. “Playing that card carried

too much risk of getting my bluff called. Instead, I appealed our case by challenging the law. You know, the whole bit about how no law is absolute and there are always newfound shades of gray and it takes a wise being to see past the rule of law, blah, blah, blah. Eventually, the Palace bought it and agreed that returning the journal to us was proper justice."

"But what about Jakki?" asked Tresado.

"She was the problem. The Palace was willing to allow me into the sanctum to retrieve the book, but I needed a distraction . . . the equivalent of pointing at something and shouting LOOK!"

"Fortunately, her aide Sparkly was a big help. I let it *slip* . . . that I recognized one of the members of a gaming party that had just arrived at the Palace. I had supposedly seen him before playing the numbers in Tresk and Ostica. He was a major player and would have a bundle of cash to drop. Naturally, Sparkly went and told Jakki right away and she went to schmooze the guy, probably by spilling soup on him, the way she did with us. While she was busy doing that, the Palace opened the door to the sanctum, and I walked right in and got the book."

Foxx turned slowly to Orchid.

"Then I came and coaxed you away from *Quilligan,* or whatever his name was, and we lit out. And *that,*" said Foxx, jabbing a finger in the air, "is how I came to possess the book. And Orchid, since you found it in the first place, and in gratitude for saving my life back in Abakaar, I thought it a fitting present for you on this most joyous of days. Happy birthday."

* * *

Citizens . . . It is my happy privilege to address the Republic on this day of remembrance and honor. I declare the annual Festival of Lights to be open!

- Imperatrix Alythya of Tresk
– 21741 (135 years ago)

Today – Western Perlan frontier

"How could you possibly know it's my birthday?" gasped an open-mouthed Orchid.

"I know many things," whispered Foxx mysteriously, "about all of you. Take care to heed that, my friends."

Three different looks reacted to Foxx's statement. Orchid rolled her eyes, Serena snarled, and Tresado smirked.

"That's kind of . . ."

"Creepy?"

"Lame?"

"Scary?"

"How about mystifying and . . . charismatic?" offered Foxx.

"Full of shit is more like it," said Serena dismissively. "Look, Orchid, we *all* know it's your birthday. What, you thought we didn't know . . . or didn't care? Of course we care, you moron!"

"Yeah, we know," added Tresado. "I didn't get you anything, but I knew."

"Me neither, I'm afraid," said Serena. "I spent my last gendrin on horse grain."

"So, we decided to donate our beer rations for one day to you for one good belt on your birthday," said Tresado. "Foxx's presentation is a tough act to follow, but . . . best we could do."

Orchid took a slow look at each of her friends' faces. "Aw, you guys . . ."

Today – The Haunted Mountains

The detour to the north to try to regain the course on the map was another slog fest through the muck. The spirits of Group Six were fairly high, though, thanks to the birthday bonding last week and the fact that it wasn't raining right now. Eventually, the slimy mud gave way to great, broken slabs of rock thrusting up through the ground. The going was rough. There was no trail per se to follow, and it pretty much prevented riding in a straight line for more than a few reaches.

"You guys will love the Treskan Imperium," said Foxx, attempting to break the monotony as their horses picked their way through the tortuous landscape.

"Yeah, so you've told us," replied Tresado. "And told us . . . and told us . . . and told us."

"Well, it's true," replied Foxx. "There are some pretty unbelievable sights to see."

"And when a con man and professional liar says something is unbelievable, you should believe him," said Orchid, always ready with a biting comment.

"You don't have to believe me. You'll see it all for yourselves," replied Foxx.

"*If* we ever get out of these mountains," said Serena from the head of the column. "Stay in single file. There's some nasty crevices that you can't see until you're almost . . ."

"That's not the only nasty thing in this neighborhood," interrupted Orchid, pointing to the partly cloudy sky. *"Look up there!"*

"What? I don't see anything . . ."

"Wait for it . . ."

A beat later, they all saw it. From behind a cloud, a dark, winged silhouette appeared. At first glance, one might think it was a bird. A second look revealed it to be something much larger at a very great altitude.

"Dragon!" hissed Serena. "We need to get to cover, fast! Quick, under there!"

Group Six quickly dismounted and hustled themselves and the horses beneath a large rocky overhang that jutted up from the ground.

"Everybody stay quiet!" whispered Orchid. "And clear your minds . . . no Magic, no thinking at all. Concentrate on the sand."

Orchid could've used a calming spell on the horses, but she knew the dragon could pick up on Magic use. Dragons could sense fear, too, but she would just have to hope that their mounts didn't realize the danger and freak out.

They waited in silence for several minutes. The only sound was the wind whistling through the rock formations. Orchid cautiously moved toward the edge of the rock slab and took a quick peek skyward. Suddenly, an impossibly fast-moving shadow eclipsed Sensang for a fraction of a beat. There was a thunderous *braaappp* sound, and Orchid was knocked back beneath the rock as though she had been kicked by a wild lumba. A flapping sound like a hundred whips being cracked at once echoed through the canyon. The dragon was heading back up to altitude. It had passed less than three reaches above their heads.

Serena looked up from the sand to see a strange, greenish-brown figure squirming on the ground next to her.

"Orchid . . . Orchid! You okay, girl?"

The slimy figure struggled to its feet, frantically trying to wipe the evil-smelling substance off itself.

"THAT STUPID DRAGON JUST SHIT ALL OVER ME!"

Orchid shook herself like a dog, scattering slimy dragorrhea everywhere. She shook her fist at the diminishing dragon flying off toward the southeast. A reptilian cackling sound accompanied it as it headed back into the clouds.

"I'll get you for that, you . . . you DRAGON!"

Nobody had any words at the moment. The others held it in for as long as possible. It was the Northlands sense of humor that first broke the silence with a long snort through Serena's nose. Foxx and Tresado couldn't help but follow suit. Within two beats, all of Group Six was doubled over with laughter, including Orchid.

"Dragons," she said. "Most of the time they try to eat you, but sometimes they just like to screw with you."

CHAPTER 3

These Eryndi impress me. My research indicates that, in the distant past, Macai were seen as an inferior form of life and useful for nothing but as beasts of burden. Today, Eryndi and Macai live together equally in the city of Tresk and beyond. It shows how magnanimous and tolerant the Eryndi are . . . despite being the superior race on Lurra . . .

-Imperator Merak – Commentaries: Book 1, Chapter 1, paragraph 3

* * *

Today – The Haunted Mountains

"Why couldn't it rain now?"

"Or at least shift the wind direction."

"Anybody got any nose plugs?"

"Oh, gripe, gripe, gripe," called Orchid, who was just about to get back on her horse. "The weather is clear now. I thought you all hated the rain."

"Oh, clear weather is great," said Foxx wryly. "The air has a certain . . . *air* about it."

"Okay, fine. You want rain, hang on a minute."

Orchid peered up at the partly cloudy sky. She closed her eyes and concentrated. Her Worldly Magic went to work coalescing the moisture in the air to a more concentrated form. Within a minute, miniature cumulus clouds formed a tight ball above her head. Another minute later, it was pouring rain, but only on Orchid and Dinky the Horse. A pool of nasty, greenish liquid ran off her body and pooled around her annoyed mount's hooves. Orchid had removed most of the remains of this morning's dragon attack, but there was still enough left to offend the noses of her companions. With a little scrubbing, a quick comb through her chocolate brown hair, and she was relatively fresh as a daisy, if not dry as a bone. Her fingernails could use a cleaning, but the rest of Group Six was satisfied.

"Thanks, *Putrid,*" smirked Tresado.

"Her name's Orchid, you cad," said Foxx. "Calling her names is a pretty *offal* thing to do."

"Yeah, you don't want to *muck* around with Orchid," Serena joined in. "Or you'll be up *shit* fjord without a wash cloth."

"You know," said Orchid calmly, "you three really ought to take your act on the road."

"We *are* on the road," quipped Tresado, trying to get in the last word.

"Speaking of that," said Serena loudly, "now that Nature Girl doesn't smell like a monkey in a meat grinder anymore, let's get *back* on the road!"

Without waiting to see if the rest complied, Serena turned her horse around and continued on to the north.

"You heard the General," said Foxx. "We have to find this *Perkin's Pass,* or whatever it is."

Orchid just ignored him.

Group Six continued for most of the day, picking their way through boulder fields and around gullies. Aftermidday considered the idea of changing into Evening. In response, the shadows decided to get longer and the breeze cooler. The farther north they traveled, the rougher the way became. Immense slabs of striated rock, three and four reaches thick, were thrust up from the ground like wood chips in a pile. The gigantic blocks were leaning in all directions, some across each other forming mighty arches. It appeared that, in some ancient time, the ground had violently heaved up the crust of rock like the broken eggshells in a mica bird nest.

Serena continued to lead the pack, carefully keeping her horse on solid rock footing wherever possible. The other members of Group Six followed slowly, trying to keep on the same path.

Tresado's horse, a mare named Guppy, picked this moment to deviate slightly. While trying to step over a fallen tree trunk, she lost her footing and found herself on a steeply slanted rock slab. Her hooves could find no grip, and she started sliding into what looked like a bottomless fissure. Guppy's equine scream of terror pierced the dusk. The great, rocky crack in the ground smiled in anticipation of its next meal. A half-beat before plunging into the unknown depths, horse and rider came to a sudden halt in mid-slide. The wild-eyed mare gaped in panic at the yawning chasm below her. A fist-sized rock, dislodged by the horse's stumble, rolled into the opening. There was no sound of an impact. Suddenly, her direction slowly reversed, and Guppy the Horse was lifted by an invisible force and gently set back on the precarious game trail they had been following.

Tresado phew-ed out the breath he had been holding and canceled the levitation spell he had frantically used to save his horse and his own life. He flashed an 'okay' sign, and Group Six continued fighting their way through the rugged, hostile landscape. Behind them and far below, a presence stirred, not a creature with limbs and flesh, but one made of bloodlust, Magic, and memory. It awoke others. A single thought spread . . .

SAVAGES!

Trippin' down the trail,
Skippin' thru the hail,
Laugh 'em off, laugh 'em off,
Send 'em back to jail!

- Travelogue of Dementus the Mad Treskan

* * *

Today – The Haunted Mountains

The next morning, most of Group Six was nervous for some reason. Usually, when such a thing happened, there was a reason: a prowling mountain tiger, a digger bear, or an enemy ambush. But there was nothing. As a matter of training and habit, Orchid kept up a constant awareness of the life surrounding them. There seemed to be nothing but birds, lizards, and gophers. She saw or smelled no big turd piles, half-eaten skeletons, or any other evidence of large predators.

The horses were fine. The four nags ambled along without a care in the world. Orchid and Tresado were visibly twitchy, and Foxx was dozing fitfully in his saddle, as was his wont. The only one not affected was Serena. She looked back at her nervous companions with just a bit of disgust. Her horse stepped on a dry branch, snapping it with a loud crack.

"HUH? WHAZZAT?"

Foxx almost fell off his horse as he suddenly awoke. Orchid and Tresado had also nearly shot out of their saddles from the startling noise of the broken branch.

"What the hell is the matter with you?" shouted Serena. "You're all acting like scared bunnies!"

"You don't feel that?" replied Foxx, who was white as a sheet.

"Ohhh, whatsa matter, Foxxy? Did we have a bad dweam?"

"I'm telling you," said Foxx, looking behind him, "there's something . . ."

"What he's telling you is that we're being watched," interrupted Orchid. "Tresado and I feel it, too. I can't believe you're not sensing it. You're usually pretty good at that."

"Only when there's something to *sense!*" said Serena, looking around anyway.

A moment later, there was plenty to sense. An ominous whistling sound was descending from the sky, a sound that Serena had heard many times in her homeland.

"Arrow volley! Get to cover!"

A dark, shimmery cloud of pointed shafts flew down upon Group Six, falling all around them. A few must have missed them by mere fingers. Foxx could have sworn that one arrow should have impacted his horse's neck, and Orchid thought she should have been hit in the arm, but there were no wounds among them. They were apparently mistaken and very lucky.

Serena wheeled her horse about and headed for the nearest cliff face where there were overhangs to shelter beneath. The arrow barrage stopped after only a single volley for some reason. Now another sound rumbled in the air. A force of fifty or sixty Eryndi cavalry soldiers was heading toward them at full gallop. Some were so swift that they appeared to fly over the uneven ground, unmindful of trees, boulders, and other obstructions. A hundred reaches behind them was what looked like a battalion of infantry soldiers charging in. There was a lot of yelling going on as the army moved in to attack. One particular phrase often heard was, *"Kill the savages!"*

Serena always knew she would die in battle. That was her hope, anyway. But this battle was just too one-sided. Being outnumbered a few hundred to one didn't do a thing for her.

"Quick, through here!"

Serena had spotted a narrow fissure in a gigantic boulder that had cracked in half in some ancient time. Through it was a dark space of unknown size. It was their only chance for a defensible cover. The crack was just wide enough to allow a person to get through, but not the horses. There was no choice. Group Six all dismounted and started squeezing one at a time through the opening. Orchid quickly retrieved Dementus's journal from her saddlebag and her even more precious staff. Their four horses that they were forced to abandon fled in terror, directly in the path of the oncoming cavalry. Foxx's horse dropped dead from a burst heart, but the other three scattered into the mountains, not to be seen again.

Tresado was the last in line for the fissure. In an effort to stall their certain death, he gathered Magic into a projectile of explosive fire and launched it into the midst of the approaching horse soldiers. His missile exploded violently, shooting flame and rock shards across the landscape. The cavalry was unfazed. No one fell. They just kept coming. More mass yelling began to erupt everywhere around them. Down from the mountain peaks in all directions came massive hordes of more warriors. These were not uniformed Eryndi like the others. Thousands of Macai were streaming down into the fray. Their weapons were primitive, their clothing was simple animal pelts, and their demeanor was definitely unfriendly.

Serena, Orchid, and Foxx were through the fissure. Tresado had more trouble than the others, but he took a deep breath, sucked in his gut and somehow managed to squeeze through. The last thing he saw before he disappeared inside was all of the soldiers, Eryndi and Macai alike, clutching their heads and hitting the ground. One important-looking Eryndi in a decorated uniform fell off his horse and crawled over to another man, who weakly raised his head. The one in uniform collapsed while the other turned his head and looked directly at Tresado before fading out completely.

Tresado popped through the opening like a rockfruit seed, his eyes big as ballberries. The rest of Group Six was within the dark cavern, ready to rumble. Suddenly, all was quiet. The war cries had stopped. The galloping hooves had stopped. The far-off rumble of thunder was all there was to hear. Serena cautiously approached the opening and peeked out. After a few beats, she sheathed her sword and rejoined the others.

"There's nothing out there."

"What do you mean, nothing?" asked Orchid.

"I mean nothing . . . the Ernie soldiers are gone, the Macai caveman-lookin' guys are gone. Unfortunately, our horses are gone, too, along with all our food."

"No food?" added Tresado piteously.

"Well, for that we have Foxx's horse. He's layin' out there with his eyes bulged and his tongue hangin' out.

"Ew."

"Ew."

"Ew."

"Whatever . . . it looks like another storm is building," replied Serena. "At least we can shelter in here."

"Let's take a look and see where we are first," said Tresado. A quick spell later, and a hovering Magical light appeared above their heads.

"Oh, wow!"

"Would you look at that?"

"Holy goat crap!"

"Looks like we finally found it."

The illumination from Tresado's spell showed them that this was no natural cave. Group Six was in a large tunnel cut into the body of the mountain.

* * *

> *In the time before men, the Northlands were home to The Dawn Folk. We know not what these creatures called themselves, indeed if anything. Perhaps they had no words at all. Legend says they were wee little buggers, scurrying about in the hours of the dark, only to return to their burrows deep in the ground upon Sensang's rising. Some say that even today, during the dark of the Orb, the spirits of the Dawn Folk emerge to visit our living children as they sleep and feed upon their dreams . . .*
>
> - Vingrid the Shadow – Bedtime stories

Today – The Tunnel

The tunnel stretched deep into the mountain, well beyond Tresado's light source. The air had a sour smell, but there was a very slight, though definite, breeze coming out of the mountain. Group Six felt reasonably safe for the moment, so they took this opportunity to get up a good, long-winded discussion.

"Any ideas on what all that hoo-ha was about?" asked Foxx, finally addressing the lumba in the room.

"Ghosts," replied Serena simply.

"I sensed no life," said Orchid.

"But we heard the yelling, the sound of the hoofbeats, the arrows whistling through the air," said Tresado.

"This may sound weird," said Foxx, "but I thought I saw some of those riders come out of the ground."

"Like out of a cave?" asked Orchid.

"No, like right out of solid rock in the side of a ridge."

"And I thought I saw some of the foot soldiers running a couple of reaches above the ground," replied Tresado.

"Ghosts," repeated Serena.

"They were real . . . we all sensed them coming," said Foxx.

"Everyone but Serena," said Tresado.

"And the horses," added Orchid.

"Then they weren't active minds," said Foxx.

"Huh?"

"There were no living brains," replied Foxx. "If the soldiers were flesh and blood, Serena's Northlands senses would have picked up on it. It was nothing but Magic. Serena doesn't use Magic. Neither do the horses."

"Ghosts."

"Are you saying someone cast a spell to create fake soldiers?" asked Tresado skeptically.

"I think someone cast a spell, all right, but I don't think it was any time recently," said Orchid.

"Why do you say that?"

"Did you get a look at those Macai?" replied Orchid. "They were wearing skins and carrying clubs. Unless there has been a major fashion change, nobody has looked like that for a thousand years."

"Ghosts."

"And I don't think it was intentional," added Foxx.

"What?"

"The spell. As you say, it must have been cast a long time ago." Foxx stroked his beard in thought. "If so, what we saw and heard had to be a . . . *reflection* of what happened way back whenever. That's not a normal effect of Magic use. Something must have gone wrong."

"That's impossible," scoffed Orchid, "at least with Worldly Magic."

"Absolute Magic, too," said Tresado. "Except maybe . . ."

"Right," nodded Foxx. "Influential Magic is a form of Absolute, but it doesn't affect the physical world, just the mind. I don't think that whoever cast this spell meant for this to happen. When I was teaching myself my Knowing Spell, the Influential Magic books I was studying warned against the danger of *geometric progression.* Something about attempting to influence large numbers of people and how multiple minds can amplify the Magic out of control. I've never had any problems like that, probably because when I use it, it's only on one or two players sitting opposite me at the gaming table. But if somebody tried it on a large group, say a hundred people or so, it might just overload the available power of Magic."

"But Rastaban controlled thousands of people in Abakaar," said Orchid. "The only problem he had was temporarily losing control of so many. Nothing overloaded."

"But Rastaban was using those medallions that were individually coded to each victim," replied Foxx. "They kept things in check. Maybe whoever cast *this* spell just directed it to a large group and it expanded out of control."

"And if that happened," said Orchid, "everything from the beginning of the spell to its termination could have just *frozen.*"

"Ghosts," repeated Serena urgently.

Tresado nodded enthusiastically. "Yeah . . . *yeah*. Everything that occurred during the spell duration, the encoding, the combined components, the outcome itself were all permanently burned into the fabric of Magic."

"When that spell amplified out of control, the flash of expanding Magical energy preserved the actions and images of all the living things affected," said Foxx.

"And it was triggered to 'replay' somehow," said Orchid somberly. "I wonder how many times that battle has been fought."

"The Eryndi soldiers, the Macai, the cavalry," Tresado had a habit of repeatedly snapping his fingers when talking about Magical theory. "Their bodies were all destroyed, but their images remain. Everything happens exactly as it did long ago. The land has changed, so that's why we saw them both above and below the current ground level."

"GHOSTS!"

"Serena," said Tresado in a patronizing tone, "there are no such things as ghosts. We've just postulated how such an occurrence might happen, using logic, knowledge, and experience. There are no ghosts. What we saw was merely an afterimage – a distant memory of something that happened a long time ago, imprinted on the fabric of Magic."

Serena's raspberry was nearly as loud as that of the dragon the other day.

"Pig piss! I know ghosts when I sorta see them! No matter how much Ernie-splaining you throw at me."

"You know, this is starting to sound familiar," said Orchid. "I think I've heard this story before somewhere . . . *Quintell!*"

"Orchid, *language!*" admonished Foxx.

"No, no. Quintell is the trader who told me about Prakin's Pass. I think what happened here is the fable that he tried to charge me for."

"Well, we just got a front row seat for nothing," smirked Foxx. "What a bargain."

"So, what'll it be . . . back outside or the tunnel?" asked Tresado.

"My vote would be for the tunnel," replied Foxx. "It'll be easier going."

"I don't know," said Orchid. "I think I'd rather be outside."

"That's Nature Girl for you," snorted Serena. "It's probably where the ghosts live, but I say tunnel. We don't have horses anymore and if it's part of this old road we've been looking for, it might take us right where we want to go."

"The tunnel it is, then," said Tresado.

Their footsteps echoed creepily off the stone walls. Tresado's hovering light made for eerie, shifting shadows as it followed them through the seemingly endless tunnel in the mountain. The members of Group Six spoke little, and when they did, it was in whispers, as though normal speech was somehow forbidden. The artificial light made it difficult to tell how late in the day it was getting, but their internal clocks told them that it would be time to bed down soon. Foxx was on the verge of suggesting just that when a sudden rush of hundreds of tiny wings over their heads forced a girlish squeal out of him instead.

"Steady, soldier," teased Orchid. "It's just a colony of marble bats, completely harmless." An evil smile lit her face, and she added, "Unless, of course, they get tangled in your hair and lay eggs in your ears."

"You know," said Tresado, sniffing the air, "even though it's laced with bat pee, I think the breeze is getting stronger. There must be an opening somewhere ahead."

"Let's keep going a bit longer and see if we can find it," said the perpetually non-tired Serena.

"My ears?!" muttered Foxx nervously.

Another half-hour of walking brought Group Six to a pile of rubble that half-filled the tunnel. The ceiling had a wide crack in it, from which the debris had fallen. A handful of scraggly bushes and some mushrooms grew painfully from the heap.

"Well, here's your opening," said Tresado, gazing up at the ceiling. "I'll take a look."

The Eryndi formed his usual invisible harness around his body and levitated himself up to the jagged crack. He hovered for a moment and then entered. A mere eight beats later, he emerged and floated back down to the ground.

"It narrows down to nearly nothing. I could only fit in so far, but I think I saw a star."

"So we're not getting out that way," said Foxx, wrinkling his nose. "Let's go a little farther and try to get beyond the stench. It smells like my Aunt Winnie's house around here. She has twelve cats."

It didn't take much walking. The breeze evidently originated from the ceiling crack and exited behind them where they had entered the tunnel. The bat smell ceased only twenty reaches beyond the crack.

"This doesn't bode well," said Orchid. "We might end up having to go back the way we came."

Ponchos for blankets and rocks for pillows had to suffice, but the night passed uneventfully. About a half-hour before dawn, the bats returned to their ceiling crack home. Foxx, who was on guard duty, pulled his poncho up around his ears defensively. Soon, a faint light began to filter through the ceiling.

"Wake up, everybody," said Foxx, grateful to have survived another night in a world filled with bats, snakes, and spiders. "Breakfast time."

"It would be, if we had any food," whined Tresado, whose stomach growled menacingly.

"We could have had plenty of horsemeat," replied Serena. "But no, that was too icky for you pusses."

"Hey, that horse carried my ass all the way from the Crystal Palace, and you just wanted to eat him?" said Foxx.

"I would have washed it first."

The no-breakfast discussion broke up, and the trek through the tunnel continued. After another ten leagues of marching, the air grew fouler and fouler.

"Amazing that the Treskans could dig so long a tunnel," said Foxx, coughing from the thick air.

"According to the story that Quintell told me, it was the . . . *Yessuans,* I think he said, the ones that were destroyed."

"Probably both," said Foxx. "According to your braided friend, Tresk sent caravans through here, too. When we get there, we should research it."

"Gonna be a while, it looks," said Serena, on point as usual.

Ahead, the glare of Tresado's light showed the tunnel to be completely blocked by fallen rock and debris.

* * *

Class, I have a problem for all of us to discuss and solve together. Now this story. Serena . . . SERENA! No throwing daggers in class. Now listen, a Northlands warrior and a barbarian are battling and fall into a pit together. The walls are too smooth and straight to climb and just a bit too high to jump for the ledge. With them at the bottom of the pit is a large, solid gold statue. It's worth a fortune but too heavy for one person to carry. What do these two combatants do?

-Hrolvad the Berserker Elementary School;
Miss Herkimer's third-grade classroom.

Today – The Tunnel

"Can you levitate these rocks out of the way?" asked Foxx of Tresado.

"Too heavy. They're jammed together and it's too tight."

"You lifted those big stones to make our shelter back in the crater zone."

"But you remember how powerful the Magic was in that area. I could've . . . funny, I don't quite remember much about those few days."

"I know what you mean," answered Foxx. "It's mostly a blur for me, too."

"Best ignore it, then," said Serena quickly. "Is there any way we can get past this?"

"I couldn't possibly gather enough wind to move those boulders," said Orchid.

"What about summoning lightning to crack them into something smaller that I could move?" asked Tresado.

"I don't have access to the open air and the weather. And, by the way, I don't summon anything! I alter potentiality, I interchange temperatures, I encourage, I invite, I request, but I don't summon!"

"Yeah, yeah, I'm sorry . . . just an expression," said Tresado. This was an old argument between them.

"Wait . . . *temperature,"* said Serena. "In the Northlands, it gets cold. Then it gets warm again."

Foxx opened his mouth, but Serena intercepted him.

"And before you make some smart-ass crack that will get your nose broken, just listen. Around the first of the year or so, usually in the month of Karaya, there's a time we call *Icecracking.* The weather will warm just enough to melt the snow on the cliff faces, which runs into cracks in the rocks. Then we'll get a snap freeze when the Nor-westers roll in. The water turns to ice again and busts the boulders apart. One year, when I was a kid, a whole section of glacier broke loose and slid down the slope. The Torgaldsons' herd of bergalo got pulped, but then the whole village was treated to a hash festival."

The other three members of Group Six waited blankly for the story to come to a point. Orchid was the first to realize what Serena was driving at.

"Of course! Serena, you're a genius!"

Orchid outlined the plan, and she and Tresado prepared their spells. Orchid focused on the moisture present in the tunnel. She condensed it into flowing water, which she Magically directed into the tight spaces between the boulders at the base of the pile. When she had gathered as much as she could, Orchid called upon Worldly Magic to kindly ask heat to move out of the way so as to let the cold in to do its job. The water quickly froze and expanded. There was a deep popping and crackling sound as the pressure of the ice forced rocks immobile for a thousand years to get a little exercise. Tresado then activated a kinetic spell (his specialty) to aid the process. He extended his hands as though physically pushing the boulders apart, but it was Magic that was doing all the work. Going through the motions aided his concentration and hence the efficacy of the spell. Beads of sweat popped out of his Eryndi forehead as he exerted more power.

"Everybody get back . . . here we go!"

With a final grunt, Tresado flung the broken shards of rocks at the base of the pile to either side. There was a loud rumbling, and the entire wall of fallen rock collapsed onto itself. Through the dust cloud, streamers of glorious Senbeams burst into the tunnel.

"Welcome back to the outside world!" exclaimed Tresado triumphantly. "Ladies first."

Orchid bowed and took the lead in scrambling over the pile and out of the tunnel into the Senlight. Tresado fell down twice but got through with just a skinned knee. They were greeted by foothills, sparse trees, and even a small stream. No structures or people could be seen, but it did indeed appear that they had come to the end of the mountain range they had been struggling through for days and days. There were also some wild pucka bushes growing nearby. Their fat, gummy seedpods tasted like stale bread but alleviated hunger. In the distance, a thin road could be seen winding across the landscape.

"Well, that's better," said a gleeful Tresado. "Looks like civilization is not far off."

"Let's find it," said Foxx.

"Back behind me, hotshot," said Serena. "You know I always take point."

"Not that I'm complaining," asked Foxx, "but why is that?"

"In case we encounter something dangerous that you need to be protected from. You know, like a swarm of roly-poly bugs, or a mouse army, or something."

"You should see me in a game of Yanevan Wild Draw."

"I never could get into gambling with little pieces of cardboard. Give me a good axe-throwing tournament, any day. I remember once . . ."

Serena was interrupted by a brilliant flash of green light which corresponded to a heavy blow to her face. The Northlands Warrior tumbled backward, landing on her butt. Before anyone could laugh, suddenly, from behind rocks and trees, there emerged a score of fierce-looking Eryndi soldiers. Their green-colored breastplates shone like great emeralds in the Senlight. Every one of them was armed with a matching crossbow aimed in the direction of Group Six. An impressive-looking Eryndi, an officer, judging by the extra decorations on her uniform, drew her short sword and approached.

"I am Primus Lucillia Manginus, Commander of the Third Cohort of the 38th Forward Legion. Welcome to the Treskan Imperium. State your business."

PART II:
THE IMPERIUM

CHAPTER 4

1332 years ago – the founding of Tresk

YEAR OF THE CITY – 1

"Elder, they have arrived!"

The aged Eryndi looked up and squinted at his aide, who stood holding one tent flap above her head. It took a few beats for his eyes to refocus from studying the documents before him. Treska hated getting old.

"Very well, Farinnia. I'll be along presently."

His air of calm was just an act. In truth, Treska was bursting with the news of the fleet's arrival. If all the supplies had been delivered safely, the work could continue. He took another long glance at the plans laid out on the makeshift desk in his makeshift tent. Someday this would be a city to rival any of Lurra, a testament to the spirit and ambition of the Eryndi people. It was a vision to cause one's heart to sing. But such a display of emotion would damage his reputation of imperturbability before his subordinates, and that wouldn't do.

Elder Treska stood, straightened his robe, and forced himself to casually walk out of his tent to greet (make that *inspect,* for appearance's sake) the supply barges. He did a quick count – twenty-four.

Excellent – they didn't lose a one.

Each vessel was heavily laden with crates and bundles of supplies of all kinds. The Great Hearth back in the home city of Mennatu had produced a full array of tools, equipment, foodstuffs, everything one would need to begin building a great city completely from scratch. There were no lumber or stone building blocks. The land would supply those.

A tall figure directed the work of several burly Macai beasts of burden as they stood in knee-deep water, hauling on lines to pull the barges up onto the sandy beach. There was something familiar about him.

"*Zarosen?* Is that you, my lad?"

The man turned and snapped to attention when he saw who had addressed him.

"Elder Treska . . . reporting with your requested supplies."

"Oh, relax, boy. Now get out of that water and come greet an old family friend."

Zarosen waded ashore and gripped the outstretched wrist offered to him.

"By Quiseron, the last time we met, you were but a snot-nosed, teenaged smart-ass. Who'd have thought you'd grow into such a fine figure of an Eryndi?"

"Thank you, Elder. It's good to see you, as well. Wait, I have something that I was ordered to place directly into your hands. Arko, bring the purple box."

A large Macai had just toted the first of the cargo ashore, a crate full of block and tackle pulleys. He heaved the heavy load off his shoulder and gently placed it upon the sand with hardly any effort.

"Okee, boss."

"He answered you!" Treska's surprise at the idea of the livestock parroting Eryndi speech was evident. "How very amusing! Did it take long to train him to do that?"

Zarosen merely shrugged and smiled. The man went back to the barge and returned a moment later with a gold-trimmed chest. A stylized figure of a bull decorated the top. Treska recognized it immediately.

"Taussian Bergalo Sausage! No need to reveal who ordered you to deliver this! Tell me, how *is* your mother?"

Zarosen smiled. "Of course it has been months since I saw her, but she was well. Sometimes I worry about her sanity. She sees to the distribution of goods to the citizens throughout the entire Domain. It's horribly taxing. Hopefully the burden will be eased soon. They were about to start construction on the new upriver Magic Infusers when I left. They will add to the available power for the Matrix."

"I remember," replied Treska. "They'll need them. Every city in the Domain was clamoring for more and more free goods . . . and the hordes of citizens moving out of the outlying cities and farms to take up residence in Mennatu. Everyone now demands the life of complete freedom that the Hearth offers. I don't envy Jarayan her duties. I have to say that I prefer this far-flung frontier life."

"I think Mother secretly agrees. She often jokes that maybe she'll just build a villa in the hills and retire early. Get away from all these demands."

"And we share in those demands, I'm afraid," said Treska with a glance at the enormous bounty that had just come to him.

"Elder, your requests were given the highest priority. This project was on all tongues when I left."

“Well, we’ll try to give justice to the Domain with our little camping trip here. Come, let me show you the future site of the city.”

Zarosen looked back at the fleet of barges with their still-unloaded cargoes.

“Elder, I thank you, but I really must . . .”

“Delegate, my lad, *delegate!* Now I insist. Come.”

“Your will, Elder. *Barom!* Will you see to the unloading, please?”

A dour-looking Eryndi still aboard the lead barge waved in acknowledgment and began pointing and grunting, trying to get cooperation out of the Macai livestock, who didn’t seem to understand him that well. Zarosen sighed and turned back to Treska. The older man took him by the arm and led him up the beach toward the wide river delta that flowed out from between two sheer cliffs towered a good thirty reaches over their heads.

“The port facilities will, of course, be located along this beach,” said Treska, pointing out into the large bay. “The main city will be atop these cliffs.”

“On which side of the river?” asked Zarosen.

“Both. My plans are for a series of bridges spanning the canyon to connect both halves of the city. Can you think of a more defensible position? From atop those cliffs, we shall command the entire bay! No enemy can possibly threaten by sea!”

“And if an attack comes overland?” asked Zarosen.

“My boy, why must you ever play Krinol’s Advocate? The answer is simple. We shall expand, ever pushing the frontiers further and further into the interior. It may take centuries, but, mark my words, this southern Domain will someday spread across the face of Lurra!”

* * *

Lieusé Foxx – "You guys will love the Treskan Imperium."

- Orchid's 'List of Stupid Things People Have Said'

Today – Breeos Province of the Treskan Imperium

Serena staggered to her feet, mad as a muddy mica bird.

"Why, you . . ."

"Greetings!" said Foxx, quickly stepping between Serena and the soldiers. "We come as visitors to the Treskan Imperium. Hail Imperator Merak!"

Tresado and Orchid gripped Serena by both arms, doing their best to hold the warrior woman back before she killed someone and subsequently got Group Six killed.

Primus Lucillia Manginus, Commander of the Third Cohort, regarded them for a moment, sizing up these visitors. The blonde woman seemed like a threat from the vicious-looking scimitar at her hip and the vicious-looking snarl on her face. The other three *looked* harmless enough, but one could never be sure of anything in this crazy world. The male Macai in red had a . . . *way* about him.

Foxx turned slightly toward Serena and began a second Knowing Spell manipulation toward her. This version, as opposed to the simple trusting spell he used on the officer, had a calming element to it. Both spells took effect nicely. Serena shook off Tresado's and Orchid's grasps and signified that all was jake with her. The Treskan sheathed her sword and visibly relaxed. Foxx inwardly gloated to himself.

Damn, I'm good!

Primus Manginus turned around, whistled loudly, and made a motion to someone behind her. A beat later, there was a green flash, briefly illuminating a gigantic, squat shape stretching many reaches beyond the officer and her soldiers.

"Follow me, please," said Manginus.

The soldiers fell into formation surrounding Group Six and escorted them forward. After a dozen steps, there was another flash of green light, and the glowing dome shape reappeared for a couple of beats, this time above their heads, then vanished again.

"That's what you ran into," whispered Orchid to Serena.

The Treskan and the armed escort led Group Six around a nearby hill and onto a footpath. They were not restrained, just watched very, very closely. Soon, an amazing vista came into sight. Nestled behind the hill was a good-sized tent city. Treskan soldiers wearing identical green armor patrolled the perimeter, tended to horses, peeled potatoes, or just lounged around, depending on what today's duty roster read. As they proceeded through the tents, the Legionnaires saluted their Primus with the standard gesture, a clenched left fist striking the breastplate, then held level with the ear. The group approached a large tent with soldiers coming and going from it.

"Varyus, break out the Tallyer."

"Yes, Primus." The young Legionnaire scurried ahead. Manginus followed, slowly leading Group Six through what they learned was the administration tent. Several soldiers were busily at work filing records, delivering messages, and saluting a lot. Varyus had just pulled a metallic box from a metallic supply trunk, both of which matched the metallic shelves, metallic tables, and metallic tent poles.

Standard military issue, thought Serena.

Varyus opened the box and retrieved a quite ordinary-looking metallic tray, then sat down at a desk. He touched a tiny knob on the side of the tray, and a green glow began to play along the top rim. He then spat a tiny bit into it and swirled it around. Whatever the tray was made of was very slippery. The droplets of saliva skittered around effortlessly until they fused into a single drop. When that was accomplished, he set it down and tried to make it as level as possible for some reason unknown to Group Six. Tresado, ever curious, opened his mouth and was about to ask about it, but was interrupted by a low hiss and a tiny shake of the head from Foxx. The spittle drop stubbornly stayed on one side of the tray, so Varyus took a couple of sheets of scratch paper and slid them under one corner. The drop moved to the center and stayed there, which seemed to satisfy him. Next, he dug into the box again, retrieved a heavy leather envelope, and pulled out four sheets of, not paper, but some filmy-looking material with text and ruled lines on them.

"While that's warming up, I need to ask you some questions. You," he said, pointing at Foxx. "We'll start with you."

The soldier then proceeded to ask questions of Group Six, the answers to which were written on the forms. It was all very basic stuff – name, place of birth, reasons for visiting the Imperium, etc. Something about the procedure was familiar to Foxx, but he couldn't place why until the questioning ended. Varyus took the four forms and placed them in the tray, one at a time. With each sheet, a brightly glowing green line appeared and tracked back and forth across the page. Varyus picked up the sheets and examined them. His eyebrows shot up in surprise.

"Primus!"

Varyus quickly walked over to his superior, who had been talking to a pair of soldiers during the questioning. He showed the forms to Manginus, and the two of them entered into a hushed conversation. When they were through, the Primus approached Group Six all smiles.

"You must be hungry," said the Treskan. "Varyus, take our guests over to the mess tent and get them a good meal. Please, my friends, if there is anything you desire or need, do not hesitate to ask. We will prepare some quarters for you. Once again, welcome to the Treskan Imperium."

The Primus's hospitality was gratefully accepted by the tired and hungry Group Six. However, there was something they did not know. At the same time their documents were being examined, on a console many hundreds of leagues away, three colored lights came on: one blue, one red, and one green.

* * *

Always greet your customers with a smile. They may think you're up to something, but it will put them at ease and smooth your deal . . . especially if you're up to something.

- Professor Abadiah Generax, 21862

1330 years ago – the founding of Tresk

YEAR OF THE CITY – 3

"No, no, that is completely unnecessary!"

"But Elder, no one has done more toward the creation of this city than you!"

Treska snorted as only an old, cranky Eryndi could. "Farinnia, I would not even venture to call it a city as yet. We only have four permanent buildings."

"I'm only telling you what the Conclave of Builders has decided."

"We would have *five* buildings, but if you remember, the grain silo burned down."

"Elder Yurzan called you a 'monument unto himself.' Everyone agrees."

"Then that windstorm pushed what was left of it off the cliff."

"Elder, more than once, I have heard you say that this will be a great city one day. Such things take time. Mennatu was not built in a day."

"Nor will this city. Not in a day, not in a year, not in a hundred years, or any time in the foreseeable future if we don't receive any more supply deliveries. There should have been at least three more shipments in the last two years."

"We should hear something soon from the reconnaissance ship, Elder," said Farinnia. "They departed for the homeland more than four months ago to find out what is wrong."

"I would hardly call it a *ship,* Farinnia," replied Treska. "The *Seeker* was not much more than a big raft. Remember the nor-westers of Tono? They could very easily have broken up and been driven into the lee shore. For all we know, the wreckage is a mere ten leagues to the north of us."

"But . . ."

"Farinnia, we are just going to have to accept that something catastrophic happened to Mennatu. We all felt it."

"If that is the case, Elder, then there's nothing for it but to continue to build Tresk on our own."

"Don't call it that. Say, how are your sister and her husband doing? That little boy of theirs must be almost a year old now."

Farinnia had finally had enough of her boss's humility. Besides, she still had work to finish before nightfall.

"Stop trying to change the subject, Elder. It's already done. Like it or not, the Conclave has made its decision. We are now all citizens of the city of *Tresk.* Long Live the Mennatuan Domain!"

"Hoo-ray."

Today – Breeos Province of the Treskan Imperium

"It isn't the gourmet food from the Crystal Palace, but I got to admit, the chow here is not bad at all," said Serena around a mouthful of bergalo sausage and beans.

"The Treskans are known for their cooking skills," said Foxx. In a lower voice, he added, "They're also good at secret-keeping."

"Do tell," said Orchid, equally quietly.

"I don't know what it means, but we have been classified as *triples.*"

"What does that mean?" asked Tresado, instantly regretting his words.

"And where did you pick up that tidbit?" asked Orchid.

"When the fellow that filled out our forms showed them to the Primus, they talked about us being triples. They were excited. It seemed to mean something important. She then sent the courier off with a message to some General."

"You heard that from across the tent?"

"One of the many skills I learned from Professor Generax

and His Traveling World of Wonders was lip-reading. It comes in handy at times."

"Well, aren't you just a red-silk-coated bundle of talents?"

"Thank you, Orchid. You're too kind." Foxx took a long swig from his mug of mulsum.

"You know what else is weird?"

Tresado's mouth opened, but Foxx cut him off.

"Rhetorical question. Did you take note of how they processed our forms?"

"You mean the *tallyer?"* answered Orchid. "That metal box with the green light?"

"Exactly. Does that process seem familiar at all?"

"Now that you mention it, they did something similar when we got dragged into Abakaar. Whats-her-name . . . Naomi!" Orchid's eyebrows went up. "Yeah! We answered pretty much the same questions and she put the answers in that metal tray with the red light!"

Serena, who seldom participated in her three companions' verbose discussions, brightened with a memory.

"And remember when we first went into the Crystal Palace? That tart at the door asked us stuff and stuck the answers in a box. A blue, glowing box."

"I don't suppose we should ask the Treskans about this?" said Tresado in a low voice.

Foxx shook his head. "Probably not. I don't think they'd have an answer for us."

"Well, if they're going to keep secrets from us, we should keep one from them," said Orchid. "I say we don't mention Prakin's Pass or the tunnel."

"Agreed," said Tresado and Serena together.

"Triples, triples," pondered Foxx. "What could they mean by that?"

"You sure your lip-reading wasn't off?" snarled Serena. "Maybe he said we were *trouble.*"

"Or typical," said Tresado.

"Or tribal," added Orchid.

"Or shut your fat gobs and take my word for it. He said, 'triples.'"

"Triples. Hmm, maybe it means . . ."

"Hsst!"

Foxx's warning to Tresado sounded none too soon. Primus Manginus was striding to their table, beaming a smile as bright as her polished green breastplate.

"Well, friends, have you had enough to eat? Is there anything you require?"

"You do us great honor, Primus," said Foxx with his best Treskan accent. "We have been treated well."

"May I ask what your travel plans are?"

"Primus, we are here as visitors to your Imperium," replied Foxx. "I myself have visited the capital once before. My friends here have not had the privilege. We hoped we could take in all the culture by starting in these eastern provinces and traveling west until we hit the great city of Tresk, the Pearl of Ocean herself, Praise to Ayendea!"

"May her currents guide us," responded Manginus. "I am intrigued by this bold plan. You seem to have no horses or supplies."

"Our horses ran off on us," said Orchid. "I tried to talk them out of it, but they wouldn't listen."

"May I ask where you came from?" inquired Manginus. "You are not Breeosian. You are not Treskan. You seem to have just appeared out of nowhere."

Group Six paused ever so slightly, then spoke at once.

"Through the mountains."

"The mountains."

"Yeah, the mountains. We came from . . . the mountains."

"Through the tunnel!"

Tresado, Orchid, and Serena froze in silence as they stared at Foxx for blurting out what they thought should be a secret. At this exact moment, a soldier came up to Manginus, saluted, and whispered in her ear.

"Indeed? Thank you. Dismissed."

Primus Lucillia Manginus turned to Group Six.

"Would you care to tell me about this tunnel?"

CHAPTER 5

1301 years ago – Tresk

YEAR OF THE CITY – 32

Sensang was just below the eastern horizon. Magical glowing orbs that hovered over the gathering lit the way for the crowds who were just arriving. The entire Eryndi population of Tresk, all four hundred twenty-eight of them, according to the sixth Lustrum, was gathering in anticipation of this great event, half on the North Bank, half on the South. For the first time in many years, the faces of weathered workers and long-suffering colonists shone with optimistic hope. The Macai workers weren't there for the celebration, of course, but had been granted a half-day rest. They were in their enclosure munching on celebratory dried grape snacks. They would be back to work in the Aftermidday.

The chatter of the crowd dimmed to a murmur when a slightly bent figure approached the podium. So that all could hear, Elder Yurzan's whispery voice was amplified by a Magical resonance spell directed at the air in front of his mouth.

"In honor of our dear friend and mentor, Elder Treska,

whose passing last year touched all our minds, we dedicate this magnificent structure which was his dream. As Chief Elder, I hereby christen and declare open *The Starshine Bridge!*"

With that cue, Parralon and Querokan, a pair of government Magicians, unleashed a barrage of spectacular fireworks. The Magical blossoms of color erupted from prepared canisters of powdered Morray Crystals and dried flint plants. Parralon's job was to produce the Absolute Magic energy that launched the canisters into the predawn sky and, once at altitude, exploded them into glorious displays of color and sound. Querokan then used his Worldly Magic to manipulate the wind eddies and sculpt the flaming streamers into luminous depictions of animals, landscapes, heroes, and monsters of myth. The grand finale was a glorious representation of Dyhendra, the great feathered bird of Mennatuan creation myths.

The Eryndi crowd cheered as the two great stone drawbridges on each side of the Erim River rumbled to life and slowly lowered to meet each other in the center with a mighty *kah-thud*. The structure was seventy-four reaches long when joined together, spanning the Erim River some thirty reaches below. The permanent link between North and South Tresk was complete. Ululating Eryndi cheers echoed up and down the steep rock walls of Bastion Canyon. The citizens joyfully ran from one side of the river to the other and back again, just for the sheer fun of doing so. Some people stopped midway on the bridge, keeping a tight hold of their children as they leaned over the railing and gazed down at the rushing waters of the Erim River below. Elder Yurzan raised a slow, shaky palm and spoke in a slow, shaky voice.

"My fellow Treskans, you have all heard the stories, the rumors, the warnings. Many are untrue, but alas, many are not."

The crowd emitted a long, muffled moan as this straightforward statement sank in.

"We have verified the presence of large numbers of Macai savages massing in the Jarayan Mountains to the east. Our exploratory expeditions up the Erim are hereby suspended until the Macai threat can be investigated. It may very well be that there is *not* an attack imminent. Perhaps the influx of Macai is merely a migratory phenomenon among these curious creatures."

Parralon turned to Querokan and muttered out the side of his mouth.

"The old boy sure can drone on, can't he?"

"He was my instructor in Midpoint School," replied Querokan quietly. "He used to eject any student he caught sleeping during sessions. He once lectured my class for over three hours and never paused once. There weren't many survivors."

"But, no matter the reason," the Elder droned on, "Tresk is now impregnable. Our position above the shoreline is unassailable against an attack by sea! Our mighty fortress wall, completed last year, surrounds our city. And now the Starshine Bridge connects South and North Tresk. Troops and supplies can be quickly and easily transported from one side to the other without having to rely on the cliff cranes. Our citizens and defenders are assured of lifetimes of security from any land-bound aggressors. The bridge can even be raised in the ridiculously unlikely event that one-half of the city is overrun by invaders!"

Yurzan's voice actually rose slightly in his excitement, causing several already-dozing spectators to snap back to attention, if only for a beat or two. The droning continued on, with the Elder repeating several points he had already made.

"Are you buying these stories about Macai savages?" asked Parralon.

"I don't know," replied Querokan. "It doesn't seem likely. The only Macai I've ever seen are the workers and they're gentle as kitties."

"But what about the Homeland? Macai destroyed everything!"

"You know," said Querokan, "when I was about twelve or so, I think, we had Grendoram over for evening meal once. He was one of the crew of the *Seeker*."

"Wasn't that the boat that sailed back to the Homeland?" asked Parralon.

"Yeah. He said that it took them months and they only made it as far as Ostracantrica. There had been some huge fire that had wiped out most of the city. The people were all gone, but there were a few Macai living in the ruins and they always fled when any Eryndi got near them."

Parralon looked confused. "That's not what I was told. In fact, Elder Yurzan himself taught that the Gods sent the Macai hordes to take over the entire Domain . . . to punish us for our greed, or something."

"I'm just telling you what Grendoram told us," said Querokan.

"He drinks a lot, doesn't he?"

"SSSHHHHHH!"

The frowning little girl standing in front of the two Magicians turned back toward the podium to try to catch the rest of Yurzan's speech.

". . . and with our fair city now secure, our armies shall venture into the mountains to scout out and learn what evil deeds are brewing there. May the Gods guide their steps!"

Querokan whispered this time so as not to arouse the ire of the little girl again. "What armies? There are only about thirty or so soldiers, and they spend all their time manning the wall."

"Doesn't matter," sneered Parralon. "Cacks with rocks and sticks are no match for trained Eryndi with steel weapons."

"Just so long as the Eryndi aren't outnumbered a thousand to one."

"MOM, make those two guys shut up! I can't hear the Elder!"

* * *

A lie can be your best course of action – unless you know you're gonna get caught. In that case, you might have to fall back on the truth, no matter how much it hurts. Oh, quick, son, hide the jug. Here comes your mother!

- Salimoré Foxx, Father of Lieusé, 21859

Today – Breeos Province of the Treskan Imperium

Group Six had finished their meal, answered more questions, and was now free to stroll about the camp within the confines of the green-tinted energy dome that encased and protected the cohort. The only restriction placed upon them was a warning not to approach the large tent at the center. Of course, once told that Group Six could not resist getting at least a peek at what was called "Guardian." It was a large, green tent made of thick, heavy canvas reinforced with bands of copper lattice. A rope warning barrier was stretched around it in a twenty-reach radius. Well-armed and vigilant Legionnaires patrolled its perimeter.

"Nothing says 'valuables' like a show of force," said Foxx, noting all the security. "A flashy display like this can't help but to tempt a clever entrepreneur to sneak in and investigate."

"Hold on there, superthief," said Tresado. "What are you considering?"

"Worry not," Foxx replied. "I'm not considering anything, just . . . musing."

Orchid was still pissed. "Were you musing before when you told them about Prakin's Pass?"

"I didn't," said Foxx. "I told them about the tunnel. I said we discovered it by accident, while traveling through the mountains. That is the absolute gods' truth."

"That must've been painful for you," offered Serena.

"It's just not what he's used to," said Tresado.

"But why tell them at all?" pressed Orchid.

"We were picked up only a quarter league from the tunnel," said Foxx. "They were going to find it, anyway."

"He's right," said Tresado. "When those rocks came down and opened the entrance, it made a hell of a noise. They couldn't help but hear it and investigate. That's probably what the Primus was doing when they ran into us."

"And," Foxx continued, "if we are going to be in the Imperium for a while, we need to stay on good terms with the Treskans. They run a fair and orderly society, but they can be . . . stern with lawbreakers. If they think we're spies, or even just hiding something, they can make our lives inconvenient."

"How inconvenient?" asked Orchid.

"Well, there's fines or incarceration . . ."

"Yes?"

"And for more serious crimes, there are things like ankle hanging, group flogging, sword gauntlets, stuff like that. Oh . . . and then, of course, there's Stadium."

"What's Stadium?" asked three voices.

"The largest entertainment attraction in the whole Imperium. Right in the heart of central Tresk. It's a huge arena where they hold gladiatorial matches, executions by wild animals, even dragon fights."

"That's awful!"

"How repugnant!"

"Cool."

"Well, on slow days they have hovercarriage races, boingball tournaments, and concerts," added Foxx.

"I still don't like it," repeated Orchid. "Quintell said that if the old road through the mountains was discovered by the Treskans, they would use it to invade the countries east of here."

"Well, if that's true, then they're gonna get invaded," said Serena. "The Treskans will use this new advantage as soon as they can – before any of those countries find out and fortify their borders. That's what I'd do."

1287 years ago – Tresk

YEAR OF THE CITY – 46

The party of fifteen Treskan explorers/soldiers had finally exited the mountain passes some 250 leagues east of the city. Their mission had mirrored that of the dozen previous ones over the years – push farther, learn all. Ahead of them now lay open prairie with a gentle slope leading up for uncounted leagues. Evidently, the lands farther inland were part of an immense plateau stretching for who knew how far. The Erim River, their constant companion on this trip, flowed faithfully on their right.

There was plenty to see on this expedition. The mountains were full of wildlife. Lumbas and packs of fire wolves that preyed upon them were the largest. There was also a smattering of wild goats, feather harts, and a type of weird, flightless bird that could run faster than a horse – not that that meant much to this expedition. Only one of their number, Detricos, was old enough to remember such things from the Old Domain. No one from Tresk had seen a horse in almost 50 years.

The other indigenous wildlife in the Jarayan Mountains seemed to be the most plentiful but the most seldom seen – wild Macai. There were many signs of them: abandoned fire pits, broken stone tools, and the butchered remains of animals. It was well known to the Eryndi that thousands of the beasts infested those craggy peaks. There had been skirmishes between them and the past Treskan expeditions that continued to push eastward from their seacoast city, but the current group of explorers had not seen a live Macai until only a week previous. They had come around a bend in the river and surprised a small herd of the creatures who had been collecting shellfish from the waters. The female who first spotted the Eryndi howled a warning. The rest of them snatched up a few juveniles and scattered into the hills. One big buck remained long enough to heave a large rock at his enemies before he too turned and fled. That had been several days ago, and now that they were coming out of the mountains, signs of the Macai dwindled and vanished.

This had been as much a scientific mission as a military one, which is why it took so long to come this far. Side trails were explored, and local flora and fauna, known and unknown, were identified and cataloged. Mineral wealth and other resources were noted. And, of course, the Macai threat had to be verified and documented. Querokan, the leader of the expedition, called an early halt. His people had been struggling through the unforgiving mountains for the last 47 days. They deserved a few days of rest as a reward. There appeared to be little danger on this prairie, and even if some should appear, the wide-open spaces would allow them to see it coming from leagues away. Even so, a strong, protective barrier of thorny branches was erected around their camp, and a blazing fire was kept going night and day.

Two women, Parmonera and Jerraica, had drawn watchguard duty that evening. They slowly walked the inside perimeter of the barrier, circling in opposite directions. They met at one of the two thorny gates and paused. Jerraica shook the branches to test the strength of the makeshift door.

"How are the feet?" she asked of her partner.

"No worse off than anybody else's, I guess," replied Parmonera. "After more than a month of those mountain trails, it'll be good to kick back." She glanced at the rest of the expedition members in the enclosure, who were napping, cataloging notes, or writing in journals. Jonculus was busy honing his sword to a fine edge. The rhythmic scraping seemed to soothe his nerves. Jonculus had always been wound a bit tight.

"Well, it won't be long now," said Jerraica. "We'll be relieved at Sendown and I'm looking forward to trying some of those gourds that we found." She nodded in the direction of the central fire, where a man was squatting before an iron pot. "Karvenos has been slow-cooking them for the past few hours."

"They do smell good, don't they?" Parmonera hadn't realized how hungry she was until Jerraica put the thought into her head.

"One good thing about this trip," said Jerraica, glancing out toward the endless prairie. "We've always had plenty to eat. Those mountains were crawling with game and there were always grapes and veggies."

"Maybe they chased it all there from the prairie."

"Maybe something chased the Macai there."

"Maybe . . ."

Jerraica's newest speculation was interrupted by the thorn gate next to her suddenly coming unfastened and swinging wide open seemingly by itself. Both women quickly readied their bows and peered cautiously out the opening. There was nothing there.

"Maybe you should stay more alert in case something unexpected happens."

The voice behind them came from Querokan, who stood there with the slightest of frowns on his Eryndi face. The Magician had apparently used his Worldly skills to manipulate the organic fibers of the thorn gate and cause it to open.

"Let's get back to keeping watch, shall we? That prairie may look empty, but we won't know what's out there until we see for ourselves, correct?"

"Yes, sir!"

"Yes, sir!"

Jerraica and Parmonera quickly separated and returned to their rounds, both blushing with embarrassment.

After two more days of rest and the stocking up of food rations in the form of dried fish from the river, the expedition was ready for the next phase of the journey. The going was continuously uphill on a gradual slope. Even so, the walk was much easier, traveled three or four times more leagues per day than when they were in the mountains. They continued to follow the river upstream, which continued ever eastward. Since exiting the mountain canyon, Erim slowed down its rushing flow and became a wider, shallower, and much calmer river. Sensang rose and fell, rose and fell, and the days seemed to merge into one long, boring trek up to the immense plateau before them.

Querokan was privately considering calling an end to this mission and heading back. There was nothing here. The threat to Tresk's security was behind them in the form of the Macai hordes that infested the mountains. Perhaps some future expedition would care to traverse the entirety of *Perpetual Plains,* as they had been named.

Suddenly a hand signal from Jonculus, who was far ahead on point, brought the group to a halt. He was perched atop a rock formation, squinting into the shimmering heat waves caused by the morning Sensang. He stood motionless for a few beats, then hurried back to rejoin the rest.

"What's up, soldier?" asked Querokan, who had snapped out of his reverie and back to reality.

"Large body of water ahead, sir," the soldier replied. "There is also a dust cloud between here and there. It was difficult to see clearly, but it might be a herd of animals, coming this way."

The riparian strip along the riverbank provided some concealment in the form of trees and shrubs. Querokan quickly ordered his troop to take cover in case the animals were something dangerous.

"Dunnelia! Shag your ass and get to cover!"

The last member to do so was always the last when it came

to moving quickly. Dunnelia was a rather corpulent Eryndi whose primary duties were the cataloging of plants and animals. She was a naturalist and artist, not a soldier or a sprinter. Her pudgy legs pumped as fast as they were able and finally took her to a hiding place behind a large seramin tree.

The dust cloud was approaching fast. Soon, the vibration of many hooves could be felt in the ground. As they got closer, it became apparent that there were at least twenty of the animals, whatever they were. The herd had been paralleling the river but turned quickly to the left just as they were opposite where the Eryndi were hiding. The dust cloud dissipated as the animals skidded to a stop. Several of them uttered a loud laughing sound that only Detricos, the oldest member, recognized.

"HORSES," he whispered loudly to Querokan on his left. "Those are horses!"

That was not the most astonishing thing, though. The horses were being ridden - by Eryndi!

CHAPTER 6

Better to grab the grilk by the balls than by the horns.

- HROLVAD THE BERSERKER, C. 20640

Today – Breeos Province of the Treskan Imperium

"PREPARE TO MOVE!"

The repeated announcement rolled through the camp at dawn, stirring the Treskan Legionnaires to action. In well-practiced maneuvers, tents were pulled down and stowed on wagons, supplies packed up and loaded on more wagons, and horses were saddled. The whole tent city was uprooted and ready to roll in less than half an hour.

"Those are some well-disciplined soldiers," observed Serena.

Guardian was apparently being saved for last. Foxx and the others were curious to see what might be inside, but before the fortified tent could come down, a party of mounted soldiers approached them. They were led by Primus Manginus, who greeted them warmly from horseback.

"My friends, I have a few things for you." She produced four thick, green-colored cards with gold printing on them. "These are your transport passes. They will assure your safe passage across all the Imperium. If ever asked about your identities by Treskan officials, simply show them these. They may also be used as grain and wine vouchers in any Treskan city."

Orchid's eyes lit up. "You mean we can get free wine with these?"

"It entitles you to a ration of bread and wine," explained Manginus. "It is the Imperator's wish that no citizen should suffer from hunger. Of course, that means one loaf and one cup . . . once per day."

"Oh."

"So, we're citizens now?" asked Tresado carefully.

The Primus smiled. "Certainly looks that way. Now, I must take my leave of you. The cohort is moving out. Varyus!"

Her aide came forward, leading four saddled horses.

"These mounts should be sufficient to get you to the railhead. Otherwise, it would be a long and dangerous journey on foot. Once there, your passes will allow you to board the Conveyor. It can take you all the way to the Imperial City, if you wish. A squad of Legionnaires will escort you to the railhead. This region is not without its hazards. Safe journey, my friends."

Primus Lucillia Manginus saluted and headed into the Guardian tent, barking orders the whole way. A confused Group Six stood there with their customized passes in one hand and the reins of a horse in the other. The escort squad leader, a man named Rockus, approached the group on his own horse. He was a good-sized Eryndi but still not nearly as tall as Serena, who boasted a full reach in height, or even Foxx, who wasn't far behind.

"If you folks are ready, we should depart. The railhead is over 150 leagues distant and we have a river to cross."

Before Group Six could ask any dumb questions, Rockus and his soldiers surrounded them.

"Shall we?"

They all glanced at each other, shrugged their shoulders, and hoisted themselves up onto their loaner horses. It took the roundish Tresado took two or three tries, as usual. His idea of exercise was levitating himself back to the food larder for thirds or fourths. Group Six and their escort of eight Legionnaires started west.

"So, what is this thing we're heading for?" asked Tresado. "What did she say, the railfoot?"

"Railhead," answered Foxx. "I've seen it in Tresk. It's a long pipe that runs along the ground. It starts in the Imperial Residence and branches off outside the city. Somehow the Magic within it propels a kind of carriage that they call a Conveyor. They use it as a fast transport. I didn't know it came this far east. From what I was told, only Imperial troops and supplies are allowed on it. I don't know why we're being taken there."

"Excuse me, sir," said Orchid, addressing Rockus. "How far did you say we will be traveling to this railhead?"

"About 150 leagues. The rail terminates at the far side of this province, although I'm told there is a project in the works to extend it to the mountains."

"Well, only a 149 and a half leagues to go," said Tresado. "That'll take us what, about a week?"

"Given favorable conditions, we should have you folks to the railhead on day six."

"Any good restaurants along the way?"

Before Rockus could answer, Tresado's cone-shaped ears perked up.

"Wait. You hear that?"

From behind them came an ominous sound, one that Serena had heard on many occasions.

"That's the sound of war."

The bulk of the army had just begun to head east toward the newly-opened tunnel entrance. Their green armor glistening in the sun was now competing with flashes of light from another source. The Treskans were under attack!

1232 years ago – Tresk

YEAR OF THE CITY – 101

It was a glorious time to call oneself a Treskan. The Centennial Celebration was in full swing with twelve full days of feasting and games. The streets were filled with Eryndi from all the other lands of the Coalition. The Horanese and Deci must have emptied their respective countries to join in the festivities in the city. There were even Talfians, Lumusites, Thalians, and many others who had traveled nearly five hundred leagues from the delightful shores of the Serin Sea to join their Eryndi cousins. Every private home and farm housed guests from the far-off provinces. There was scarcely a bed to be found among the Treskans, but somehow accommodations and many new friendships were made.

While the Charter stipulated that all member countries

were considered equal, there was an unspoken rule that everyone knew. To be from the founding nation was to be envied and respected. Many even considered native Treskans to be just naturally better-looking, too. Most of the Coalition's ruling families and elected Assembly Presiders were Treskans. The wealthiest businessfolk were all Treskans. It was not undeserved. When the countries of the First Coalition discovered each other over fifty years before, it was clear even then that the Treskan technology, Magic adeptness, and wisdom were generations ahead of all the other Eryndi peoples living in these pleasant lands. A partnership was reached very early, with no conflicts ensuing.

The Talfians, famous for breeding the finest livestock in the known world, brought with them over two hundred prime Macai to be traded, sold, or leased out for stud service, a duty that the hearty Macai bucks much preferred over manual labor. Treskan wines flowed like the Erim River. Gourmet seafood, prized *dirkova,* and exotic fruits and veggies were brought from the interior to delight Treskan palates. There were also, of course, many varieties of Decian fungus and high-grade jambabud products brought in by enterprising sellers. While such intoxicants were not exactly illegal, their use was considered to be base and crude, with only lowlifes indulging in them. Most citizens of all walks of life secretly bought and used them anyway, though they tried hard not to admit it.

Chief Presider Constanzia made the first of several speeches, announcing new expeditions to the south and east to make diplomatic contact with the Eryndi nations known to exist in those far-off lands. There were promises of expanded territory, secure borders, and health and prosperity for all. The Macai raids were largely over as the tribes were gradually integrated into a safer and more comfortable existence as beasts of burden and servants; all in all, it was a glorious time to be a Treskan.

* * *

Octavia, why do pigs always chase me up trees?
A question that you already know.
That's it . . . that's it! Ham hocks and beans for supper . . . right right?
Right right.

- Travelogue of Dementus the Mad Treskan

Today – Breeos Province of the Treskan Imperium

"Rebels! Quickly, we must get to cover!" Rockus wheeled his horse around and aimed its nose at a rock outcropping that thrust out of the ground.

"Shouldn't we go back and help?" asked Tresado, peering back at the battle.

"Yeah, what are we waiting for?" Serena hadn't been in a good fight since the Battle of Zanteryne Castle, and she was eager to mix it up.

"They will be all right," said Rockus. "We, on the other hand, are exposed. My orders are to let nothing happen to you, so MOVE IT!"

The squad began strategically retreating and herding Group Six along with them. They snatched glimpses of the battle from over their shoulders as they headed for cover, but the only things they could see from this distance were arcs of light being launched from the surrounding foothills and descending upon the Treskan army.

Rockus and his squad led the way over and through the outcropping until they reached the center. The pointed crags surrounded them on all sides, creating a relatively defensible shelter in the event the battle came to them. Serena pulled out her looker, an expandable tubular device that allowed her to see a great distance. Of the many fancy presents her people had given her when she had been declared *Queen of Honor and Love*, it was the only one she had kept.

"Holy stink rat sweat!"

"What?" said Tresado, reaching for the looker. "Let me see!"

Serena stomped on the Eryndi's foot without missing a second of the action. She could now see more clearly what was happening. The spears of light they had seen were actually large arrows or javelins being flung at the Treskans. They glowed with some kind of eerie Magical luminance. When they struck, a small explosion kicked dust and rocks into the air, as well as the occasional Treskan Legionnaire. A signal horn sounded, initiating a well-rehearsed move on the part of the soldiers. Immediately upon hearing the horn, the soldiers halted their march, tightened up their formation, and closely surrounded a curious, metal-framed wagon in the center. A beat later, a green, glowing tendril emerged from the top of it and expanded to cover the entire cohort in the familiar short dome shape they had seen before. Now the onslaught of explosive javelins, or *bang-bangs,* as Group Six later learned they were called, impacted harmlessly on the outside of the dome. The Treskans, not to be outdone, launched volleys of arrows from the inside, right through the energy dome as if it weren't even there. Several of the attacking force went down. In a last-ditch effort, the Breeosians launched a coordinated volley of bang-bangs, all targeting a single spot on the dome. The combined explosions did indeed open a bit of a hole in the shell, allowing two or three javelins to get through. They couldn't maintain a constant enough attack, though. As soon as the volley was over, the hole reformed itself with the shell again intact. Another handful of attackers were struck by the Treskan arrows, and the ambush party melted back into the hills whence they came.

"Who were they?" asked Orchid.

"Breeosian rebels," replied Rockus. "This province was annexed only last year. For some unfathomable reason, a few malcontents are not in favor of joining the Treskan Imperium."

Once the supposed danger was past, Rockus and his squad resumed the march to the west, dragging Group Six with them. They did not feel like prisoners but rather were treated like valuable cargo that needed to be guarded against theft.

The day wore on with no more emergencies. The well-used road smoothed their way through the rough country. The ragged foothills gradually changed to gently rolling countryside. Rock outcroppings became hardy oak trees, glorious in their fall colors. They passed through the wilderness as well as a few farms, all of which were abandoned and their fields and orchards stripped.

"This is nice country," said Orchid, happily drawing in a deep breath of wildflower-scented breeze. "I wonder why these farms are empty."

"Ha-hem!"

When Foxx's throat clearing drew Orchid's attention, he pointed at the soldiers with his eyes, a clear warning to not discuss that subject.

Just as Horizon's head tickled Sensang's bottom, Rockus called a halt for the night in a tight grove of trees near a small stream. For the next hour, the soldiers got busy hanging branches and thorny bushes from the boles of the trees surrounding their camp. Once the area was as secure as they could make it, the tents were pitched and cooking fires lit.

Chow that night consisted of cooked beans and sausage, the exact same food they had eaten in the Treskan mess tent, but it still tasted good after a full day's ride. The soldiers set up watches of two men for two hours each all night. Group Six offered to take their turns, but the Treskans wouldn't hear of it.

The sky was a dark one, as Nyha was taking a break for the next few nights and the light cloud cover obscured most of the stars. Far off in the distant hills, a few points of flickering light could be seen – other campfires from other campers, most likely. Who they were was a mystery.

Group Six sat staring into their own fire and contemplating their future in the Treskan Imperium. A far-off cry sounded in the distance, a strange, two-toned sort of sound. It began as a deep, rumbling cough. The second half was more of a high-pitched squeal.

"What the hell was that?" asked Foxx, the city boy.

"Predator and prey," answered Serena simply.

"Comforting. Well, I'm going to hit the sack. They set up two tents for us." Foxx rubbed his hands together vigorously. "Who wants to be my bunkmate tonight?"

"That would be Tresado, hotshot," replied Serena. "Orchid and I will be in the other tent. Just remember, I sleep with a scimitar. That tent flap moves and someone will be minus his gizzard." Serena made sure she said that last bit loud enough for the soldiers to hear it, as well.

"You're such a tease," replied Foxx with a charming smile.

"But I was, in fact, joking." He gave Tresado a prod with his foot. "Come on, bunkie. Good night, ladies."

TENT 1

"That green dome is really something," remarked Tresado as he pulled off his boots and emptied the dirt out. "I just can't imagine how so much Magic could be controlled like that."

Foxx took a quick peek out of the tent to make sure all seemed well before bedding down. "I think they call it 'The Shell.' I've heard of it, but never seen one operate before. It gives them a huge advantage over enemies. No wonder the Treskans have conquered so much territory."

"Serena said it seemed to emanate out of a metal wagon," said Tresado. "That must have been what was in the Guardian tent. I wish she would have let me see through her looker. I might have been able to analyze the Magic in use."

Foxx nodded. "She is pretty stubborn."

Tresado answered. "Opinionated."

"Hostile."

TENT 2

"Foxx is such a pig, at times," snarled Serena, wrapping the thin blanket around herself.

"He talks big, but can still be a gentleman," answered Orchid. "When he's not casting his spell on you."

"What, that Numbing Spell, or whatever he calls it?"

"Knowing Spell."

"Whatever," scoffed Serena. "No, he knows better than to try that crap on me. It wouldn't work. It's you that he casts it on."

"Whaaaat?"

"Orchid, he uses it to talk you into things that you're too smart to do on your own."

"No, you're wrong. I would know. And, trust me, he's used it more than once to . . . calm you down occasionally.

"Pig piss."

TENT 1

"Now, wait a minute," said Foxx. "I seem to remember that several months ago, you were pretty crazy about the Queen of Love and Honor."

"You know damned well that was because she was inhabited by that spirit. *Everybody* was in love with her."

Foxx's eyes twinkled. "Just messing with you, bro."

"Yeah. And don't think I haven't caught you sneaking a few peeks at both her and Orchid on occasion."

"I'm just a growing boy." Foxx paused and turned down the oil lamp. The two friends lay on their mats, contemplating the flickering shadows on the tent walls. Occasionally, the shape of a Treskan Legionnaire on guard duty passed by.

"But you know, I gotta say," whispered Foxx from the darkness, "both of them are okay in my book."

"Yeah," answered Tresado. "In my book, too."

TENT 2

Orchid sat cross-legged on her mat, idly flipping through the stained pages of Dementus the Mad Treskan's journal. Some parts were written in fine ink calligraphy with a clear, steady hand, while other passages looked like a First School kid had used a lumber crayon.

"What's so interesting?" asked Serena through a yawn.

"Oh, just this crazy diary," Orchid sighed. "I'm beginning to think our friend Dementus was not right in the head."

"Gee, you think maybe that's how he got his name?" Serena rolled over with her back to Orchid. "Eryndi are all not right in the head, Dementus and Tresado included. Now turn down that lamp, girl, and go to sleep. We still got a lot of riding to do tomorrow."

"Yeah, all right," said Orchid. She took one last look at the page she was on, which contained a bizarre poem, something about Tironian woven art, creamed flicken soup, and a bathtub. Orchid shook her head in utter confusion and addressed the book.

"What the hell does this mean?" she mumbled. "What are you saying here?"

She slammed the journal shut rather harder than needed out of frustration. What she didn't notice before it closed was the extra wording that, at this moment, was writing itself.

CHAPTER 7

1014 years ago – the Treskan Coalition

YEAR OF THE CITY – 319

Tersian, son of Prellit and Danniba, gratefully sat down on a low wall. His sandals had seen better days, and they did little to protect the young Eryndi's blistered feet. It had been a long, grueling trip all the way from Tresk on Ocean coast to the shores of the inland Serin Sea. But this was where the work, the adventure, and the girls were. Oh sure, there were plenty of opportunities back in Tresk if you wanted to work in the vineyards, as a trades apprentice, or join the army. If you were well-connected, a cushy post in the government could be had. Senators and wealthy business types traded favors all the time, such as hiring someone's child as an aide.

But that wasn't Tersian's idea of a full life. He had been told back in Tresk that the job market was so good in the interior that they would meet the caravans as they arrived and hire workers on the spot, even bid on them. And they were right. Hookers, hawkers, hucksters, and hirers crowded the entry port to the city of Surrana in the province of Talfia, all appraising potential customers or employees, each for their own reasons. There were merchants selling trade goods, treasure maps, passage on boats, mining tools, fishing equipment – some of it legitimate, much of it not. The hookers were there to relieve them not only of money but of the stress of the trip, or so they said. The edge of the city also contained gambling dens, watering holes, whorehouses, and a barbershop.

The Serin Sea was the gateway to prosperity. Its waterways led to motherlode mines in the northern mountains and forests full of rare and valuable spices and exotic woods. And, of course, the waters themselves overflowed with profit in the form of the dirkfish.

Tersian's plan was to make a lot of money in a short time. Simple plan, what could go wrong? With that in mind, he headed over to a small tent belonging to the Telachapook Fishing Consortium. He had heard of them from travelers. They were a group of several fleets of trawlers that had banded together. Big money in the dirking business, his friends had told him. You may smell like fish, but you'll be rolling in dough. Girls like to roll with guys in dough.

The recruiter gave Tersian a quick once-over and asked very few questions. They needed youth and muscle. Other matters, such as criminal records or debts, were mere trifles that couldn't be bothered with now. Besides, if there was a delay, like from checking backgrounds, some other outfit would snatch the prime workers away for themselves.

Two weeks and three days later, Tersian accidentally filled his loincloth when he was nearly disemboweled by the thrashing dirkfish on the deck. He and two shipmates had been knocked on their butts when the fish leapt three reaches out of the water and landed on the deck in the middle of the bare-legged dirkers.

The fish's sharp tail, fins, nose, whiskers, and teeth lashed and thrust in all directions. It is said that everything on a dirkfish is sharp. The dagger-pointed nose sliced cleanly through Tersian's leather sash, a hairsbreadth from his tender tummy skin. Three of the sailors and a Macai worker received some deep cuts before Chief Bonashonn managed to plunge a sharp boathook through the fish, pinning it to the deck. Even run through, the vicious creature continued to try to slash at the Eryndi, who were wise enough to keep out of range. These carnivorous nightmares were incredibly dangerous and feared, but the tiny, dark green eggs the females carried were considered one of the greatest delicacies known.

"Ungas, Patree . . . dispatch this beauty. We might just knock off early today."

The two Macai workers hesitated for a mere half a beat but did their duty. While Ungas distracted the infuriated and perforated fish, Patree grabbed a sledge. He waited for his opportunity when the fish would pause in its gyrating for a moment. When it did, he quickly moved in and, using the big hammer for its designed purpose, bashed in the head of the dirkfish. In gratitude, it lashed out one last time with its serrated tail and gave Patree a scar to be proud of across his calf.

Chief Bonashonn prodded the fish to make sure it was dead, but even then was cautious. Dirkfish have been known to play dead, suddenly sever a limb, then grab it up and dive back into the water. The boat chief ran a hook through its gills and hauled it up with the deck hoist. It was a beauty, all right. The dirkfish measured one reach eleven fingers from its needle-sharp nose to its razor-sharp tail. It would yield over ten stone of delectable meat. But, most importantly, it was a female.

"Get me a spiny, quick!"

One of the sailors was already on it and had just pulled one from the live well. It was an urchin-like creature whose feeding habit was to envelop its food and "save" it for later digestion. Some chemical in the spiny's body was a natural preservative that kept its food from spoiling, for weeks sometimes. Bonashonn stuck his thumbs in the rubbery body and opened it up. When he was ready, he squeezed the dirkfish in just the right spot. A torrent of tiny green eggs squirted out, and he carefully caught every one of them in the spiny. When full, the creature sealed its body back up, secure in the knowledge that it would have plenty to eat over the next few months. What it didn't know or understand was that the dirkova within it was destined to be sold for exorbitant prices and the spiny discarded. The shares from the sale of just this one fish's eggs would be enough to feed and clothe each of the crew and their families for weeks.

"SCHOOL!"

The cry from the masthead alerted the crew that limitless profit was just a league away. To the northeast, the water was being churned into whitecaps. It was a school of dirkfish, all right, and they have been known to travel together in the hundreds. Woe betide any creature in the water with such a large number of hungry predators. The first thing Tersian was told when he was hired was, "Whatever you do, don't fall out of the boat!"

"HELM, ALTER YOUR COURSE, KEEP US TO THE STARBOARD OF THAT SCHOOL. EXTEND THE BOOMS! STAND BY WITH THE IRON NETS!"

The proper ropes were pulled, changing the angle of the sails, and the rudder was put over. The trawler came around two points and was soon on the trail of the school. Chief Bonashonn continued to bark out orders to his dirkers. He rubbed his hands together in anticipation of the profit to come. This school was enormous. If they could bring in a full load and not lose too many of the crew, they would all be rich as kings, or at least princes.

"DECK THERE. SCHOOL HAS DISPERSED!"

The lookout was right. The water had ceased churning, and it seemed the dirkfish had sounded for some reason. That reason became apparent to the Eryndi very soon. There was a heaviness to the air, a sudden drop in air pressure, followed by an equally sudden rise. The waves fluttered with fine ripples as though being vibrated by some unknown force. Then came . . . *the feeling.* Within the space of five beats, every Eryndi on board suddenly felt a hollowness and a deep sense of loss. Something terrible had happened somewhere.

Today – Breeos Province of the Treskan Imperium

The next dawn had the soldiers up and ready to hit the road. Tresado had to be pried out of his bed, as usual. He always did like to sleep late. Breakfast consisted of cold wafers made of dried meat and grain. It was hard as a rock but filled the belly.

As Group Six rode along with their soldier escort, civilization seemed closer and closer. The road got better maintained and there were signs of logging in the woods. Sensang was nearly at zenith when more farms started appearing. Some had farmers hard at work in the fields and others were decimated and burned out. One couldn't help but notice that the functional and thriving farms were the ones displaying crisp, new Treskan Imperium flags. They were green with a stylized bear head in the center.

The horizon ahead was capped with a thin gray line over a thin blue one. The blue was the Big Bree River, the main water source for the town of Arkay. The gray line was a wall on the opposite bank of the river, a typical stone wall used by so many cities and towns to either keep its citizens in or an enemy out. In this case, it was the latter, but it didn't seem to have been very effective. The city gates, charred and blackened, stood wide open, with Treskan soldiers guarding the entrance.

Normally, one would cross the river to get to the town using Forsten Bridge, but alas, there was no more bridge. The only things remaining of it were two sets of charred posts on each bank. Now there was a stout rope line stretched across the water. Group Six and their entourage had to dismount and wade their horses across the chest-deep water, using the rope to steady the mounts. It took a good hour to get all the nervous creatures through the choppy waters. Tresado fell down sixteen times. He didn't nearly drown every time, just eleven of them.

A quick check-in with the guards and another whispered reference to the "triples" got Group Six immediate admission. They entered Arkay and were escorted to the other side of town. While crossing, they saw more evidence of recent violence. Many buildings had been torched or knocked down. A few citizens wandered the streets intent on their own affairs but giving the Treskans the respect that was no doubt demanded of them. When they reached a large villa, Rockus made the signal to dismount.

"I hope you will be comfortable here. We shall resume the trip at first light."

"We're staying here?" asked Orchid, who was eyeing the large mansion.

"Affirmative," replied Rockus. "This house used to belong

to a mayor, or governor, or some such thing. As premium guests, tonight it is yours. The servant master is inside and will see to your needs. We will call for you in the morning. Rest well."

"Rest well, he says," said Tresado, watching the soldiers ride off. "How fortunes change. A few days ago, we were starving and struggling, now we're 'premium guests.'"

"I don't know how many other people are staying here," said Orchid, "but you could fit a whole legion in this place. C'mon, let's go meet the servant master. I could use a drink."

* * *

The similarities between Ma Kahy and the native Ern are astonishing. Who would guess that two different species from two different worlds should evolve so much the same; two eyes, a nose with two nostrils, hands and feet with five digits, and a very similar internal layout and cellular structure. Bodily functions, dietary requirements, even the skeletal layout and dental formations are nearly identical . . . nearly. Nucleotide sequences are different by a mere 0.87 percent. Almost identical, but different enough. From my studies of these people, I have learned that much of their behavior is similar to the early Ma Kahy also. Their rituals and societal structure are much the same as our own early development. Reproduction is performed just as our ancestors did before Syndrome and the advent of uterine cloning. It would be impossible for our two peoples to reproduce, but the sex act would be performed in the same manner. I hope we will be welcome on this world.

- Doctor Comisa Maneret – personal journal

Today – Breeos Province of the Treskan Imperium

The accommodations in the Arkay villa had been luxurious but did not include sleeping in. As usual, Serena, the early riser, did the kicking out of bed for those who needed it. Rockus and his soldiers were waiting impatiently at the door of the villa at first light, and the party set off immediately.

The next four days were a bit monotonous: towns, farms, and the occasional burned structure or field. Several times they met other Treskan Legionnaires on patrol. In each case, Rockus would briefly confer with them and exchange intel. The farther west they got, the more something like "all is secure" was heard.

Finally, they arrived at a fair-sized city. The gates were open but heavily guarded. Soldiers kept a close eye on everything and everyone as they passed through. Just ahead of them, two Legionnaires were shaking down what appeared to be a Breeosian laborer attempting to leave the city. He was roughly pulled off his cart and cast down into the dirt. One of the Treskans pressed the tip of his pilum into the man's back to hold him down. His partner used his own weapon to prod the load of garbage on the cart. On the third thrust, a loud yelp was heard.

"Got one!"

An arm protruded from the trash pile in the universal gesture for "okay, I've had enough." A beat later, the rest of the Eryndi appeared, clutching her punctured thigh that was bleeding profusely. A Treskan officer appraised the new captive.

"Danikan Tyre! We are very glad to see you!"

At the sound of that name, Group Six's escort murmured to each other.

"Did you hear that?"

"Danikan Tyre!"

"They got her!"

"Pipe down and eyes front!" barked Rockus. "Let's try to look like soldiers!"

Two more guards from the gate joined in restraining the woman from the trash heap and the man driving the cart. Their mood was jubilant.

"Take her away and bandage that wound," said the officer. "Then put her with the others."

"Someone you know?" Foxx's question to Rockus had just a touch of Knowing Spell piggybacked on it. He wanted to know how the Treskan felt about what they had just seen.

"Danikan Tyre has been wanted for months," he replied. "She's been stirring up trouble amongst the Breeosians. Some even say she's the leader of the Durii, the local underground, and that she planned the Kryssan Massacre last year."

"What will they do to her?" asked Orchid.

"That'll be up to the Magistrate, I would guess. Interrogation, most likely - punishment definitely. Anyway, welcome to the city of Traelar, Provincial capital of Breeos. Your journey will be much easier from here on."

There was a lot going on here. There were Treskan soldiers and civilians everywhere. Commerce seemed to be flourishing in the bazaar. Treskan merchants sold a variety of goods, mostly to other Treskans. Socially, Breeosians seemed less regarded, whether they were Eryndi or Macai. On a hill overlooking the city, Breeosians toiled away, cutting and hauling stone blocks for the half-finished Fortress of Kasata, the future seat of Treskan administration here. Another large work party was busy constructing a heavy framework made up of twin rows of triangular braces that snaked their way down the hill from the fortress. A pair of strange-looking, metallic tubular rails were being laid across the top of them and securely fastened. Looking beyond it, Group Six could tell that it would eventually lead to a large, round building ahead, which seemed to be their own destination as well.

"We're here," said Rockus. "And it looks like you're in luck. The weekly Conveyor is just loading up. You shouldn't have to wait at all."

Group Six dismounted and their horses were led away to the stables. There was heavy security to get through before Rockus was allowed to take his charges into the building. The proper papers and travel passes were produced and examined by no less than three tiers of Treskan soldiers. At first, they were all suspicious of the civilian strangers, but once their status had been verified, the guards were as friendly and accommodating as any hostess at the Crystal Palace.

They were ushered into the building and shown around. This was most definitely a military establishment. There were no civilians to be seen other than themselves. The building was round with several large, open doorways. Each one had a pair of rails entering and terminating in a complex series of loops leading to other doors. Atop some of them were peculiar-looking coaches attached to each other single file. A number of troops were being methodically unloaded and marched out under the orders of their commander. Another smaller group was waiting to board as soon as the incoming soldiers were cleared out. These troops all showed evidence of battle injuries. They had been expertly dressed and bandaged, but some were seriously wounded. More than one soldier was missing an arm or leg. Orchid sized them up quickly but saw that there was little more she could do. Eryndi healing had stabilized them nicely.

"There will be just a short wait while your accommodations are prepared," said Rockus. "In the meantime, there is a PX right over there if you should require refreshment."

He didn't need to tell Orchid twice. "Time to test this sucker out." She quickly pulled out her travel pass and headed over. There was a large assortment of wines and spirits to be had, but the larger jugs required cash, of which she had none. Fortunately, the Imperator's Portion, as it was known, doled out a reasonably large cup of wine and a modest loaf of hoba bread. She smacked her lips in appreciation.

"Damn! For a handout, this is some tasty wine!"

"There's no finer wine anywhere than Treskan Firellian," said Foxx.

"I can believe it," said Orchid, downing the last of her cup in one gulp. "And it's free, too! Next town we get to, I'm getting another cup."

"Good luck with that," said Rockus, who had just returned. "Check your travel pass."

Orchid looked to see that the gold lettering on her card had turned gray.

"Twenty hours from now, the pass will reset and you'll be able to get another ration."

"A whole day?" Orchid pouted.

"Welcome to the Treskan Imperium," he smiled. "In the meantime, allow a simple soldier to buy you a drink. We have just enough time before your Conveyor departs."

"Well, lead on, handsome," said Orchid, grabbing his proffered arm.

849 years ago – The Treskan Coalition

YEAR OF THE CITY – 484

"Sire, Sen . . . Sen-a-tor Bal-a-tine is here. Wants have speaks with you."

"Balatine, eh? Ugh, do I have to?" In his own manner of protesting, Tersian took a large swallow of Firellian from his large glass that was always on the large side table in his large villa on the balmy eastern shore of the large freshwater lake known as the Serin Sea. Bora, his large, overprotective Macai servant, clucked her tongue in disapproval.

"You drink such much, Sire. Bad for you."

"It helps me deal with blowhards like Balatine," said Tersian. "Show him in."

Bora snorted and headed for the entry parlor, just fast enough to avoid a rebuke from her employer, but no faster. It was her way of letting Tersian know she was crabby and annoyed. She was that way all the time, though, so he paid her no mind.

Tersian grunted out of habit, rising from his comfy chair. At 180 years old, he probably could still do a full day's work but hadn't done so for many years. As the owner of the largest merchant fleet in the Serin Sea, he didn't have to. He was also the largest employer in all the Coalition, save for the military. But he wasn't fifteen years old anymore, as when he got his start in this business. That was 165 years ago, the same year Prakin's Pass and Yessua had been destroyed. He had packed on more than a few stone in that time. A wave of nostalgia washed over him as his mind drifted back to those grueling days working the trawlers and . . .

"Senator Balatine."

Bora's announcement snapped him back to the present. An officious-looking Eryndi was ushered in. He was a craggy-faced, silver-haired, walking picture of importance.

By *Krinol's Hairpiece, what a self-serving fish head of a man*, thought Tersian.

He and Balatine had grown up together back in Tresk. While the adventurous and very broke Tersian left to pursue his fortunes in the interior, Balatine used his family's influence to insinuate himself into the political arena in the capital. Now Tersian was rich and Balatine was influential.

Better to be rich; then you are automatically influential.

"Come in, Senator. Pour you a glass?"

Tersian knew that if the answer was no, whatever the man was about to say would not be welcome. If yes, this was either a social call or the Senator wanted a favor.

"Yes, please. You're very kind."

Wants something . . . and from that compliment, something big.

Balatine looked around at the spacious, airy rooms in the villa. A light breeze scented with scarum blossoms and herbs drifted in from the open garden windows. The fine furnishings were of a nautical motif, functional and sturdy, but retained the typical Eryndi elegance of style.

"You have a delightful home, Sire Tersian."

"I know. Have a seat."

"Thank you," Balatine sighed. "Yes, most delightful."

Get on with it!

"What brings you down to the beach, Senator?"

"You control a wide variety of water vessels, I believe."

"I own a boat or two."

"I wish to discuss a proposition."

"You discuss, I'll listen."

Tersian freshened up his glass of Firellian and settled back into his comfy chair. This was going to take a while. He made a conscious and obvious gesture of craning his neck to look at the water clock in the corner, a clear signal to the Senator to get to the point quickly.

Balatine took the hint. "You're familiar, no doubt, with the Noxus River?"

"I know it's a shallow, sand-clogged, piss-poor excuse for a river, poisoned with waste and rotted plants."

"Yes, there is that," said Balatine, sipping his wine delicately. "And beyond the river?"

"Nothing but hundreds of leagues of sand dunes and spark beetles."

"And beyond that?"

"Senator," Tersian sighed, "the point, if you don't mind."

Balatine smiled in understanding. "The Assembly wishes to charter your vessels and your expertise."

"For what? Or is that a state secret?"

"In a way, it is, so we will count on your discretion for now." Balatine paused as though he was either thinking through his answer or deciding whether to proceed at all. "We're going to make the greatest discovery in Eryndi history – the secret of Magic itself!"

Today – The Treskan Imperium

The Conveyor sped smoothly along its track with remarkable speed. It was at least as fast as a galloping horse and didn't require rest or feed. The car, as it was called, was plain and functional on the inside, understandable in that it was supposed to be for military use only. This particular car held forty seats and some bins and racks for the soldiers' weapons and packs, but Group Six had it all to themselves. There were twenty cars connected together. Most of the other ones were filled with wounded Legionnaires and crates of supplies headed for the capital. That's what they were labeled as, anyway. In reality, the boxes contained spoils of war taken from Breeosian homes and cities.

Group Six watched the landscape change with every league. The newest Treskan province of Breeos was swiftly left behind. The countryside became one of pleasant, rolling hills and carefully landscaped orchards, vineyards, and expensive villas. There was no wilderness as such. Every square reach of ground had been cultivated, landscaped, or urbanized. The area had been civilized for a great long time. Such was the province of Dralia.

At these speeds, if the Conveyor train had headed non-stop for Tresk, they could have made it there in just over a day, but there were a lot of towns and cities to stop at. Military cargo and passengers were unloaded at each stop and replaced with new ones. A scheduled stop usually lasted less than an hour while transfers were made. This gave Group Six a few short opportunities to stroll about, stretch their legs, and take in Treskan culture. They visited a museum dedicated to Macai antiquities and caught the first ten minutes of a play at an outdoor theatre. Unfortunately, there was never enough time to tour these places properly, as a loud air horn always announced that the Conveyor was about to depart again.

Two days later, as Sensang headed to Her gigantic four-poster bed just over the western horizon, the Conveyor stopped after pulling onto a side rail in the city of Burdeon. The soldier in charge announced that this would be the last stop of the day. During the night, something called core replacement was to take place, whatever that was. Tresado, ever curious about such things, stuck around to watch the process. Foxx, Orchid, and Serena left him to his hobbies and went to check out the bazaar.

As usual, arrangements for this night's billet were made. A wealthy family had graciously agreed to put up Group Six in their own home, again courtesy of their "triple" status. They seemed to have no idea why these four foreigners were so important, but they were compensated by the Imperium for their trouble. Tresado came in late, just as the evening meal was beginning. The lamb roast was succulent and the baked pebble bean casserole deliciously spicy. After dinner, they were shown to a comfy parlor with comfy furniture. Their hosts made a last inquiry to see if they needed anything, then excused themselves to retire early.

"Where were you all evening?" Foxx asked of Tresado.

"I was watching them service the Conveyor," replied Tresado. "It runs on a sort of Magical energy source. The Treskans use these infused spheres that react with the rail that the cars run on."

"Like the fuel coins you had to drive *Enchanter*?"

Tresado smiled fondly at the memory of his Magically-fueled catamaran that had carried Group Six on their first adventure together.

"Not exactly. If you remember, those reacted chemically with water to produce propulsion." Tresado's eyes got big as he got to the good part. "These cores, as they call them, somehow have the opposite polarity as the Magic in the rails. They allow the Conveyor cars to float just above and propel it forward."

"I didn't know Magic had a polarity," said Foxx.

"All of nature runs on polarity," added Orchid. "It's what allows lightning to strike and plants to grow."

"But I've never heard of Magic being used in this way," said Tresado. "It's so different from any method I'm familiar with."

Serena was stretched out on a plush divan. Her contribution to the conversation came in the form of a quiet snore. She always found these long-winded discussions about Magic boring as hell. Tresado lived for them.

"So, what are these cores made of?" asked Foxx.

"I don't know – dull black spheres about the size of a boingball. I only saw them taking out the spent ones and storing them away. I didn't get a chance to see the new ones installed."

"Why not?" asked Orchid. "I'd have thought you would have stuck around for that."

"Didn't want to miss dinner," burped Tresado, patting his generous belly.

* * *

People spend their lives searching for the big score, the winning hand, the buried treasure. These things are tough to find, but if you're not willing to go after them, then you'll just have to be content with living a boring life and then dying.

- Professor Abadiah Generax, 21862

CHAPTER 8

849 years ago – the Treskan Coalition

YEAR OF THE CITY – 484

Everyone who lived his life on the teeming Serin Sea knew to avoid the Murtez Estuary on the southeast coast. A constant battle was waged between the clean, fresh waters of the Serin Sea and the influx of the tainted Noxus River. Its water was unfit to drink or even wash in. It was contaminated with heavy concentrations of brimstone, poison shemak, and lead. There was no riparian plant life along the riverbanks. The toxic water embraced its only ally, the endless sand of the Zinji Desert, giving travelers a choice of dying slowly from poisoning or thirst. There were no predators or any other dangers that might kill instantly. Death was patient here.

Tersian was a businessman interested only in profit. He had been promised that this expedition should probably yield much. He was not a scientist, a Magic adept, or even an explorer, but he was in co-command of just such a bunch of people. This was the thirty-second day of struggling up the Noxus River. Teams of lumbas plodded along on the banks, harnessed to tow cables to move the cumbersome fleet upstream. Burly Macai workers sweated with oars, poles, and ropes to assist. It was certainly not a pleasure cruise. The Noxus was calm and slow-moving but aggravatingly shallow. All the vessels carrying the researchers were strung out single file behind the lead boat. The two tankers were the troublesome ones. Holding a thousand buckets of fresh water each, they weighed in at almost 1,600 stone. Four huge pontoons gave these behemoths a relatively shallow draft, but they still got constantly hung up on sandbars. At least six times a day, Tersian had to call a halt while one or both of the tankers were hauled off and refloated. This also meant unloading the six horses from their respective barges to add pulling muscle. There was no choice. Fresh water had to be carried with the expedition. There were Worldly Magicians along who could normally produce rain, but here, the dryness of the air precluded acquiring large amounts and the tainted water of the river could not be purified enough.

This was an expensive venture, to be sure, and one that was absolutely not guaranteed a return on Tersian's investment, but the Coalition was paying a preset hefty fee for the use of his boats, so he should at least break even. His contract also promised a generous percentage of any valuables found during the expedition. By the look of the forbidding Zinji Desert that stretched for unending leagues in all directions, the chances of that seemed pretty negligible.

One would think there would be no reason on Lurra to want to explore such a dreary and deadly place – until recently. A team of Treskan scientists and Magic adepts had made a remarkable discovery. Among the nasty chemicals in the river water, there were also occasional bits of decayed plant matter found drifting downstream. Nothing unusual there, but these scholars had discovered something that was interesting to them. Tersian had been briefed on their findings, but all that Magical mumbo-jumbo was quite beyond him. In short, the Magic found in the decayed plants was said to be many thousands of years old. Why that meant anything was also not on Tersian's list of things to worry about. What he did worry about was some of these fish heads getting themselves killed by doing something stupid.

Like now. Burtenal, a young researcher, was leaning far over the railing of the command barge, trying to snag something in the water with a boat hook. Another Eryndi and a Macai worker were hanging on to the back of his pants, trying to keep him from tumbling into the corrupted water. It was a close one, but Burtenal managed to get his prize aboard. He proudly held up a horrid-looking, slimy black mass. Tersian scowled at the oily corruption that was dripping onto his immaculate deck.

"What in the name of Rookus's Rot is this bilge?" he roared.

The scientists did not acknowledge him immediately but were gathered around the new find and jabbering excitedly. Dexos, leader of the academics and Tersian's co-commander of the expedition, came forward.

"My apologies, sir. It's just that . . . well, have a look for yourself."

Tersian scowled again, one of his best tricks, and pushed his way through the small crowd of clueless lubbers. Burtenal, rechristened *Boathook Boy* in his mind, was still holding up the slimy thing with his namesake. On closer inspection, he could see that it had at one time been a pinecone. There were still a few bits of it intact enough to recognize it as such. But what a pinecone! One of the researchers stretched a measuring ribbon and pronounced it to be one reach, seven fingers in length. Another fish head was mumbling to herself and doing some weird thing with her palms.

"A trace, a strong trace!" exclaimed the excitable young woman.

"Same as the originals?" asked Dexos.

"Yes, sir! Most definitely!"

"So now what?" asked Tersian wearily. "Do we cook it for dinner?"

"Oh, no," Dexos answered, not getting the sarcasm. "No, no. This is a great find! Proof that we are nearing our objective. The Magic trace in this specimen is consistent with other samples taken in the past!"

"So it's a Magic pinecone, is it?"

Dexos finally caught on that he was being talked down to. He shook his head slightly at his provincial sailor co-commander. He tried not to sound patronizing, but some things just can't be helped.

"This specimen confirms that there is an incredibly ancient source of Magic somewhere ahead of us. I'm *sure* you realize the significance."

Tersian looked back at him over the top of his Senlenses.

"Perhaps you'll tell me – and be sure to use small words, please."

The sarcastic tone could have melted the pitch in the planking.

"Praxan," Dexos said, addressing the young Magician, "this is your specialty. Perhaps you'd care to explain to Commander Tersian."

"Yes, sir," she gulped. Talking to crazy rich people always intimidated her marginally and annoyed her considerably

— something to do with their life-and-death power over other people's lives. "This plant matter is of a sort that, for some reason, has a kind of memory in its component bits. It seems to store traces of Magic in the structure."

"Fascinating," deadpanned Tersian. He eyed the young Eryndi woman, noting her nervousness. He moved in closer, using his taller-than-normal height of eighty-eight fingers to assert his authority.

"Anything else?"

"As a matter of fact, there is." Praxan may have been intimidated, but she was not one to put up with a bully's bergaloshit for very long. She now had an edge to her voice for all to hear. It essentially said *Stuff your arrogant snottiness*.

"We know that Magic has been around for many thousands of years of Eryndi history, *Commander*, but no one knows exactly how long. Some say it was created by the First Hibestian Empire about 25,000 years ago. Others believe that Magic has existed since the beginning of time."

"That is foolish, of course," interrupted Dexos with a snort. "Calculations of the ephemeral decay rate suggest a much more contemporary origin. If we can locate the source of that pinecone, it may be possible to vector in the initial point."

"Exactly what I was thinking," said Tersian, "but I believe young Praxan here was doing a good job of explaining. Heave away, baby-face." Tersian respected anyone who stood up to him.

Praxan brightened at the veiled compliment, whatever it meant.

"Commander Dexos is correct. In layman's terms, if we can find where that pinecone came from, there may be a way to triangulate the strength of the samples we find and trace the origins of Magic."

"Not unlike charting a course by the stars," replied Tersian. "Now forgive an old dirker's ignorance and tell me why learning this is so important."

"If we can understand where Magic comes from, we might be able to utilize it more efficiently, more productively."

"Think of it," interrupted Dexos again. "Magic power harnessed and controlled and available for all people everywhere to use safely."

Tersian still didn't quite understand all this Magic bilge, but he silently nodded and wandered back to his cabin to do some thinking. He was on his fifth shot of Firellian when a call from the lookout brought him back to reality.

"Fog bank ahead!"

It must have rolled in quickly. In the time it took Tersian to heave his bulk out of his hammock and head out on deck, the thick, white mist had completely enveloped the fleet of barges.

* * *

Seven weeks later, Hupyric of Lumus was supervising his crew of Macai workers in the digging of a relief channel off the left bank of the Noxus. If some of this poisoned water could be diverted into a leach field, then more of the delta land could be reclaimed for productive use.

"Boss . . . boss!"

A Macai who was working atop one of the temporary crane towers was pointing upstream at a strange mass slowly approaching. The small floating island eventually showed itself to be a tangle of planking and casks bound sloppily together with about a league of ropes. A dash of color on one edge caught Hupyric's attention.

"There's somebody on that mess. You there on crew five, get some lines on it and haul it in to shore!"

Two Macai jumped into kayaks and sped out to attach lines to the debris. One of them slipped and fell into the river. He had to be immediately pulled out before the poisoned water could do any harm. Despite this delay, the floating junkyard was pulled over to the bank. Hupyric jumped aboard and made his way across the precarious mound of shattered wood. A figure was lying face-down at the edge, one arm up to the elbow in the water. Hupyric turned the body over to look into the face of a young Eryndi woman. Her arm, was soaking wet, swollen and wrinkled but still had a faint pulse.

"Take her into my office, and find Healer Bronchus."

An hour later, thanks to Eryndi medicine, Praxan the Magician came back to semi-consciousness. Her fluttering eyes darted about in terror.

"Not . . . not."

"Now take it slowly," said Bronchus soothingly. "Take a sip of this tonic."

"Not the . . . not the source . . ."

"Not the source of what, dear?"

"Not . . . the source . . . of Magic . . ." The wild-eyed Praxan grabbed the healer's lapel and pulled him close, "but of madness!"

PART III:
TRESK

CHAPTER 9

Today – Tresk

YEAR OF THE CITY – 1333

As the Conveyor plunged deeper into the heart of the Imperium, cities and rail stops became more and more frequent. Three days later, after twenty-seven stops, three mountain passes, two rivers, and all the breathtaking snow-capped peaks, sprawling vineyards, gorgeous scenery, and fascinating culture they could stand, Group Six was finally approaching their destination.

The Conveyor slowed to the pace of a fast walk. The rail swung to the west and paralleled the north side of a deep canyon with a raging river below. Two heavily-trafficked roads flanked it on either side. A large and ancient stone wall lay ahead. A great iron portcullis hung over the canyon. It appeared that the heavy grating could be dropped down to the water, sealing off the river channel. There were also heavy gates on the two roads. When asked, the soldiers explained that the walls, of which there were several, were used in ancient times to protect the city from enemy incursions. They all ended up being unnecessary because, in all the centuries since the founding of Tresk, there had never been a battle within its walls. The gates had not been closed within living memory. Such was the famous lasting peace of the Imperium. The Conveyor rail rose in altitude and the cars proceeded smoothly and silently over the wall and entered the great city of Tresk.

Such sights to see! People from all walks of life and all parts of the known world hustled and bustled about their affairs. Group Six watched from the windows in fascination at the civilization around them. Magic was in use everywhere. In other cities, horses, bergalo, and similar beasts of burden were used to do the heavy work. Here in Tresk, even the humblest of businesses used hovering carts to move goods, grind grain, or crush gravel. Levitating, glowing signs floated above their heads, advertising eateries, entertainment parlors, and wine shops; even a tiny flower boutique had a floating fire poppy dancing about its open door.

The city was bisected by the fast-flowing Erim River in a deep canyon below. Ancient stone bridges crossed it in several places. They looked as though they were designed to raise and lower, probably during times of emergency. Like the iron gates, they had not moved in a long, long time.

After crossing the fourth and most ancient wall, the Conveyor entered what was known as Old Town. Some of the buildings in this area were well over a thousand years old. The architecture and the military seemed to be largely Eryndi, but the citizenry was a refreshingly mixed lot. Both Macai and Eryndi integrated and moved about equally. A quintet of citizens garbed in the robes of Senators strolled imperiously down the street. Two were Macai and three were Eryndi.

The Conveyor slowed and came to a full stop at a large,

bustling depot. A tone sounded and all the soldiers on board began to file out. Apparently, this was the end of the line. Near the end of the Conveyor train, another group of people exited the last car. They were shackled and under heavy guard by soldiers and were quickly led away.

Group Six stepped out of their private car and into the Senlight. Two enormous buildings flanked them. Just to the north of the rail was the largest edifice any of them had ever seen. The massive stone structure looked to be almost 150 reaches wide. The prisoners were taken inside.

"Twigs!" exclaimed Orchid. "What is that monstrosity?"

"That, my lady, is Stadium," replied Foxx. "The most popular hotspot in town. I'm told the Imperator had the old one torn down and replaced with this new and improved model."

"That's where they have the gladiator and dragon fights, isn't it?" asked Serena.

"Among other attractions . . ."

"Sounds like a hoot," said Serena. "And what's that other big-ass building, there?"

She pointed to a huge, nine-sided building just to the west. Unlike the elegant but functional Stadium, this one was adorned with scintillating, twisted spires, massive gold-trimmed windows, marble statues, fantastic murals, and exotic, flowering vines climbing about every surface.

"Imperator Merak's house," replied Foxx.

"Cozy. Do you suppose he has a spare room we can bunk in?" Orchid was never impressed with opulence.

"As a matter of fact, he does."

The unfamiliar voice came from a pleasant-looking Eryndi woman holding a clipboard box.

"Greetings, friends. My name is Feelia Efficious. Have I the pleasure of addressing," she said, pausing to glance at her clipboard, "Orchid, Serena, Foxx, and Tresado?"

Before Foxx could smarm his way in, Tresado quickly stepped forward and answered.

"You do, indeed. That's me . . . I mean, this is we . . . or . . . yes, you're correct. That's us."

"It's nice to meet you," she said, extending her left hand, palm forward in the Treskan way. Tresado, not familiar with the local custom of interlacing fingers, awkwardly attempted to match what she was doing, stepping on her toe in the process. The other members of Group Six stood by in restrained silence as they winked at each other and watched this hilarious display of Eryndi discomfiture.

When he finally got a grasp of Treskan handshaking, Tresado couldn't help staring into the soft hazel eyes of this most delightful woman who was holding his hand. His Eryndi connectivity reached out. He could feel not only her fingers but her essence, her place in the universe. Time stopped. This was so right, so ordained. All was as it should be with the world. The moment lasted forever until the spell was broken by Feelia's subtle attempt to squirm her fingers loose from Tresado's grip.

"I'm so sorry," she said with easy grace. "I should have remembered that you come from outside the Imperium. Some of our customs must seem strange. Well, hopefully we can remedy that. I have been sent to be your personal guide and advisor for your stay in our lands."

"That's wonnnnnderful," sighed Tresado. "I really want to learn your ways . . . TRESKAN . . . I really want to learn Treskan ways like they do things in Tresk. It's the Treskan way."

"As grace and charm are Tresado's way," interjected Foxx,

who finally decided it was time to rescue his friend from himself, no matter how amusing it was. "We thank you, my lady. Your offer is, of course, accepted."

"Splendid. Your quarters have been arranged. I can see you there now, if you wish."

"Lead the way," said Serena in her usual authoritative tone.

Feelia led them down the street to a hub where passenger hoverchariots awaited customers. She hailed a large one with multiple seats. The driver, who was better dressed than any of them, Foxx included, smiled widely.

"Where to, my friends?"

"The Orblight Villas on Comatusian Way, unless . . ."

"Unless what?" asked Tresado, his voice trembling a bit.

Feelia flashed him an irresistible smile. "Unless you would care for a quick tour of the city first."

Without asking his comrades or even really being aware of them at the moment, Tresado nodded vigorously.

"Yes, yes! A tour would be . . . great!"

"A tour it is, then," said Foxx with a surreptitious glance at the ladies, who were both in mid-eye-roll.

"Here, allow me," sputtered Tresado to Feelia. He offered his hand to help her into the chariot, but instead, clumsily managed to knock the clipboard box out of her hands. It hit the paving stones on one corner, shattering the thin material. A cloud of brilliant green sparks shot out of the interior, setting aflame the several sheets of thin paper in the clip.

"Oh, my. Oh my!" Feelia wanted to stamp out the flames, but her bare legs and open-toed sandals prevented her. Also, the fine, flowing robe she wore looked just as flammable as the paper. A small brouhaha ensued as everybody tried to either stamp or smother the fire at once. It resulted in nothing more than a shin-kicking contest as the flames continued to be fed by something within the broken box. Tresado, thinking quickly, grabbed the floppy hat off of Foxx's head and tried to beat the flames out with it. The green sparks were evidently very hot because the fuzzy, red velvet caught fire in his hand. Tresado squealed like a piglet from burned fingers and flung the flaming chapeau away. The infamous Tresado bad luck curse kicked in as the hat landed in a nearby planter.

Soon, a decorative green pillow bush was ablaze, sending an oily smoke wafting across the plaza. The small purple berries on the bush started exploding like party favors. Foxx lunged after his hat as soon as it was thrown and collided with an amused Serena, who had calmly stepped backward to enjoy the show. Foxx and the Northlands Warrior went down in a tangle. Treskans enjoy spectacles, so a small crowd began to gather and press in close. Tresado tripped over a pair of children who had rushed over to find out what was going on. Finally, Orchid collected herself and humbly asked Worldly Magic for a very localized rain shower upon the flames. They were quickly extinguished and the green sparking ceased a couple of beats later.

Tresado, like everyone else in the plaza, was now wet. His knee was skinned, his fingers were blistered, and he turned his bedraggled face to Feelia.

"Does this mean the tour's over?"

33 years ago - Tresado

"C'mon, don't be a puss, it's harmless."

Tresado looked down at his friend Marmosel's hand and the carved wooden pipe it contained.

"I don't know. I don't want to end up being hooked on it, like Pennaka."

"Pennaka was a goose brain long before she ever started smoking jamba."

"I'll stick with the punch, I think."

"You're braver than I am, my brother. I already know the punch is full of rockwine. And I think somebody might have also slipped in a little Nightroot. That mix will twist your puzzler worse than this stuff. Jamba doesn't make you stupid. In fact, it gives you advantages and insights, more than you can realize right now."

"Oh, yeah, right." Tresado tried his best to look wise.

"No, really. It lets you see just how crapped up Lurra really is."

"Why would I want that?"

The noise level at the illicit party had been steadily rising. Now, it reached a crescendo from a game of Kiss or Drink that was going on in the next room.

"C'mon, Tres. Let's go out back. I want to show you something."

"I really ought to head home. If my parents knew I snuck out . . ."

"Okay, fine. Head home, but come out back, first. I really want to show you something."

"Well . . ."

"C'mon. It will only take a few beats."

Tresado shrugged and followed his friend out of the overcrowded house. Marmosel's uncle, whom he lived with, was gone until tomorrow after midday. What better chance to throw a teen party?

Nyha was three-quarters full, providing ample light, but

was still dark enough to remain discrete about certain things. An old black owl watched the two young Eryndi approach and secrete themselves behind the bole of the tree it was sitting in. Black owls don't care about such things, so it went back to looking creepy and mysterious.

Marmosel took out the pipe again and held it in his open palm. His eyes closed for a beat as he concentrated. An orange glow emanated from the pipe's bowl as the jamba ignited. A tantalizing smell like that of roasted corn mixed with stink rat grass sought out Tresado's nose. At first he recoiled, but after Marmosel took a long drag from it and exhaled more smoke, Tresado couldn't deny it had an intriguing scent.

"Is that what you wanted to show me?" asked Tresado, trying to remain aloof. "My folks were both Worldly Adepts. They taught me how to start a flame when I was eight."

"And now you're twelve. Time to learn something else."

Marmosel closed his eyes and opened his palm. The pipe gave a slight shudder and slowly lifted itself into the air. It hovered unsteadily for a beat, then moved smoothly up to the young Eryndi's lips. He took a deep drag and held it, eventually expelling a cloud of blue smoke at Tresado's face. The hovering pipe turned itself around and floated over in front of Tresado's face.

"Sure you don't want to try some?"

"That's Macai Magic!" Tresado's volume dropped and he quickly glanced around for fear that someone had heard.

"Yeah, so what do you think?"

"Where did you learn this? Does your uncle know?"

"Doesn't matter, and no. Now you answer my question. What do you think?"

"About what?"

Marmosel's eyes rolled. "About what, the price of Ophanian griffleberries in winter! About *Absolute Magic!* What do you think about Absolute Magic?"

"I think you're gonna get in a lot of trouble."

"That all you think, Tres?"

"You could lose your seat in school, your folks could kick you out, you could . . . you could . . . show me that trick again."

Today – Tresk

The tour was, in fact, over, or at least delayed. The incident with the broken clipboard box was apparently more serious than it seemed. Feelia, with the help of Group Six, carefully gathered up the shattered, burned, and soggy remains. She insisted that every scrap, even the burned bits of thin paper, be salvaged, and it took forever to locate all the pieces. They finally boarded the long-waiting hoverchariot with the snickering driver, who couldn't help being amused by the spectacle. No doubt all the details would amuse the man's family at dinner tonight. Instead of the city tour or even Group Six's assigned villas, Feelia instructed him to take them straight to the Imperial Palace.

"Hey, I was only joking about that," said Orchid. "Or is this part of the joke?"

"Not at all," replied Feelia. "You have all been invited to attend a session of the weekly town meeting. Unfortunately, we lost much time after the *mishap* in the plaza." She shot a quick smile at Tresado, who melted at the sight. "We must enter the residence soon."

"Oh," deadpanned Orchid. "That sounds . . . exciting."

"It certainly is," Feelia said. "A great honor, as befitting your status."

"As triples?" asked Foxx quickly. He was fishing, and his Knowing Spell focused on the Eryndi woman to gauge her mental and physical reaction to the word. Her response was merely one of slight surprise at their knowing the term. Nothing unusual there. Foxx did not pick up anything nefarious or covert about Feelia. She was whom she appeared to be—a pleasant, helpful, and honest person, just doing her job.

The carriage rolled smoothly down Imperial Boulevard toward the opulent edifice ahead. The main entrance was an enormous, pillared opening large enough for a herd of lumbas ten abreast to pass through without scraping a hairy shoulder. Immense, gold-trimmed doors stood wide open with a score of Eryndi Legionnaires standing guard. They were magnificently armed in brilliant, highly-polished green breastplates that shone in the Senlight like emerald tortoises. Their matching swords and pole arms were encrusted with gems and inlaid gold filigree depicting stylized bear heads. The carriage did not enter here but rather rolled past and came to a stop at another, smaller entrance.

"Come with me, please," said the very patient Feelia. "There is still time before the meeting for you to clean up and change clothes."

"We have no other clothes," said Foxx, who glared at his good friend Tresado. "I don't even have a hat."

"Don't you worry about that," replied Feelia. "We'll provide you with something proper."

"Our clothes might be wet, but they aren't good enough for a town meeting?" asked Serena in her blunt way.

"There is a dress code."

"I hope they don't make me wear a tie," muttered Tresado under his breath.

Feelia led Group Six down a long corridor and stopped in front of doors seventeen and eighteen.

"Here you are," said Feelia. "Girls in here, boys in there. There are attendants within to assist you. Now, if you will excuse me, I must get changed myself. Can't appear at a town meeting wearing rags, you know."

Half of Group Six shrugged at the other half, and then each went into their assigned chambers, where they were besieged by armies of Eryndi retainers, each with their own specialties. They were washed, scrubbed, steamed, oiled, powdered, coiffed, and mani-pedi-ed half to death. The whole process was overseen by the watchful eye of a twitchy Eryndi man named Sequious Finnik, who carried the title of Propriety Monitor. He flitted back and forth between rooms, checking on every detail. When the grooming was finished, it was time for the clothes, racks and racks of them. There was no choosing for themselves, though. Sequious personally went through the inventory and made selections for each guest, clucking his tongue with each discarded choice. As respected triples, Group Six's original wet, singed, and torn clothing was taken away and burned. Sequious claimed it was just too tacky to impose its presence on polite society any further.

The men were given fine silk robes and assured they were the height of Treskan fashion. Foxx cut a dashing figure in his black silk wraparound trimmed with silver fibers. A broad magenta sash over his shoulder and tied at the waist directed the eye to his handsome features. His short beard and eyebrows had been trimmed in the Treskan fashion.

Tresado was dressed in an equally striking white and aqua garment designed to flatter any wearer. It didn't work on him, though. Even in fineries, Tresado still looked dumpy. Sequious just sort of threw up his hands as if to say *I've done all I can.* Two and a half hours after Group Six had entered the dressing rooms, he pronounced his creations complete.

Foxx and Tresado were led back into the corridor. The door to the women's dressing room opened at the exact same time, a tribute to Treskan efficiency. Serena and Orchid looked absolutely glorious. The women were decked out in spectacular gowns that accented their femininity and showed off more than a little skin.

Orchid's shimmering, forest green dress had a wide, off-the-shoulder bodice and a flowing train accented with silk flowers and a subtle leaf pattern in the material. Her chocolate brown hair was curled into ringlets and decorated with aromatic orchids in honor of her name. The newly formed curls danced across her bare shoulders with every step. Her makeup, perfectly applied, gave her a healthy, full-of-life sort of look, befitting her deep connections to the natural world. Even her ever-present staff had received a buffing and oiling. It purred and scintillated with a subdued pastel light show. Her dresser had advised her to leave the artifact behind, but Orchid would have none of that. Her argument was that the elegantly carved wood went well with her green silk gown. She finally lost the debate when she was told that weapons of any kind were not allowed and quite unnecessary, anyway.

Serena's dark blue dress was a perfect match for her lapis-colored eyes. It was cut from a strange, almost metallic fabric, every bit as glossy and delicate as silk, yet not silk. It clung tantalizingly to Serena's athletic body like a second skin. A halter neck bared her back and a deep v-cut down the front accented her magnificent diamond and equally impressive cleavage. Her usually tangled mane of blond hair had been done up in an elaborate, swirling steeple, adding to her already towering height.

Both women were sporting borrowed jewelry to accent the clothing, emeralds for Orchid, sapphires for Serena. A small fortune hung from their necks, fingers, and ears.

"I can't decide which of you cleans up better," said an admiring Foxx.

"Thanks," replied Tresado.

Further discussion on fashion was interrupted by the appearance of Feelia and an officious-looking official. Tresado audibly gulped at Feelia's appearance. Her clothing was just as alluring as that of Serena and Orchid. The male Eryndi accompanying her frowned sternly and strode forward to meet Foxx nose-to-nose.

"Well, well, if it isn't Mister Foxxus Veracitus with two exes! By the filthy fingernails of Shalaki, what prison did you escape from?"

"Sticky, you old degenerate!" exclaimed a surprised Foxx. "What are you doing here?"

"My job, which is making sure the Imperium is not overrun with thieves and conmen, but I see I'm too late. How's it going, Lucy?" The man's features softened as he clasped hands with Foxx in the Treskan manner.

"It's good to see you, my friend," said Foxx. "Last I heard, you were an intern or something for some senator?"

"My first real job. Mostly, I fetched wine."

"But, not anymore?"

"I'm still technically classified as a Senatorial Assistant, although with a different client," replied the Eryndi.

"Well, you seem well dressed, Sticky," grinned Foxx. "You must be earning a decent living, for once. You certainly were a piss-poor card player."

"Against you, maybe, but you always seemed to have the luck of the gods. I never did figure out how you knew I was bluffing on that last hand of the Blitzkrieg tournament."

Foxx cleared his throat self-consciously and changed the subject. "My friends, let me introduce to you my old friend, Stickitus Owtus. Sticky, this is Orchid, Serena, and Tresado."

"Charmed, utterly charmed," said Sticky, overtly ogling the two women. "I'm sure everyone will appreciate some new faces . . . and figures."

Foxx turned to the others. "Mister Owtus and I met when I visited Tresk years ago. We had some good times."

Sticky and Foxx each winked at the other and tittered lasciviously at some secret joke.

"It's obvious you're a friend of Foxx," said Orchid, a bit on the sarcastic side. "Just who is going to be at this town meeting, anyway?"

"Everyone who is anyone," said Feelia.

At this point, another Eryndi dressed to the nines hustled up and whispered something in Sticky's ear.

"Excuse me, friends. I'm needed elsewhere," said Sticky. "Do try to stay out of trouble, Foxxus." The two Eryndi hustled off down the hall, leaving Feelia with Group Six.

"Shall we go in?"

CHAPTER 10

Today – Weekly Honor Day School – City of Merakia

"Settle down . . . settle down . . . Nawshuss! Fulius! Put down the icons and take your seats. Now class, we'll do our reciting of The Treskan Creed. Who wants to start?

I believe in the Gods and all Their Children;
And in Dyhendra, The Great Bird of Creation;
Shalaki and Quiseron, Soil and Water;
Dajari and Heitus, Forest and Mount;
Great Ayendea, Eternal and Vast;
Vistaria, Of the Infinite Horizon;
Veratu, Sustain Me Now;
Jeruma, Sustain me Hereafter;
Dramin and Kermin, Find Me Love;
Parakline, Make Me Remember;
Comatus, Make Me Forget;
Rookus and Krinol, Ever Present and Inevitable,
Grant Me Patience.

"Very good. Now, for this Honor Day Class, let us remember the basics. So many people are caught up in their everyday affairs that they forget what started it all. Who can tell us the story of Dyhendra? Yes, Teenia?"

The little girl who always had her hand up answered excitedly.

"Dyhendra was a bird . . ."

"A really BIG bird."

The interruption came from a scrawny Eryndi kid with droopy ear cones.

"And she wanted children . . ." continued Teenia.

"So she laid an egg," said the pest.

"So she laid an egg," repeated Teenia angrily.

Magister Petrarus was an infinitely patient man, but this little butthead had been disruptive and intrusive and his own personal demon ever since this semestris began.

"And that was . . ." said the brat.

"Shut up, Dorfus!"

"Dorfus, let Teenia give the answers," said Petrarus tiredly.

"Yes, Magister."

"Go ahead, Teenia."

"And that egg became our world of Lurra," she continued.

Dorfus butted in again. "Tell him about the feather."

"I'm getting there! And Dyhendra plucked a feather out of her own tail and made it into the first Eryndi."

"My Pater says that then She pooped and that became the first Macai."

The class was now officially out of control from laughter.

"All right, that's it!" shouted Petrarus over the tumult. "Dorfus, go check the hallway for icebergs. Don't come back until you either find one, or you can act respectfully in class. Go!"

Dorfus gathered his scrolls and headed for the door,

making a silly face at his two fellow class clowns on his way out. Order was soon re-established.

"Very good, Teenia. Now, everyone open your scrolls to the tenth stanza and we will review the lessons of Dramin and Kermin and the history of prejudice."

Today – The Imperial Palace of Tresk

Feelia led the way through the door into the meeting hall. Group Six was expecting something like a lecture hall or council chambers. What greeted them upon entering was a cloud of jamba smoke and music. They entered an enormous, domed room with exotic tapestries, draperies of gold threads, mosaics depicting scenes of every means of partying imaginable. There were no tables, but rather short platforms no more than ten fingers high and surrounded by infinite piles of pillows and furs. Treskan citizens and politicos filled the room, lounging, drinking, smoking, snogging, and generally having a good old debauch. A team of highly-skilled dancers performed in the center pit, their scant silks swirling to the alluring music amidst a Magically created light show.

"This way," said Feelia. "Our reserved place is right over here."

There were so many pillows scattered about that there were no open paths on the floor. Feelia and Group Six were forced to pick their way carefully, stepping over several meeting attendees who were too engaged to move aside. Several probing hands reached up, trying for a quick feel as Serena, Orchid, and Foxx moved through the crowd. Tresado was apparently not worthy. The stoned senator that grabbed at Serena's thigh received a broken finger as a reward, but scarcely felt it.

Since there were no chairs, meeting-goers were required

to lounge on the many pillows. Serena had trouble keeping the split in her dress closed. Scantily clad servers of all sexes and races floated about the room, serving drinks, food, intoxicants, and even themselves if requested. A young Eryndi woman approached the table guiding a large, hovering silver platter, heavily laden with many types of mood-altering goodies. Anything was available, from the rare, expensive fireberry liqueur that Orchid requested to the stein of northern ale for Serena. Tresado opted for makara brandy with a jamba pipe chaser, while Foxx stuck with the local Firellian wine.

"When in Tresk," he said, eyeing the local scenery that filled the room.

"Yeah," said Tresado, perusing the various hors d'oeuvres and smacking his lips. He took a plate and filled it with flicken liver pate, pickled mica bird eggs, and a heaping pile of mashed spudkins with butter and green gravy.

"Hungry?" asked Orchid.

"As a matter of fact, I am," answered Tresado. "Won't you join me?"

"Well, maybe a bit of this rockfruit pudding."

Serena and Foxx also helped themselves to the gourmet food. Refills on drinks and pipes came quickly and often.

"I wonder when the 'meeting' starts?" asked Tresado around a mouthful of food.

"I'd say fairly soon."

"Why do you say that?" asked Orchid.

"Remember out in the hall, when that fellow came up and whispered in my old friend Sticky's ear?"

"Gee, you mean way back about three minutes ago?" asked Serena. "Yeah, I think I can dredge up that memory."

Foxx ignored the crabby Northlander. "He said, 'The Imperator is ready.'"

"Your lip reading?" asked Tresado.

"Yup."

As if to verify, the towering double doors at the far end of the room opened and a fanfare of Treskan trumpets erupted. A huge floating platform slowly moved inside. Everyone in the room stood (if they were able) as Imperator Merak graced the meeting hall with his presence. The crowd erupted in chants of "Hail, Merak" and "Imperator" and whatever else was thought to impress their leader and gain his favors.

The absolute ruler of the Treskan Imperium was a huge Macai, tipping the scales at well over thirty stone. He lay reclined upon a massive, ornate floating chair, fully tricked out with a built-in hookah filled with the best jamba, trays of delicacies, and no less than four drink holders. Merak held a large mug of some kind of heavy beer in one hand and a triple-decker lumba steak sandwich in the other. He took a large swig from the mug, half of the beer running down his three chins and washing away the glob of scarum sauce from his sandwich.

His aide, Stickitus Owtus, followed as closely as he could, stumbling over all the pillows and bodies as he tried to keep up with his Imperator. Merak maneuvered his floating throne of smorgasbord throughout the room, pausing to pass pleasantries with some senator, or actively chew out some military officer. His demeanor seemed to change from happy joviality to red-faced rage at a moment's notice. No one in the room was exempt from his attention. He even had the audacity, and evidently the power, to actively grope two Treskan women with impunity, leaving sandwich and beer stains on their gowns. Their husbands stood right next to them, but were powerless to do anything other than smile and bear it. Merak drifted slowly around the room, trailing dropped food and spilled drink.

When his sandwich was fully consumed, the mighty Imperator took a long toke from his hookah and immediately reached for a tray of dirkova canapes. There was always more of everything on the well-stocked Imperial Throne.

The meeting continued on into the evening. A couple more dance and acrobatic acts took their turns on the stage, as well as fire jugglers and a trained spearcat act. Booze was guzzled, food devoured, jamba smoked, and spit swapped. Such was the Treskan Weekly Town Meeting.

Two and a half hours later, the meeting was still in session, but winding down. Not that anyone had left. It was considered bad form and really not a good idea to leave while the Imperator was present. Things were winding down only because about half the room was passed out by now.

Feelia was dozing, as was Tresado, whose head had somehow found its way into her lap. He quietly burped in his sleep as he and his distended belly snuggled even closer.

Serena had priorities of her own as she slapped away the probing hand of yet another drunken meeting attendee who was interested in either her or her diamond. Her restraint was impressive, considering that a year ago, the Northlands warrior would have split someone in two for trying either. It helped that her scimitar had been left back in the changing room. She dealt with the situation by folding her arms across her chest and pretending to be asleep.

Orchid was on her seventh goblet of alcohol and pleasantly gregarious. She tried telling what she considered to be a bawdy joke to Foxx, but he was too busy with the serving girl in his lap. She sighed out of boredom and signaled for another drink. Her waving hand caught the attention of the Imperator, who immediately ceased his fondling of Senator Miriamia and headed in the direction of Group Six's table.

Feelia must have sensed his approach somehow and came awake immediately. She struggled to her feet, causing Tresado's head to fall off her lap and collide with a soft pillow. He didn't even wake up. Feelia prodded him and signaled to the others to stand up and pay obeisance.

The Imperial Throne floated slowly up and the giant man perused his newest guests.

"Ah, what have we here?" Merak gurgled. "A pair of Macai lovelies and their bodyguards, no doubt." He guffawed at the hilarity of his own words.

"Imperator, we are honored by your attention."

"Feelia, my treasure," replied Merak. "You are looking stunning as always."

"Thank you, Imperator," she responded. "May I present Mister Foxx, Mister Tresado . . ."

"Welcome, gentlefolk," he said, scarcely acknowledging the men. "I would hear the ladies' identities from their own gorgeous mouths."

Merak looked up and down at the stately Serena, who, despite the clothing and jewelry, still held herself like the proud warrior she was.

"I am called Serena the Free."

"Glorious, glorious," unashamedly ogling her chest. "You must tell me of your unique bit of jewelry."

"Long story, your Imperator-ness."

Another juicy guffaw and some remnants of half-chewed fish eggs burst from Merak's mouth. He turned to Orchid, who was swaying slightly.

"And who is this vision of Lurran perfection?"

"Orchid, daughter of Mishanna and Revinal, Imperator."

"Ah, Eryndi parents," Merak replied. "Do tell, what are your stories?"

"Imperator," said Feelia, "my friends here call themselves Group Six, and I believe they have many wondrous stories to tell."

"Group Six, eh?" Merak paused to shove an entire pebblegrape scone into his mouth and then wash it down with a gulp of wine, half of which ran down his three chins. He turned to Stickitus. "Have I heard of them?"

Sticky, ever-present at his Imperator's side, answered immediately by holding up three fingers.

"Ah, yes . . . *triples!*" He slapped his pudgy knee gleefully. "A fine score for me! Crystal Palace and Guraba?"

"Actually, the Crystal Palace and Abakaar, Imperator," said Sticky.

"Abakaar . . . ABAKAAR? HA HAHA HAHA!" Merak's outburst drew every head in the room. Having the Imperator in a good mood was generally good for everybody.

"You know of Abakaar, Imperator?" asked Orchid.

"Never been there, but I will! HA HAHA HAHA!"

Orchid, now quite tipsy, laughed along with Merak.

"Now that was an adventure!" she said loudly. "We saved the whole realm! Defeated the Vizier, who had taken it over. We saved Queen Minore, too! We saved everybody!"

"Yes, I know," replied Merak with a strange smirk. "Tell me, how did you do that?"

"Well, Foxx here found out those red medallions were controlling everybody and making them not want to leave. We got into a battle with . . . what was his name, Ramalama or something?"

"It was a weird name," replied Serena. "Ras-ta-ban, I think."

"Yeah, that was it!" shouted Tresado, who was just now starting to sober up enough to follow the conversation. "He tried to call all the soldiers to the castle, but we fought them off, didn't we, my friends?"

"That was sweet!" shouted Orchid, in her drunkenness. "He was about to kill the Queen, but we blasted him and that crazy, floating whale slug thing he was flying in!"

The once-jovial Imperator now had a scowl on his face. Foxx noticed and tried to surreptitiously shush Orchid, but to no avail.

"The pig deserved it! That one shot of yours took off his whole hand and wrist! Queen Minore even preserved it and hung it on the wall of her throne room! I love that lady!" Orchid threw back her head and laughed loudly.

Merak's face was now five shades of red. In his fury, he flung his pudgy legs out, trying to rise from his floating throne. It took three tries, but he managed it. He perched on the edge of the seat and leaned forward. His fleshy eyelids opened fully and he glared at Group Six with hatred and fury. A pair of onyx black eyes peered at them; they had seen such a pair of eyes on another occasion.

Foxx stared back in shock and horror.

"Rastaban?!"

The other three members of Group Six realized it at the same time. There was no mistaking those eyes, and also the voice. It was deeper, but had the same resonance as their foe from Abakaar. All four of them leapt to their feet and prepared for treachery. They were too late, though.

"Code Green – table six!"

That call came from Stickitus Owtus. As soon as the words left his lips, a green glow emanated out of the floor and coalesced into a hemispheric dome that covered the table, trapping Foxx, Tresado, Orchid, Serena, and also Feelia within.

107 years ago – the Treskan Coalition

YEAR OF THE CITY – 1226

The man wearily walked through the city gates. The guards gave him a once-over, noticing his odd clothing. He held their gazes for probably five seconds longer than normal, but they did not stop or question him. The morning heat was rising and the man was starting to sweat. His feet felt like lead and his shoulders ached from the weight of his backpack. He had walked almost three kilometers from where he had left his pod in the dark of night. It was well hidden and wouldn't be found by any of the locals. He took a little box from out of his pocket and spoke quietly into it when no one was watching.

"Mama always said I needed to eat less and exercise more. I'm sure glad to finally be away from her nagging. I'll show HER . . ."

The man had entered the city on the northeast side. He passed a contained tract of land cultivating some kind of vine with clumps of little green and red globes clinging to them. There was a series of wooden pipes and valves snaking amongst the vines, apparently for irrigation. There were no pumps, however. The water was pulled from the ground another way.

"My initial covert survey of this city indicates a civilization with relatively sophisticated technology as well as skillful vorennial field manipulation, both passive and active."

The man eventually came to the north rim of the deep canyon that split the city in two. He sat down to rest for a few minutes at an observation area. He munched on a ration pack and perused the swiftly running river far below. When he was finished eating, he hoisted himself off the bench, grunting with the effort. The man followed the canyon's edge along the north side of the river. He strolled through the bustling streets, marveling at the complexity and ingenuity that these two species were capable of when using what they called Magic.

"The Magic-powered lifts that hoist cargo and supplies up and down the cliff faces to and from the port are particularly ingenious," he said to the box. "They work very well, but require a Magician to operate them every time. Well, I'll just have to devise something a little better."

The man moved through the bustling city, taking in all the sights. As he toured the metropolis, he saw bazaars, wineries, merchants selling all manner of goods, and also many edifices dedicated to the worship of mythical deities.

"They may be civilized, but still cling to old superstitions," the man said to his little box as he passed the Temple of Dramin and Kermin, where a wedding was occurring. "That is one thing that I won't screw with. The fear of divine displeasure will prove to be useful in maintaining my token's integrity."

The further he penetrated into the heart of the city, the more ancient the architecture. He passed through four different walls, built centuries after one another as the city grew. They were now nothing more than curiosities. The Coalition, as the locals called it, had expanded considerably. It now encompassed several ex-countries, which provided a huge buffer against any invasion from inland. All these lands had apparently joined voluntarily. When the Macai had been granted full equal rights a few hundred years ago, their vigor and energy combined with the wisdom and sanity of the Eryndi, making for a well-regulated and serene civilization. The populace seemed reasonably happy and content, and therefore less likely to rebel. They had an apparent love of order and discipline.

"This realm will make an excellent opening gambit."

The man halted his walk and sat down on a public bench. He pushed some studs on the box and a series of lighted green characters appeared on the face. "Ascendency opening move input." Another series of characters appeared on the box, this time in red. He chuckled to himself and tapped out a response, mumbling each word to himself as he entered them.

"I know you wanted this token, but I won the toss. Your turn, my brother."

He was about to make another oral entry when a group of people approached his position. He quickly palmed his little box and allowed them to pass. They were chattering back and forth, which, of course, he didn't understand. Once the crowd passed him, he accessed the translation function. Their words were repeated in his own language. All of them were discussing their eagerness to hear a public address by someone called Imperatrix Alythya. Someone important, apparently.

As they got closer to the western and oldest section of the city, the crowd gradually increased. It seems the whole city was gathering to hear this Alythya. Eventually he came to a large building with a balcony overlooking a plaza. Everyone had stopped here and was looking upward in anticipation. The crowd buzzed with conversation. The man surreptitiously slipped a pair of tiny hearing servos into his ears and re-activated the translation function of his little box. In time and with help from his tools, he would learn their speech for real.

"All the people of this place speak the same language," he said to the box. "That suggests some kind of extraordinary connectivity between the natives. Mama theorized that the vorennium-infused core had something to do with it. Perhaps so. A mystery for later investigation."

His musings were interrupted by cheers erupting from the crowd. Alythya, Imperatrix of the Treskan Coalition, stepped out onto the third-story balcony. She was glorious. A wide smile beamed from her beautiful Eryndi face as she waved and blew kisses to the crowd. Despite her efforts to quiet them so she could speak, the populace continued the unending cheer. Finally, after several minutes, she managed to settle them down.

"Citizens," she called out, "as usual, I am thrilled and honored by your support. It is most gratifying, is it not, when one's family and loved ones actually like you? How rare is that?"

The crowd erupted in a round of laughter and cheering, again. The Imperatrix's speaking style was friendly and easy-going, as though she were one of the masses herself. The man listened in rapt attention to her speech, which dealt with important issues of the Coalition. It was a little difficult for the man to follow every nuance, as the translator always ran a few seconds behind the spoken words. Also, he had no idea who or what some of her topics were. It didn't matter, though. This woman was glorious.

The man's mind, abnormally skewed by its recent changes, whirled with strange attractions and urges that he barely understood. The bulk of the prepared speech was over and now Alythya was just being herself. She focused on a Macai family near the front of the crowd, a mother, father, and two children.

"That is a lovely shawl, citizen."

The woman blushed at the compliment and bowed her head in thanks.

"I think I would like a closer look, if you don't mind."

Alythya smiled broadly, athletically hopped up onto the

balcony's railing, and leapt out into space. The crowd gasped in fear until a shimmering Magical effect coalesced into a tall brass pipe reaching to the ground. The Imperatrix deftly grasped it in midair and slid gracefully to the ground, spinning about the three-story conjured pole with a handsome leg extended and her musical voice crying out a long "woo-hoo."

The crowd cheered wildly at both the performance and their ruler's warmth toward the family. She again complimented the woman on her shawl, then took a few moments to talk to the children, who were shyly hiding behind their Dad's legs. Alythya then moved through the crowd, talking to people, clasping their hands in an unusual but apparently customary way. She had no body guards and apparently did not need them. The crowd loved her.

The man watched this local ruler with increasing rapture. This was truly a leader of the people, friendly, supportive, yet still regal and imperial. He could not take his eyes off her. The object of his fascination was approaching. Alythya stopped in front of him and smiled brighter than the star itself.

"Greetings, my friend," she said. "That is a most interesting tunic you are wearing."

She was referring to the strange, metallic-looking one-piece jumpsuit the man was wearing. The translator provided her words, but not a proper response. He merely nodded his head and smiled. She was intrigued by the man's eyes. Never before had she seen such black eyes on a Macai. They drew her in like an inescapable well of darkness.

"What is your name, friend?"

The translator, of course took a couple of moments to repeat her question in words he could understand, but this was one he was able to answer.

"Merak."

Today – Tresk

The shimmering, green dome completely encompassed the table area that Group Six occupied. Tresado and Orchid immediately tried their various Magical skills to either dispel it or break through it, but there was little effect. Tresado tried his kinetic specialty to push away the shell barrier, but found his spell had no more power than a kitten pushing a lumba. Orchid's attempt at a windstorm produced only a pathetic wheeze.

"This thing is taking up all the Magic from the air!" shouted Tresado with a panicked look. He didn't like being deprived of his abilities.

The shell that they had observed being used against the Breeosian rebels had protected the Treskan Legionnaires from outside attacks while allowing them to launch their own from inside. This one that encased Group Six was the exact opposite. It was designed to keep troublemakers such as themselves harmlessly confined. Its ability to allow deadly missiles to enter from the outside was confirmed by the score of guards who quickly appeared and surrounded the table, pointing crossbows at them.

The soldier in charge looked to his Imperator for instructions. Merak's face was red as a rockfruit and there was a vein standing out on the side of his head that you could tow an ore wagon with.

"Imperator?"

Merak could only manage to spit out one word between his gritted teeth.

"Stadium!"

"Imperator! IMPERATOR! What about me?" Feelia was close to panicking as she tried to push against the barrier.

Merak, with his usual penchant for justice, answered her.

"You brought them here. You may join them. Stadium!"

Primus Kapatius Ampol, the soldier in charge of the Imperial Guard, was not fazed. He had seen his Imperator in action before.

"Bring their belongings. They're going to need them."

A low-level grunt saluted and ran out of the room.

"Guards, stand ready!" barked the Primus.

The soldiers cocked their crossbows in a meaningful way. Each member of Group Six, including Feelia, now had at least two or three barbed bolts aimed at their midsections.

"Criminals, it is my duty to advise you of your rights," said Kapatius. "You have none. Do not resist and no harm will come to you in front of all these good people." He glanced back at Stickitus, who nodded back.

"Code white, table six."

At Sticky's command, the shell disappeared.

"Prisoners, the order of the day is cooperate or die. March them out, Chief."

There was nothing any of them could do. Their brains conjured several plans, but all the scenarios ended with numerous puncture wounds. Group Six was led out of the meeting room and into the hall. The Imperial jeweler, Kartia Scintillus, who had supplied the ladies with their borrowed fineries, waited there. At her request, the soldiers halted just long enough for her to remove the emeralds and sapphires. She made the mistake of also reaching for the fabulous diamond embedded in Serena's sternum. In a move that could scarcely be followed even by Eryndi eyes, Serena's head snapped forward. Kartia yelped in surprise, looking down at her left hand that now had only four fingers.

Ptooie!

The missing digit spat from Serena's mouth to land on the Chief's foot. The guards' laughter nearly drowned out Kartia's screams of pain as she fled down the hall.

"Oh, you'll do well in Stadium!" said the snickering Chief. "Now MARCH!"

Group Six and their well-armed entourage marched down Imperial Boulevard toward the massive Stadium. A crowd of curious citizens trailed behind the strange sight. Treskans were quite used to seeing criminals taken for punishment, but not such well-dressed ones. The slight breeze billowed Orchid's and Serena's silky garments about them. Orchid did her best to keep her dress in place. Serena, on the other hand, marched proudly with head high and a defiant look on her face. Feelia was in shock and gently sobbing as they plodded along. Tresado kept a tight hold around her waist. Otherwise, she would have simply collapsed from the sheer horror of it all.

The Legionnaires marched Group Six up to a special gate on the west side. The Chief halted and pulled on a lanyard. From somewhere deep in the bowels of Stadium, a gong sounded. A trio of guards approached the gate from within. The head jailer, named Ternkeus, carefully scrutinized the group. After recognizing the Chief, he grunted a greeting.

"Are we having a fashion show before the executions, Chief?"

"Evening, Ternkeus. You're looking at tonight's guests for the executions. Open up, please. I need to get this bunch squared away ASAP." The Chief lowered his voice a bit. "They're here at the Imperator's personal orders."

"Truth?"

"Truth," replied the Chief.

Ternkeus and the other two guards snapped to attention at the mere mention of Merak. He quickly produced a large iron key and unlocked the heavy bars. The gate swung open. A dark stone stairway going down yawned ahead of Group Six. A cold draft brought the acrid scent of predatory animals and unwashed bodies. Those who were sensitive to such things also detected feelings of despair and fright coming from below. The five prisoners were herded through the gate, which slammed shut behind them with a loud bang.

"Go ahead and take them below," Ternkeus said to the soldiers. Serena made a sudden move of resistance, but the experienced guards were prepared for such a thing. She was quickly clubbed from behind with the haft of a pole arm. Serena sank to her knees, stunned but still conscious.

"Trust me, prisoners. We are very good at this. Any more resistance will be met with sterner measures." Ternkeus nodded to the guards, who proceeded with their orders.

"And prisoners," he added, "welcome to Stadium!"

PART IV: STADIUM

CHAPTER 11

Alythya, my treasure;
I swear to be faithful and true;
To love and protect you and your subjects;
To rule justly by your side;
I swear this by all the gods of Tresk;
Till death shall separate us . . .

-Imperator Merak
– Bonding ceremony, 21771 (105 years ago)

* * *

Group Six and the still-terrified Feelia were taken down the ominous stone steps and into a room with more guards. A stern-faced Centurian named Pharox sat at a desk.

"When your name is called, step forward! Chonk Boy!"

All heads turned to Tresado.

"By the Gods! That is not my name," replied the incensed Eryndi.

"I'm the only god you need to worry about now," said Pharox. "Now get your fat ass over here!"

A shove from a guard gave Tresado the motivation to step forward. While doing so, he concentrated on a kinetic spell that would have wall-walloped the guards into pulp. But nothing happened. Now he knew why this place filled him with such dread. There was no Magic at all surrounding him.

It must be shielded or negated somehow, he thought.

"Well, that answers my question," smirked the Centurian. "So you're a big scary Magician, are you? You're not going to be pulling no rabbit out of your ass in here. Save it for the sands."

He took a piece of green parchment, wrote a big number two on it, and handed it to one of the guards. The man stuck a long pin through it and not-so-gently attached it to Tresado's chest – literally. The thin silk of his robe did little to protect his thin skin beneath.

"What does this mean?" winced Tresado, who started to reach up to the paper.

"It means you'll get beaten within a finger of your life if you try to take that label off."

"Okay, okay." Tresado continued to very carefully pull the pin out of his skin while not removing it from his clothing. "But what does the number two mean?"

"It means that as a big scary Magician, you get the honor of single combat with a single opponent. Now shut up and step back."

Pharox pointed at Orchid. "You're next, PeeWee. What's your skill – floral arrangement?"

"Why don't you let us out of here and I'll show you?"

"Another toughie. You look like a number three to me."

He made the appropriate label and a soldier pinned it on her dress.

"Step up, Boobie," he said to Serena, who was rubbing the back of her head and shooting daggers out of her eyes.

The Eryndi guards kept a very close watch on Serena. She

towered over them. They could tell she could break them in two if given half a chance.

"No need to ask what we have here," said the Centurian. He turned to his guards. "Barbarians like this usually don't do so good, too undisciplined and stupid." That made the boys snicker at the Northlander's expense.

Serena's cheeks burned with the insult. To her mind, a barbarian was one of the deformed mutants that she had fought against in her homeland.

"Even so," he continued, "maybe if you survive the first round, we'll put you in a single opponent bout. The crowd likes to see knuckle draggers like you get their arrogant smiles carved off their faces by professionals."

Serena was given a number one to wear, defining her as a non-Magical fighter. That left just Foxx and Feelia. Pharox didn't even bother calling them up.

"These other two are a waste of skin. Birdseed for both of them."

"NOOO!!" Feelia cried piteously, then collapsed in a swoon. Tresado tried to rush to her aid, but was held back by guards. While Foxx and the prone Feelia were being labeled as number fours, another guard entered from the staircase carrying a large sack over his shoulder along with Orchid's staff in the other hand.

"Their possessions, Centurian."

"Good, let's have a look."

He opened the bag, which had the hilt of Serena's scimitar sticking out of the top, and examined each article. He efficiently set aside all weapons, including Serena's sword and stiletto, Foxx's and Orchid's belt knives, and Orchid's staff. The rest of the stuff consisted of their backpacks, Serena's looker tube,

Orchid's usually empty flask, Tresado's snack stash, various backpack stuff, and Dementus's and Orchid's journals. The Centurian tossed them aside without looking at them.

"You've got no need of books for the rest of your life, which, in case you're curious, is about one day. Stow this junk in locker number six. Take them to the hospitality suites."

The man took the bag and put it in a large storage bin, which he closed and locked. At the Centurian's orders, another guard gathered up the weapons and followed the well-guarded Group Six deeper into the bowels of Stadium. They halted at a T in the hallway.

"One and four wait here. Two and three, follow me."

CELL 1

Tresado and Orchid were taken down the passage to the right and hustled into a large, caged holding cell. There were several other prisoners held in different cells up and down the hall. There was no Magic to be found anywhere, so they had no choice but to get locked in.

"You getting anything?" Tresado asked as soon as the door slammed shut and the guards retreated down the hall.

"Nothing. Somehow, they're blocking or dampening Magic. I wouldn't be able to do much in this stone dungeon, anyway. I need access to the open air, or plants, or animals. Not much of that down here," said Orchid, looking around at the bleak stone walls.

"What do you suppose Rastaban is going to do with us?" asked Tresado, with just a bit of whine in his voice. Tresado was no coward, but he was used to using Magic to get by in life. To him, being in this dungeon was one of the most frightening experiences ever. Not being able to cast even the most basic spells was like losing a sense.

"You mean Merak?" replied Orchid.

"I just don't know. Something's fishy. Doesn't make sense."

"He sure looks and sounds like Rastaban," said Orchid.

"Except that he seems to have gained about fifteen or twenty stone since we saw him."

"He also seems to have grown his hand back," said Orchid.

"Yeah, about that," said Tresado. "That seemed to be what set him off. Maybe you shouldn't drink so much when in the presence of a powerful head of state."

"Says the brandy-breath guy who passed out from overindulging."

"We were honored guests until you mentioned the battle – just sayin'."

"Oh leave me alone," whispered Orchid. "I have a headache."

Tresado ignored her and continued wrestling with the puzzle. "We all saw those eyes and heard that voice, but Queen Minore said that Rastaban had been her vizier for years. Merak has been ruling Tresk for like a hundred years or something."

"But that doesn't make sense, either," added Orchid. "Merak is a Macai. How could he be the Imperator for a century? He should be long dead."

"If he was an Eryndi, it would be possible," said Tresado. "But he is definitely no Eryndi. Eryndi don't get nearly that large."

"At least . . . not from lack of trying."

Tresado looked down at his oversized (for an Eryndi) belly and winced. "I've been too busy studying Magic all my life. I'll leave the healthy living and exercise to the Serenas of the world. Too much work."

At the mention of Serena, Orchid got a worried look. "I hope she's all right."

"Yeah," Tresado agreed. "And Feelia and Foxx, too."

Now more angered than fearful, Tresado put his face to the bars.

"If you hurt that woman, YOU'LL HAVE TO DEAL WITH ME!"

"SHUT UP DOWN THERE!"

The shout from the guard down the hall elicited hushed whispers from the other prisoners.

"Quiet . . . keep it down . . . don't piss 'em off . . . if you get beaten, we ALL get beaten."

"Maybe we should go for the not get-beaten option," whispered Orchid.

Unnerved as he was, his basic Eryndi wisdom kicked in.

"Yeah," Tresado said, quickly lowering his voice. "You're right. We're stuck here, and I don't see where there is anything we can do about it until . . ."

"Right," whispered Orchid. "Until what?"

CELL 2

Foxx and Feelia were taken down a long corridor, which, from the distance they walked, led to the far side of Stadium from where they entered. Feelia was no longer hysterical, but rather numb. She plodded along with a blank look, unable to process the horrific fate that the gods had inflicted on her so suddenly.

A sour smell began to assault their nostrils, distinctly bird-like. Foxx sneezed more than once. He was allergic to feathers. Some animal pens came into sight. Long, pointed beaks poked out from between the bars, at least a reach and a half above the stone floor.

Hurdlebirds!

Foxx had seen them before when he had visited Tresk the first time. They were used in an exciting and dangerous sport, chariot racing. In past centuries, the birds pulled bulky, two-man chariots around a track. In these modern times, sleek hoverchariots took the place of the old-fashioned wheeled variety. To make the race more exciting, random dangerous objects were scattered about the course for the racers to avoid; spear clusters, fire braziers, swinging pendulums, even wild animals. The driver controlled the birds with a bit and bridle. The huge, fast-running birds were directed to either go around the obstacles, which lost the racers a bit of ground, or to leap over them, the hoverchariot trailing behind and hopefully clearing the danger. It was a very popular sport in the Imperial City, and wheelbarrows of coins changed hands at the betting booths.

"Halt!"

They stopped in front of a large enclosure containing about twenty wretched-looking prisoners. The place smelled like a monkey house from unwashed bodies. The other source of stench was the overflowing waste bucket in the corner. Two of the guards thrust their spears through the bars to keep anyone from approaching the door while it was opened. Foxx and Feelia were pushed into the cell and the door quickly relocked behind them.

"What are you going to do with us?" shouted Foxx.

One guard, an expert at clever humor, answered.

"You're to provide amusement to our entertainment-starved populace, assuming your fellow prisoners don't eat you first. Enjoy your stay!"

Foxx looked around the cell, appraising the other convicts. One Macai fellow had legs the size of tree trunks and a huge scar on his throat. The man grinned, revealing a row of sharpened teeth. The other prisoners, Macai and Eryndi, male and female, all had a look of malevolence about them.

Thieves and murderers all, thought Foxx. He gathered up Feelia, who had immediately assumed a fetal position, and moved her as far as possible from the others, which wasn't very far. An Eryndi woman with spiked hair and incredibly long nails approached. Foxx had no weapon, no Magic to defend himself with, and his fighting skills were notoriously poor.

"Oh, you poor dears," the woman said. "How did two fine citizens such as yourselves end up in this place?"

Foxx looked down at the fine silk suit he was wearing and Feelia's elegant gown and compared them to the ragged clothing of the prisoners. They did tend to stand out a bit. Even though using his Knowing Spell was not an option, he still possessed a fine gift of gab and the self-taught ability to fit into any situation. When he answered her, he used the same regional accent that she had.

"By pissing off the Imperator."

"Well, that'll do it, all right. Let me get you some water. Severus, hand me the jug, will you?"

The dude with the teeth picked up a clay amphora and passed it over.

"Go ahead and help yourself," he lisped through his pointed teeth. "They'll be bringing more later."

"Thanks, many thanks," said Foxx, who tried to hide his surprise at not getting shivved right away. He took the jug and gently washed Feelia's tear-streaked face. She blearily looked up at him with reddened eyes.

"Where am I?"

"It's all right," said Foxx. "Here, take a drink of water." She sipped at the jug. The water was stale and warm, but it brought her around a bit more. She looked around her at the fearsome faces and the heavy iron bars on all sides. The horror started to well up inside her again as she remembered the awful events of the last hour.

"Take it easy," reassured Foxx. "You're safe for the moment. Why don't you lie back and relax. I'll look after you."

"Thank you. I've forgotten your name."

"Foxx. That's with two exes," he said, crossing his arms and fingers in his signature gesture.

One of the prisoners, the one with the painful-looking 'T' for thief branded into his forehead, handed Foxx a musty blanket.

"Here, use this."

"Thanks, friend," Foxx said. He folded it and gave Feelia a place to lay her head. "Now you try to relax, while I find us a way out of here."

He stood and quietly addressed his fellow convicts.

"IS there a way out of here?"

"Only one that I know of," said the spike-haired woman. The other prisoners grimly nodded their heads in agreement. "And right before they brought you in a guard told us that happens tomorrow night. We weren't scheduled to be executed until the Kondo Honor Day Games, but I suspect your arrival pushed that forward some."

CELL 3

Serena's arms were held tightly by four guards and she had a loop of wire on the end of a pole around her neck as she was marched along to her fate. The muscles and tendons of all her limbs were as tightly wound springs ready to unleash destruction at any second. She towered over the Eryndi guards, by a full head in some cases. These soldiers were undoubtedly used to handling dangerous prisoners, though. They were treating her as though they had a full-grown razor lion in their custody.

Eventually, their trek through the bowels of Stadium came to a halt in front of a cell full of warrior types. Two burly Macai guards stood watch as the prisoner escort approached. While Macai soldiers were rare in the Treskan Imperium, they weren't unheard of; every army had a use for brutes who could carry the heavy weapons, or dig ditches all day long, or guard dangerous prisoners if they were stupid enough, and the one named Ruglum was definitely stupid enough.

"Whoa, look what Heroic Hare brought me from Present Land!"

"I'd leave this one alone, if I were you, Ruglum," said the guard holding the wire loop around Serena's neck. "She took a finger off a chick in the Residence." He clacked his teeth together in a meaningful way to augment his warning.

"Well then, you just hold that pretty head still. I want me a closer look. Whoa, what is that?"

Ruglum's hand stretched out toward Serena's chest. Her arms and head were tightly held to prevent a repeat of the biting episode. This was about the twentieth guy today that tried to take her diamond, and she had had quite enough. As soon as his ragged fingernail touched the jewel in her sternum, the coiled spring that was Serena's body unleashed itself. She dropped her weight onto the four Eryndi that were holding her arms. Her stomach muscles tightened and her powerful right leg kicked upward with a sledgehammer blow right between Ruglum's legs. The heavy whump was accompanied by a squishing sound that brought winces and a communal response from everyone in the room.

"Ooooooh!!"

When all legs had been uncrossed, Serena was hustled into the cell. The defiant grin never left her face as the door slammed shut. Ruglum was on the floor, blubbering like a child.

"Get him to Suturus," ordered the head guard. Ruglum couldn't walk on his own, so a pair of soldiers hauled him out, whimpering all the way. The guy in charge turned to the smug Serena.

"Promise me something, barbarian. Don't die too soon tomorrow night. You do have a way of making me smile. All right, let's go," he said to his squad.

"See you later, Headless," Serena called to the guard's retreating back. "I'll be giving you that nickname personally, by the way."

As soon as the guards had disappeared down the hall, Serena's cell erupted with applause behind her. The rest of the prisoners were apparently quite amused at the new arrival's antics with the much-despised Ruglum. An Eryndi woman limped forward, favoring her right leg, which was bound by a cloth.

"Well done, warrior. A lesson well taught."

The woman's wrists and ankles were covered in shackle bruises. Serena narrowed her eyes. "Don't I know you from somewhere?"

"We rode the same Conveyor," the woman replied. "Although, while you and your friends were up front getting waited on, I and a few of my friends were several cars back where the service wasn't quite so good."

"You were the one they dragged out of the garbage cart up in Breeos."

"Danikan Tyre." The Eryndi extended her left hand in the Treskan manner. Serena paused for a half-beat, but took it.

"It seems I know your name, too. Is it true what they say about you?"

"Just the bad stuff. The rest is all lies."

Serena did indeed have a sense of humor, if a grim one. She got jokes. She just didn't like them unless she told them.

"Uh-huh. Whatever. Do you know what these green clowns plan to do?"

"Well, it's like this," said Danikan, turning to indicate her convicts. "We're all criminals against the state. All different, too. We got a couple of road workers, an apothecary, oh, and three, that's *three*, artists. Art can be politically dangerous, you know. And various real crooks of all kinds. But still criminals of the state. Criminals of the state get publicly executed in Stadium."

Serena's hard face got harder. "Nobody's gonna execute me without a fight!" she growled.

"That's the idea," said Danikan.

"Huh?"

"Criminals are expected to fight back. Nobody wants to just see heads lopped off. They want action, entertainment, thrills. The mob wants a good show."

"Can't say that I blame them," Serena said. "What do they give you to fight with?"

"Your own weapons if you got 'em. If you don't, they give you something."

"Hmmm. One of the guards said something about putting me in a single opponent bout."

"Oh, yeah?" said Danikan. "Me, too."

"What about the rest of these jailbirds?"

"They'll go first. They always put the less interesting matches at the beginning. No offense, guys," she said to the rest of the cell. "You'll be taken out onto the sands and they'll send out an equal number of gladiators to engage you."

"We'll try to give a good accounting of ourselves," said one guy with battle scars all over his body.

"I've got no doubts, Puggnayshus," said Danikan. "If you fight as well as you did at Kryss, the crowd will get one hell of a show." Danikan now addressed everyone in the cell. "The one thing to remember is to never surrender. No matter what happens, no matter how hopeless things look, keep fighting until your last breath. We have to show these invading creeps that we know how to die!"

Danikan's pep talk lifted a few spirits. She was obviously a natural leader. Even though everyone had been telling Serena this was to be a sure-thing execution, she couldn't help liking this plan.

"That about sums it up. Um, come over here, I want to talk to you. Cover us, guys."

Danikan took Serena by the arm and pulled her to the back corner of the cell. The other prisoners understood and moved away. Their conversations got a bit louder to cover whatever was about to be said from the guards down the hall. She looked over the Northlands Warrior.

"You seem to be a capable fighter."

"Now how would you know that?"

"I'm good at sizing up folks. I'll be blunt. What are you in for, dressed like that?"

"Long story."

Danikan bored into Serena's lapis eyes. "Did you kill someone?"

"Well, uh . . . when? What about you?" asked Serena, changing the subject. "They said something about you being the leader of a terrorist group."

"I'm sure they did."

"You planned massacres."

"That's harsh."

"Your followers are cold-blooded killers."

"Maybe you shouldn't believe everything you hear."

"Never do."

"Besides, if I had a bunch of devoted followers, you'd think they would've busted me loose by now."

"Maybe you shouldn't put your trust in followers you don't have."

"Maybe you're right. I guess we'll just have to trust in ourselves."

"Works for me. So, after I've killed my opponent, what then?"

"I like you, barbarian. What's your name?"

"Serena the Free. Although the last time I fought before a crowd, I went by Diamond Girl," she said, indicating the fabulous gem in her sternum.

"So which is it?"

"I think I'll go with the first one. I kinda need to show these bunghole Treskans something."

"Me too, barbarian, me too."

CHAPTER 12

The next day – Stadium

It was past five in the Aftermidday. The shadows were lengthening and citizens were already starting to trickle in, although the evening's games weren't due to start for another two hours.

A stooped figure, painfully walking with a cane, approached a little-used portal where a single guard was on duty. This was where the losers and their severed body parts were taken away at the games' end.

"I'm sorry, lady. You'll have to go around to one of the main entrances."

"Oh, hello, young man. Perhaps you could help me."

The little old Eryndi lady pulled back her hood to reveal a smiling, kindly face. She looked like someone's Grand Nana who bakes cookies at the slightest provocation. She pulled the crocheted doily off the woven basket she carried to reveal that was exactly what she was bringing. The aroma of fresh baked goods wafted out of the basket and assaulted the guard's nose. His mouth watered immediately.

“I’m not here for the games. My favorite nephew works here and I was hoping to bring him his favorite snack.”

“I’m sorry, lady. I can’t open the door and let you enter here.”

“Oh, I really didn’t want to fight the crowd. I don’t get around very well, as you can see.”

“It’s against regulations. I have no way of knowing what’s in those cookies.”

The woman tittered in the cutest way, “Well, goodness, dear, they’re not poisoned, if that’s what you think. Here, I’ll show you.” She reached into the basket and took out a cookie. She bit into it and a hot thread of sweet chocolate yumminess stretched out from the still-warm cookie as she pulled it away from her mouth.

“I added extra butter and parthonut extract,” she said around a mouthful, “so they’re a little gooey, but they’re definitely not poisoned. Would you care for one? I won’t tell my nephew.”

“I, um . . . we are not allowed to accept gifts, but I suppose I could take the basket in for you.”

“Oh, would you? You’re a dear.”

The guard looked about furtively and quickly unlocked the gate. He opened it just enough to allow the smiling old woman to pass him the basket. As she did so, she concentrated on a silent Worldly Magic signal directed at the basket. A brownish finger-like object shot out from under the similarly-colored cookies and touched the guard on the hand. The pinkie snake neurotoxin worked fast. The man tried to pull back, but found that he was suddenly dead. The body collapsed in a heap.

“Thank you, dear. That was very sweet of you.”

The bent little old Eryndi lady athletically hopped over the body, without the use of her cane, and waved to someone outside. From the shadows, bushes, and trees, a score of furtive figures approached. Some were carrying pry bars and heavy hammers. One of them immediately started stripping the dead guard and transferring the green armor and equipment to his own person. Once the others were inside, he closed and locked the door with the dead guard's keys and took his place as sentinel. The little old Eryndi lady concentrated again and the little pinkie snake emerged from the cookie basket and affectionately wound itself around her wrist.

"That's a good girl, Slinkie," she said. "Let's get this job done, shall we?"

* * *

> *TONIGHT AT STADIUM! SEE MAN MOUNTAIN NEMOSTHENES DEFEND HIS TITLE AGAINST SAMMY THE SCREAMER IN THE ULTIMATE GRUDGE MATCH! SEE ALL YOUR FAVORITE GLADIATORS PURIFY OUR SERENE REPUBLIC WITH THE EXECUTION OF STATE CRIMINALS FEATURING A SPECIAL MYSTERY GUEST VILLAIN! THINK YOU KNOW WHO? FIND OUT IN A SPECIAL NIGHTTIME PERFORMANCE. ACTION AND THRILLS ABOUND! GLADIATORS! HOVERCHARIOTS! HURDLEBIRDS! AND OF COURSE, YOUR FAVORITE – SUPPERTIME FOR SERESIN! BRING YOUR SKETCHPAD! FREE ADMISSION TO ALL CITIZENS! TONIGHT AT STADIUM!*
>
> - Treskan Imperial Town Crier

Today – Stadium

The betting booths all had long lines. While always well attended, tonight's special performance looked to be standing room only. A large chalkboard listed all the scheduled bouts and the names of featured artists.

"So, who is this Serena the Free?" asked one fellow with a handful of coins that he was just itching to lose.

"Don't know," replied another. "Anybody know this Serena?"

No one in the crowd of Macai had ever heard the name before. A couple of Eryndi also pleaded ignorance, but had heard rumors. The crowd pressed them for any info they might have. Eryndi were known to be shrewd bettors and usually came out on top. It was fortunate for the Macai that only a small percentage of Stadium's audience were Eryndi. Macai usually outnumbered them by about twenty to one, despite the Eryndi majority in the Treskan Imperium. Macai just seemed to like these blood games more.

"What kinda rumors?"

"Well, I heard that some criminals were caught trying to assassinate the Imperator. Maybe she's one of them."

The other Eryndi had another theory. "Well, I got it from a friend of mine, whose cousin works in the Palace. She said that," the Eryndi glanced around and lowered his voice, "Merak went dragonshit crazy because his food wasn't right or something. There was a temper tantrum and he sent the whole kitchen staff to Stadium. Maybe this Serena the Free is one of the chefs."

"She better be more than that," said the Macai with the scraggly beard. "They got her paired with Marcellya. She'll be a pin cushion."

"But," said the Eryndi, "they wouldn't put her with a champion like Marcy unless they thought she had a chance. They like to keep things even, or at least looking even."

"And look," said the other Eryndi. "Serena's odds are at 22 to 1." He paused for a moment, in the contemplative way that Eryndi do. "I think I know who I'm betting on."

The Macai, who are easily influenced by crazy ideas, started agreeing as a mob. There was a frantic rush to the booths to place their bets.

A smooth, melodious tone began to echo through the halls. It was the sound of fifty Eryndi Stemhorns surrounding the uppermost tier of the gigantic arena. The games were about to begin. At the same time as the horns, several banks of Magical lights slowly brightened, illuminating the crowd. Regular goers knew this was the moment to cheer, even though nothing had happened yet. It was just one of those weird traditions that Macai loved so much.

There were no empty seats. These games, very popular with the mob, as many Senators called the populace, were always well-attended. This special nighttime show had excited the fans with curiosity. Sixty-two thousand four hundred and seven of them were either crammed shoulder to shoulder in their seats or forced to stand. The guards finally had to close and lock the gates when the overflow started spilling into the aisles.

"Gotta keep these cacks safe," muttered an Eryndi guard.

The stadium lights dimmed. A dazzling colored light show erupted out of the Imperial Balcony. At the same time, the Stemhorns blared out a fanfare fit for the Imperator Himself. Merak's hovering throne Imperiously floated out onto the large balcony, where a dozen other bigwigs and servants were already standing and giving the standard salute of touching the left fist to the right shoulder, then raising it next to the ear. The Son of Dyhendra, as Merak sometimes liked to call himself, waved and blew big, spitty kisses to all his adoring fans. His enormous silk robes billowed about him in the warm evening breeze. His throne set down on a circular collar built into the floor of the balcony. The chair itself now began to tilt forward, easing the gigantic Imperator to his feet.

And the crowd went wild. Tens of thousands of throats screaming at once is an awesome sound, especially when you are the Imperator and they're all screaming for you. There was a smattering of boos heard, but those voices were quickly silenced.

He strode slowly forward to the balcony's railing. The cheering reached its height as Merak waved to the crowd. After soaking up a few minutes of that, Merak motioned to his left. A servant opened a small box and a shimmering, metallic object floated out and sped over to Merak, hovering just below his three chins. The Amplifier, as the Imperator had named it, was just one of the many innovations that came from the brilliant mind of the greatest leader in Treskan history. His Imperial voice boomed out across all of Stadium.

"Citizens! I salute you on this special night. I have no doubt you will enjoy this evening's entertainment!"

Merak paused for an applause session, then raised his palms. The cheering ceased immediately.

"LET THE GAMES BEGIN!(burp)"

Another burst of Magical lightworks exploded across all of Stadium. The Imperator returned to his throne and ordered a deep-fried lumbasteak and salted kohlrabi strips. A servant hurried off to accommodate His Imperiousness.

The stadium lights now changed their angle and narrowed

their beams to illuminate the arena floor. One of the many portals opened, the one directly below the Imperial Balcony. A strange figure emerged. It was Jeruma, Goddess of the Dead! She was dressed head to toe in brown, signifying the soil of Lurra, where all Eryndi would someday lie face-down on their way to the afterlife. Her many-layered garment flitted about as she moved in a sinuous dance to the center of the sands. She turned and bowed low to Merak on his balcony.

"Imperator! I await your offerings!"

The crowd responded with an ominous low moan, as was customary when sending souls to the afterlife. Merak gave the expected, traditional underhanded wave, and the figure of Jeruma vanished in a Magical lightshow of otherworldly brilliance, presumably back to the Underworld to wait for impending arrivals.

The Emcee of the proceedings, Vocalus Projectivus, entered the arena, standing in an elaborate hover chariot. He also had a Magical voice amplifier at his command.

"Welcome, citizens, to the Imperator's Games! HAIL MERAK!"

The crowd responded in kind, as was expected and required.

"We begin tonight with the execution of eighteen state criminals – criminals whose perverse ways and traitorous plans threaten the security of our serene republic. Justice shall be served. FOR THE IMPERATOR!"

The crowd cheered and the hoverchariot quickly whisked Vocalus out of harm's way. As soon as it disappeared into the portal it came from, a set of doors opposite it opened. A herd of nervous prisoners, blinking in the glaring stadium lights, uncertainly entered the arena, prodded on by the sharp pilums of the guards. Foxx and Feelia were among them. A huge wave of laughter and boos oozed out of the crowd like a toxic mud slide.

The sand-covered floor of Stadium squirmed in several places. Small doors opened and eighteen stout posts about a half reach tall, with heavy ring eyes on the end, emerged from the sand. They were two groups of nine spaced equally apart, one on the south side of Stadium floor, one on the north. The guards connected shackles to the prisoners' right wrists and attached the other end of the two-reach-long chains to the posts. When this was done, the head sadistic guard faced the Imperial Balcony and saluted Merak. Then he and the rest of the guards retreated back into the portal.

The prisoners all stood in their shackles, some catatonic, some sobbing, some wetting their pants. The only movement they were allowed was a two-reach radius around their respective posts, which were just far enough from each other to not allow two prisoners to touch. Foxx and Feelia were coincidentally next to each other in the southern section.

It seemed Feelia was done being weepy and catatonic. She had had the night to think about her situation and was now just pissed off. Out of frustration and anger, she jerked her chain a few times to test the strength of her shackles. All it did was to anger her more and bruise her wrist.

"Save your energy, Feelia," said Foxx. "We're going to need it. I'm not sure what's about to happen, but all we can do is our best."

"I know, Mister Foxx," she replied. "I'm just so angry! How could the Imperator do this to me? I've served Him well and faithfully for over four years!"

Foxx's heart went out to the charming Eryndi woman. He

could accept death for himself, mostly because he was perfectly aware that he deserved it for some of the stuff in his past. But Feelia, he was quite sure, was about as innocent as they come. She was putting up a brave front, but behind the anger was still much fear.

Wait a minute . . .

There IS fear . . . I SENSED IT!

His self-invented Knowing Spell was functioning! There was Magic operating on the arena floor. With the proper concentration, Foxx could sense the moods of most of the other prisoners, except for those farthest away. He tried an experiment. He sent a subliminal suggestion to Feelia, one encouraging her confidence and bravery.

"Four years!" Feelia said to no one. "Four years I worked for that fat frog! Well no more! I QUIT!" She now turned to face the Imperial Balcony. "You hear that, Imperator?" Her words dripped with contempt. "THIS IS MY OFFICIAL NOTICE, YOU BLOATED DUNG BEETLE!"

It works! thought Foxx.

Any plan he may have been devising was interrupted by three of the stadium doors, the ones closest to them, opening. There was a rushing sound and three hurdlebird-drawn hoverchariots burst out. It looked as though the chained prisoners would be immediately trampled. They backed up as much as their shackles allowed, but it was not necessary. The chariots, each containing a driver and a weapons wielder, veered away at the last beat and sped off around the track in the opposite direction. This confused Foxx at first, but their strategy became clear a few moments later. When the three chariots were about halfway around the track, the doors opened again and another three chariots emerged, then another three.

Now there were nine hoverchariots circling the track. The first three were just rounding the last turn and headed right for the helpless prisoners.

The driver on the outside pulled her bird to the wall, aiming at the chained prisoner on the end. The bird was headed directly for the post and it seemed as though a deadly collision was imminent. The driver pulled up on the reins and the hurdlebird leapt completely over the post. The hoverchariot was pulled along in the leap, clearing the post by several fingers. The doomed man tried to dodge his oncoming death, but wasn't agile enough. As the chariot passed over his head, the man caught a glimpse of a grinning face leering down at him. It was the last sight his eyes would see. The perfectly timed javelin, thrown by the weapons wielder, penetrated the man's neck, driving down through the collarbone and into the chest cavity below. Two other prisoners were equally unlucky. One was killed by trampling and another by a long pole arm that nearly severed his body at the waist.

Foxx and Feelia were lucky in this first round, but the hopelessness of their situation looked apparent. The second wave of three chariots was approaching swiftly. And, of course, the first three would make another lap and come at them again – if there was anything left for them.

The woman with the spiky hair called out to her fellow prisoners.

"Don't worry, they make no more than three laps. All we have to do is to survive until then!"

Foxx didn't have time to consider how comforting that may have been. The next wave of chariots was approaching fast. The one in the middle seemed to be aiming directly at Feelia. Foxx reached out with all his mental might, attempting to get at the mind of the driver. He had only a few beats, but managed to plant a suggestion. While he couldn't create the mental illusion of an actual danger, like a monster or a flame or something, he simply inserted the ideas of *look out! turn! avoid!*

Without knowing why, the driver of the hoverchariot suddenly pulled the reins violently to the side. His hurdlebird squawked in protest and threw itself to the right, where it collided with another bird. The long legs of both birds tangled and they went down, taking the two trailing chariots with them. Both vehicles' hover capabilities couldn't keep up with the birds dragging them to the ground. They smashed nose-first onto the sands, flinging their passengers out like sling stones.

The third charioteer targeted Severus, the dude with the sharpened teeth. The weapons wielder behind the driver was readying a powerful short bow. She had just drawn back when her world ended. Severus stood defiantly to the left of the post at the full limit of his chain. The instant the hurdlebird started its jump over the post, Severus leapt to the right, ducking down behind the post. With a speed belying a Macai of his size, he swung a loop of his chain upwards and, at the same time, quickly put another loop over the top of the post. The pointed beak of the hurdlebird, just clearing the top of the post, thrust through the loop and pulled the chain tight, all within a single beat. The bird's neck broke with an audible pop that carried all the way to the audience, who cheered in appreciation. Severus didn't get his hand out of the way quite quickly enough. The lightning-fast tightening of the chain nipped off his little finger at the first knuckle. That was nothing compared to what happened to the chariot's occupants. The driver went face-first into the top of the iron post, pulping his head. The wielder, being farther back, was pitched straight up into the air. Her drawn bow launched the arrow meant for Severus harmlessly across the arena floor. The archer's body spun crazily in the air and belly-flopped hard onto the sands beyond the chained prisoners. Every breath of air in the woman's lungs fled from her body and she lay there thinking about her surely broken ribs. There was nothing else she could do.

The score was tied at three each: three prisoners dead, three hoverchariots destroyed. Another wave of chariots was rounding the track once again. There was little to do other than to try the same tactics again. The next wave had as their weapons wielders another archer and two soldiers with long lances. The wielder with the bow was drawing a bead on the woman with spiky hair. The prisoner danced back and forth on each side of her post, hoping to fake out the archer. It didn't work, however. That tactic was well known to the hoverchariot execution squad. The archer anticipated Spiky's move and led the woman expertly. The arrow was loosed when aimed at nothing, but in the half-beat it took to travel, Spiky moved exactly into its path. The feathered shaft penetrated her ribcage directly through her heart. The bloodied arrowhead protruded from her back and had time to drip a single drop of blood before the prisoner collapsed like a sack of hobo clams. The hurdlebird lived up to its name and jumped effortlessly over its victim, to the cheers of the appreciative crowd. Spiky had an odd smile on her face as she died, as though she was glad this crap was finally over.

The next two chariots were not close to one another as before, so Foxx couldn't use the same trick a second time to get them to collide. This time, his focus was on the weapons wielder. The man was just leveling his lance at Foxx's chest. The Knowing Spell now persuaded the man that his target would try to duck under the needle-sharp weapon. To compensate, the wielder dropped the point of his lance, but Foxx's spell caused him to dip his weapon too far and the point stabbed into the ground. The other end flew out of the man's hand and lodged under the railing that ran around the rim of the open chariot. It was like a log being thrust in the spokes of a moving wagon wheel. The hurdlebird found itself half strangled by the sudden drag and went down, taking the chariot and its two occupants with it.

There were now four destroyed hoverchariots and seven dead executioners. Another of the prisoners died from the lance of the third chariot. There was nothing to do to stop it.

The remaining five chariots now regrouped into a single formation with the intention of finishing this execution.

The crowd was going wild with these unexpected events. In most simple executions like this, the prisoners would all be dead before even one complete circuit was made. No one suspected Foxx as the cause of most of these deaths. He was not seen to have done anything. It just looked like operator error in those three crashes.

The remaining charioteers were now targeting Severus, who was the only prisoner that anybody had seen defeat any executioners. Foxx did not seem to be in any danger on this lap, so he tried his original trick again. He sent a suggestion to one of the charioteers in the middle of the pack to quickly turn to avoid some imaginary obstacle. Just as before, it worked like a charm. The driver swerved to her left and collided with another chariot. Two more down, three to go, but it didn't look good for Severus. The remaining executioners were just zeroing in on him when suddenly the three hurdlebirds went down in rapid succession with arrows protruding from their chests. Foxx, as well as every member of the crowd, looked with astonishment at the slight figure on his left. Feelia stood holding a bow that she had evidently picked up from some of the wreckage. She looked back at him and shrugged.

"I took second place in an archery tournament last year."

"That's show biz!" yelled Foxx, grinning widely. He crossed his arms in front of his chest and gave Feelia a crisp, jaunty Foxx salute, which she happily returned. The crowd went absolutely dragonshit crazy. No one had ever seen a defeat of the hoverchariots before. There were the occasional executioner deaths, it being a contact sport and all, and there were sometimes survivors amongst the prisoners, if they were lucky enough to evade all three waves of chariots, but never a complete rout.

Foxx turned to the roaring crowd and, being the showman that he was, rallied the survivors and led them in a group bow. The mob was practically pissing themselves with exuberance and he milked the applause for all he could. The more popular he could make himself, the better chance he might have of talking his way out of this mess, the way he always did. It seemed to be working a little. From the roar, Foxx could hear the occasional "Mercy!" or even "Free the prisoners!"

A troop of guards came out onto the sands to escort the prisoners back to their cells, followed by a crew to clean up the carnage for the next event. As they were being led off Stadium floor, the guard escorting Foxx mumbled to him.

"Don't worry, slick. You'll still die tonight, just so you know."

"Are you sure about that, Commodore?" replied Foxx with a smirk.

"Very sure."

Foxx used his Knowing Spell on the guard the same way he would on another card player, to see whether his opponent was bluffing or not. He was dismayed to discover that the guard was not.

CHAPTER 13

Today – Stadium

The little old Eryndi lady led her band into the bowels of Stadium. She stayed on point and used the same trick with the yummy cookies and the deadly snake. It worked like a charm. If there's one thing prison guards can't resist, it's homemade chocolate parthonut cookies. In the event she encountered more than one guard, the extra ones were taken out by silent mini-crossbow darts dipped in sleeper bush poison from the two stealthy figures following her in the shadows. At last they came to the final staircase, which led to the lowest level of Stadium. A faint, green glow and a low hum came from whatever was at the bottom of the stairs. The commandos silently descended and, at a count of three, burst through the double doors. There was a score of Eryndi within the large room, all tending to some massive banks of machinery. One ambush later and there was a score of unconscious or dead Eryndi littering the floor. The little old Eryndi lady pointed to a massive conduit leading up from the machinery and into the ceiling.

"That's it, my brothers and sisters. We need to take out that column."

Four of them stood guard, while the rest picked up their sledge hammers and pry bars and went to work on the strange, metallic tubing.

Today – Stadium

Vocalus Projectivus, the emcee for tonight's games, floated out upon the sands in his hoverchariot just as the crews were clearing away the last of the wreckage and the corpses.

"Did we not promise you thrills and excitement?"

By its raucous cheering, the crowd heartily agreed. If the opening executions, which were usually pretty boring, were this exciting, the later spectacles should prove thrilling beyond words. Their bloodlust was stirred and they wanted more. They would not be disappointed. The best was yet to come.

"We offer you more of the same. We now invite you to witness something with a little more skill and finesse involved. Twelve, count them, twelve more state criminals, all of whom took up arms against our Serene Republic, shall meet their deaths at the hands of your favorite gladiators. ENTER THE GLADIATORS!"

A fanfare of Stemhorns blared out as doors opened and a dozen heavily-armed warriors strode out.

"Presenting, Kollonos of Talfia, AKA The Fisherman!"

A tall Macai wearing scaled armor and carrying a long trident raised his weapon over his head and growled defiantly. Portions of the crowd cheered, other sections booed. Everyone had their favorites.

"Nicodemus, the Butcher!"

An Eryndi armed with two huge cleavers and wearing a bloody apron over his armor also elicited cheers.

Vocalus continued to announce the rest of the names. There was The Salamankan Slayer, Epsos the Tiger, Punisher, Pietra the Pirate, Jabana the Virgin Beast, Herakus the Horrible, Eruptus the Volcano, Yareena the Horanese, and two twin sisters, Marilos and Larimos of Tresk.

All these gladiators were familiar figures to regular Stadium-goers. The names had been previously posted at all the betting windows. It was well known and assumed that all the gladiators would be victorious and achieve a kill. The challenge was selecting who would triumph first, or third, or dead last; whether it was a clean, swift kill, or if the prisoner would have to be finished off; whether a limb was severed or a head removed. You could bet on nearly anything at Stadium.

"You've met the heroes," announced Vocalus. "Now meet the villains!"

The Stemhorns played a comical, derogatory tone as the twelve prisoners were escorted out under close guard. None wore armor, but all were armed in some way. Just before the door opened, they were each given a weapon of some kind. Most of the prisoners had the look of experienced fighters, but a few hardly knew which end of the sword to hold. The crowd laughed, booed, hissed, and generally expressed disapproval of these people that were about to die for their entertainment. Many pieces of rotten fruit and broken wine bottles were flung from the stands.

"We have murderers, traitors, and terrorists. We know how badly they can rob and murder, now let us see how well they can fight and die! Long Live the Imperium!"

Vocalus, as usual, wasted no time turning his hoverchariot around and getting the hell out of harm's way. The gladiators spun on their heels and turned to the Imperial Balcony.

"Hail Merak!" they shouted in perfect harmony. Some of the prisoners also paid their respects to the Imperator in the form of raspberries and/or obscene gestures.

The Stemhorns sounded again, in a short fanfare that everyone knew meant Begin. Each gladiator had singled out an opponent. They advanced and the killing commenced. The few prisoners who knew nothing of combat went down immediately, to the elation or disappointment of the crowd, depending on how they had bet. Some of the more seasoned fighters managed to survive for a few beats, but with no armor, they didn't last long.

The one exception was Puggnayshus, who was paired against Pietra the Pirate. Pietra, an Eryndi, fought with a cutlass in her left hand and nothing in her right, including a hand. Attached to the stump end of her right arm was a jagged, triple-bladed long dagger. Puggnayshus had been given a long pole arm, a kind of bill with three opposing points. It was a cumbersome weapon, but long enough to keep Pietra at a distance. She feinted and attacked, trying to get under Puggnayshus's weapon to get in close and finish him. He realized that he could not keep the pirate gladiator at bay for long. One of these times, she would avoid his parry and skewer him with her fake arm dagger. Puggnayshus tried a gutsy move. He thrust the point of his bill directly at Pietra's chest. She easily sidestepped the attack and would have pressed the advantage, but Puggnayshus immediately pulled backward for all he was worth. The smallest point on the bill was a short, inwardly curved hook. It was designed for use by a foot soldier to pull a mounted opponent out of the saddle. The quick jerk snagged Pietra by the ribs and sent her plunging forward face-first into Puggnayshus's knee. The impact broke the pirate's nose, stunning her. Puggnayshus quickly unhooked his weapon and swung it against his opponent's neck. The sharpened steel cut easily through bone and sinew, sending Pietra's head rolling across the sands, much to the delight of the crowd. He quickly turned to see if he could be of any help to his fellow prisoners, but Herakus the Horrible was just finishing the last of them off with his heavy, spiked mace. The Stemhorns sounded, signifying the event's conclusion. Puggnayshus was quickly relieved of his weapon by guards and sent back into his cell, but not before managing a couple of quick bows to the crowd.

The corpse crew returned to gather up the bodies and their various disconnected parts. Vocalus came out again.

"Well, I don't know about you, Gentlefolk, but I made a little money on that event. How about the rest of you?"

There was a mixture of cheers and boos from the crowd, but still an enthusiastic response.

"Before we get to our main events, we bring you a special presentation. Our Imperator, the Divine Merak, is pleased to announce a great victory in the ongoing defense of our Serene Republic. She was a plague upon the Treskan way of life, the Treskan love of life, and the ideals of decency and fair play!"

There were more than a few titters amongst the crowd at this speech, but nobody cared. The crowd was here to see some blood, not engage in political debate.

"She was a scourge upon our citizens, murdering hundreds in the name of her radical agenda. A terrorist, a murderer, and a traitor to the Imperium and the Eryndi race. And now she is here, ready to pay the ultimate price for her crimes, all for the satisfaction and entertainment of you, the people. Citizens, I give you the enemy of the people, the worst of the worst, Danikan Tyre!"

One of the doors opened onto Stadium floor and Danikan limped out. The crowd erupted with excitement and surprise and lots and lots of boos. Danikan Tyre was a name they had heard for years, but few had knowingly seen her in person. The Eryndi woman wore no armor, but carried two standard-issue Treskan short swords. She pointed one up at Merak in the Imperial Balcony. With the other, she made a gesture of a throat being cut, a clear message of what she'd like to do to him. The crowd guffawed at this brazen bit of disrespect.

"And now, by special order of His Imperial Magnificence himself . . ."

Another door opened and a figure stepped out. It did not look like a typical, heavily armored gladiator. The woman was tall, blonde, and impeccably dressed.

"Presenting her opponent, from the farthest reaches of the northern barbarian lands, Serena the Free!"

Today – Deep below Stadium

The little old Eryndi lady played with Pinkie, her deadly pet snake, who affectionately curled itself through her fingers. Meanwhile, her burly compatriots continued to hammer and pry on the metallic column that disappeared up into the ceiling. Their efforts weren't producing much progress. Whatever the material was, it resisted the strongest blows without a scratch.

"All right," she said, "we're not doing any good here. We need another plan."

"It won't be long before someone shows up down here and sounds an alarm," said one of her gang.

"All of you, come on down off of there."

The workers gratefully jumped down off their perch. One of them tossed his sledge hammer ahead of him. It hit the stone floor, but didn't make what should have been a solid thud. Instead, there was a distinctly hollow metallic sound. The little old Eryndi lady stepped over there and carefully examined the floor. Her excellent eyesight and Eryndi senses picked out a very fine, almost invisible seam in the stone floor. She tapped on it with her prop cane and a smile lit her face.

"I think I have another plan. Bring your pry bars."

The gangsters went to work on the floor. They soon discovered that it was not stone at all in this particular area, but rather metal ingeniously colored to match the blocks that Stadium was built out of. A little bit of progress was made, just enough to allow the point of a pry bar to wedge in the opening. Eventually, a section of the floor was lifted away. It was now apparent that it was actually an access portal meant to be camouflaged. They didn't have whatever key, if any, was meant to open this, but brute force worked nicely. Once the opening was big enough, the agile little old Eryndi lady hopped down inside. She found herself in a large chamber. In the center was the bottom half of the column they had been attempting to destroy. Surrounding the column were six long racks, each one holding sixteen metallic spheres. A heavy metal clamp held each of the spheres in place. It was obvious that these also required a key of some kind to release the clamps, a key they did not have.

"Ah, here's our new plan. It'll take longer, but we'll just have to do it bit by bit. Bring your pry bars."

Today – Stadium

Serena strode onto the sands with a pissed-off look on her face, which was absolutely normal for her. She had heard the announcement about her opponent just after she finished buckling on her weapons.

Were it not for the grim circumstances, her appearance would have been laughable. Serena's elegant gown shimmered under the Stadium lights. It really did not accessorize well with the sword hanger that swung from her left hip and the long stiletto on her right. Her own weapons had been given back to her to amuse the crowd with. The first thing she did with them was to cut off the flowing train of her dress so as to free up her legs.

Danikan plunged both her swords into the sand and faced the Imperial Balcony.

"I won't fight this warrior," she shouted up to Merak. "She has done nothing to me. Bring out some gladiators and let us spill a little Treskan blood!"

The crowd watched Serena carefully. This would have been an easy victory for the tall Macai. Her opponent's back was to her and was unarmored. Serena disappointed everyone by siding with her would-be opponent. She strode forward and linked arms with Danikan.

"My friend is right! I am a Northlands Warrior. I fight for honor and country, for revenge, even for pleasure. But I don't fight for the amusement of a Stadium filled with pathetic voyeurs like you! That includes you, Porky! So why don't you send out the best gladiators you got, or better yet, bring your own greasy-ass carcass down here yourself! We'll show you how warriors fight!"

This arrogance brought a wave of boos from the crowd, but laced with excitement. The mob was eager to call this upstart's bluff. Their cries quickly settled to a murmur as Merak furiously slammed down his goblet of Firellian at this challenge, spraying sticky wine all over Senator Flavia, one of the bigwigs whom he had invited to join him. He hoisted himself to his feet and moved to the edge of the balcony. The Imperator rarely addressed lowly prisoners.

"As you wish, you impudent peasant!" Merak screamed. His face was red as a rockfruit and a big vein was sticking out on his temple. "I expected such crudity from a barbarian! Your *real* opponents were already booked hours ago," said Merak with an evil grin. "I've been looking forward to this all day. You will be the first of your pathetic *group* to die. The others will follow soon enough. I may lose a few points, but crimes against kin are the most heinous of offenses and will be dealt with accordingly. Let justice be served . . . NOW!"

The Stemhorns sounded again and a door opened. Four fearsome gladiators strode out. The crowd recognized them immediately, but Vocalus Projectivus gave them each a proper introduction.

"Citizens, for your viewing pleasure, I give you the Merakian Mauler, Sixtus Manlius!"

Coming from a newly-built resort town in the foothills to the south, Sixtus liked to sport a touristy look. He wore a bright, flowery print shirt, a pair of green Serin short pants with lots of pockets, and topped it off with a jaunty sun hat. The costume was just for show. Beneath all that was chain mail and steel shoulder guards. Also belying his casual look was the wicked-looking barbed sword in his right hand and the round spiked shield in his left.

"Next," shouted Vocalus, "from the Barrier Isles, we have the Island Menace, Humfrey of Tord!"

Humfrey was short, squat, and a mass of muscle. His only weapon was a reach-long hammer with a head the size of a brandy cask. His specialty was systematically breaking his opponents' arms, legs, feet, hands, and face, in that order.

"And the darling of the sands, three-time and current champion of the Women's League of Warriors, Marcellya of Tresk!"

The Eryndi woman raised her arms to the crowd, encouraging their cheers, and the mob was happy to oblige. Marcellya, affectionately called Gunboat Marcy after the armed patrol craft of the Serin Sea, carried a standard short sword, but her main forte was arrows, lots and lots of arrows. She had mini-crossbows strapped to each wrist and a powerful short bow strapped to her back, along with a bulging quiver filled with sharp-pointed death.

"Finally, I give you the current Heavyweight Champion of the Sands. You know him, you love him, Man Mountain Nemosthenes!"

The crowd had begun applauding before Vocalus was even finished with the intro. Nemosthenes was everybody's current crush.

"Whom, as you know, is one-half of tonight's main event. You'll see him again later as he takes on the challenger, Sammy the Screamer, for the title of Champion of Stadium. Despite that, Nemosthenes actually asked to be part of this execution squad; said he wanted to get in a light workout before his main bout."

The crowd loved the humor and they loved him, especially the women. The stands of Stadium echoed with thousands of wolf whistles and the cries of citizens offering themselves to whatever his pleasure might be. Nemosthenes was one reach, eleven fingers tall and weighed in at twenty-seven stone. His smooth, bronze skin rippled with muscles with not a scar to be seen. His straight, black hair hung loose with bangs in front. He liked to show off his looks, too, even to the use of blush and guy-liner. He wore no armor, not even a helmet to hide his handsome Macai features. A scant iron codpiece was his only clothing. Nothing was to get in the way of that much beauty. Nemosthenes carried a huge, two-handed battleaxe that he could swing equally well with either hand.

"Ladies and Gentlemen," intoned Vocalus, "your Execution Squad!"

The crowd cheered for all they were worth, encouraged by the superstar Gladiators. The long pause gave Serena and Danikan time to chat.

"Think we can handle them?" asked Danikan.

"Oh, sure," replied Serena. "When do they bring your opponents out?"

"Funny. We were originally supposed to have one opponent each. I think I was paired with Sixtus, and I heard a guard talking about betting on you against Marcy."

Serena narrowed her eyes, sizing up the gladiators. They were all tough, capable, and ruthless-looking.

"They must have thought they needed backup and added the extra two at the last minute," she observed. "They'll try to flank us, one taking us head-on and the other maneuvering behind us. Can't let 'em."

"We could charge them right now while they're getting their applause." Danikan's eyebrows went up in a question.

Serena paused for only half a beat. "Works for me."

Stadium now echoed with Serena's powerful Northlands war cry. She and Danikan raced forward, swords swinging. Danikan leapt up behind Sixtus Manlius, slashing down with her twin Treskan short swords. The first one put a deep slice into Sixtus's shoulder. He was able to pivot in time to take the second sword on the guard of his barbed weapon.

Serena's attack was not quite as effective as she had hoped. Her target was Marcellya, whom she considered to be the greater threat. She swung for the junction of her neck and shoulder. The blow of the razor-sharp scimitar would have nearly bisected the Eryndi woman. In the last tenth of a beat after she swung, Serena realized her near-fatal mistake. Her shadow from the Stadium lights betrayed her attack from behind.

Rookie mistake! Serena chided herself.

Marcy, with her Eryndi senses, was able to duck below the blade's path and twist about, extending a wrist. The small crossbow bolt spat out. It was only because of Serena's own lightning reflexes that she avoided it. Her sword, for the umpteenth time, saved her life. She followed through with the swing and brought her sword up in a defensive move. The bolt impacted on the folded steel of her scimitar, deflecting it nearly straight up. About eight or ten reaches above their heads, the arrow collided with an invisible barrier and fell harmlessly back onto the sands. For a beat after impact, the form of a green dome covering the floor of Stadium appeared and quickly dissipated.

There is one of those shells protecting Stadium!

It only made sense. If they were going to have armed combatants, especially bitter, resentful ones that might lob death and destruction up into the stands or the Imperial Balcony, then protection must be provided. This was another one-way shell like the one Group Six was briefly imprisoned in when they were arrested at the meeting hall. It kept what was inside from escaping, but still allowed foreign objects to be thrown onto the floor from the stands. This was evidenced by the already large amount of rotten fruit and other projectiles littering the sands. This shell apparently covered the entire floor of Stadium at a height of maybe ten reaches.

The crowd booed at the criminals' despicable sneak attack. The gladiators turned to their foes, annoyed that they had lost some audience time because of these cheating criminals. They and the crowd were out for blood now.

Marcy attempted to back up, so as to keep Serena in crossbow range. Serena instinctively moved in to prevent that. Her scimitar was best used in sweeping, slashing attacks. When in close, its length could be a hindrance, but when paired against an enemy who specialized in multiple arrow shooting, it was best to stay in tight. Marcy pulled her own short sword, trying to fend off the attacks of the Macai, who stood a full head taller. With typical Eryndi quickness, Marcellya parried Serena's powerful attacks. She feinted with her short sword, causing Serena to take a half-step backward. Marcy then jumped back and fired her other wrist-mounted crossbow. The small bolt was headed directly for Serena's midsection. She managed to twist her body to get her vitals out of harm's way. Instead, she took the bolt through her right side. Penetrating no muscle, the barbed point entered her skin just below the bottom of her ribcage and exited a few fingers back. Marcy took advantage of the momentary distraction to leap backward a step, whip her short bow from her back with her right hand, and pluck a trio of arrows from her quiver with her left. Gunboat Marcy earned her name and the continuing cheers from the adoring crowd as she launched three arrows in rapid succession, any one of which could have meant death for the Northlands Warrior. But out of pure showmanship, Marcy had meticulously targeted her three arrows with diabolical accuracy. The first two penetrated

Serena's calves in the fleshy parts. The third transfixed her left shoulder. They were not designed to kill right away, but to prolong the performance for the cheering crowd, whose entertainment was why they were all here tonight.

Serena stumbled backward and went down on one knee. A shadow from behind appeared a fraction of a beat before a heavy iron pommel tapped her on the back of the skull. Serena pitched forward on her face, kissing the sand. She pulled herself to her elbows and painfully looked over her shoulder. The grinning face of Man Mountain Nemosthenes stood above her. His all-steel battle axe had a heavy, curved blade nearly half a reach long. His grin turned to a mask of pure pleasure as he raised his axe. It hovered for a half-beat before plunging down toward Serena's head.

Today – Deep below Stadium

It was tedious work, but the little old Eryndi lady's crew of saboteurs had made a bit of progress. They had managed to pry loose eleven out of the ninety-six spheres. Her slight frame not being suitable for this kind of work, she sat back, playing with her snake and passing out encouragement.

"Keep it up, people, keep it up."

She was interrupted by a "hsst" from one of her men standing guard in the room above. Using Eryndi sign language, he indicated that someone was approaching. She signaled for silence and the work stopped immediately. Soon the footsteps were audible to everyone – at least five, maybe six people. The four sentries she had left up there were all armed with the sleeper bush crossbows. Less than three beats after the door opened, there were six unconscious technicians. Their limp bodies were dragged inside and relieved of their lunch boxes. Evidently, they were just reporting for a work shift of whatever it was that they did.

"Good work, lads," said the little old Eryndi lady. "Back at it, we're putting a dent in Merak's shell. Keep it going!"

Today – Stadium

Sixtus Manlius, the Merakian Mauler, howled in rage after Danikan got in that sneaky first blood. He spun to his right with his barbed sword swinging, but Danikan was no longer there. After her initial attack, she hit the sand and rolled under his swing, mindful of where the other gladiator was. It was well she did, for Humfrey of Tord was waiting for her. She stopped her roll just in time as the gigantic hammer head slammed into the ground a hand's breadth from her own head. The monstrous thing was capable of tremendous damage, but was slow and unwieldy. Danikan rolled away before Humfrey could raise it up for another swing. Meanwhile, Sixtus pressed his attack, leaving her little time to recover. As she came out of her roll, she thrust out a sword, just to keep him honest. It allowed her time to spring back to her feet with typical Eryndi nimbleness. She met his long, curved sword with one of her short ones and deflected his blade away. She followed through with a thrust to the ribs, which connected, but didn't penetrate to a life-threatening depth due to Sixtus's armor beneath his colorful shirt. Now he was really pissed. This upstart terrorist had gotten in two palpable hits, both putting holes in his favorite shirt. The large Macai approached the slight Eryndi, slowly swinging the wicked, barbed sword side to side. It had a vicious slashing potential, but the really gory detail was the barb. If used in a stab attack, the harpoon-like point penetrated skin and tissue. When ripped out, it left a horrid, jagged wound, pulling out tissue and organs with it.

Sixtus launched a devastating attack on Danikan. He swung his sword with his right hand and used the spiked shield on his left arm both to defend and attack. Danikan was forced to back up, and still fended off his swings, but the half-healed wound in her leg hampered her agility.

Humfrey held back and acted mostly as support to Sixtus. Nemosthenes was doing the same in the battle with Serena, leaving the main attack to Marcellya. What few knew at the time was that those were exactly their instructions. Sixtus and Marcy were the original scheduled opponents for Danikan and Serena. Someone, presumably Merak, wanted to make extra sure of these criminals' deaths, so Humfrey and Nemosthenes were added as insurance. The bookmakers were not happy with this arrangement. Had they known ahead of time of the additions, they could have adjusted the odds accordingly.

Finally, Sixtus saw his opening. A strike with his shield impacted mere fingers from her bandaged leg wound. Searing pain shot through every nerve in Danikan's body. The shock caused her guard to drop ever so slightly. Sixtus spun theatrically, giving his swing momentum and pleasing the stuffings out of the crowd. Even in her pain, Danikan saw the move and lunged backward, but not quite far enough. The point of Sixtus's sword carved a neat line across her stomach. As it was, it left a deep laceration, cutting through the skin and abdominal muscles. Had they been a quarter-finger closer, her intestines would be spilling on the ground now. Sixtus backed up and had a quickie with the crowd, who roared in appreciation at the martial skill being demonstrated, or maybe they just liked to see blood.

Sixtus turned back to his opponent, who was staggering now. It was time to administer the death blow. He jauntily saluted Humfrey, who returned it with a nod. This would be a tag-team effort. Sixtus roared and charged Danikan, who was just pulling herself together after her latest wound. Sixtus leaped into the air, swinging his sword. She tried to deflect it with her two short swords, but in her weakened state, she couldn't resist the momentum of the Merakian Mauler's plunging blade. His sword slipped between her defenses and delivered a long, deep slash across Danikan's chest. At the same time, Danikan followed through with a quick single thrust of a short sword directly into Sixtus's left eye socket. The Mauler collapsed in a heap, the hilt of Danikan's sword sticking out of his face and wobbling back and forth. The exchange sent Danikan stumbling backward right toward the waiting Humfrey of Tord. He swung his massive hammer in a level arc and caught Danikan on her left side. The heavy hardwood fractured her shoulder and sent her tumbling across the sands of Stadium. Danikan's broken body came to a halt five reaches away and lay still.

CHAPTER 14

When confronted by a possible defeat, it's time to get absolutely berg bear vicious . . .

- Hrolvad the Berserker, c. 20642, describing his famous battle with Chieftain Gramdam the Forktooth.

* * *

Today – Stadium

Serena rolled to her left barely in time to avoid a battle axe to the face. The highly-polished steel blade plunged into the sand less than a finger from her ear. A substantial lock of her blonde hair was not so lucky. Serena lashed out with her scimitar in a sweeping move that forced Nemosthenes to leap above the whistling blade. She used the energy from her sword's momentum to help her get to a more defensible stance than lying on her back.

Serena rolled to her feet, ignoring the searing pain of her wounds in the manner of a Northlands Warrior. Nemosthenes was kind enough to back up and let her. Per orders, his partner,

Marcellya, should take over now. Marcy stood with a smug look on her face, holding her bow with an arrow nocked and ready to loose. She could kill Serena at her leisure, but that move was not a crowd pleaser.

Serena had fought against Eryndi martial arts once before. They're fast and agile, but if caught in a clinch, the superior Macai strength will win out. This time, though, deception was the key. Serena turned away and leaned on her sword, pretending to be seriously wounded, which was not far from the truth. Bleeding from her wounds, she let Marcy get closer and closer, monitoring her movements through the sounds of her equipment, the movements of shadows, even smells. At the precise moment, Serena forced every fiber of strength and speed she had left in a sudden, furious attack. Surprised, Marcy stepped backward, but Serena would have none of that. Marcy had the agility, though, and tried to maneuver into bow range.

Serena, hoping for just such a move, was ready. The tip of her scimitar licked out just as Marcy was about to loose an arrow and neatly cut the taut bowstring. The laminated five-stone bow snapped straight with a loud *sproing*, throwing her off for a split beat. In that time, Serena launched her real attack, going for Marcy's gut with her stiletto. She had spotted what looked like a seam in Marcy's chain mail where it attached to another layer. Seams are weak spots. The long, triangular blade slipped between the mail rings and entered Marcy's ribcage up to the hilt, piercing her liver. Serena savagely twisted the tang in a circular motion, making mush of Marcy's innards. Before she even pulled the blade out, Serena spun and thrust behind her with her scimitar, plunging the point into the throat of Humfrey of Tord, who had tried to sneak up on her . . . but nobody sneaks up on Serena the Free.

The crowd roared at the double kill. This unexpected turn of events was what the mob lived for. Fistfuls of coin were exchanged between individuals who had made private bets. But Serena's victory looked to be short-lived. Three of the four gladiators had been disposed of, but there was still one left.

Man Mountain Nemosthenes approached slowly, grinning like a cooncat and casually tossing his battle axe, which must have weighed at least three or four stone, back and forth between hands.

"I appreciate a tall woman, especially one without armor," said a leering Nemo. "Like me, nothing but steel and flesh. You like *this* flesh?" He smoothed his hair back in a narcissitic manner. The crowd had seen this before. The catcalls and whistles increased. The end was near.

Serena pulled herself together and waited for his attack, letting him come to her. She was familiar with the use of the giant battle axe. It was the preferred weapon of many of her fellow Northlanders, as well as the Axenite barbarians. The handle was steel, rather than wood, and so could resist cuts. Both ends of the axe were deadly. The pommel was a big sphere of steel, like a heavy mace. The axe was a slow weapon and Serena was normally lightning fast with her scimitar. Her wounds and fatigue from battle were taking their toll, however. The two arrows protruding from her calves and the ones stuck in her side and shoulder hampered her movements and slowed her reflexes. Nemo started his swing, aiming for her mid-section. There was no deflecting a weapon as heavy as that axe. The only thing Serena could do was to evade and get under his guard as best she could, but now that Nemosthenes was fighting in earnest and not showing off for the crowd, that wasn't so easy. He handled that weapon like it was a toy. He slashed over and over at a downward angle, Serena ducking to the side each time. She had to hit the sand and roll to avoid his last attack. She came out of the roll with a slash to Nemo's right arm, severing a few tendons. He merely smiled and transferred his weapon to his left hand. Finally, he managed a vicious sideways swing that there was no avoiding. The blade impacted on Serena's sword, numbing her right arm and sending her scimitar whistling across the floor of Stadium. Serena sprawled on the sands and landed on the arrow sticking out of her side. It wrenched itself crossways and triggered a dizzying wave of pain.

The battle appeared to be over. Nemosthenes backed off and did a little more love-making to the crowd. Blown kisses and hip thrusts thrilled the audience, especially the women. The mob began to chant, "Kill, kill."

Serena lay upon the bloodstained sands of Stadium, breathing heavily and fighting to remain conscious. While Nemo was busy flirting with all of Tresk, she slowly began to gather her legs beneath her, summoning up every last bit of strength in her body. When the time was right, Serena launched herself in a low dive at Nemosthenes, sliding between his tree-like legs. His tender bits were protected by the iron codpiece he wore, but her target was a bit lower. During her slide, Serena thrust her thin stiletto into his inside upper thigh and was immediately shot in the face with a thin stream of blood. She had hit the artery as planned. She knew it would not be an instantly fatal wound, so after coming out of her slide, she wisely backed off to regroup and to evaluate her opponent. Nemosthenes looked down at himself, noting the spurting blood.

"You've killed me, bitch. But I shall die on the sands of Stadium. It's what every gladiator wants . . . and expects. But

I also intend to kill you with my dying breath. That will make you my eternal slave in the Afterlife. Just so you know."

All out of strength, Serena hurled her stiletto as a last resort. The thin blade stuck in his ribs, but he simply pulled it out and tossed it away. The giant gladiator slowly advanced on her, raising the axe with his one good arm.

Serena collapsed onto her back, weaponless and completely spent, but not beaten - never beaten. She lifted her chin and started mentally preparing the speech to her god, Crodan, whom she would be meeting in a moment. Nemo stopped and slowly raised his axe above his head. A large pool of blood was collecting under him from his wound. His axe moved backward slightly as he started his swing. Serena's unfearing eyes calmly watched. If they hadn't, they would have missed seeing the bloody point of a Treskan short sword suddenly protrude from Nemo's chest. His handsome face went blank. His last act was to plunge forward, swinging his axe for the last time. The blade buried itself in the sand between Serena's legs. Even as he died, he did so dramatically - for the sake of the crowd.

As Nemo's huge corpse collapsed, it revealed the bloodied form of Danikan behind him, one arm hanging useless and the other just letting go of her sword hilt. She staggered over to her partner and collapsed to her knees, then fell all the way face-to-face with Serena.

"Feeling okay, barbarian?"

"Never better, terrorist. You?"

Danikan winced. "Got a bit of a headache. Been kind of a long day."

"I'm afraid it ain't over yet. C'mon, let's take some bows before they haul us out with the dead."

The crowd had gone silent with suspense while the two

women lay on the sands, just as unmoving as the other corpses that littered the floor. Suddenly, they saw Serena's hand move. She sat up, then got dizzily to her feet, reached for Danikan's hand, and hoisted her upright. Now the crowd truly roared. Serena even heard her own name being chanted, though Danikan's not so much. The Northlands Warrior turned and panned her gaze across the packed stands. A sudden flash of memory slammed into her brain like a mental gong. She had seen and heard this before. She had BEEN here before. How was that possible? It wasn't. Only a few beats passed, but in that time she remembered.

The old Eryndi woman in the cave!

A few years previous, while she was leaving her own people and country behind, Serena had encountered the woman Bata, some kind of a strange witch who spoke always in three word sentences. While enjoying the hospitality of Bata's cave, she had experienced all kinds of strange dreams or visions. One of them was . . . this! This place, these circumstances, the roar of the crowd, the blood. In Bata's cave, she had been shown this.

This strange recollection in her brain was overruled by the pleas from Serena's body. A shroud of dizzying blackness overtook her, and she knew no more.

Today – Deep below Stadium

It was hot, sweaty work, but progress was being made. Some of the workers were starting to experience strange side effects from handling the Magic-infused spheres. One of the terrorists claimed he was receiving visions of a place where the sky was a pinkish color and smelled of burning oil. Another found that she was hearing voices. They were babbling nonsense words, but somehow she understood them. The little old Eryndi lady had anyone exhibiting such symptoms trade places with the sentries above. She also gave each of them a cookie to ease their minds.

"I know it's rough, but we're doing it! You're more than halfway there. A few more of those spheres gone and Merak's shell will turn to wet pasta. That's when the fun begins. Keep it up!"

Today – Stadium

There was music playing, and singing, and light filtering through Serena's closed eyelids.

The world beyond . . .

Opening her eyes would put her at the gates of Crodan's Keep, where only the worthy are admitted. Warriors must prove themselves by their deeds in the mortal life. She was worthy. That last battle and victory with the gladiators in Tresk should look pretty good on her resume.

Man, whichever one of Crodan's Daughters is singing is a real hootysnorter . . .but I won't tell Him that.

The first thing she should see would be the fearsome face of Crodan Himself. It was time. Serena had prepared herself and was ready. Her eyes opened. Strangely, Crodan bore a striking resemblance to her friend Orchid.

"She's coming around. Serena. Serena! Are you with us?"

I would have thought the Warrior King, God of all the Clans, would be more butch.

"SERENA! That's it. C'mon, wake yourself up."

Orchid? What are you doing here? Get outa my Afterlife!

"You're gonna mess this up for me!" shouted Serena, while swinging a fist. She didn't connect with anything though.

“Hey!” shouted Orchid. “Will you settle down, please? You’re being held together with wire and a torn-up bedsheet.”

Serena looked down at herself and her head finally cleared completely. There were bandages around her lower legs, her ribs, and a heavy one wrapping her left shoulder, but she was alive – a bit disappointed, but alive.

“You patch me up?”

Orchid smiled. “Along with this gentleman, here.” She motioned to a haggard-looking Eryndi wearing a bloody apron. Even his long, stringy beard had flecks of blood in it. “Serena, this is Suturus. He’s the . . . sorry, what was it?”

“The Assigned Imperial Agent for Stadium Asset Damage Repair and Maintenance,” said the bloody man. “Pleased to meet you while you’re conscious.”

“That means it’s Suturus’s responsibility to heal wounds so they can be re-inflicted.”

“Harsh, but basically true,” replied Suturus.

“You had us both worried for a bit, you’d lost so much blood,” said Orchid. “But thanks to some brilliant innovative muscular bonding techniques of Healer Suturus, you’re gonna be fine soon.”

“It wouldn’t have been nearly as soon if not for Healer Orchid’s very intriguing use of regenerative herbal catalyst agents,” replied Suturus excitedly. He turned to Serena.

“You see, you had lost a lot of blood from multiple punctures and lacerations.”

“Yeah, I got that, but . . .”

“Orchid here showed me a method for infusing various herb solutions with a very clever dose of Worldly Magic in a slow-decaying fashion. Time release, if you will. That solution is introduced to the wound, again using Worldly Magic to push the tiny droplets into the surrounding area. Once the mist has been thoroughly absorbed, the Magic discharges in full, flooding the tissue with regenerative healing energy."

"What about . . .?"

"Healer, you make it sound like it was all my idea," countered Orchid. "You were the genius who thought of gasifying the solution for quick and deep insertion. That was positively brilliant."

"HEY!" shouted Serena. "What . . . happened . . . to DANIKAN?"

"Oh, she's fine," Orchid responded off-handedly. "But, Healer Suturus, how do you maintain control of the vapor flow once it's penetrated below skin level? You can't see it then."

"Ah, that is accomplished through a mimetic enhancer. Your wonderful mixture samples damaged cells on the surface of the wound and repairs them. The enhancer copies that process and guides the medicine into the tissues, seeking more of the same. But how do you specialize the Magic to do certain repairs? How does it know the difference between a nerve and an artery?"

"Is she here someplace?" asked Serena, half sitting up and looking around.

"Part of the mixture is a bonding agent derived from the Sporka vine," said Orchid. She produced her precious herb kit, that had been given back to her along with her staff, and showed Suturus the various bottles and envelopes. She pulled out a small glass vial containing something that looked like ordinary sawdust.

"This is it," she said. "The ratio of Sporka to Tomaleaf powder is the key. It must be measured very precisely to heal a certain type of injury. Then the Magic is added. It reproduces the energy that you get from ingesting food, but in concentrated form. There are many formulae for multiple applications: one for blood replacement, another for bone knitting, tissue regeneration, and on and on."

Serena sighed to herself. *On and on, indeed. What is it about Magic types, anyway?*

While the two healers continued the lively discourse, Serena slid her sore, bandaged legs off the cot and onto the floor. In a tray near her, she noted the clipped-off, bloody arrowheads that had once been sticking out of her. She saw many other cots with recovering criminals and even a few gladiators and charioteers. At the far end of the room was a score of heavily armed Treskan Legionnaires ready to deal with any act of defiance. As Serena persuaded her battered body to move about, a curious sensation coursed through her aching bones. It made her hurt more, but somehow felt good.

Maybe there was some merit in all that Magical gobbledygook.

Serena continued her search for Danikan. Finally she spotted a cot on the far side of the room off by itself. The soldiers were keeping an especially close eye on it.

That has to be her.

"Hey, terrorist, when do they burn you at the stake?" said Serena, limping toward her.

Danikan had been half dozing, but turned her head when she heard the familiar voice.

"Barbarian, it's you! Haven't they fed you to the hurdlebirds yet?" replied Danikan.

"No, that was us."

Foxx and Feelia stood there, smiling, but looking a bit bedraggled.

"I wondered what happened to you," deadpanned Serena.

"Not as much as what happened to you, it seems," said

Foxx, looking at Serena's bandaged body. "We pretty much heard all about it from the guards who saw your fight. You're the talk of Stadium."

Serena's head still hurt. "And what about . . .?"

"HEY GUYS!"

Tresado's plump form came pushing his way through the crowd of prisoners, eliciting angry growls from a few of them.

"BOY, IT'S GOOD TO SEE YOU GUYS!"

Serena's headache just got worse.

"Orchid and I have been worried sick about all of you," said Tresado, taking Feelia's hand. "Especially you, Feelia. Are you all right?"

"I've been better," Feelia replied, "but I'm alive, thanks to Mister Foxx here."

"And I'm alive, thanks to Feelia's archery skills," said Foxx, returning the compliment. "She's quite the badass when she wants to be."

"Speaking of badasses," said Feelia, "who's your friend?"

"She's a friend, all right," said Serena. She carefully put a palm under Danikan's back and helped her sit up. "This is Danikan, who saved me by killing Man Mountain What's-His-Ass."

Danikan winced from the pain in her shattered shoulder. It had begun the healing process, the same as Serena's wounds, but still hurt like a mother.

"You killed him first," she said, gripping Serena by the forearm. "I killed him the second time."

"Wait a minute," said Feelia. "Danikan? Danikan Tyre, the traitor?" Feelia turned to Suturus. "You actually helped her?"

Suturus looked at Danikan with an expression like he had smelled something really bad.

"Yes, even her," replied Suturus. "My Paraklinian Oath obliges me to care for the wounded, no matter who they are, or what."

"Uh, yeah, we had to work on you for a while," interjected Orchid, trying to change the subject. "You had some severe bone breaks and deep lacerations. Now that you're awake, can you feel anything odd?"

Danikan looked down at herself. "Yes, I think so. It's sort of tingly."

"Yeah, me too," said Serena. "In my legs and chest."

"That means the process is working. This is kind of new, so I . . . we aren't sure how long you'll be recovering, but damn if it didn't work!" said Orchid, giddy with self-congratulation.

A soldier, resplendent in her green armor, entered with two escorts. She did a quick pan of the room, noting the lack of screaming and dying sounds.

"Suturus, report on asset status."

Suturus surreptitiously winked at Orchid with a slight grin. He consulted a scroll. "Eleven gladiators with minor wounds, seven charioteers, and all surviving prisoners treated and recovered."

"No deaths?" asked the soldier.

"No one who was dragged in here alive is anything other than imminently recovered."

The soldier looked annoyed, whether it was from disappointment or the fact that she kind of had to do the math at Suturus's last statement. As a soldier, she hated having to figure things out. She preferred orders.

"It is my duty to inform you that, in light of . . . recent events," she glared at Serena at that point and returned to the scroll, "all scheduled bouts and bookings are hereby canceled while a new schedule is devised. In the meantime, The Imperator has graciously declared a Hiatus of Comatus."

The soldier nodded curtly to her two escorts. They snapped to and opened up a cask of Firellian. The open barrel and several cups were left on a stone table.

"Even criminals and traitors," said the soldier, rolling up the scroll. "Let's go."

"I think she means me," said Danikan after the soldiers had gone. She was on her feet, now, unsteady but functional.

"That mean what I think it means?" said Orchid thirstily.

"Free wine for all within Stadium," said Foxx. "They also put on a kind of half-time show to keep the mob from getting bored."

"So that's where that awful singing is coming from," said Serena. "I thought maybe they were slaughtering a sheep."

As if on cue, the singing came to a halt and was replaced by occasional laughter. There must be a clown show or something going on. Suturus interjected his medical opinion.

"I recommend everyone lie down and get as much rest as you can. There's no telling when they start the games up again, or what they'll have you facing. So, come on now. Back to your cots, everyone." He shot a foul look towards Danikan. "Except you. Feel free to bash your head against the stone wall, or fall on your sword, anything. Just so long as it's something I can't fix."

Suturus turned and moved off haughtily.

"Popular, aren't you?" said Serena.

"I kind of like it," said Danikan. "Keeps me from having to talk to people."

Although Orchid's medicine seemed to be working, Serena felt that a nice nap would be just what the doctor ordered. She looked around for Orchid to thank her first for all she'd done, but she was busy emptying the wine cask. Several prisoners were gathered around for their share, but she wasn't making it easy.

Serena sat on the edge of her cot and massaged her bandaged calves. They were starting to feel a lot better, but there was still some stiffness. The pain had reduced from mind-numbing to a dull ache. Her shoulder was a different matter. Serena found she couldn't raise her left arm at all. But the tingling was still going on.

Tresado, Feelia, and Foxx wandered over, along with Danikan.

"So, what's new with you guys?" Serena asked.

"Oh, you know, just hangin' out," replied Tresado.

"They haven't made you fight anyone?" asked Feelia.

"Not yet," said Tresado. "Orchid neither. I get the impression they had us set up to battle some Magicians of some kind. But now, with the death of the champion, their schedule is all screwed up. Thanks for that, by the way," he said to Serena and Danikan.

"Had nothing better to do," said Danikan, who was still in a fair amount of pain.

"Merak must be throwing a temper tantrum about us surviving," said Foxx.

"He sure was pissed about something," said Serena. "One second we were treated like kings, the next . . ."

"It was right after Orchid mentioned me blowing Rastaban's hand off," said Tresado.

"Oh, I forgot. This was all MY fault," said Orchid, throwing back the last cupful of wine.

"There's something fishy here," said Foxx, in his thinking pose. "Merak and Rastaban? How are they connected?"

"Remember at the town meeting?" asked Orchid. "Merak

seemed real pleased at first when we talked about Abakaar. Like he was happy about us defeating Rastaban."

"But when Orch . . ." Tresado paused. "I mean, the conversation turned to how we did it, that's when he freaked out."

"Merak did say that weird thing right before our bout," said Serena. "Something about crimes against kin."

"And he also said something about losing points," added Danikan. "What did he mean by that?"

"Let's sum things up," said Foxx. "Merak, who looks just like Rastaban, except a lot heavier, clean shaven, and two-handed, would seem to be in competition with Rastaban. Merak was happy about his defeat, which he already seemed to know about. But when he was told that Rastaban had been seriously injured or even killed, he became furious. That implies that maybe it's a friendly competition. Merak mentioned losing points and avenging kin."

"Any of you have siblings?" asked Orchid.

"Just cousins," said Serena.

"A sister," replied Tresado.

"Yeah, me too," said Orchid. "Several, in fact. You ever play games with them?"

"Spear the Barby," answered Serena. "You choose up sides and pick one guy who has to play the barbarian, and then you . . ."

"What's your point?" asked Foxx quickly.

"You play games with your sisters, your friends, you choose up teams to play on and to root for," she gestured. Orchid always did talk with her hands. "My two brothers were really into boingball in school. Their team took first place. We were all ridiculously happy about that. But when you come right down to it, sports goals are essentially meaningless. Getting a ball over a line or into a hole. The competition is the point, rather than the act itself. You cheer for the team you like and you boo and talk smack about the ones you don't like."

"But you don't want anything bad to happen to the other team," interrupted Foxx, who had suddenly grasped her meaning.

"Exactly," said Orchid. "Merak only went crazy after he heard about our attack."

"Back in Abakaar, I sensed that maybe Rastaban was playing some sort of game," said Foxx. "I think we just found out who he's playing against."

"Someone who looks just like him," said Tresado. "Brothers?"

"Good," said the ever-impatient Serena. "Now that we figured that out, let's figure out how we're gonna get out of here."

"There is no way out of here," said Danikan sadly. "The Treskans have seen to that. You probably noticed there are areas where your Magic doesn't work. The Shell keeps Magic contained on the Stadium floor. There are other select rooms that are shielded from Magic use. Makes prisoners like you easier to handle."

"There is Magic here in this room," said Orchid. "We used a lot of Worldly for the healing."

"That's because this room connects directly with Stadium floor to allow immediate treatment of injuries." said Suturus. "Its official designation is Asset Maintenance, also called the Narthex. It's pretty much my office."

"What we need is outside help," said Foxx, turning to Danikan. "Didn't I hear a rumor about you being the leader of a large terrorist organization?"

“I’m sure you did,” said Danikan, “although we call it The Durii. Named after . . .”

“What’s in a name?” Foxx interrupted. “My point is, I don’t suppose you have access to hordes and masses of soldiery ready to bust in and save us all?”

“Don’t hate me for this, but . . . I ordered them not to. Too dangerous to risk lives just to save mine.”

“Never hurts to ask,” said Foxx.

The ominous sound of the Stemhorns drifted in from outside. A moment later, a squad of soldiers entered and started herding the prisoners together. The wounded Treskans were allowed to stay in their cots and fully recover.

“Ready, Centurian,” said one of the Legionnaires to his superior.

“Right, stand by,” said the Centurian, who appeared to be listening to something that no one else could hear.

The magnified voice of Imperator Merak echoed off the stone walls.

“Citizens, welcome back. I hope you enjoyed the Midgames Entertainment.”

Merak paused to allow the crowd to applaud. They did so half-heartedly.

“And the wine.”

Now the mob responded more enthusiastically (and drunkenly). Merak was pleased when crowds were pleased with him.

“Your enthusiasm and loyalty have earned you what you want on this night. For the second half of tonight’s games, I hereby declare . . . a Treskan Holiday!”

Now it was time for wild cheering. Merak had the volume of his Amplifier increased to full.

"LET THE GAMES CONTINUE!"

"Open the doors," the Centurian ordered. The large portal on the south side of the Narthex creaked ominously open. The noise from the crowd increased. The soldiers advanced with their spears and pole arms, prodding the prisoners to exit onto Stadium floor.

"What's a Treskan Holiday?" whispered Tresado.

The rest of Group Six didn't know, but Feelia did.

"A bloodbath."

As they were led out the door, the Centurian gave them a final piece of advice.

"Die well, prisoners, die well."

CHAPTER 15

I am devastated. The loss of your Imperatrix and my beloved wife has thrown all our lives into chaos. The mysterious wasting disease that claimed her has been determined to be completely alien to our Republic and will not return. Our lives and our way of life must go on. The past sorrows are gone. The future is all that matters. Henceforth, this is the last time the name of Alythya shall be written or spoken. It is my order and my manner of ruling as your Imperator. Also henceforth, the term Coalition is abolished. Long live the Treskan Imperium!

-Imperator Merak – Commentaries: Book 4, Chapter 1, paragraph 1

* * *

Today – Deep below Stadium

No one heard the light footsteps coming down the stairs at first. It was Callya, the young daughter of Ducius, the work crew leader who now lay sedated and unconscious from sleeper bush poison. Callya was used to hanging around in the bowels of Stadium. She had practically grown up here and was coming to see her father to ask his permission to go on a boat ride with her friends the next morning. She had to talk to him now, because it would be her bedtime soon and it would be too late to ask. When she entered the room, she was surprised at the sight of her father and a number of others lying about, seemingly dead. Her high-pitched, girly scream startled the sentries, who had failed to detect her presence. Callya did the smart thing and immediately turned and fled back up the steps. There was no stopping her before she escaped. The little old Eryndi lady realized that time was quickly running out.

"She's going to bring help. Quickly, get the rest of those spheres free! Move!"

Today – Stadium

"Citizens," bellowed Vocalus from his hoverchariot, "Your victims!"

The prisoners were driven onto the sands of Stadium. It was a toss-up among the crowd. Half were booing and half were chanting, "Serena, Serena."

"Well, aren't you the popular one?" said Orchid. "How is your healing coming along?"

"Shoulder still stings a bit," replied Serena. "The calves have stopped aching and I think the skin on my side is all healed."

"And how about you, Danikan?"

Danikan painfully tried to raise her left arm. It only went about halfway. "That's the best I can do on that side. The chest wound is nearly all closed."

"It'll take a little time," said Orchid. "Your whole shoulder was shattered. Meanwhile, get plenty of rest and drink lots of fluids."

"Yes, Healer," answered Danikan with a smile.

The Stemhorns sounded again.

"And now, your heroes!"

A set of doors opened and two score of armed gladiators sashayed onto the sands. There were many familiar faces, including Screamin' Sammy Soultaker, the challenger in the title bout against Man Mountain Nemosthenes that didn't take place. Vocalus quickly introduced them one at a time, but the crowd knew them all.

Serena and the few surviving prisoners readied their weapons and prepared to make a stand, although they were seriously outnumbered and out-muscled. Serena's sword and stiletto had been returned to her, but the scimitar had a serious groove in one side from Nemo's axe.

That's gonna take forever to buff out, thought a resentful Serena.

Following the gladiators was a trio of curious-looking beings. Two were Eryndi women and the third was a Macai man. They were costumed in bizarre, personalized outfits decorated with strange symbols and letters.

"And now let me introduce to you, in no particular order, the Ice Queen, Megana of Decium!"

One Eryndi woman raised her arms. A blizzard of ice crystals formed between them, coalescing into a dozen spiked balls of death which she sent exploding outward. The multi-pointed icy projectiles stuck into the sand, surrounding the prisoners in a perfect circle – just for demonstration purposes.

"And I believe you know that little firecracker, the Toaster with the Moster, Pyroxemus!"

The other woman, smallish even for an Eryndi, stepped forward. Pyroxemus was dressed in a bizarre black and white costume with no discernible pattern and chaotic black and white facial stripes to match. She pointed a finger at the air and traced out her name with letters of flame that appeared and hung in the air for a few beats. The blazing banner spun about a couple of times, giving the crowd plenty of time to admire it and her. It finally exploded in a shower of fire and sparks.

"And last we have, from the far-off Kingdom of Muringia, that Gentleman Magician, Squire Buckminster Gold."

The Macai stepped forward and adopted a strange stance with strange motions. Anybody who knew much about Magic knew that movements and gestures were unnecessary. Magic was formed in the mind. However, they did help the Magician maintain and control a spell by aiding in concentration. Not only that, but they made for a better show. The result of Bucky's squirming involved the sands of Stadium rising from the floor to form a huge, mostly Macai-shaped creature with long, sharp claws, no eyes, but a mouth full of needle teeth. His creation stood nearly three reaches in height and adopted a warrior pose with all sharp things extended, looking especially fierce. Buckminster bowed regally to the crowd and his sand creature mirrored the gesture.

"Phase One of the Treskan Holiday begins . . . now!" Vocalus, as usual, quickly spun his hoverchariot about and got the hell out of harm's way.

The Stemhorns sounded and the small army of gladiators rushed forward, brandishing their weapons and screaming bloody murder, as was their intent. The small number of pitiful prisoners would be no match for such an overwhelming wave of muscle and steel. But a Treskan Holiday was meant to be anything but fair. By putting Magicians in the fray, it changed the odds dramatically.

Tresado saw the tragedy about to happen and immediately launched a kinetic spell, his specialty. He sent a wave of force lashing toward the lead warriors. Several of them were knocked down and skidded backward on their butts, filling their loincloths with sand.

Orchid joined in the fun by creating a funnel cloud that snaked amongst the gladiators, blasting sand in their faces and knocking several off their feet.

Serena stood by, ready with her scimitar, but so far, no gladiators got through her companions' Magical barriers.

"HEY, you gonna let me help, or what?"

"We're doing fine," shouted Orchid. "Shut up and heal!"

"Phase two!" Vocalus's announcement boomed out from behind the safety of one of the heavily gated doors. It was the signal for the Magicians to begin their attack.

Pyroxemus began by launching a thin finger of flame toward Tresado. He tried to get out of the way, but his own pudginess slowed him down. As he turned to jump to the side, the fire caught him on his retreating posterior, igniting his butt. Tresado yelped in pain and stumbled. Fortunately, his roundness caused him to roll, immediately extinguishing the flame, but there was a definite smell of singed Eryndi in the air. Mad as hell, he quickly sprang to his feet, ready to initiate a kinetic spell that would have pulped Pyroxemus, but she wasn't there. She was nowhere.

Invisible . . . Pyroxemus is invisible.

Buckminster's sand creature ambled forward, intent on harming whoever got in its way. Of course, it had no mind. It was controlled by its creator. The behemoth strode clumsily in Serena's direction. She unleashed her Northlands Warrior battle cry and leapt to the attack. Her left shoulder was still stiff, but like most Macai, she was right-handed. As the sandman stooped to reach for her, Serena swung her trusty scimitar, connecting with the thing's "wrist." The hand dropped off and hit the ground, leaving a pile of sand. It didn't bother the thing, seeing as it had no life, but it did slow it down. It paused for a moment to allow Buckminster to add a little power to his spell. The pile of sand flew back up, reconnected to the arm, and became a big, sandy hand again.

Serena saw that she couldn't harm the thing, but maybe she could bring it down. With her bandaged calves now fully healed, she sprinted between the legs of the sandman. It tried to reach for her, but couldn't match her warrior speed. Two swipes of her sword severed both "feet," causing the thing to slowly pitch forward. Buckminster tried valiantly to reassemble it, but was prevented by the Northlands Warrior. Serena had realized that fighting the creature was useless. Better to chop off the snake's head, instead.

The second-to-last thing Buckminster saw was the tall, blonde warrior rushing toward him with murder in her eyes. The last thing he saw, just for a beat or two, was a worm's eye view of his own headless body collapsing in the sand. Then the lights went out forever.

Meanwhile, with Tresado distracted, it fell to Orchid to continue to hold off the gladiators. The funnel cloud she created was doing a good job. The mini-twister bowled over the bad guys like twelvepins, but the gladiators separated widely, making it difficult for Orchid to keep them all at bay. Two of them managed to evade the funnel and engage Danikan. Serena rushed forward to help her, but an aerial flame attack struck the ground in front of her, forcing her to skid to a stop.

Orchid saw the danger to Danikan, who was still dealing with the pain of her injuries. She was holding her own, but weakening, and a third gladiator was heading her way. Orchid sent a surge of power to her funnel cloud, which slammed into the bulk of the gladiators, bowling them all over. She directed the mini-tornado over the large pile of sand previously known as Buckminster's conjured creature, which had collapsed along with its creator. It picked up the pile and dispersed it in the air, creating a concentrated sandstorm. Buckminster's head was inadvertently picked up as well. It swirled around in the funnel, its tongue hanging out and its dead eyes staring blankly. The crowd loved it. Using the natural forces at work, Orchid politely asked Magic to increase the potentiality in the cloud. A couple of beats later, directed lightning bolts issued from within. The two gladiators fighting Danikan were both struck and writhed on the sand from the shock to their systems. She smiled at her own ingenuity, knowing that trying to use the funnel itself to drive off Danikan's attackers was dangerous to her, as well. The lightning could be directed much more accurately.

Orchid didn't have any more time to congratulate herself. A stinging barrage of hailstones began to pummel her mercilessly. The Ice Queen, Megana of Decium, stood with arms raised and her face stony with focus. The hailstones formed in front of her and quickly sped to their target. She was dressed all in white, including white face makeup. Her hair was silver with blue streaks. Her lips were painted blue, as were her fingernails. She had singled out Orchid to be her target and kept her under constant attack. Concentration couldn't be held under such an assault. All Orchid could think about was getting out of range of those projectiles. Her funnel cloud collapsed as a result. The gladiators who were able regrouped and once again charged the survivors.

Tresado saw the spear of flame hit in front of Serena. He followed it up with his eyes. It seemed to originate about five reaches above the sands. There was no Magician at the source. Of course, a Magician doesn't channel Magic through his body, but alters what is in the air. Pyroxemus could be anywhere. But Tresado watched carefully and the source seemed to shift a couple of reaches, changing the angle of the flame attack.

There IS somebody up there!

The flame stopped abruptly. Tresado launched another kinetic wave at where he thought the source was. But there was nothing. Pyroxemus was not where she used to be. He did not feel his spell impact on anything but the shell, which momentarily glowed green when struck by his Magic.

Invisibility! Tresado had studied such a thing back in his early years. True invisibility is impossible, but there are ways around natural laws. A skilled Magician could conceivably cloak herself by reflecting her background or even bending an enemy's eyesight completely around herself. Such a feat would have one fatal flaw. The Magician would not be able to see. If images are not making it to her eyes, there would be nothing to see.

The flame stopped. Serena took advantage and leapt forward to help Danikan, who was fighting with only one short sword a shattered left shoulder that was not completely healed. The two gladiators she was fighting had been taken out by Orchid's lightning bolts, but there was a half score more heading their way. The one in the lead howling like a banshee was Screamin' Sammy Soultaker, the original opponent for Nemosthenes.

Serena charged to meet him, belting out her own impressive

war cry. Hers sounded a bit like a vicious "HOOOAGH!" Sammy's was more of a "NI-NI-NI-NEAGH!" The two crashed together in a flurry of flashing blades, both of them screaming their lungs out. This was one of the noisiest one-on-one sword duels ever.

Orchid snatched up a large shield from one of the downed gladiators, giving herself some protection from the hailstone barrage. She needed a few beats to concentrate enough to defend herself. Tresado was still playing cat and mouse with the Toaster, attempting to locate the invisible foe. Serena was battling Sammy in a thrilling exhibition of swordsmanship from both parties. Foxx was given a sword at the beginning of the Treskan Holiday, but soon cast it away, having no skill with such things. He attempted to use his Knowing Spell wherever it was most needed, confusing or distracting their foes. Feelia had the same bow and quiver of arrows she acquired in her last battle, using it to pick off gladiators. The other prisoners were doing their best, but losing. The odds were against all of them, but they were holding on for now.

"Phase three!"

At Vocalus's announcement from safe behind steel bars, a dozen other doors in Stadium's inner wall opened, releasing a stampede of snarling, deadly creatures. Razor lions, spiny apes, and splitzards poured out of the openings and rushed toward the closest food source. It didn't matter if they were gladiators, Magicians, or prisoners. They all tasted the same, and the creatures were all hungry.

* * *

Magic's computational disposition can be compared to a snowflake naturally forming six points, or crystals in their uniformity, water seeking its own level, etc. Nature taking the easiest path, as it were. A Magician connects with the Magic in the air, the soil, the plants, everywhere. His brain waves are read as to what kind of "'spell'" is being cast. That is broken down into a binary code. Energy from the belt is reconfigured into the algorithm necessary to transform one's target into . . . say . . . a lumbaslug.

- PREFACE TO *SPELLCASTING 101*,
BY CEDRIC SIGGERSOL* - FORMER PROFESSOR OF MAGIC, PARMELAX ACADEMY,
QUARAN, C. 24639 – 24663

**Dismissed due to allegations of radicalism*

Today – Stadium

A razor lion clamped its enormous jaws around the upper leg of a burly gladiator and gave the man a vicious death shake. The leg separated from pelvis in a shower of tendons and blood. A spiny ape, smelling the blood, rushed forward to try to grab the bulk of the body, which was still sort of alive and screaming. Despite the fact that there was potentially a lot of fresh meat on the sands of Stadium, the razor lion was unwilling to let such a brazen theft take place. Lion leapt upon ape and a vicious tussle ensued.

The splitzards, resembling two-reach-long salamanders, were more willing to work collectively. Dividing into packs of about four or five, they systematically fanned their groups out, each one claiming an area of Stadium and all the food that resided therein. For being vicious carnivores, they were very cooperative.

The spiny apes, on the other hand, were just here to party. Being mostly herbivores, they had little interest in eating the victims. But also being higher primates, they got great giggles by chasing, catching, torturing, and killing their victims and when in a group like this, even more so. They seemed to like outdoing each other. The troop of twelve apes whooped and wailed in joy when they first saw the scattered gladiators and prisoners.

Another blast of flame came out of the sky with no seeming source. It struck the unfortunate Puggnayshus just as he was beginning to battle the gladiator Eruptus the Volcano, whose signature was loud farts while swinging his spiked mace. Both of them went up in colored methane flames to the delight of the audience.

Orchid recovered herself behind the shield she had appropriated. Her own Worldly spell was designed to counter the ice queen's hailstorm. Summoning a highly localized wind, she managed to blow the ice balls right back at Megana, who was forced to retreat herself.

Tresado continued to carefully watch for the source of the flame spells from the air.

There!

A brief glimpse of something! It was tiny, but whatever it was definitely showed itself intermittently.

Eyes!

It was a set of two eyes levitating about. Tresado realized he had been right earlier. Somehow, Pyroxemus was deflecting the sight of her body away – everything but her eyes, which enabled her to see. The flaw was that it left her not quite totally invisible. Tresado carefully prepared his next spell, waiting for his target to present itself. The eyes appeared again in a different spot and Tresado quickly launched one of his favorite spells, a giant, invisible grasping hand. Through the spell, he could feel the fist close around Pyro. Grunting with effort, he Magically threw her up into the shell. Instead of bouncing off a hard surface, as he expected, a green, Magician-shaped dent appeared in the dome. It remained for a beat, then the black and white form of Pyroxemus reappeared and fell toward Stadium floor. The dent in the shell slowly smoothed out and the green glow vanished. In a half-beat, Pyroxemus regained her wits and fired off twin flame columns straight down that slowed her descent to the ground. Tresado, still mad about his singed butt, did not opt for the sportsmanlike thing to do. Before Pyro could reach the ground, he sent a kinetic wave which launched the flaming Eryndi woman straight into the ape and lion that were still fighting. Pyroxemus was effectively shredded by tooth and claw.

The greasy fur of the spiny ape caught fire and it bolted, causing more mayhem as it careened through a group of splitzards that were attacking a pair of gladiators. One of them got in a good lick with his sword. The splitzard purposely tore itself in two. Its front half reared up on its two legs and continued to attack with vicious bites. The back half stood up on its back legs and attacked with brutal swipes of its needle-pointed tail. How it could see what it was doing was anyone's guess.

Orchid tried to reach the minds of the creatures in an attempt to calm them, but they were too hungry and fired up with bloodlust. The same could be said when Foxx tried to Magically influence the gladiators.

When everyone and everything on Stadium floor was

engaged in either defending their lives or trying to take others, Vocalus deemed it was time.

"Phase four! SUPPERTIME!"

It was what the crowd was waiting for. All of Stadium was consumed in bloodlust. The mob began to chant.

"Suppertime, suppertime!"

The stemhorns sounded a different refrain, one specific to Phase Four. The final door opened and a huge, silvery head poked its way out. It looked about for a beat or so, summing up the situation, then the whole creature showed itself. It was a magnificent dragon. It lumbered out onto Stadium floor and stopped. For the benefit of the crowd, she stood on her back legs and reared up. The dragon, known as Seresin, spread her mighty wings and roared out a deafening challenge.

CHAPTER 16

Today – Deep below Stadium

The little old Eryndi lady had her wrinkled hands full. The staircase was a narrow enough bottleneck that only a couple of soldiers could come down it at once. Several of them lay unconscious at the base of the stairs, victims of the tiny crossbow bolts. But there seemed to be an inexhaustible number following them. Three of her own had already gone down from sword and arrow wounds. She had ten left that could fight. The remaining three were desperately needed to pry loose the last few spheres. There were dozens of loose spheres rolling about the room. She decided to put them to good use. Using levitation Magic, she flung them one by one at the guards. They were heavy and caused a lot of damage when they hit. Fortunately, there was much Magic in the air down here. One wouldn't think so, considering their depth underground, but the spheres seemed to have something to do with the atmospheric saturation. The little old Eryndi lady had a lot of power to her spells in this place. Even so, the saboteurs were slowly being overrun.

"Don't give up, lads! It's do or die now!"

In a last-ditch effort, she placed the backs of her hands over her eyes and concentrated on the soldiers, probing deeply into the very substance from which the gods had made them. It was a difficult spell and very demanding. She shrieked with the effort. In her inner vision, she entered their tissues, their blood vessels, seeking out the many fluids there. The six guards on the stairs suddenly dropped their weapons and began screaming. Their blood, their spinal fluid, even the pee in their bladders began heating up to the boiling point. The little old Eryndi lady kept up her vicious attack. In her mind she could sense the deaths of trillions of cells as they boiled away into husks. The horrible stench of steamed Eryndi filled the corridors.

"Last one!" shouted one of her men. The final sphere came loose and rolled onto the stone floor. The persistent hum faded to nothing. The shell was disabled!

The little old Eryndi lady collapsed onto the floor. It took a few beats for her to recover her senses. She was helped to her feet and took stock of their situation. The guards had ceased coming for the moment, but more would be along soon.

"Time to get out of here, lads."

Today – Stadium

"Suppertime, suppertime!"

The chanting continued and Seresin the dragon loved it. She was used to it. She had been with Stadium for thirty-two years, having been captured when still a scaling. Now, from nose to tail, Seresin measured sixteen reaches, seventy-two fingers. She was not quite as large as Gleam, whom Group Six had met at the Crystal Palace, but he was older. It was said that Seresin's win/loss record in Stadium was 96/0. Dragons don't lose.

In the same manner as the gladiators, Seresin bowed and blew kisses to the crowd. They responded by throwing balkur flowers through the shell and onto the sands – an old custom. But now it was time to get down to business. Seresin put her reptilian fingers together and cracked her knuckles. She took a look around at all the potential suppers and decided to start with a couple of the beefy gladiators. As she didn't care for the taste and texture of steel armor and pointy weapons, a little food prep was necessary. She focused on the two guys charging across the sands bent on some project of their own. Her dragon eyes glowed with an eerie green luminescence as she concentrated. The gladiators stopped in their tracks, dropped their weapons, curtsied to each other, then to the crowd. Using a dance move known as the Wriggle Rag that was popular in the Imperium, they both began stripping off all their clothing. The crowd cheered and whistled at the two beefcakes doing their alluring dance. One guy was pretty good. His final move was twirling his now-removed loin cloth around his foot and tossing it in the air. Once fully naked, they both took their bows, then dutifully strode up to Seresin and presented her with the first course. There was a lot of well-marbled meat on these musclemen. Seresin took her time and savored every bite. She always saved the heads for last. Crunchy on the outside, and rich and chewy on the inside – like the griffleberry on top of a frozen whalecream sundae. Such things should always be eaten last.

Meanwhile, the free-for-all battle continued. Spiny ape vs. gladiator vs. razor lion vs. prisoner vs. splitzard. None of the gladiators had ever participated in a Treskan Holiday before. That's because usually nobody survives such a thing. They accepted the fact that they would probably die. It's what gladiators do. Besides, everyone knows there is a very special place in the afterlife reserved to gladiators, one filled with drinking and debauchery. They were all just fine with that. The blood continued to flow and the body count escalated. Group Six and friends managed to stay relatively unscathed, due to Orchid's and Tresado's spells.

Seresin had eaten her fill and wasn't interested in more food, but she was still having a blast manipulating the survivors. Her Magical suggestive powers were formidable. She talked a group of splitzards into dividing themselves and fighting their other halves. Those members of the crowd who still had betting money left wagered back and forth on the victors. The front halves prevailed until Seresin declared the fight over by stomping them into pudding. In triumph, the dragon spread her wings and flew up to the center of the dome. She extended her claws and dug them into the invisible barrier until she had a secure foothold. The shell glowed green in protest. This was something the crowd expected. It was a familiar move on the part of Seresin. What they weren't expecting was when one of her feet suddenly protruded all the way through the barrier. The dragon seemed as surprised as anyone when this happened.

"Look at that," said Foxx, pointing up.

"Is that supposed to happen?" asked Tresado, shading his eyes against the bright Stadium lights.

"Maybe," said Orchid. She looked over at Foxx and they both said the same thing at once.

"The shell is weakening!"

"Can you reach her?" asked Foxx. "Maybe we can convince her to help us."

No one had ever talked with a dragon. They had no speech that anyone could decipher, but they were known to be highly intelligent creatures. Orchid and Foxx both concentrated. Orchid was better with animals than Foxx, but this was an animal with intelligence. Dragon Magic was closely akin to Foxx's Knowing Spell, only more powerful. Foxx made contact first. It was relatively easy. The dragon's psyche was sophisticated and well developed. He sent a greeting.

Hello . . .

There was no response from Seresin, but she did pause for a couple of beats. She peered down at the puny Smallthings who were making so much noise in her head. This time both Foxx and Orchid were getting through.

The shell is weakening!

You can escape!

We can ALL escape!

You can be free!

Together we can take revenge on our captors!

Will you help us?

Seresin snorted in annoyance at the Smallthings. She understood what they were saying. The Smallthings had spoken of revenge, and that had appeal, but other callings had been tugging at her for some time now. The shell was gone now and there were far more important things to do.

Foxx and Orchid could tell they had the dragon's attention, but there was no response from her yet. They continued to send mental messages of friendship and promises to punish her captors if she would just help the prisoners escape. Finally, Seresin seemed to make a decision. She tossed away the mangled remains of a splitzard that was smeared all over one of her front feet. Taking a firm grip in the softening shell, Seresin pushed with all her might against the barrier with her pointed nose. It was like forcing her way through thick gelatin, but after a few beats, she struggled through the shell completely, finding herself in the open air for the first time since she was a little scaling. Her huge wings opened and clawed at the air. At last she had momentum and took to the skies. The crowd screamed as one and tried to stampede out the nearest exits in a frenzy to get away from the mighty predator that was suddenly in their midst. Seresin circled Stadium a couple of times, roaring in triumph at the fleeing crowd. She then peered back down at Orchid and Foxx, who had looks of betrayal on their faces. Seresin gave them the dragon equivalent of a nose-thumbing, took a big, slimy dump on the fleeing crowd, then soared off to the south and disappeared into the night.

"Well, there's dragons for you," harrumphed Orchid.

The Stemhorns blared out a tone that was meant to announce that the event was over. A small army of guards and animal wranglers rushed out onto the sands, attempting to gather surviving prisoners and wild animals and restore some kind of order. Needless to say, Group Six actively expressed a reluctance to be retaken back into custody.

Serena was still fighting a protracted battle with Screamin' Sammy. Both had displayed excellent prowess with their swords and seemed equally matched. Finally, after a brilliant feint, Serena got through Sammy's guard and thrust her scimitar under his green Treskan breastplate, ending his career forever. Serena threw up her arms in triumph.

"I am Serena!" shouted the Northlands Warrior to the crowd. She beat her chest with the hilt of her scimitar. "Serena . . . THE FREEEEE!"

The remaining crowd slowly began chanting.

"Serena, Serena!"

The pace and the volume picked up as she stood victorious upon the sands of Stadium, her dripping scimitar raised to the sky.

"SERENA! SERENA!"

Suddenly from above there was a flash of green light and the shell vanished completely. The Stadium lights also went out, plunging the arena into darkness. Evidently they were powered by the same source as the shell. The only lights were the few fires that were still burning on the floor and the half-orb in the night sky. No one within Stadium had a clue why any of this had happened. All anyone knew was that now, the remaining razor lions and spiny apes were leaping up the walls and into the stands where people were trying desperately to flee. There was pandemonium in Stadium. The crowd was either trampling themselves to death trying for the exit tunnels or being torn to pieces by wild animals. Imperator Merak had disappeared from the Imperial Balcony at the first sign of trouble.

"I think it's time to leave," suggested Foxx.

Group Six, along with Feelia and Danikan, headed back into one of the open doors on the floor. While making their way through the passageways, they encountered guards several times, but they were not interested in prisoner control. They were trying to get out of the building themselves. Eventually, thanks to Tresado's Eryndi sense of direction, they found their way to the first room they had been brought to. The storage locker where their belongings had been stowed was on the far wall. Foxx quickly squatted in front of it and examined the mechanism.

"I can pick this lock." He looked around for some kind of tool to do such a thing. He found somebody's uniform rank pin on the floor next to the overturned table where the Centurian had sat.

"Now, this is a standard, pin-type lock. Not to worry . . . it just takes a little . . . damn! Let me try that again. This time, a little pressure to the left and . . . okay . . . almost there. Just have to . . ."

"Oh, for crap's sake!" cried an exasperated Serena, who drew and swung her sword faster than the eye could follow. The angle and force were exactly what was needed to shear away the hasp.

"HEY!" shouted Foxx, falling backward. "I need all my fingers!"

"I'll argue that," she said. "Now grab the stuff and let's get on with the escape!"

The stuff consisted of their packs, the contents of which seemed undisturbed. Orchid checked first for Dementus's journal, which was safe. She opened it to a random page to see some nonsensical poem about hornet nests and hair gel.

"Now I know why they called him *The Mad Treskan.* This place would make anybody crazy."

Suddenly there was the sound of running feet behind them and a group of armed people appeared. Both groups stopped and stared. Since neither side was wearing soldier suits, there seemed no reason for violence. Danikan stepped forward, recognizing several of the people.

"What are you guys doing here? You had strict orders not to . . ."

The little old Eryndi lady pushed her way through the men and smiled at Danikan, whose eyes widened in astonishment.

"MOM!?"

* * *

MEMO TO: Mama
FROM: Zaurac
cc: Dispatch buffer
DATE: 1313.75
RE: The Effect of Lurran Magic Upon Casalian Genreps

Observation: Analysis of implant relay telemetry indicates substantially altered brain and glandular functions in Genreps Rastaban and Merak.

Hypothetical cause: Interaction with metaphysical field known by the locals as magic.

Source of magic: Energetic orbital belt

Prognosis: Prolonged exposure may cause erratic or irrational behavior.

Recommendation: Genreps return home for observation and possible treatment.

Today – Tresk

Danikan was aghast.

"How did you . . . ? When did . . . ? Why are you here, Mom? Thuseus, explain this!"

Thuseus, one of the saboteurs, dug in a pocket and handed Danikan a crinkled-up, hand-written note. It read, "New developments have arisen. I have vital information that could bring down Merak once and for all. Disregard all previous instructions. Imperative that you get me out. – Danikan Tyre."

"I didn't write this!" Danikan exclaimed. "This is a forgery! Who . . .?" She looked over at her mother and it dawned on her. "You did this! Only you could forge my signature like this!"

"It worked, didn't it?" said the little old Eryndi lady. "It's your own fault, you know. Didn't I tell you when you were a little girl that you should've studied Magic?"

"Ah, Mom, I hated studying that stuff."

"No, you always wanted to play with swords. How do you expect to make a decent living or attract a mate with a sword?"

Danikan glanced over at Group Six. "Mom, do you think we can talk about this later?"

"No, it's settled. We'll have no more argument about this, young lady. You're free now, and I expect you to stay that way. I can't come running to your rescue every time you get yourself into a jam. Now I want you to apologize to all these nice people who were put out by your shenanigans."

"All right," Danikan sighed. "I want to thank all of you for your sacrifices and loyalty."

"I said apologize," Mom interrupted sternly. "Not a political speech. Well?"

"Okay . . . sorry!"

The sounds of chaos and animal roars came drifting up from somewhere in the interior of Stadium.

"I think we should finish escaping now," said Danikan.

Everyone agreed and ran up the steps and into the open air. There was smoke rising from Stadium and terrified people running through the streets. Green-armored Legionnaires were rushing to the scene to try to restore some order. The crowd was all trying to get as far from the scene as possible, which was also where Group Six and the terrorists wanted to be, so it was easy to blend in and follow. The echoing voice of Stickitus Owtus boomed out from Magical amplifiers mounted on the green-globed streetlight poles throughout the city.

"Attention citizens: An incident has occurred at Stadium.

At this time, citizens are advised to avoid the area, return to their homes, and stay off the streets until this minor security problem is under control. Thank you for your cooperation."

About that time, they witnessed a spiny ape chasing a screaming teenager down an alley. A few beats later a horrible slavering and growling sound was heard. The screams stopped soon after.

"Well, I'm glad they have things under control," said Danikan, with a big grin on her face.

The fires within Stadium were spreading. An orange glow and a billowing smoke cloud lit up the night sky like an eerie vision of Eternal Damnation. Bodies littered the street and chaos still reigned.

"We need to get out of the Imperium," said Foxx.

PART V:
FLIGHT

CHAPTER 17

I seem to be in a mountain environment. There is frozen dihydrogen monoxide everywhere and jeepers, it's cold! Not that it bothers me, doncha know, it actually helps my brain work better, but I worry about my boys. I know they're alive, cuz they've gone and started a new Ascendency. Yah, well. They think they're all grown up and independent and all, but they still need me to adjudicate. Crazy kids. When I find those little nixnutzes, I'll take a switch to their backsides. If I could only move . . .

- MAMA'S NOTEBOOK – DAY 2

* * *

Today – Tresk

"We could steal some horses, maybe," suggested Serena.

"We'd be too exposed in the open. Merak will have soldiers looking for us," said Foxx.

"Well, we're on the coast," said Tresado. "Maybe we could stow away on a boat."

"Same problem. To get to the shore, you have to ride the lifts down the cliff face. They'll be watched."

"What about striking out cross-country?" Orchid suggested. "We could travel by night and hide out during the day."

"You saw the countryside as we were riding the Conveyor coming here," said Tresado. "We're in the middle of an empire. From what I can tell, there aren't any wild lands anywhere within hundreds of leagues. It'd be like trying to escape across a thousand backyards with watchful landowners."

"The Conveyor!" cried Foxx. "If we could get aboard one, that would be the safest and the *fastest* way out of the Imperium."

"Sounds good," said Serena. "Let's get to one while it's still dark out."

"It'll be tricky getting on board," said Foxx. "The Conveyors are supposed to be for army use only."

"I think our status as honored *triples* has expired," said Tresado.

Group Six, along with Feelia, Danikan, the little old Eryndi lady, and the remaining members of the Durii set out to find a Conveyor. The problem was, most of the Conveyor lines ran through the city and terminated in the Imperial Palace, but nobody wanted to go back there.

"There have to be other spots where we can sneak onto one of the cars," said Tresado, thoughtfully.

"There might be," ventured Feelia. "In the northeastern district of the city, there are storage depots where they stockpile things like weapons and equipment meant for the Legionnaires in the frontline provinces. The City of Tresk is the industrial center for the whole Imperium. Most mass-produced goods come from here. It's all taken to the depots and stored until needed. The Conveyors load up there before heading to the interior."

"That's excellent," said Tresado adoringly. "Do you know the best route, Feelia my, er, I mean . . . *Feelia?*" He might as well have been wearing a big sign with glowing green letters and flashing hearts that said *I have a crush on Feelia.*

She looked about for a bit and got her bearings. "This way," she said, pointing. "Imperial Thoroughfare runs there nearly directly."

"If we're being hunted, it's best not to travel on a major road," said Serena.

"It's about a league and a half or so using the main streets," said Feelia. "I think I can get us there taking back alleys, but it'll be farther and take longer, probably a lot longer."

"It's about four hours to Senrise," said Tresado.

"Then let's get started," said Foxx with determination.

The route was safe, at least from crime. This outermost section of Tresk was well patrolled by squads of soldiers, but that was what slowed them down. Several times Group Six and party had to hide until the coast was clear. They would elude a patrol, then only minutes later have to evade another one. Everyone spaced themselves out, which looked less suspicious than one large group. Danikan and Feelia were in deep discussion as the group moved through the streets and back alleys, trying to remain inconspicuous. It wasn't too difficult. There were still plenty of panicked citizens either fleeing monsters or just trying to make it home.

It took them well over three hours, but they finally made it to a row of dense bushes near the perimeter fence that protected the depot. There was enough of it for the whole group of fugitives to hide behind temporarily. Guards and more guards patrolled inside and outside the fence.

"It's crawling with these green goons," said Serena. "Hmm,

they seem to be on the alert. I wonder if something happened somewhere?" she added, smirking and winking at Danikan.

"Which brings up another subject," Danikan replied. "I really didn't plan on this happening. In fact, I left specific orders not to try to rescue me in the event of capture, but we know how *that* ended up."

The little old Eryndi lady produced a professional and well-executed Mom Look.

"The bottom line is, we're not going with you," said Danikan.

"Any particular reason?" asked Orchid.

"I started this fight when the Treskans invaded Breeos, my homeland. And I was content to fight them there, but now I realize the real fight is *here.* It's not the Treskans that are the enemy. It's *Merak.* We've won a great victory today, but we have to keep the momentum going. Now that we're here in the capital, we must take the fight directly to the Imperator. We get rid of him, maybe Tresk will become civilized again."

"That's a big maybe," said Foxx.

"Maybe," replied Danikan with a smile.

"And I'm going to join them," said Feelia. This was directed specifically at Tresado.

"WHAT?"

Tresado's mouth gaped open like a hobo clam in the sun. He made several attempts to form something like *what* or *why,* but it just wouldn't come out. Feelia saved him the trouble. She took his hands and looked him in the eye.

"Yes, that's right. I'm going with Danikan and the others. I think I can do a lot of good here."

"But I thought . . . didn't you call her a traitor or something?"

"We've been talking," replied Feelia. "It seems we each did some growing after recent events. We found we've a lot in common in our goals. Now that I know her, I *know* her. It's an Eryndi girl thing."

"B-but it's too dangerous!" said Tresado, finding his voice at last.

"Not any more so than for these other patriots," Feelia said indicating the Durii. "I know a lot about the inner workings of Merak's palace: the layout, schedules, even secret doors."

"But . . . fighting in a revolution? Feelia, do you know what you're getting into?"

"I do know how to handle a bow," Feelia said, letting go of Tresado's hands. "I have to do this. I'm sorry, Tresado, but . . ."

"Yeah."

A patrol marched past, forcing everybody to shut up for a few minutes until the soldiers got out of earshot. Danikan carefully poked her head above the bushes.

"Looks like it's as clear as it can get. We need to leave now."

Foxx shook left hands with Danikan, as did Orchid and Tresado, in the Treskan manner.

Serena, not to be left out, grasped Danikan in a berg bear hug.

"So long, terrorist. Good luck. Good luck to all of you," said Serena to the Durii.

"Same to you, barbarian," said Danikan. She took a quick look at the fenced compound before them.

"If you're to get through that fence and sneak onto a Conveyor, you're going to need a diversion. I think we can provide that for you."

"What are you going to do?" asked Tresado worriedly.

"You'll know when. Just be ready to move."

Danikan and the Durii disappeared into the shadows. Feelia was the last one and cast a sad look backward at Tresado before also fading away into the dark.

Foxx put his hand on Tresado's shoulder. His friend of years looked like he had been punched in the gut.

"I'm sorry, bro."

"Yeah, me too." Tresado squared his shoulders, picked up his pointed chin, and met the eyes of the rest of Group Six.

"Let's get ready to board that Conveyor."

The others nodded in agreement and waited for the signal. It came in the form of sounds of pain and terror. Eryndi are notorious for their high-pitched screams. A beat later, a fiery cloud rose in the west, illuminating the night sky. Groups of Legionnaires were running toward the scene, leaving a momentary gap in their guard posts.

"Now's our chance," whispered Foxx. "Let's go!"

Group Six quickly scaled the wire fence and dropped down inside the compound. Tresado landed butt first. About fifty reaches beyond the fence, a Conveyor car sat with its door open. A stack of crates lay on a platform, waiting to be loaded. There was no point trying to sneak across all that open space. There was no cover. Their only choice was to sprint as fast as possible across the compound and hope no one spotted them. It worked, barely. Just as Group Six piled into the open car and hid behind some already-loaded crates, a couple of guys walked around the corner and resumed their work. The boxes sitting on the loading dock were smaller than the coffin-sized crates the fugitives were hiding behind. After they were all loaded, one guy checked something off on a clipboard, closed and locked the door, then moved on to the next car.

It was pitch dark in the car where Group Six was hiding. Tresado could have produced a Magical light, but it might have spilled out of the door crack, revealing their presence. After ten minutes more of loading, which they could hear going on in the next car, the Conveyor gave a slight jerk and started moving. Foxx tried to make himself comfortable on the hard floor.

"I guess now we sit back and enjoy the ride to . . . wherever."

* * *

Starfish has grown out of her maidenhood and come to full maturity. She's progressing admirably. I'm so proud of her. Not to say there are no issues still to be dealt with. For one thing, adapting the Mogritron to function with a magical energy source will be difficult, but conventional fuel sources were nearly used up from material fabrication. If I want a crew, I guess I'll have to try to adapt a standard power converter, somehow. It won't be easy. I've had trouble concentrating of late, especially during the headaches. The drone has returned from its fourth search, but still cannot locate Mama. I sincerely hope she is okay, wherever she ended up.

- *Starfish* ARCHIVAL SPHERE 01

Today – The Conveyor

Half an hour after boarding the Conveyor, Tresado announced two things: that it was Senrise and they were traveling east.

"We seem to be steadily moving," said Foxx. "And if it's daylight now, we could probably risk a little light in here."

"Coming up," said Tresado. He concentrated for a moment and a glowing light sphere appeared near the ceiling of the Conveyor car. It was carefully attenuated to produce just enough light to see, without risking some Imperial Magician detecting the spell. The car they were hiding in was more than half-full of crates of all sizes. All of them, including the large ones they had been hiding behind were labeled 12th Forward Legion.

"Let's take a look and see what we have here," said Serena, pulling at one of the big crates. "I could use a change of clothes."

"But that dress looks so good on you," said Orchid.

"Except that it's full of holes and stained with blood," observed Foxx. "I didn't see your first battle, but you sure were a mess afterward."

They didn't have tools of any kind, but between Tresado's kinetic spells and Serena's great strength, they managed to pry the wooden lid off the box. There were clothes in it, all right. All identical, all green, and all military. This crate contained several stacks of the standard issue green breast plates that Treskan Legionnaires wore. Other boxes held boots, tunics, and other standard issue equipment. There were no weapons. Maybe those were in another car.

A woo-hoo scream of sheer delight issued from Orchid's delicate lips. She immediately clamped her hand over her mouth, but couldn't help dancing a little celebratory jig. Her green eyes were lit like a pair of emerald lanterns.

"It's WINE!" was all she could manage to croak out at the moment. She was pointing at one of a stack of 24 identical boxes, all marked Firellian, also meant for the 12th Forward Legion. Orchid immediately started clawing at the lid of one of them with her fingers, breaking a nail in the process. Before anyone could offer to help her, she had ripped the lid off. The boxes each contained 40 pre-filled field canteens of the robust wine.

"This could be a big problem," whispered Tresado to Foxx.

* * *

How Come They to This Place of Joy;
Of Peace, of Love, of Bliss;
Embracing All as Kin Long Gone;
Yet Never to Know Home's Kiss . . .

- Trianna of Sylvas,
Poetess to the Glades

Today – The Conveyor

The Conveyor traveled on, non-stop. Apparently, this train was for cargo only and did not stop for the night, or any other time. It also seemed to travel at a slower speed than the one they were on before. Maybe it took less Magical energy or was cheaper or something.

Who knows why the military does anything? thought Tresado.

Group Six had gone through all the boxes in the car with them. Now they all resembled properly outfitted Treskan Legionnaires, right down to the standard issue army socks. Resembled, perhaps, except that none of the uniforms fit Tresado properly. His breastplate hung off his protruding paunch like a loose roof tile. The other exception was Orchid. Her uniform fit perfectly, as there were many Eryndi with the same small stature, but disciplined Treskan soldiers did not get as drunk as Orchid. Despite her companions pleading with her to try to maintain sobriety, she had just emptied her fourth canteen of Firellian wine. She now lay curled up in the corner of the Conveyor car, snoring slightly and clutching one of the empty canteens.

"Do you have *any* idea where we're going?" asked Tresado.

Foxx adjusted his newly-acquired Treskan helmet with the prominent bear head design. Somehow, a bear was supposed to represent Merak, but he didn't see it, personally.

"Not exactly," answered Foxx. "If we're still headed east, we could be going to the Serin Sea, which I think is unlikely. There's nobody for the 12th Forward Legion to conquer around there. The Serin Sea and the surrounding countries have been part of the Imperium for centuries. I'd say that, after we clear the Jarayan Mountains, we'll either turn north or south. My vote would be north, back the way we came. I would lay odds these supplies are for the Breeosian campaign." Foxx stood back with his arms folded and a smug look on his face for his brilliant, insightful conclusion.

"Sorry to bust you up, genius, but that's not the 12th Forward Legion up in Breeos. It's the 38th Forward Legion."

"And how do you know that?" asked a suddenly doubtful-looking Foxx.

"Weren't you listening?" countered Serena. "That smilin' bitch in the Treskan camp introduced herself. She said they were part of the 38th Forward Legion."

Orchid suddenly came awake with a bleary-eyed snort. She stood on wobbly legs and thrust forward the empty canteen in her hand, bonking Tresado on his pointed chin.

"To Group Six," she slurred. "Long may they wave . . ."

Orchid immediately passed out again, and collapsed

face-first atop a crate. A limp arm hung down on each side of the box and she resumed her snoring.

"So, what were we talking about?" asked Tresado, rubbing his chin.

"We were talking about where we're going," answered Serena.

"Well, wherever the 12th Forward Legion is, I think we can assume that it's a battlefield somewhere," said Foxx. "We're not out of the Imperium yet."

Foxx sat down wearily on a crate. He picked up Serena's bloodied dress that had been exchanged for the Treskan uniform. He poked his fingers through the various sword and arrow holes that had been put in it.

"My friends, I have to apologize. It was my idea to come to Tresk. I wanted to show you all a good time. Instead . . . all the death and injury. I am so very sorry."

"It wasn't you," replied Tresado. "It was Merak. Feelia was right. Merak is solely to blame for everything that happened."

"Don't beat yourself up," said Serena. "Personally, I had a hell of a good time."

Foxx's and Tresado's eyebrows raced each other to the ceiling. They looked at each other and immediately broke out in nervous laughter. The sheer lunacy of everything that had happened in the last days could no longer be contained. At first, Serena looked pissed at the response to her remark, but then couldn't help joining in the tittering. Even Orchid giggled along with the rest, without regaining consciousness.

The conversation died down while everyone swam in their own thoughts. Tresado picked up one of the unused Legionnaire breast plates and examined it closely.

"That's weird."

“What is?” asked Foxx.

“This armor,” Tresado replied. “It’s not metal. It’s light and flexible, but it’s not steel or bronze or anything else I can recognize.”

“And they’re all exactly the same,” said Foxx. “I’ve seen others that were made of steel, but those were the fancy ones for officers. These are standard issue for the troops.”

Foxx looked closely at the one Tresado had and compared it to another. “Look at this,” he said, pointing to a slot designed to have a leather strap running through it. “See how this oval hole is slightly crooked? It’s a minor flaw, but all of these others have the exact same mistake.”

“Feelia said that most mass-produced goods in the Imperium come from Tresk,” said Tresado. “It must be Merak’s doing. He has unbelievable Magical resources.”

“So did Rastaban,” said Serena. “All those red things we wore, and the thing he shot Foxx with. Maybe he and Merak are in cahoots, somehow.”

“They’re competing with each other, but still brothers,” said Foxx thoughtfully. He paused for a moment, making motions in the air as though moving gaming tokens. “Did you ever play *Takeover*?”

“That game where you move armies and take over countries?” answered Tresado. “Yeah, some Macai friends in cram school taught me. Most Eryndi prefer *Kings and Queens*. *Takeover* is kind of a Macai thing.”

“The kids play something kinda like it in the Northlands,” said Serena, “only ours is called *Raid* and *Slay*.”

“This may sound wild,” said Foxx, “but I think these guys are playing their own version of *Raid and Slay*, only with real armies and live people.”

"But Rastaban is in . . . or he *was* in Abakaar. Merak is in Tresk," said Tresado. "Those places are many hundreds of leagues apart. How would they know what venture cube roll the other guy gets?"

"Somehow, I don't think it's quite that simple," said Foxx thoughtfully.

"I know what you mean," said Tresado. "I just get the impression that, in addition to the powerful Magic that those two seem to have, there's something else going on."

"Well, I'm gonna get some sack time," said Serena. "I'd advise you to do the same."

The day turned to night once again. In the middle of that night, Group Six was awakened by the slowing of the Conveyor, the diminishing momentum tugging at their bodies. Orchid rolled off the crate with the gracefulness of a pregnant lumba and landed on her knees. Her hair was a mess and she had board lines across her face from the crate. She gave forth an enormous yawn, smacked her lips at the awful taste in her mouth, and looked around.

"Are we there yet?"

From the vibration, or lack of it, they could tell that the Conveyor was coming to a slow halt.

Soon, they could hear voices and thumping about, suggesting cargo was being handled.

"All right, now remember," reminded Foxx, "we are Treskan soldiers. If we find ourselves in an army camp or something, we have to try to blend in. Be ready when that door opens."

That was probably a good plan. The only snag was the door did not open and there was no way to operate it from the inside. Group Six waited in the darkness . . . and waited. Finally, after an eternity of listening and waiting, Tresado, with his usual punctuality, announced two things.

"It's morning. Gods, I'm hungry."

12 years ago – Orchid

Orchid had never felt so nervous in her life, but she was determined not to show it. It seemed like a month had gone by while she sat interminably waiting outside the office of Elder Kazorel, Director of the Melosian Academy of Worldly Arts. The chair was hideously uncomfortable. Most likely, it was designed that way to further punish evildoers as they awaited academic crucifixion. While she waited, the other three Governing Elders strode by her and entered the Director's inner chamber. The sour looks each one gave her as they passed shriveled her psyche.

She had been summoned here, pulled out of Advanced Ethics class in front of her schoolmates. No reason was given, but Orchid had a pretty good idea why she was here. They had found out. They knew. Her crime that was not a crime was out. Technically, there was no written rule about teachers and students having relationships. It wasn't taboo, it wasn't illegal, it just wasn't done . . . by most. The other problem heaped on top of that one was the racial difference. She being a Macai and Professor Jennick an Eryndi added to the mortal sin that she was about be punished for. Interracial relationships also were not illegal, but taboo to many. It was a family thing. Most people didn't want their sons and daughters to become close with the other race. The main reason for non-approval was that children were impossible in such a relationship. As Orchid had heard one of her classmates, the foreign student from Tresk, say once, "Dramin and Kermin can't make a sandwich." She didn't know exactly what that meant, but it had something to do with Macai/Eryndi relationships being impossible, even for the gods. What ancient, ignorant nonsense! But that's the way things are on Lurra. Grass is green, water is wet, and people believe what they want.

Jennick had left her only the morning before. After thinking suicidal thoughts in the forest for over an hour, Orchid had gone back to the town and taken up residence in an off-campus pub. The proprietor, an understanding Macai, had prescribed a self-made concoction he called a *Broken Heart Special,* guaranteed to make bad memories flee in terror. Orchid had never been much of a drinker, but managed to put away five of those bad boys before passing out at the bar.

Jennick had left her! The pain of that raw wound was compounded by the fierce hangover she was now suffering heaped on top of the further heartbreak that was moments from being handed down. Orchid tried not to imagine what the consequences of her actions would be, but just couldn't help coming up with any number of worst-case scenarios. There was suspension, or maybe cancellation of her senior year credits, perhaps even full expulsion. In any event, it was sure to be disastrous.

The years dragged on. The splintery arms of the ancient chair she sat in seemed to close about her, ready at any moment to drag her down to her deserved fate. Its wicker structure squeaked with the slightest movement. From the adjacent hallway came the muffled sounds of many footsteps as students were moving between classes and most likely discussing her. The water clock down the hall dripped off the beats, seemingly getting louder and louder, adding to the tumult that threatened to burst Orchid's eardrums, or was it the pounding of her head?

At long last, the heavy office door swung slowly open. Elder Markusa's grim visage appeared and peered impassively down the hall, apparently oblivious to the terrified Macai sunk in misery. After six or seven beats, her eyes made contact with Orchid. Her wrinkled hand beckoned.

"The Director will see you now."

This was it. The walk of death. The last league. The gallows awaits.

Orchid slipped past Markusa as she held the door open. The sound of it clicking quietly shut behind her impacted her brain like a solitary confinement cell door slamming forever. Elder Kazorel sat behind his elaborate monkeywood desk, his lined, inscrutable face revealing nothing. Orchid happened to know for a fact that the Director was two hundred fourteen years old. His wisdom and life experience were beyond imagining. His ability to invent and implement the most heinous punishment must be infinite. His thin lips parted.

"Sit."

There were several unoccupied chairs in the room, including one immediately in front of the desk. Orchid took a chance and sat in that one, figuring that was where the condemned would receive final judgment. She fervently hoped she had made the correct choice, yet dreaded that she was right. The other three Elders continued to stand, reinforcing her already firm belief that this was to be an official disciplinary procedure.

Behind and to one side of the Director stood an Eryndi with a folder of papers. Without looking at him, Kazorel extended a hand and found it immediately filled with documents. He glanced quickly at them, then focused on Orchid.

"I have here your student file for the last four years. It makes for some . . . interesting reading."

This is it. This is where life takes a terrible turn.

"I'm sure you are well aware of your achievement scores," said Kazorel in his whispery but authoritative voice. "The last four years have been a difficult struggle for you. Your handicap of being a Macai was a heavy burden to bear. To be quite frank, many of our faculty considered you to be . . . *unteachable.*"

Director Kazorel glanced at the other three Elders. They all sported dour expressions. Orchid had always felt a certain antipathy toward her from several of her classmates and most of her teachers. Her mother and others had warned her of this possibility. Maybe she should have listened.

"I also have here a letter left for me by Professor Jennick before he departed on his sabbatical," said Kazorel. "I should like to read it to you personally."

More humiliation! Now intimate, personal details were about to be made public for all to gawk at and judge.

Kazorel cleared his throat and read the letter.

"Director: I wish to make known my immense gratitude and humble thanks for the opportunity to teach at the Melosian Academy. There truly can be no higher calling than the privilege of guiding and shaping young minds to prepare them for the world and its challenges. One student in particular deserves the highest praise I can muster. Orchid, daughter of Mishanna and Revinal, has proven herself to be an outstanding student and the hardest worker I have ever had the honor of instructing. No obstacle has, and I am sure *will,* prove insurmountable by her. I firmly believe Orchid shall go on to do great things after graduation. I am, in all sincerity and gratitude, Jennick, Professor of Life Empathy."

Kazorel set the papers down and studied Orchid's confused expression.

"Anything to say, student?"

"I . . ." replied Orchid with a stammer. Nothing else would come out.

"Apparently not," said the Director. "No matter. Orchid, in light of your outstanding academic record and now this glowing recommendation from your mentor, I am pleased to announce that you have been selected as the Melosian Academy's first Macai Apex Scholar for the year 21864."

The other elders made clear by their scowls that they didn't quite approve of this, but kept silent. The Director ignored them and continued.

"You shall speak for your class at graduation in two weeks. You have sixteen days in which to prepare your speech."

Orchid stood with open mouth, quite unable to function.

"Do us proud, scholar. That will be all."

CHAPTER 18

Today – The Conveyor

Whissh, thunk . . . whissh, thunk . . .

The approaching noise was caused by Bumpus, the Macai yard worker walking the length of the Conveyor and using his specialized key to open the sliding doors on each of the cars. He didn't really glance into any of them and didn't care what was in them. While he was technically in the employ of the Imperial Military, as was everybody else around here, the loading and unloading of any cargo was the concern of the troops. That was just fine with Bumpus.

He passed a group of Legionnaires who were bringing up some wagons of cargo from the wharf area. They hardly spared a glance for the lowlife Macai worker. Bumpus, on the other hand, had his usual disdainful scowl for the troops.

Idiots and their stupid uniforms.

Whissh, thunk

Why do those buttwads always schedule these things for right at shift's end?

Whissh, thunk

As he slid open the door on Conveyor car six, an empty canteen tumbled out onto the ground. Instead of picking it up, Bumpus bullseyed it with a stream of chewing jamba spit.

Not my job.

Whissh, thunk

Let them fancy-pantsed little squirts pick up their own crap.

Whissh, thunk

Little creeps. Not one of them could find their asses with both thumbs.

Bumpus heard a noise behind him and saw four Legionnaires hopping out of a car. He knew that particular car was designated cargo only and they were probably not supposed to be in there.

Don't make a shit to me.

He could have turned them in, but his shift was over in ten minutes and he needed to get out of here. The wife was making dirkcakes for Midday meal and he had to pick up the makings at three different stalls. She always insisted on fresh fish and herbs.

Whatever . . . the old bag.

Foxx watched the workman who had opened the door retreat down the rail. He seemed to be muttering to himself about something.

"Any idea where we are?" asked Tresado of no one.

"Yeah," replied Foxx, peering between two buildings. There was a narrow vista of a large and busy body of water. Boats and ships of all types and sizes could be seen. "We're at the Serin Sea. It's a huge, freshwater sea right in the middle of the Imperium. They call it *The Treskan Lake.*"

"Have you been here before?" asked Orchid.

"No, I never came this far east the last time I was here," answered Foxx. "Why?"

“I thought it might be a good idea if we knew where we are and where we should go,” replied Orchid. “Is there any way we can find a map or something?”

“This looks like a good-sized port,” said Tresado. “There’s bound to be a chart shop around here.”

“Let’s first try to figure out what city this is,” said Foxx, taking charge. “We should split up and comb the wharf for some clue as to where we are.”

“Wait, I think I’ve discovered a clue,” said Serena in her dry, deadpan manner.

“What’s that?” asked Foxx eagerly.

Serena’s cool lapis eyes regarded Foxx with a touch of pity. “There’s a sign right behind your head that says SURRANA DEPOT.”

Foxx turned and looked, then admitted sheepishly, “I’d say we’re in Surrana.”

“You’re a regular Halfklam the Navigator,” Serena smiled. Three blank expressions looked back at her. “Halfklam? Out of Frigga by Crodan? Oh, for crap’s sake! He’s the Northlands God of Raiding. When are you savages going to get civilized?”

“YOU!”

Group Six turned at the sound and found themselves confronted by an armed squad of Treskan Legionnaires.

Meanwhile, back in Tresk

Stickitus Owtus, personal aide to the Imperator, and Primus Kapatius Ampol, Head of the Imperial Guard, waited nervously in Merak’s opulent quarters.

“Any idea how long he’ll be?” asked the Primus. “I’ve got a continuing crisis to deal with.”

"The Imperator ordered both of us to report," replied Stickitus. "We daren't disobey."

They both looked at the large door at the other end of the room. A glowing, green orb above the transom warned that Merak was within and to disturb him, or even open the door, was strictly forbidden.

Their Eryndi ears could make out sounds coming from beyond the door. They could hear Merak's unmistakable voice, possibly berating someone. His tone was angry, but they couldn't make out his words. Occasionally, a scream of frustration, followed by a shout of exultation. Finally, after an hour of this, the door opened and the Imperator of the Treskan Imperium started to come out, but something back in the room distracted him. He stood, holding the half-open door and staring back within. Stickitus and Kapatius risked a quick glance while Merak's back was turned.

It was a small room, with no other apparent doors. There was no one in there. Every surface was covered in slanted counters and overhead, rectangular slates of some kind. They all displayed colored lights in either red, green, or blue.

All of that was secondary. What really drew the eye was the great translucent sphere in the center of the room. It was a glowing globe of vague shapes, rotating slowly from left to right. Its surface was covered with drifting areas of color and hundreds of tiny objects that orbited the sphere at different distances. There were little depictions of castles, ships, mountains, cities, horses, grain, gems, crossed swords, and many other things. There was a blue fish symbol and a green bear. A red snake appeared frequently. There were unknown symbols in sequences floating about the surface of the sphere. A particular set of green lights went dark and Merak exited all the way and shut the door. Stickitus and Kapatius quickly snapped their eyes front.

"Imperator!" they both exclaimed, while executing the Treskan salute by striking their breasts with their left fists and then raising them to eye level.

Merak grunted an acknowledgment and waddled over to his plush, floating throne to graze a bit on the snack table. Licking his greasy thumb, he looked Stickitus in the eye.

"Tell me more about this Group Six."

Today – Surrana Depot

"YOU!"

Group Six stared back at the squad of Legionnaires. The authoritative voice came from the soldier in front. He had a permanent scowl on his Eryndi face, which was weathered and scarred. His whole bearing said *tough as nails from a lifetime of commanding small numbers of troops.*

Non-com, thought Foxx. *They've found us!*

Foxx was standing close to Serena. He could feel the tenseness of her body in the space between them.

She's ready to rumble at a split-beat's notice, but she's the only one of us that's armed. I better try to defuse this, quick!

Foxx tried desperately to gather his wits, but the fact is, he was terrified. If they weren't killed immediately, they would probably be taken back to Stadium for execution.

"Well?" grunted the grunt. "Don't just stand there gaping like idiots! Get your asses to work and load this cargo!"

He pointed to a heavily-laden cart full of different-sized casks and barrels.

"Yes sir. *Yes sir!"* Foxx immediately scurried over to the cart and grabbed up one of the small casks. He headed for the car they had ridden in all the way here.

"Not that one, dimwit! Car four! Can't you read?"

"Oh, sorry sir," replied Foxx.

"And if you call me sir one more time, I'll kick your ass so hard, you'll be wearing it for a helmet!"

Realizing that they had not been caught, like they all had immediately thought, Group Six got busy loading the casks. Some were tightly sealed with wax and smelled like fish. Others were labeled as drinking water. That seemed odd, considering how common fresh water supplies usually were.

Maybe we're headed out to sea, thought Tresado.

The larger barrels required at least two people to handle them. Serena helped Orchid, who had the upper body strength of a kitten. Foxx and Tresado worked on the others. Tresado could have easily levitated them, but he didn't want to draw attention to himself. Finally, all the cargo was loaded into car four. Foxx looked down the train and saw the non-com barking orders at some other soldiers. In the other direction, more boxes were being loaded by some other soldiers into car six, where they had hidden. One soldier checked a clipboard and motioned to someone down the track. Bumpus, the scowling yard worker, was returning and systematically closing the doors he had just opened.

"Quick," said Foxx. "Let's get back aboard while we still can."

Everybody looked about and jumped into car four, trying to look nonchalant. They looked anything but, so it was fortunate nobody saw them. Orchid was the last one, silently grieving at her separation from the treasure trove of wine back in car six. More importantly, her staff and her pack containing

Dementus's journal as well as her own were in there, too. She had wanted to take them with her, but Foxx had reminded her that she would stand out too much.

They quickly hid behind the crates in car four and stayed quiet. They could hear soldiers checking the loading list. It apparently was proper. Bumpus was about to close the door when they could hear the non-com bellowing.

"Where are those troops who were just here?"

There were the sounds of *search me* and *I dunno.*

Foxx could barely see through a narrow crack between two crates. He saw the loud-mouthed soldier suspiciously eyeing the open car. Foxx immediately projected a thought that a stink rat was hiding in there somewhere. Orchid reinforced the notion by imitating the chittering sound made by the feared creatures. Nobody wanted to get sprayed, so Bumpus closed the door quickly and latched it. A few minutes later, hiding in the darkness, Group Six felt the Conveyor starting to move again.

12 years ago – Orchid's speech to the graduating class of 21864

Fellow students, faculty, Elders, family members, and friends. There is no way I can express the honor that has been bestowed on me. Being selected as Apex Scholar and the presentation of this year's Guiding Staff is a dream long in coming. I'm sure we can all agree that the past four years have been the most grueling and demanding that any of us have ever experienced. For me, as a Macai, it was doubly so. To be honest, I was apprehensive when I was first accepted at the Melosian Academy, especially when I found out I was to be the only Macai in my class. I worried. I worried about a lot of things. I worried about non-acceptance. I worried about competing with my Eryndi classmates. I worried about whether the teachers and Elders would give me a fair shake.

It turns out that I was wrong – about all of it. It's not about any imagined prejudice or misconceptions from my Eryndi classmates. It's not about Eryndi at all. It's about myself. It's about the misconceptions that I myself invented and believed about myself and others. And after four years, I have come to realize it was all just self-created noise. It didn't define me. I defined who I am after freeing myself from that noise. I finally accepted the notion that I am nothing less than who I wanted to be. I have always been myself. I have been the antagonist of my own story as well as the heroine. Understanding that duality within yourself is the key to your own identity.

As we set off on our individual journeys, we must never lose sight of where we are going and what we want to do, even if we have no idea what that might be. One thing I do know is that great accomplishments cannot be done alone. Surround yourself with the best people you know. Friends who love and understand you, friends who will always have your back, and friends who count on you as much as you count on them. The group is stronger than the individual. I hope you all find yours.

Today – Conveyor Car Four

The Conveyor moved along with its usual smoothness. Every so often, the train would slow down, speed up, or change directions. Group Six sat within, hidden behind the crates and barrels, most of which they had loaded themselves.

They could feel the car moving up and down over hills and around curves. They had no way of knowing that they were switching tracks and maneuvering through the complicated rail system encircling the huge Serin Sea. Numerous bridges and trestles were crossed, but Group Six was unaware of exactly what was going on. Tresado could reliably sense exactly what direction they were going, but other than that, they were clueless.

Foxx opened one of the smaller casks to find out what they had. A strong odor of fish wafted out.

"What in Crodan's name is that?" asked Serena, who held her nose with two fingers.

"Individual packets of something," replied Foxx. He tentatively opened one of them and peered inside. "It's dirkova. Fish eggs. A very expensive delicacy that Treskans seem to like. Remember? Merak had some on his throne deli. Since there's only six small casks, I'm assuming they're for the officers."

Tresado opened the end of one of the large casks. There was some kind of shipping manifest on that strange, metallic paper such as they had seen before.

"This says it's a shipment of salted dirkfish in individual packets," said Tresado. He pulled out a single pouch labeled *D RATIONS.* "They are to be used as field rations for the 12th Legion. Labeled Serin Seafoods, Ltd., a subsidiary of TersiCo Enterprises. At least we won't starve."

Orchid was getting more and more nervous by the minute. All she could think about were her precious goods presumably still locked in Car Six. She took to pacing, but could only manage a handful of steps back and forth in the crowded car. Finally, Serena had had enough.

"Would you sit your ass down, please?"

"I can't help it," said Orchid piteously. "I've got to get my stuff back, especially my staff!"

"We understand," said Tresado. "But we might not get the

chance. We have no idea where we're going or what happens when we get there. An hour from now, we might be running for our lives."

"Well then, go ahead and run," responded a now-angry Orchid. "What are you waiting for? I won't stop you, but I'm gonna get my stuff!"

"Then what we need is a plan," said Foxx calmly. As usual, a little squirt of his Knowing Spell was included underneath his statement to subtly take things down a notch.

"The four of us should be able to come up with something," said Serena.

Tresado cracked his knuckles, as he usually did when about to use Magic. "Do we want to be sneaky, or just blast our way into that car? I favor the latter."

Orchid stood frozen for a couple of beats and looked at the faces of her friends, realizing she had just made an ass of herself.

"Are you sure?" asked Orchid.

"Well, I never got you anything for your birthday," smirked Tresado.

"And I for one could use some exercise," said Serena. "I still have a bit of Treskan payback on my list of things to do."

"So you're gonna kill people for my birthday?" said Orchid with just a hint of a tear in her eye. "I'm touched."

"It's the Northlands way," replied Serena. "When Eymon the Rank, Chief of our village, held his yearly birthday festival, I gave him the head of a barbarian I had killed a few weeks before."

"Aw, isn't that sweet?" mocked Foxx. "That reminds me of . . . wait a minute! You gave your Chief a head that was weeks old?!"

"It's the thought that counts."

Today – Tresk

Stickitus Owtus brought a handful of papers to his Imperator. He had spent all night working on it, but the report on Group Six was woefully incomplete and he feared retribution. Trying to maintain a neutral face, he presented his findings to the leader of all the Treskan Imperium. Merak snatched them out of Sticky's hand, staining the papers with expensive Hanokian mustard. He perused the papers for a minute and then threw them down.

"These tell me nothing I didn't already know!"

Sticky's eyes widened momentarily. How could the Imperator know about some of the details he had just laboriously dug up? Many of the lands visited by this so-called *Group Six* were little known to Tresk. The Imperium had for years been a trading partner by sea with Ostica and the other cities of the northern coast, but the interior was hardly more than wilderness. The Crystal Palace, where the group had received their first imprinting, was far away beyond the impenetrable mountains north of Breeos. The only route there was the southern road out of Abakaar and that would be a detour of weeks. Thanks to Group Six, the legendary Prakin's Pass had just been rediscovered after a millennium of searching. Their blunder was completely unplanned and it would take some time to transfer more troops to the northeast to take advantage of it. The Breeosian campaign was understaffed as it was, thanks to the fearsome resistance by the rebels.

"I care not where this riffraff has been," thundered Merak. "What I want to know is *where they're going!* You have one more day to locate them. You know what happens to you if you fail me?"

Stickitus was smart enough to keep silent, even though he

was pretty sure of the answer. His terrified look gave him away, anyway.

"That's right!" bellowed Merak. "It's Stadium for you and anyone else who fails in this. Pass the word to all Commanders. The order is, 'Whomever finds these vermin stays alive!' Now get out of here!"

Sticky quickly bowed his way out of the Imperator's chamber. Once on the street, his mind started busily calculating his personal finances as well as the various ways out of the city.

Today – Conveyor Car Four

They planned and argued, argued and planned, but Group Six just had no way of knowing what awaited them when the Conveyor stopped. Finally they decided to play things by ear when the time came. There were just too many unknown variables.

The Conveyor cruised along for the next five days. They had the salted fish and dirkova for sustenance, but, unlike the luxurious passenger car that they originally traveled to Tresk in, this cargo car was woefully lacking in toilet facilities. An emptied out water cask was used as a makeshift commode, with which they all took turns. Serena threatened beheading for anybody who peeked.

Eventually, the Conveyor began slowing and came to a full stop with just a slight jerk. Once again, Foxx reminded the others to act like Treskan Legionnaires when the door opened. When it did, there was only the surprised face of a single soldier. The young peach-fuzz face and lack of rank pins or stripes told them that this was a newly-minted Legionnaire. He was even greener than the uniform he wore.

"Uhh, I don't get it," said the junior trooper. "What are you . . ."

Foxx took his cue from the non-com they had run into earlier.

"Well, don't just stand there, baby face!" bellowed Foxx. "Get your ass up here and start unloading this cargo. *NOW!*"

The youngster hesitated for a beat, then dutifully saluted and obeyed orders. With an unprecedented show of initiative, he paused for a beat while holding a cask.

"I'm sorry, uhh, but my orders say I'm supposed to report to . . ."

"Right now, your orders are to unload this Conveyor car," barked Foxx. "According to Regulation 17, subsection 2, paragraph 3, all standing orders are superseded in favor of Directive R179, by authority of the General. Now get moving!"

Private Baby Face looked at Foxx and the others and appeared to have made a decision. He started to turn to flee, but Serena was ready for him and gave him a gentle tap on the jaw, not hard enough to really injure him, but just to put his lights out for a short time. The soldier spun around from the force of the punch and landed face-first into Group Six's temporary water cask commode in the back corner of the car. A couple of bubbles showed his breathing was all right.

"It would have been more merciful to just kill him," said Tresado with a disgusted look on his face.

"How do you know so much about Treskan regulations?" Serena asked Foxx.

"I made all that up. I was just trying to bluff the inexperienced player at the table."

"Come on, let's go get my stuff," said Orchid impatiently.

It was fairly easy to blend in. There were Treskan soldiers

everywhere. Group Six made their way up the track to car six. The door was already open and there were sounds of voices coming out.

"It looks like someone's been squatting in here."

"What's that there?"

"It's just a stick. Toss it."

About this time, Orchid's staff came flying out of car six to clatter on the hard ground. Orchid immediately started to race for her property, but was held back by a firm hand on her shoulder.

"Easy there, Nature Girl," said Serena, who looked around at the rest of Group Six. "Shall we try some sneaky stuff, or just bust in?"

Foxx knew which option Serena and Orchid would choose, so he answered quickly.

"Let's take a moment to plan." Foxx stopped for a moment with the others following suit. "Sounds to me like there are three or four of them."

"I suggest we not get into a huge melee in the middle of all these Legionnaires," said Tresado.

"Agreed," said Foxx, predictably. Tresado and Foxx looked over at the women.

"Yeah, I guess," answered Serena and Orchid in perfect harmony.

Group Six resumed their calm, nonchalant approach to car six, which was only about five paces away. Orchid broke ranks slightly to pick up her precious staff. More voices came from within.

"Hey, somebody broke into the cargo."

"Check out those packs."

Group Six took one more look around for possible witnesses. The platform was still crowded.

"I guess this is as good a time as any," whispered Foxx. They peered around the edge of the open door. There were three Legionnaires in there ransacking their goods.

"Whoa, what do we have here?" asked soldier number one. He pulled out Serena's looker and played with it. He wasn't sure what it did. He turned it over and over, pulling apart the three sections and closing it again. Finally, by accident he pointed it out the open Conveyor door and looked through the small end. He almost wet his armor when the stern face of his commanding officer, who was across the compound, suddenly appeared. Realizing what it did now compelled him to tuck it into his armor.

"What's in those other packs?" he asked the other two guys.

"Nothing but a bunch of junk," said soldier number two. "A couple of books, a comb, a cork from a liquor bottle, a box of leaves or something . . ."

"Leaves?" asked soldier number three.

"Yeah, leaves and powders and some weird little tools or something."

"Is it Jamba?" eagerly asked soldier number three, who was known as the junkie of the outfit.

"No such luck," said number two. "I don't know what it is, but it smells like butt."

"Actually what you're smelling is a mixture of perimasis, rockwort, and saltleaf. It's used to treat bruises and contusions," said a female voice.

"That ought to come in handy," said another.

The three Legionnaires turned at the unfamiliar voices.

Four soldiers stood there, looking decidedly non-military, despite the uniforms.

Group Six leapt as one into the car. Unfortunately, Tresado's green breastplate snagged on the edge of the sliding door, pulling it shut.

A few beats later, another pair of soldiers came strolling by. They stopped at an unfamiliar sound of thumping and screaming. Car number six seemed to be rocking slightly. The soldiers walked up to the car to investigate. One of them put his hand up against the door. His mouth opened to say something, but the door was violently blown outward by some kind of explosion, smashing the two Legionnaires against a stone wall. An extremely flat Eryndi was stuck to the inside of the blasted door. He would have to be scraped off.

A couple of beats later, Group Six piled out of the car, each clutching their own goods. They looked around and discovered about fifty sets of eyes turned in their direction. Serena was massaging her right fist where she bruised it slightly.

"There'll be no talking our way out of this," said Foxx. "We've gotta get out of here."

"This way," ordered Serena.

She led the others away from the rail. It stopped here. Apparently, wherever they were was the end of the line for the Conveyor. In the distance they could see many hundreds of tents housing troops. Serena was smart enough to start off with a slow, casual walk, but too many eyes had witnessed the explosion. With the first "get them," she started to run. Serena had to pace herself, because she was the fastest runner. Orchid brought up the rear. Just ahead of her, she saw a Legionnaire point his crossbow directly at Tresado's back. The soldier was a fraction of a beat from pressing the trigger. With no time to cast a spell, Orchid did the only thing she could. As she passed, she swung her staff and knocked the crossbow up. It discharged and sent the arrow sailing away. On the backswing, Orchid bonked the man on the top of the head and he went down like a sack of fire melons. Her staff responded indignantly with brown sparks and smoke, almost as if it had been betrayed. Orchid felt a little sick at what she had done.

They ran past a couple dozen Legionnaires who were patrolling in a tight circle. Group Six eyed them as they flew past. These guys were guarding something, something familiar. Sitting nearby were three of the strange metallic boxes the Treskans called Guardians, the devices that generated the shield. Alongside, there were several pallets of the black spheres that they had seen powering the Conveyors and who knows what else.

The mob of soldiers was closing on them fast. Orchid looked to the skies and asked nature for a favor. Wherever this place was, it was hot, dry, and sandy. Orchid's psyche reached out to the elements, requesting a change of potentials in the arid atmosphere. The wind picked up, swirling the ever-present sand into little tornados. The more they spun, the greater the static charge that was built up. Soon, random lightning strikes began to discharge from the sky to the ground. Soldiers shielded their eyes and tried to find immediate shelter. The mini-sandstorm provided perfect cover for Group Six's escape. Serena instinctively ran in the direction that her nose told her to go. There was a large, makeshift corral ahead filled with horses and draft animals. Six horses stood outside the corral, fully saddled and provisioned, probably being readied for a patrol. Handlers were trying to get them to shelter, while shielding their own eyes from the blowing sand. They didn't even put up a fight when the four strangers leapt into the saddles and hauled ass out into the desert. The sandstorm quickly abated. The pursuing Treskans soon gave up and watched the fugitives disappear into the heat waves. The one in charge shook his head sadly.

"What a waste of four good horses."

CHAPTER 19

No matter the danger;
No matter the cost;
No matter the blood that's lost;
Family, Home, Hearth, and Honor above all . . .

- Hrolvad the Berserker, c. 20641

Today – The Zinji Desert

It was hot. The kind of hot that sucked every bit of moisture out of one's body. It didn't take them long to discard the Treskan armor and helmets. The heat had quickly turned these into ovens. They used pieces of fabric found in the saddlebags as head coverings against the merciless Senlight beating down on them. Serena really hated it.

I bet it hasn't snowed here for years, she thought. Serena had a hard time accepting a place without snow.

After their quick escape into the desert, they had made a wide circle to the east, finally coming back to the river which flowed past the Treskan camp. They rejoiced at first, because Orchid had been unable to gather more than a few drops of moisture from the parched air. It didn't take long to discover that the water of this river was quite toxic. The horses snorted in displeasure and refused to touch it. They wouldn't even stick their hooves in it to cool down. Not only was the water poisoned, but also very corrosive.

"Well, now that you got your Magic stick back, can you do anything about the heat?" Serena asked Orchid.

"No."

"That sounds pretty definite," said Foxx. "I thought it was a very powerful weapon."

"It's *not* a weapon," replied Orchid emphatically. "That's not what it was designed for."

"But I saw you knock that guy over the head with it," said Serena. "Laid him out cold."

Orchid blushed heavily. "Don't remind me. That's the first time I've ever used it as a weapon. I'm so ashamed."

"So what does that oaken toothpick do then, other than spark and hum?" asked Tresado.

"Nothing."

Three voices repeated Orchid's answer with a question mark.

"That's it. That's all it does. It is meant to be a constant monitor of my emotions and intentions. It keeps me centered and even scolds me if I stray beyond my oath."

"It *scolds* you?"

"Well, it will give me a mild shock, like slapping me on the hand."

"A *stick* tells you what to do?" Serena had never heard of such a silly notion.

"Yeah, it *does!"* replied Orchid angrily. "I guess you'll just have to deal with that."

"Any idea where we are?" interrupted Tresado.

"That army camp was on what looked like an estuary," said Foxx, happy to change the subject. "This disgusting river probably empties into the Serin Sea. I'm guessing on the south shore somewhere."

"I think we're a ways south of Abakaar. It's probably that way," said Tresado, pointing to the northeast. "Can't say how far, though. A long way, for sure. If there is a city or country out here somewhere, we need to find it soon."

Group Six had been on the run through the desert for four days now, and things were getting worrisome. The horses they had stolen were equipped with extra-sized canteens, a couple of dirkfish ration packs, and even a measure of horse grain. They were probably meant for a one- or two-day patrol but water consumption was getting critical. The salty fish was making them drink more than was prudent. The main problem was that this horrid desert seemed to go on forever and they had no idea how much further they had to go before encountering a less punishing environment.

"This doesn't make sense," said a parched Foxx. "That was some kind of forward Treskan camp. There were thousands of troops staging there, probably preparing to invade some other country."

"I don't see any other country," said Tresado.

"All I see is sand," added Serena.

"And poisoned water," said Orchid.

"Must be some reason for bringing an army out here," opined Tresado, "other than to kill us, that is."

Orchid shook her head. "The 219th Century and we're still killing each other."

Group Six plodded on, walking the horses to conserve their strength. Since they had no idea which direction was best to go, they kept following the river, hoping it would lead to some less inhospitable place. The fish rations had since run out, but water was the big problem. They were down to a few swallows a day. There was not nearly enough for the horses. After the fifth day, they started dropping. Tresado's mount was the first. It stopped its slow walk, swayed for a couple of beats and collapsed into the sand. The other three soon followed, and Group Six found themselves in the middle of the dry desert with no water and no hope in sight. Tresado did his daily levitation up to altitude to look around. There was nothing to be seen until the seventh day, when, scanning the horizon in all directions, he looked back the way they had come. There were flashes being reflected from something on the horizon. He pulled out the looker tube that he had borrowed from Serena. The desert heat waves still obscured his vision. Tresado floated himself as close as he dared before his spell ran out. Now the flashes had a decidedly green tint to them.

"Great gods of Lurra!" he said to himself.

Tresado immediately reversed his course and headed back to where he had left Group Six. On his way, he caught a glimpse of something dead ahead. He hovered for a moment and smiled to himself, then continued on. Fortunately, his levitation spell held out just long enough to get him back safely.

"What did you see?" asked Foxx, who saw the shocked look on Tresado's face.

"I have good news and bad news."

"What's the good news?" asked Foxx.

"Up ahead of us I could see a *wall!*"

"What kind of wall?" said Orchid.

"A huge one!" Tresado replied. "It's hard to see in the desert heat, but it seems to stretch endlessly across our path. It must be a walled city!"

"And what's the bad news?" asked the realist Serena.

"The whole Treskan army is coming after us!"

Meanwhile, back in Tresk

Merak was in his secret chamber, deep in contemplation of the ethereal, spinning orb in the center of the room. He continually monitored the position and status of all of the various symbols, lights, colors, etc. He made a few minor adjustments, all the time muttering to himself.

"All right. You . . . and *you.* You'll just have to wait for your supplies."

Another adjustment.

"Oh, no, no! You're not moving in on *me!*"

There was a lot of work to be done, and quickly if he was going to save his standing. Recent events had left a lot of holes in his boundaries. He had to patch them before they caused him to lose more status. Merak looked at the sphere again and released a very frustrated sigh. Desperate circumstances called for desperate action. He held his thumb down on a particular area on the sphere.

"This is going to cost me, but it's better than losing an entire sector."

The green lights on a large area of the sphere began to blink.

"No more isles, but they're a pain to control, anyway. Transferring two thousand units, five thousand casks of Firellian, and four thousand stellar tons of marocite ore to the central bank."

He sat back to watch the results of his reallocations. Several of the blinking green lights began to change color.

Some of them turned red, some blue. About two-thirds of them remained blinking. Merak may have just taken a loss, but his action forced the others to move against one another and weaken their resources in other areas.

"There you go," he said with a sneer on his face. "You guys just go ahead and fight over my table scraps."

It would take many days for all the changes to take full effect. After making sure the situation had stabilized itself for the moment, Merak opened access to his bank. A global locator was a good-sized expenditure, but this one was worth it. He entered the specifics and put the hound to the scent.

"There you are!"

He checked the surrounding conditions and grinned to himself. The situation could not have been more convenient. Everything he needed was already in place and in motion. Merak need not do a thing.

"How fortunate! Goodbye, Group Six!"

Merak closed down his session and exited the chamber. It was time for dinner.

* * *

*Ascendency campaign 137 - Open blue bank – authentication: Zaurac 179//squall/index999. – Transfer 7000 to ready account – BREAKDOWN: 3200 to Melosian Merchant Fleet Central; 3800 to Barrier Distributers - Manifest: 2000 hand weapons, K, R, and Q type; 450 casks Ostican pitch, 100 bales sailcloth, 80 spools #6 line, 40 spools #4 line, 300 gold tormacs, 2000 silver paleens. _ENTER_*

- *Starfish* ADJUDICATION LOG - REQUEST 1957.

Today – The Zinji Desert

"A whole army?" asked a skeptical Foxx. "I can't believe they'd send thousands of troops just to capture us."

"We did rather piss off the Almighty Imperator," said Orchid.

"And he is dragonshit crazy," added Tresado.

"Still, there's got to be another reason for all these troops to be here," said Foxx. "If there's a walled city or something like you said, I'd say that's their original target."

"We have to make it to that city before the Treskans get here," said Serena.

"How far away is this wall?" asked Foxx.

"Hard to tell," replied Tresado. "I could barely see it in the heat waves."

"Well then, let's get going," said Serena.

They were still following the poisoned river and already on a course which should take them there. They needed to hurry, but it wasn't easy. All of them were suffering from thirst, but they plodded on. They started up a slight slope, slowly gaining altitude above the river, which had carved its way through the fine sandstone over the millennia, creating a canyon of tight-packed sand walls. They couldn't stay near its sloping, sandy bank for fear of accidentally sliding into the destructive water. Far ahead, they could see a ridge line. The top of the wall was just visible beyond it.

The hours dragged on, and so did Group Six. Their mouths were too dry to speak. The only thing they could do was to press on up the hill. If they were to stop, they'd eventually die. If the Treskans caught them, they'd die in an even worse manner. Best to keep going and die somewhere else.

Finally, just as Sensang was setting behind their backs, they reached the top of the ridge, where they found themselves on the crumbling rim of a precipice. The sandstone cliff face jutted over the desert floor and the Noxus River below. They peered down with bleary eyes and tried to get a good look at the wall before them. Orchid was the first to realize it. She had felt something *familiar* the whole time. She gasped in awe. The gigantic wall was not an artificial structure, at least, not a wall such as is built by men. They were trees. Incredibly big trees. All in a perfectly straight line in the sand stretching for leagues in both directions.

The Noxus River, which they had been following, began just beyond the base of the ridge. The source of the water seemed to be a swampy morass about a league wide. Beyond the swamp was a plateau on which stood the mighty trees in an impossibly straight line.

There were occasional fissures on the cliff edge through which they might possibly descend. It was precarious and Tresado nearly tumbled over the edge, but Group Six had nowhere else to go. They slowly let themselves down the face of the ridge. The loose rocks could not keep a tight hold on the sandy face. Every foot placed upon it caused a mini-avalanche. Eventually, their own exhaustion won out. A good-sized rock pulled loose under Tresado's feet and they all lost their footing. With no energy left to resist, Group Six did a slow but painful sliding descent to the base of the ridge. They found themselves once again on the bank of the poisonous waters. A ground fog began to rise in the gathering darkness and Group Six lost consciousness.

* * *

Of all my anthropological observations thus far, the one I find most intriguing is funerary customs. Macai prefer to bury their dead face-up, so as to approach the afterlife among the stars, mirroring my own ancestral history. Eryndi dead are buried face-down, in the belief that their eternal reward resides deep underground. This would seem to have something to do with the planetary core. There is an unknown element or elements interacting with the vorennium from the impact crater. Mama taught me this during the Intervoid.

- *Starfish* ARCHIVAL SPHERE 17

Today – Tresk

The Imperator was ready to address the crowd. A small army of servants first swarmed about him, making sure his tunic was properly adjusted, his hair properly coifed, and the mayonnaise properly wiped from his upper chin. As he waited for them to finish their primping, Merak idly wondered what had become of his trusted aide, Stickitus Owtus, whom he had not seen for a few days.

It was time. He stepped forward onto the balcony to the accompaniment of a dozen stemhorns announcing his presence. The crowd below cheered loudly, but with noticeably less enthusiasm than normal. Merak stood with arms raised, milking the applause. They kept it up anyway, because to show open disrespect might earn one a trip to Stadium.

"CITIZENS!"

The crowd wisely settled down immediately upon hearing his voice. One did not interrupt the Imperator once he started orating.

"I humbly thank you for your warm response. The past several days have been trying. The terrorist attack upon our beloved Stadium was a heinous act and I promise you the barbarians responsible shall be brought to justice. Rest assured that all is under control and there is no further threat to Treskan citizens. The damage to Stadium is being swiftly repaired and the families of those who lost their lives in the attack are being adequately compensated.

"Despite these setbacks, our Imperium remains robust and ever expanding. We are nearing total victory on the northern front. Within the month, the last vestiges of resistance shall be overcome. With the annexation of Breeos, Tresk will add yet another province to Her territory. Beyond that, our brave Legionnaires have recently discovered Prakin's Pass, the long-sought-for gateway through the eastern mountains to the vast interior and the riches to be found there.

"And the Imperial expansion does not stop! I now have the honor to announce a new campaign to further our mighty cause. Representatives have been sent to the far-off region of Sylvas. Soon their vast wealth of medicinal miracles, priceless resources, and Magical wonders shall benefit Treskans everywhere. Our great nation shall shine as the jewel of civilization across the face of Lurra! Her citizens and culture shall continue to be the envy of all peoples everywhere. And I promise you this. Those who would scheme against the Imperium and plot Her downfall shall face swift justice and well-deserved penance."

Merak droned on about justice and retribution and victory and the will of the people and plenty of other platitudes designed to make the population feel better about themselves. A pair of hooded figures near the outer edge of the crowd listened with feigned enthusiasm.

"You see how vulnerable he is on that balcony?" whispered the figure in the grey hood. "A single arrow with a dose of one of your concoctions could end his career very quickly."

"Would you listen to yourself?" replied the figure in the green hood. "Not only are you going to get yourself killed, you want to drag me into your silly plans, too."

"Mom, keep your voice down. We've been over this before. You know I'm determined to bring that piece of lumba shit down. It's what I live for."

The little old Eryndi lady smacked her daughter across the lips. "Danikan Prissillia Tyre, you watch your language! You got that foul mouth from your father, but don't think for a beat that I'm going to put up with it."

"Sorry, Mom, but it's a harsh world, you know? You should know. You were here before Merak appeared on the scene. You used to talk about the golden age and how civilized the old Coalition was."

"Prissy, that was over a hundred years ago and I was just a youngster," replied the little old Eryndi lady. "But that was then and this is now. We have to play the cards we're dealt."

"Then why did you move the family to Breeos?" countered Danikan.

"That was your father's decision. You don't know anything about back then. That was many years before you were even born."

Danikan's eyes narrowed to slits as she took another look at the large, greasy presence above them. "Maybe not, but I do know about now. And I know that I have to do something to change it. And Mom, do me a favor?"

"What's that?"

"Don't call me *Prissy.*"

PART VI:
THE GLADES

CHAPTER 20

Needles of Shelter, Armor Blossoms,
Ever Safeguarding Your Charge.
Sacred Shade Defend Us . . .

- Trianna of Sylvas, Poetess to the Glades

* * *

Foxx looked about him. Something was not right. It was twilight. The shadows of trees and bushes waved about, seemingly under their own power, for there was not a breath of wind. The shadows continued their evil dance, closing in around Foxx. He felt a slight brush across his calf. When he looked, there was nothing there but the shadows. Another stroke, this one he felt on his cheek. He whirled about, trying to discover the source of these creepy touches. There was still nothing there but shadows. He peered into the semi-darkness, trying to make out something substantial. It came in the form of a sharp jab in his left kidney. As he turned, a pair of red eyes looked down upon him, reflecting the firelight, of which there was none. Another touch, behind him. This one was more of a slash to his shoulder blades, causing searing pain. This time, the eyes had more substance, nearly two reaches off the ground and surrounded by a black, snarling rat-like face. The entire creature appeared before Foxx, reaching for him with long, clawed fingers. It was a clee-at. Foxx had seen one before someplace. He couldn't place where, only that this horrid thing should have been extinct. The spiny hands seized him by the face and bent his head backward. The creature's black mouth opened. Curved, needle fangs sunk into Foxx's exposed throat, shredding his flesh and spewing blood.

* * *

Serena could not have been more proud and excited. Only two weeks ago, she had completed her two-year apprenticeship under her assigned mentor, Katrina the Defiant. And now, as a full-fledged Northlands Warrior at the tender age of fifteen, Serena was on her very first raid aboard the Raven, commanded by none other than her own father, Gunnar the Steadfast. Their ship was part of a six-boat raiding pack heading along the far northern coast toward little-known lands in search of a missing warrior, as well as booty. At the moment, it wasn't necessary to man the oars. A stiff nor'wester off their port quarter kept the pack sailing smoothly. Serena stood at the bow, watching the ocean in all directions, as was her duty. Some small black dots appeared in the water ahead. They protruded from the waves and disappeared again. Serena leaned out over the portside gunwale to get a better look. Not rocks.

Ripper whales! Always hunting, always hungry.

The pod and the pack each sped toward the other, both too proud to be the one to turn away.

"Hold your arrows!" shouted Gunnar. There were a few grumbles amongst those crewmen who would like nothing better than to spear one of them for the rich, red meat.

"We're not out here to go fishing!" Gunnar yelled back. "We have a mission and we're not going to lose days butchering a whale."

At the mention of the word 'whale,' a violent thump slammed into the keel from below as one of the angry creatures let the puny things above know just whose ocean this was. The shock caught Serena off-guard just as she was shifting her grip, and over the rail she went. She was an excellent swimmer due to her warrior training and did not panic. She trod water just below the surface while she got her bearings. A large goatfish swam up to her, giving her a surprised look. It came a little nearer, approaching Serena's face. The curious fish eyed her closely. The young warrior was quite enchanted and wiggled her finger to entice it closer. She glanced away for a fraction of a beat. In that time, there was a rush of bubbles and a pressure wave. The goatfish was no longer there. At least not all of him. His open mouth and half his head swirled before Serena's blurred vision. The one remaining eye stared at her accusingly, blaming all this on her. Serena stared back in shock, panic rising in her throat. She tried frantically to reach the surface and get back onboard, but was being pulled under by something. The bubbles cleared, revealing an open, toothy mouth of a ripper whale shooting toward her. Above her, the retreating keels of the raiding fleet faded from sight without turning back. Her father had left her. The toothy jaws closed upon Serena's face, ripping the flesh and severing her head and left arm.

* * *

The foreman's whistle sounded and Tresado moved along the line with all the other workers. Another day would be Week's End Honor Day and he could take a break. That is, unless he was called in to work again as he had been for the last three weeks. This job sucked, but he needed the work if he wanted to eat. As he reached his station, he donned his leather gloves that had holes in all the fingers. The pile of unsorted scrap was overflowing his in-bin. This was more that he could possibly do in one day. Looks like he would be working tomorrow, after all. How easy this would be, Tresado fantasized, if he could just magically cause all this junk to separate and sort itself. There was no such thing as magic, though, so he might as well get going on this pile. If he didn't make sufficient progress today, the foreman would be by to motivate him. The woman was fond of her switch, which she delighted in using on plump backsides such as his. A sound of laughter and good spirits drifted into the scrap house. A group of well-dressed Eryndi sauntered by, snickering and offering nasty comments to this army of laborers. He recognized all of them. He had gone to primary and intermediate school with this bunch. They were all former boingball athletes turned business executives who owned and operated this facility, raking in the money and women. The one in front, the one he knew as Faltonar, spotted Tresado at his work station. The man came over, sniffing the starflower in his buttonhole.

"I remember you, round boy," the man said imperiously. "You always were a worthless little turdhead. I think you need more to do."

Faltonar snapped his fingers and three cartloads of fresh junk were dumped onto Tresado's station. Faltonar and his buddies exploded in hooting laughter and catcalls. Finally the shift ended and Tresado shuffled out and headed home, which was a miserable hovel with half a roof. In front of it, a freshly dug grave gaped open. The tombstone read, HERE LIES

TRESADO – PLAIN, ORDINARY, UNINTERESTING TRESADO. He couldn't help it. His plodding steps led to the edge of the grave and Tresado tumbled in. Dirt was shoveled onto his upturned face, cutting off his screams.

* * *

Orchid was happy, so much so that she found herself skipping toward the venue entrance. There was an archway of brilliant flowers and delicate vines with the word WELCOME spelled out in Melosian carnations. A large crowd lay ahead, surrounding tables filled with yummies. Family reunions were such fun. As Orchid approached the crowd, several people cried out her name and ran to her. They hugged and kissed her, telling her how much they rejoiced over seeing her. Orchid didn't know any of them, but they all had the same shade of green eyes as her own. One woman steered her toward the buffet tables, where she was assured that all her favorite foods awaited her. None of the dishes were familiar, but they looked wonderful. More relatives came to hug and greet her. Orchid couldn't tell if they were Macai or Eryndi. Despite the newness and uncertainty of everything, it was still a joyous, most pleasant experience.

* * *

"AAAAAAAAAAGH!"

"AAAAAAAAAAGH!"

"AAAAAAAAAAGH!"

"Aaaaaaaahhh."

Three bloodcurdling screams and one sigh of comfortable happiness echoed through the canopy. Foxx, Serena, and Tresado each awoke from the most terrifying dream they had ever had. Orchid stretched languorously in the soft leaf bed and sighed with contentment. Sensang sent her glorious gifts of warmth and light filtering through the rustling leaves above. A nearby stream babbled away, whispering its secrets to all who could hear. A family of moonlarks chattered from their nest above, the mother chastising the one youngster who continually refused to eat his supper of regurgitated worms.

There's one in every family, thought Orchid with a smile.

A disturbance fully woke Orchid from her dozy reverie. Foxx had leapt to his feet. He grasped at his neck and spun around in a panic, looking terrified. Serena and Tresado were waking up just as badly.

"WHAT?!"

"GET AWAY!"

"MOMMY!"

Orchid didn't understand. Everything was all right . . . more than all right. What she was feeling now was nothing less than eternal bliss and joy.

"What's your problem?" she asked, almost annoyed at them for spoiling the mood.

"Gods!" exclaimed Foxx. "That was . . . I mean . . . I guess I had a dream, but I can't remember."

"Yeah," agreed Tresado. "Same here. I was . . . I don't know."

"Serena?" asked Orchid. "You too?"

Serena looked about wildly for a few beats, but didn't answer the question.

"Where the hell are we, anyway?"

Group Six looked around. Instead of the burning and lifeless Zinji Desert, they found themselves feeling refreshed in a garden of delights. Lush greenery ringed them in on all sides. There were bushes weighed down with berries and vines of melons that snaked across the clearing. A small pool fed by a happy, gurgling cascade of fresh spring water was filled with life. Water bugs skittered across its surface, while frogs and fish splashed and played amiably.

The ancient boles of the immense trees twisted and intertwined with each other, forming an impassable barrier on all sides of the glade. They resembled a kind of gigantic cedar tree, with their aromatic trunks and branches locked together tightly. Other varieties of trees mingled among them. There were monkeywood, rockfruit, and corkwood trees mixed in. Many of them grew out of soil-filled niches in the gigantic branches of the cedars themselves, dozens of reaches above the floor of the forest.

Huge purple and orange flower blossoms a full reach across swung on long vines anchored above on the overhanging limbs. There were spectacular butterflies, some with half-reach wide wings. The sound of their great wings fluttering could actually be heard from the forest floor. The lowest tree branches were at least twenty-five to thirty reaches above their heads and there was no telling how much above that the canopy extended. A small circle of blue sky and Senlight blinked down upon Group Six. It was like looking up a long, long well shaft.

No one had anything to say or any kind of explanation. All four of them just stood there looking around with their mouths hanging open. The situation was just so impossible. The last any of them remembered, they were dying of thirst and heat exhaustion in a merciless desert with a very angry army on their tail. Now they were here in this garden of delights. Their bellies seemed to be full and the trail-worn Treskan military clothing had been replaced with some kind of soft and durable plant-based fabrics. Even their hair had been washed and simply styled. The group's backpacks and other belongings were neatly arranged on a boulder by the stream. Finally, Serena found her voice.

"Weird."

A clicking and scraping sound from the canopy! Far above their heads, a branch was waving about from something other than the wind, of which there was none in this cavern of greenery. A loud snapping sound was heard and the branch plummeted to the forest floor. It was dry and had pine needles on the end of it, but they appeared dead and rust colored. The whole branch was about five reaches in length and fractured in the middle. The large end was cleanly cut off as though from a pruning shear. A beat later, something started crawling down the bole of the tree from a dizzying height. As it got nearer to the ground, the creature became more visible. It was a full reach in length, clutching the thick bark with heavy claws on the tips of ten thick, double-segmented legs. The armored body was mostly a dirty white with a smattering of bluish freckles. Two enormous *tusks*, for want of a better word, protruded from one end of the creature. Whether that end was its head was yet to be determined, as there were no eyes visible. The tusks waved up and down and clacked together as it descended to the forest floor. It hopped down the remaining three or four reaches and thudded to the ground.

"Is it a . . . *spider?"* asked Foxx uncertainly, backing up at the same time. He was famous for being creeped out by bats and crawlies and such.

"It's just a big bug," said the fearless Serena, not retreating a finger.

"Or a crab, maybe?" offered Tresado.

"Whatever it is, it's magnificent," said Orchid.

The spider/bug/crab thing ignored them and scuttled over to the fallen branch. Its two tusks went to work on the wood, quickly reducing it to sawdust, which it spread out onto the forest floor. When that was done, it went to the base of a different tree and began a slow ascent until it was finally out of sight.

"Whatever it is, it eats wood," said Tresado.

"Not eats," corrected Orchid. *"Mulches.* It's like a natural gardener. That branch had been cracked by something and so was unhealthy to the tree. The creature must have nipped it off with those mandibles and chopped it up. A forest housekeeper!"

The small glade they were in was only about thirty or forty reaches across. The totally confused adventurers gathered up their goods and walked the whole perimeter, marveling at the immense trees that towered above. The pool butted up against the twisted boles and, as water tends to do, trickled through the tightly packed trees to disappear into the forest. However, there was no passage large enough to allow any of them to get through. They saw a rockmunk squeeze through a tiny opening, but nothing any bigger could've made it. Tresado looked above at the dizzying heights.

"I don't think I could levitate myself that high," he said with a worried look. "Maybe if I went up in stages and hung on to something while I get my second wind. Or third, or fourth."

"Let me see what I can do," said Orchid. "I'm pretty good with plants. Maybe I can persuade them to let us through."

Before she could make the attempt, however, a flurry of movement on all sides rustled the branches above. A score of brown, fur-covered creatures appeared and quickly descended to the forest floor. They seemed to be very large monkeys, some taller than Serena. They were sleek and muscular with intelligent faces. Long, sinuous prehensile tails snaked about them, apparently as dexterous and useful as a fifth hand.

Serena quickly reached for her sword, but Orchid held her back.

"Wait. I don't think they're hostile."

The scimitar came a little further out of its scabbard and several of the monkeys reacted with hisses and baring of teeth.

"Serena, put your sword away," said Orchid in a calming voice. "Slowly. The rest of you don't make any sudden moves. They seem to be just curious."

In an incredible display of self-discipline, Serena reluctantly did as she was told and took her hand off her weapon. The monkeys moved cautiously forward, sniffing and studying Group Six. A couple of them closely examined the scimitar and stiletto on Serena's hips and reacted with low growls, but did nothing more threatening than that. After a couple of minutes of snooping and sniffing, the monkeys withdrew into a huddle, leaning back on their powerful tails as though they were barstools. There was a lot of grunting, vocalizing, and elaborate hand gestures exchanged between them. Curiously, only one monkey at a time had anything to say. They took turns speaking as though it was a regular conversation. It was mostly grunts and whistles, but Foxx swore he could hear some distinct dialogue. He was pretty sure he could make out the words good, bad, home, tree, and maybe something that sounded like names. The monkeys acted a bit agitated whenever one of Group Six make a move of any kind.

"I suggest we all just sit down and enjoy this place," said Orchid calmly. "I sense that's what they want."

"Or what they expect us to do," growled Serena. Even so, she and the others found comfortable spots in the soft grass. The monkeys seemed satisfied and moved off a bit to pursue their own interests, which involved grooming each other and snacking on the various fruit surrounding them.

Foxx picked up a small melon and sampled it. "This is excellent," he said, smacking his lips. "But it's funny. I really don't feel very hungry. I was starving while we were in the desert."

"So what'd they do, shove food down our throats while we were unconscious?" asked Serena.

"Maybe they pre-chewed it," said Orchid. "I've seen some primates do that with their young."

Tresado gagged a little bit at the thought. "Did they also strip us and dress us in these fig leaves?" he asked sarcastically.

At this point, the apes all chattered at each other. It sounded like laughter and Foxx could swear he heard a couple of them say, "Yeah."

"Oh for crap's sake!" snarled Serena. "They're monkeys. Dumb animals!"

One of the dumb animals, a tall monkey with a developing white stripe down his back, picked up a ripe melon and bulls-eyed Serena in the back of the head. Rich, yellow juice ran down her neck, soaking her back. She leapt to her feet, madder than a wet flicken, and drew her sword in a swift move. As one, the troupe of apes dropped what they were doing and formed ranks against the warrior woman. Foxx quickly used his Knowing Spell to try to calm things down, as he had done with Serena so many times in the past. He knew just what mental buttons to push with her. Surprisingly, the monkeys responded as well. Slowly, the situation de-escalated. Fangs were un-bared, melons were dropped, and Serena's sword was sheathed. Everyone returned to peaceful pursuits. It was very easy to do so in this idyllic environment.

"I guess we go back to waiting," said Orchid.

"Who said we're waiting for anything?" asked Tresado.

Orchid calmly turned to the Eryndi.

"The monkeys."

CHAPTER 21

Today – The Zinji Desert

General Prixus Scapulus squinted into the searing heat coming off the sands of the barren Zinji desert. His adjutant, Primus Barria, slowly moved her horse beside his as they plodded along.

"Are we there yet?" she asked with a wry smile on her helmeted face.

Scapulus rolled his eyes at the stale joke. Without breaking character, or even looking at his old military friend and subordinate, he gave the traditional response.

"Yes, dismount."

The casual greeting over with, Barria returned to military protocol to deliver a report.

"Another floater has broken down, General. One of the water carriers. It was nearly empty, but what remained was salvaged and transferred to another tank."

"What is that, the third one?" asked Scapulus.

"The fourth," replied Barria. "If we don't sight Sylvas soon, we might have a little trouble, maybe even have to dump some supplies."

The General swiveled in his saddle and perused his army. His cavalry of 400 mounted Legionnaires flanked him on each side with the infantry and heavy equipment immediately behind them. The massive siege towers and supply barges smoothly drifted along with them. The slight, green glow beneath their flat bottoms kept them suspended a half-reach above the sand.

The suspension fields under each barge were the latest fantastic innovation provided by Imperator Merak. There was no way a large army such as this could move through the hostile desert environment without them. A dozen Guardian shell generators also floated along on their individual fields. But they were not infallible. The heat, the sand, and the rigors of many days of rugged travel were taking their toll.

Barria shielded her eyes from Sensang's burning kiss. Something was moving ahead on the heat-distorted horizon.

"Looks like our scouts are returning, General."

Two dusty Legionnaires came riding up to Scapulus and saluted.

"Report."

"We followed an incline up to a ridge, General," said Pondarus, the large Macai corporal. "The river runs below in a canyon. A league beyond the ridge is a wall of trees."

"Really gigantic trees," added Krimen, the young Eryndi private with him.

"Any signs of life, other than the trees?" asked Barria.

"No, Primus," answered Pondarus. "There's a kind of stinky bog or marsh this side of the trees. The river seems to originate from there. Other than that, there's no smoke, no buildings, no roads. Just the trees."

"Anything else?" snarled Scapulus.

"No, General."

Krimen fidgeted a bit in the saddle.

"Something to add, Private?" asked Barria.

"I don't know, sir. It's just that . . . I don't know. Something just seemed . . . ominous."

The General looked over at Pondarus, who seemed a little annoyed at Krimen's impertinence, but said nothing. Scapulus was inclined to trust the young Eryndi's judgment over that of the more experienced Macai, but didn't say that in so many words.

"Very well, Legionnaires," grunted Scapulus. "Well done. Report to the mess barge and get yourselves something to eat."

"Thank you, General," replied both in unison. They saluted and walked their horses back to the rear of the column.

Barria turned to her superior with relief crossing her face. "Looks like we've arrived, General."

Scapulus grunted a non-committal response. He of course knew what to expect. His sealed orders had informed him of what little intel they had on the area known to the Treskans as Sylvas. Included in those secret documents was a description of an incident that had occurred over eight hundred years previously. The story had never been generally known to the public since the old Coalition had designated it as secret. The original mission was to scout the area, mistakenly believing it to be the source of Magic. Through interviews and tests of the single survivor, those old-timers had pieced together her story. The expedition had succumbed to a hellish mind attack that left all the victims dead of fright or hopelessly insane. Whatever this power was, Imperator Merak wanted it as well as the valuable natural resources that he claimed were there. He had also assured the General that the 12th Legion would be adequately protected from a similar fate. Tomorrow or the next day would tell.

Today – The Glades

"So you're talking to monkeys now?"

Serena's snotty question to Orchid elicited a couple of snickers from Foxx and Tresado.

"More like they impart images and feelings to me," said the slightly-annoyed Orchid.

"And what are they saying?" asked Serena. She was now a little more inclined to believe her than the others.

"Just that we, meaning us and the monkeys, are waiting for something to happen," replied Orchid.

"Like what?" asked Tresado.

From above came the answer. One of the giant flowers on its vine was gracefully lowering itself to the forest floor.

"What's that inside the petals?" asked Foxx.

"Looks like a cocoon, for want of a better word," replied Orchid.

The flower gently rested itself on the ground. The "cocoon" started unwrapping itself. It appeared to be a huge leaf with several layers protecting whatever was inside. The cocoon eventually fell away and a woman stepped out. She was Eryndi, slightly built, with ephemeral brown hair that seemed to wave about, despite the lack of any breeze. One might think she had an almost greenish tint to her skin, or maybe it was just the presence of all the flora around them.

"I am Trianna, Poetess to the Glades."

She looked directly at Orchid, then twirled around and addressed the canopy above.

"O, Lords of Wood and Shade;
To Kin of the Floral Folk,
And Sister of the Green Menace,
Bid Welcome Greetings and Joyous Meetings."

An invigorating wave of pollen scent wafted down from the canopy, tickling Orchid's senses and imparting a glorious sense of well-being and homey good feelings. Foxx sneezed.

Once again, Trianna turned her hypnotic gaze back to Orchid.

"You and your friend are both welcome. In deference to Your Honored Selves, safe excisement shall be granted to these other three."

Tresado looked at Foxx and Serena and quietly mumbled out of the side of his mouth.

"You think she means us?"

They both shrugged their shoulders, indicating they were just as confused as Tresado was.

"Have no fear," said Trianna, looking around the glade. "I humbly ask you to show yourself, friend."

Trianna's voice had a tinkling musicality to it. Orchid stared back at green eyes, much the same as hers. She had a thousand questions for this strange woman, but for a few beats could not think of any. At last she found her voice.

"My . . . my friend?"

"Two names, one heart," Trianna said, looking around. "I do not see her. It is all right, precious one," she said. "You may come out of hiding. You are safe and most welcome."

"Who the hell is she talking to?" asked Serena in her blunt way.

Foxx, ever the diplomat, stepped forward and put on his most charming of airs.

"Your pardon, My Lady. My name is Foxx. This is Serena and . . ."

"I am befuddled," interrupted Trianna, as if Foxx weren't

even there. "All our senses tell of her presence, except those of our eyes."

Orchid glanced over at the rest of Group Six, who seemed as confused as she was.

"Trianna," said Orchid, "there are only the four of us. No one else."

The woman of the trees let go with a delightful little giggle. Apparently Orchid had said something Trianna had found cute and amusing.

Suddenly, one of the monkeys began to chatter excitedly. He pranced about, pointing at the small pile of Group Six's belongings. The other monkeys joined him and seemed to agree on something. Now, several of them were repeating the same grunt and all gesturing at Orchid's backpack.

Orchid slowly approached the group of primates. Despite their fearsome appearance and demeanor, they parted for her deferentially. Serena started to step forward to see what was so interesting, but the monkeys were having none of it. As soon as she took a step, they turned and bared teeth. Serena didn't like it, but she stopped.

Orchid continued on. The monkeys were showing her no hostility, but rather seemed pleased by her presence. Several of them sidled up to her bashfully to receive a little scritch behind the ears. Orchid looked at the ground where several sets of monkey eyes were focused. Her backpack - it was her own backpack that held their attention.

"What's so interesting about my bag? Is it the herbs you smell?"

Orchid reached for the bag and opened the flap. She began to remove items one at a time, starting with her herb kit, knife, a few basic necessities, and finally her own journal and that of Dementus the Mad Treskan.

"You know," Orchid said jokingly, "you should never ask to look in a lady's purse. It's . . ."

She glanced up at the monkeys, who were all now frozen in rapt attention at what she held in her hand.

"This?" Orchid held up Demantus's journal. The monkeys immediately reacted, emitting long, low tones that had the sound of reverence to them.

Trianna tilted her head in an odd way and gracefully moved next to Orchid. It was almost like she glided rather than walked. Her feet touched the ground, of course, but scarcely made a rustle, or even bent a blade of grass.

"I feel Her, but all I see is a . . . book?"

Orchid held the journal out to Trianna. Foxx tensed for a moment, but held himself in check.

"It is a travel journal, written by an Eryndi known as Dementus," said Orchid, handing over the book.

Trianna shied away at the sound of the name, but only for a moment. Again, she addressed the immense plant life around her.

"Tis a name well known,
From tomorrow and before,
Parter of Hearts, Savior of One . . ."

The poetry over for the moment, Trianna took the book in her arms, its weight staggering her slight frame a bit. Immediately, her green eyes went wide and she held the book out at arm's length. The grasses at their feet began to rapidly grow and morph themselves into a kind of waist-high altar. The tree woman reverently placed the book upon it.

"This is a thing not understood."

Trianna paused and leaned closer to the book, as though taking a second look.

"She is here."

Trianna danced about in joy, laughing and cavorting with the monkeys, who also jumped for joy. Orchid felt pretty joyous herself, although she had no idea why. It must be contagious.

"Come, my friends," said Trianna to Orchid. "You have come home at last."

Orchid, her own face lit with a broad grin, examined this compelling woman of the trees. She knew nothing about Trianna, no idea who she was or what she represented. Orchid's own life experiences, a series of joyous times and hard knocks, told her wisely to trust no one, be wary, question all. However, her gut instincts said to trust Trianna implicitly.

Trianna reverently picked up Dementus's journal from its altar and handed it back to Orchid. At the same moment, the great flower lowered itself as before, to the forest floor. With the same odd tilt of her head, she held out a delicate hand to Orchid.

"Come."

"Where are we going?"

"We are already there. It is my great joy to show the two of you your forever home."

Orchid, fascinated by those green eyes, eagerly took Trianna's hand and stepped up into the welcoming petals of the gigantic flower. They curled around the two women, forming comfortable, sweet-smelling seats. The flower stalk smoothly rose toward the canopy far above. About a third of the way up, two of the immense boles shivered slightly, then bent themselves apart, leaving a gap. The two women then disappeared into the dizzying heights. Some of the monkeys took to the trees and followed along. The rest saw them off, waving and chattering and cutting the wildest capers.

Meanwhile, with the celebration at its peak, Foxx, Serena, and Tresado were huddled in quiet conversation.

CHAPTER 22

106 Years ago – The Hall of Perception, The Treskan Coalition

YEAR OF THE CITY – 1227

The whisper-thin Eryndi stood at the back of the crowd and looked with manic sadness at the sight of his beloved Octavia's Royal body upon the lattice of carefully prepared monkeywood slats.

It was all his damaged brain could do not to throw himself upon the rising flames. Octavia's body, lifeless but still radiant, lay face down upon the intricately-laid pattern of monkeywood logs that made up Her funeral pyre. The flames, fanned by the Worldly Magic of the Dajaran Temple Matrons, burned with a brilliant, white-hot intensity. The logs were consumed quickly, gently lowering the remains into the center of the coals and the grave below. At the proper time, the Matrons concluded their death song and cooled the flames. The marker slab was maneuvered into position and lowered on top of the prepared stone vault.

The Matrons began their Mourning Dirge. The lyrics spelled out the typical kind of farewell common to all Eryndi and Macai alike. They spoke of remembrances and acts of kindness. The story of Octavia and her grand and special ways rang out from the sacred halls and spread via word of mouth to all in the City and the many lands of the Coalition beyond.

Dementus was dressed not in finery, as all the others gathered in Memorial Common, but in his worn travel clothes. His Travelogue, the Eryndi's most valuable possession, now infinitely more so, lay safely secreted in his new leather backpack, a gift from the Imperatrix Herself.

The Matrons were just wrapping up their dirge, offering the prayer to Dajari, Goddess of the Forest. Octavia had been studying for the Priestesshood herself. She and her twin sister Alythya were both children of the wood, as they liked to call themselves. They had been born in the forests of the Jarayan Mountains, near the lovely alpine city of Laylya. Being members of the Royal Family did not allow them to stay there beyond childhood, however. Alythya currently served as Imperatrix and Senate High Minister. She stood nearby, tears running down her perfect cheeks. She was clutching the arm of her consort, the strange Macai known as Merak.

Alythya spotted Dementus at the back of the crowd. She fixed her gaze on him until she was sure he was looking back at her. After making eye contact, the Imperatrix gave him the slightest jerk of her delicately pointed Eryndi chin, indicating that he should get the hell out of there, as she had advised him earlier. He returned a pleading, sorrowful look, but managed to remember her warning. And so, Dementus, AKA The Mad Treskan, hitched his new pack higher on his shoulders, picked up his also new steel-tipped walking stick, and continued the journey he had started many years earlier. This time, however, he would not be alone in his travels.

Dementus passed through the heart of the city until he came to the Vistarian Gate on the northeastern part of Unity Wall. The massive edifice still had hundreds of Legionnaires stationed there, but the great gates themselves had not been closed in living memory. In all of Tresk's long history, no invading army, whether by sea or land, had ever attempted to breach Her walls, had not even come close. Beyond the gate stretched the Arterio Treska, one of the main roads leading from the city to the great continental interior. Dementus passed through and then paused in his steps. He moved off the road and sat down on a stone bench. He sadly looked back at the city that he thought was going to be the end of his journeys and his forever home. Vendors in wagons and booths lined the avenue, hawking every product and service imaginable. Travelers of all races and nationalities busily jammed the road, leaving and entering the city to see about their affairs. He would miss the place terribly.

Dementus sighed and opened his pack. He fished out his journal and opened it to a random spot.

"Well, we're on our way," he said to the calfskin page. It contained a list of all the gin joints in the town of Ras that he had written many years ago. As he spoke, his words wrote themselves in the middle of the list of pubs, pushing the existing words out of the way to make room for the new text. He cleared his throat and spoke again.

"If ever a man was in tatters,
For certain now nothing much matters,
But there's good news it seems,
Cuz in all of my dreams,
We're together forever and that . . .

"Octa, what rhymes with matters, but isn't matters, and means matters?"

Nothing does, the book wrote in a fine hand.

"Nothing doesn't rhyme with matters."

The book in his hand paused ever so slightly before responding, again the new text inserting itself into the middle of an existing sentence.

You're a loony, but I love you.

Today – The Glades

The flower stalk lifted Trianna and Orchid high above the small portion of the forest floor that Group Six had found themselves in. The monkeys sped up the trunks just as quickly, finding plenty of hand, foot, and tailholds in the half-reach-thick bark. Even at this height from the ground, the massive tree trunks were still all around them. They entwined together, their sinuous branches interlocked with each other, forming a solid, circular wall of ancient wood. Orchid mentally compared herself to an ant inside a regular-sized hollow tree.

Their floral conveyance moved closer to the boles and slowed. It gently touched the junction where two great trees met and stopped. Orchid estimated their height at about twenty-five reaches and the tree continued up for at least another forty or fifty more.

Trianna rose from her sweet-smelling seat. Without any kind of gesture or spellcasting apparent, two giant boles shifted and twisted themselves apart, forming a kind of tunnel between the two trees.

"Amazing!" said Orchid. "I'm pretty good at manipulating plants, but these giants are well beyond my abilities"

Trianna chuckled in her tinkling way. "Nothing is manipulated here. The trees are here to help, as are we all. Let us proceed."

Trianna lightly skipped through the tunnel, humming some little tree tune. Orchid and the monkeys followed suit. She tingled with excitement. Orchid had no idea what she was about to be shown, but she couldn't wait to find out.

A couple of dozen skips later, they came to the opposite side of the two trees. This area was more open. It was still heavily forested, but the trees were smaller and farther apart. A smaller, but still big, tree grew, not out of the ground, but from a gigantic knothole in one of the others. Over the ages, soil had accumulated in that knot, allowing a completely different species of tree to take root. It was a kind of broadleaf nut tree. Scattered around the base of this tree were several large, discarded nutshells. The shells looked like a kind of gigantic koofa nut, but in size they were more like a reach-long wooden boat. Trianna merely touched one of them and it righted itself to rest on its "keel."

Trianna picked up some handfuls of spongy moss and placed it in the bottom of the nutshell. She climbed in and extended a tiny hand to Orchid.

"Make yourself comfortable."

Without any reservation, Orchid accepted Trianna's invitation and sat down in the little nutshell dinghy. A moment later, trailing lianas snaked their way under the bottom and smoothly lifted it and its two occupants up and away, passing the job over to another tree. Orchid and Trianna were carried along at an impressive, fast-walk speed through the middle terrace of the forest. The monkeys flanked them, swinging easily from branch to branch.

Orchid was treated to some marvelous sights as they traveled along. They passed a large nest with a mated pair of booger birds caring for their brood of little ones. The hatchlings clucked and chirped for their parents to feed them. Several reaches beyond the nest, Orchid saw a flash of red in the concealing foliage as they passed. It was a scarlet panther, stealthily sneaking up on the nest. He was a magnificent beast, fully two reaches long from his tomato red nose to the tip of his triple-forked tail. It took note of them as they went by, but seemed unconcerned with anything other than his potential lunch. A few beats after they passed came the snarling victory cry of the panther, the death scream of his prey, and the panicked chittering of the chicks. Orchid didn't blame the panther for his nature; in fact, she shared the cat's fondness for booger meat. Trianna and Orchid both understood that the life and death cycle is inevitable, eternal, and no right or wrong attached to it.

The nutshell dinghy and its monkey escort traveled on. Orchid refrained from asking where they were going or any other questions. She was just enjoying the trip too much. She leaned back, snuggling herself into the soft moss bedding. The birds and other creatures lulled Orchid to doziness with their blended musical performance – a symphony of the forest. Soon, the composition altered slightly. Orchid snapped fully awake when she realized she was now also hearing the voices of people mixed in with the song. She looked over to Trianna with questioning eyes.

"Yes," the tree woman said, "we are approaching the hamlet of Shurzy."

Their conveyance slowed and passed through several bushy branches that parted for them. Beyond was a village, small homes, walkways, a sheltered common gathering area, even a marketplace of sorts with bins full of food. And there were Eryndi, going about their business, greeting each other, having meals, playing games, even making love, all apparently living their entire lives many reaches above the forest floor. Nothing was built. No saws or hammers had ever touched any of this. All of the rooves were formed from intertwining branches with large overlapping leaves or sheets of bark to keep water out. The walk paths connecting the homes were the titanic branches themselves, flattened on one side for ease of walking. They curved and intersected, just like the streets in any village, only with handrails. There were very few walls. People's homes were all open to view at all times.

Without any kind of obvious effort, Trianna had the vines set the dinghy down on a firm branch at the edge of town.

"Would you care to walk about and meet some of the tree people?" she asked Orchid.

"I would like nothing better."

"Here comes one now," said a delighted Trianna.

A kind of monitor lizard about a half-reach long came bounding toward them along the branch. It excitedly emitted some barking sounds and slithered around Trianna's legs. She picked it up and it nuzzled her face with a long reptilian tongue. When it was through with Trianna, it jumped over to Orchid and gave her affectionate lizard kisses, too.

Orchid giggled in delight. "So, you're a tree people, are you, little friend?"

"We are all tree people," said Trianna. "We, the Trimmies, the crabblers, the birds, everyone."

Trianna and Orchid strolled amongst the walkways of Shurzy. Every Eryndi they met was friendly and outgoing. Most were surprised to meet Orchid, a Macai. They were fascinated and curious, but none suspicious or fearful. Everyone knew Trianna, of course.

"Greetings, Poetess."

"Happy Day, Poetess."

Trianna knew all of them, too. She always asked about their health, their relatives, how their children were doing, etc. Orchid estimated that this village housed roughly three or four hundred Eryndi. No one appeared to be homeless or poverty-stricken. In fact, it didn't appear that anybody worked. There was no construction or maintenance to be done. The dwellings were all formed from the branches and bark of the trees. Here, where people lived, food was literally right outside the window. Every home had fruit trees next to them. Vegetables were grown in soil-filled hollows in the branches. There were even varieties of animal flesh available, mostly great snails and crustaceans. Everything came from the forest.

"Oh, here is my favorite sight!" said Trianna with a cute little squeal. She ran forward across an aerial walkway to a small enclosure in the branches. Seated in a circle were several young Eryndi mothers with nursing infants. The mothers greeted Trianna with hushed tones. A few of the babies were being bottle-fed using gourds. Orchid approached a woman who was crouched next to a burning hearth and stirring a little cauldron.

"Happy day to you," she said. "I am Orchid."

"And to our visitor," the woman responded. "My name is Kory."

"I am curious. May I ask about this mixture?"

"Certainly! Come, see for yourself," the woman said. She lifted a dripping wooden spoon and offered it to Orchid to sample. "It is a blending of eyepods, pine nuts, loga beans, and Font water, of course."

Totally trusting, Orchid took a taste and smacked her lips. This stuff was wonderful and left a tingling sensation on her tongue.

"We of the trees call it Sustenade," said Trianna. "It is fed to babies as an aid to weaning. For infants, it is kept diluted in a liquid form like this. We make a thicker paste for toddlers. It is very nutritious and helps the little ones develop. You and the others were as babies when the Trimmies brought you into the Glades. The desert had nearly taken your essence. Sustenade restored you."

Everyone is so friendly and helpful here, Orchid thought. She had not said that aloud, but Trianna still responded.

"All are helpful in the Glades. Even to nobelongs such as yourself, but of course you are an exception."

"Nobelongs?" asked Orchid. "I don't know that word."

"Apologies, I did not mean to offend," said Trianna. "That is something the trees refer to. A nobelong is unwelcome or unasked for, like fire mites or dragons or pigs or horses. They also refer to certain food crops as nobelongs, as well as . . . Macai, of course. Again, no offense is intended."

Orchid wasn't quite sure how to react. She hadn't been too fond of dragons of late. Twice in as many weeks she had been screwed over by them, having once being denied aid in Stadium and the other time being shat upon. She also didn't care for being compared to fire mites or pigs, so she changed the subject.

"I see. What is this Font water that Kory mentioned?"

"That is our next stop," whispered Trianna, so as not to disturb the babies. "Come and I shall show you the most sacred place in all the Glades."

CHAPTER 23

Orchid and Trianna bid good-bye to the mothers of the hamlet of Shurzy and headed back to the shell boat. The trees obligingly picked it up again and resumed the task of passing it on to subsequent trees. As soon as they were underway, the Trimmies moved along with them, unerringly swinging and leaping from tree to tree.

"They are so very agile," said Orchid. "And so suited to their home."

"As their home is suited to them," answered Trianna. "This part of the journey will take a little time. Might I converse with your friend?"

Orchid was confused for a beat, but then realized what Trianna meant and handed over Dementus's journal. She accepted it and lifted it up to present to the Glades.

"Big sister from afar paces her cell,
Not seed, nor root, nor spore,
Have you soil to grow a flower matured?
What say you, oh home of us all?"

Trianna clutched the book to her chest for a beat, opened it to a random page, and settled back on the moss padding.

Orchid didn't understand how, but the trees continued passing the shell boat along with their branches. It didn't seem like Trianna was actively concentrating to cast a spell as Orchid and other Worldly Magicians would do. Somehow the trees seemed to know where she wanted to go and took up the project on their own.

Total communion with the plants, thought Orchid. *Astounding!*

Trianna flipped through the pages, not saying a word, at least not out loud. Occasionally she would giggle at something and then become morose to the point she seemed about to cry. She nodded her head, rolled her eyes, and furrowed her brow, just as though she was gossiping with a lifelong friend, but not a spoken word passed her lips.

The journey continued for another hour. Trianna closed the book and turned to Orchid.

"'Tis a sad story these pages tell. Octavia is a wondrous soul."

"Octavia?" said Orchid. "Who is Octavia?"

"Why your friend in the book," said Trianna with an amused look. "You know of her from the writings."

"Dementus's writings? My friends and I have all looked at the journal. None of us have ever been able to fully understand them."

"But it is as plain as moss upon bole," said Trianna. "See here." She pointed to a passage that described the nest-building methods of the Werin Atoll Dung Pigeons, but then in the middle of a sentence, it spoke about some kind of cupcake recipe from Dementus's Great Aunt Caloria. Halfway through the ingredients list the writing turned to several tables of numbers. At the bottom of that same page was a crude drawing of someone playing boingball.

"Octavia kept a close watch upon her man," said Trianna

with a small smirk on her tiny face. "Never was there a mate with such a penchant for trouble. Her scolding and advice kept him from serious harm half the time and the other half he counted on his unerring luck to save himself – just as it says here."

Orchid shook her head in complete bewilderment, but she believed Trianna.

"Dementus and this Octavia were lovers? But how can a person exist in a book? How are you able to understand the writings? I have a zillion questions."

"Indeed you do," said Trianna. She again seemed to reach out to the trees in some unfathomable way and a sly look crossed her face.

"I have been misinformed," Trianna giggled. "Conifers can be such pranksters, but the Oaks have put in their two leaves' worth. 'Twas mushroom gas that fibbed to the Pines. Now we know the truth."

Orchid's head was awhirl in an eddy of confusion. "*What?*"

"*The traveler finds a restful home,*

While the lonely still seeks.

Arboreal health awaits an answer."

The Poetess giggled after her recitation and then settled down in the shell boat for a quick nap. Orchid shook her head and just enjoyed the trip. The boat continued briskly through the forest. They passed other villages, receiving waves and friendly greetings.

"This truly is a happy place," the wide-eyed Orchid said to herself. She often giggled with delight at some charming scene. Usually she wasn't much of a giggler, except when drunk, but Trianna's childlike demeanor was contagious. At last the forest began to thin as they moved eastward. The trees became farther apart, thus slowing the rate at which the shell boat could move. Finally the last tree was behind them and the boat settled to the ground. The branches supporting it returned to their former positions.

"'Tis but a short walk from here," said Trianna, waking up from her nap at exactly the right time. They both hopped out of the boat and stretched. Ahead of them loomed a large, cone-shaped hill that first appeared to be striped like a limpet rat. After walking for a few minutes, Orchid realized it was due to many streams and rivulets flowing down its slopes.

The two women were heading in an easterly direction, following one such bubbling stream up the incline. The farther they walked, the less abundant became the plant life. The ground was a curious light yellowish-gray. A strong but pleasant combination of odors wafted up from the water. Trianna read Orchid's expression.

"Taste it."

Orchid knelt and scooped up a palm full of water. It was quite warm and smelled funny, but a slurp later, Orchid grinned.

"Delicious, invigorating!"

"Come," tittered Trianna. She skipped lightly up the hill with Orchid close behind. About a hundred more reaches brought them to the top where a steaming pool covered nearly the entire plateau. A foaming fountain of hot water continually erupted from the hilltop, filling the pond to overflowing and producing a radial series of streams that flowed down the hill on all sides and entered the surrounding forest.

"This is Font," said Trianna. "She flows from here to nourish all the Glades."

Orchid was fascinated at the sight. The spray of water

was turned into a fine mist by the breeze. It made for a warm, enveloping fog that tickled all her senses.

"This is the only source of fresh water in the Glades?" she asked.

"Aside from the occasional rain shower, but those are rare," answered Trianna. "The Font is all we need. Its water is our lives. It is the basis for Sustenade, with which we feed our infants."

From atop the mound, Orchid looked out upon the relatively small but fully self-sufficient ecosystem that radiated out from the life-giving Font. Even at this highest land point in the Glades, the giant trees in the distance still towered above them, like a protective wall on all sides. As far as she could tell, the Glades was roughly twenty or thirty leagues across and surprisingly hexagonal in shape. She estimated that the entire Glades was only about six or seven-hundred square leagues, a tiny oasis of super-life in the middle of the barren Zinji Desert.

Trianna and Orchid walked the perimeter of the pond, which was about half a league in diameter. A few birds and insects flitted around, occasionally landing to take a drink. There were none swimming or even flying near the center. The water coming up from the steady geyser was just too hot. Trianna began to look a bit anxious by the time they had come full circle.

"Is everything all right?" asked Orchid.

"Oh, yes," replied Trianna. "I find all this open-ness and steady Senlight to be somewhat overwhelming. Let us go back to the comforting closeness of the trees."

They made their way back to the shell boat and soon were once again moving through the branches at a speed that would have been impossible on the ground. After about twenty minutes, they passed over a small clearing. Trianna looked below, and immediately the branches slowed the boat and began to lower it. It halted a few reaches above the ground and held there. Trianna spoke to the forest.

"As the morning petals,
The drama below unfolds;
Join in and feel;
Who shall win?"

Orchid looked over the side at the forest floor, where there were dozens of large, brightly colored, dead birds. Their splendid feathers were spread sloppily out from oddly bent wings; some lay on their backs with their feet in the air. Orchid was alarmed at first, until she saw one of them twitch a leg. She looked around the clearing and saw hundreds more of the same variety perched in the branches of an oak tree. That tree had several ropes of sakola vines, a separate plant, snaked about the bole. Dark pink berries hung in clumps. She nodded to herself in understanding. Trianna had noticed Orchid's initial concern.

"No worries, no cares. The parrotoids but guard their peers."

"As soon as I saw the sakola vines," said Orchid, "I realized the parrots were just drunk on the berries."

"Behold, the drama begins."

Orchid looked down. The leaves on one of the ground bushes quivered and a nose poked out. A brown and yellow striped Vermian Weasel, over half a reach long, slowly emerged and looked cautiously around. Satisfied that the coast was clear, the weasel dashed out, intending to snatch up one of the inebriated birds. Before he even came close, several of the sober parrotoids launched themselves down to the rescue. With flapping wings and powerful talons, they angrily encouraged the weasel to go find himself a meal elsewhere. As he disappeared back into the brush, the parrotoids gave one last defiant screech that was the equivalent of AND STAY OUT!

The other parrotoids began a cacophony of triumphant calls. The monkeys joined in with the victory cheers. Orchid couldn't help but be enchanted and laughed along. When it quieted down, she turned to Trianna, who was peering at her with those familiar but disturbing eyes.

"Thank you for showing me this."

There was no answer from Trianna, only that intense, gentle stare. Orchid looked down at the parrotoids again. One of them was stirring. It slowly pulled its disheveled wings about itself and struggled to its feet. The bird shook its head, as though to clear it. As soon as it had its bird wits about it again, the parrotoid spread its colorful wings and laboriously flapped its way into the air to join its buddies in the tree. Some of the other birds clustered around it and offered aid. A couple of them teamed up to groom the drunkard's feathers. Others offered some nutty bits and sips of water from some nearby dew-covered leaves. Gradually, the bird's faculties began to return, but it still had a hangover. The other parrotoids in the trees collectively cheered for the restoration of their fellow bird. Some of the other passed-out creatures on the ground were beginning to stir also. According to Orchid's trained senses, the flock as a whole had somewhere else to go and something else to do, but was content to hang around until everyone was fit to travel.

Orchid, the Trimmies, and the parrotoids were still celebrating, but Trianna was a little downcast.

"Something wrong?" asked Orchid.

Trianna looked up at the ever-present greenery.

"One goes on, one goes without,
One to live today till tomorrow's final call,
The other to hunger till fated reckoning.
When another shall feed the soil."

Orchid puzzled over Trianna's poem, then understood.

"You're saying the parrotoid lives today, but tomorrow it will die anyway and the weasel will kill something else?"

"Such is the way of the Glades."

"I understand, but how do you know that?" Orchid puzzled. "Do you see into the future?"

"Such is the way of the Glades," Trianna repeated simply, as though such a thing should be obvious. She looked again to the forest around her and nodded. "To know the way of the Glades, one must become the Glades."

"How must I do that?" Orchid asked. "Is there a specific spell I need to learn or . . .?"

"Open your mind to the trees. Hear what they say." Trianna used a patient tone as though she was talking to a four-year-old.

"I already have," insisted Orchid, "as soon as I found myself and my friends in this forest. It was the first thing I did. That's what I always do. That's what I was trained to do."

Orchid summoned up all her experience at school, at home with her adopted family, even what she had learned traveling with Group Six. She strained every intuitive cell in her brain, focusing on one of the giant trees. She was aware of its primitive plant mind, but no more so than that of a dandelion on the ground.

"Your Macai senses limit you," said Trianna. "The trees are here to help, as all the tree folk are. To listen is not enough. You must live their lives, enter their bark, their roots, their sap. A single tree knows nothing. The forest knows all."

Orchid drew a breath and let it out slowly. She relaxed her mind into a semi-trancelike state. A sudden urge tickled the back of her head, something she hadn't considered before.

"Give me the book," she said. "I'll ask for help."

Orchid took Dementus's journal in hand. She opened it to the last page, which contained The Mad Treskan's final words before the Water Spirit took him. "Octavia, it is I, the Lady of the Emerald Eyes. Tell me what I need to know."

Orchid's emerald eyes suddenly went wide. Her mind was aflame with a flood of thoughts and feelings. There was a lifetime of images, words, songs, history, regrets, anger - all too overwhelming to process just yet. On top of it all was love . . . strong, pure, unwavering love. She saw people, vague and undefined, but for three exceptions: a loving man, a sister of great energy, and a man of great menace. Orchid's eyes opened to the smiling face of Trianna. She hadn't even realized they were shut.

"Rejoice, Woman of the Trees. You now understand all!"

Trianna suddenly gave Orchid a strange look, one of pity and sympathy.

"You have been exposed to much sorrow. The draining of the Ring has damaged you. But you are of the trees now. The healer shall be healed."

She didn't know how, but Orchid sort of understood what Trianna meant, or she thought she did.

"You're referring to Absolute Magic?"

"A foul term for a heinous practice."

"I would not think you know of such things here in the Glades," said Orchid.

Trianna got very serious. "I know and believe what the trees tell me."

Trianna again seemed to hear something they said.

"What nourished kills,
What empowered weakens,
Nurturing Ring,
Sapped and spent."

Trianna slumped in sadness. The sound of the forest life dipped in volume for a few beats, then the shell boat resumed moving again and turned to the west. As they were passed from tree to tree, they kept gaining altitude.

"Why have you asked the trees to take us up?" said Orchid.

"I have not," replied Trianna. "Octavia has. As I have said, the trees are here to help." Her head tilted again. "Octavia wishes us to see something."

The shell boat was passed to one of the largest giants, which lifted it higher and higher, until finally it was supported by only the most slender upper branches. It swayed slightly at the dizzying height of over eighty reaches above the forest floor. Orchid looked about when she found the courage to take her hand from in front of her eyes. She and Trianna were looking down upon the western edge of the Glades. Immediately beyond the line of giant trees, which arced away into the desert mists on both sides, lay a league-wide morass which seemed to encircle the whole of this life-filled land in the midst of the barren wilderness. Orchid could see rivulets of brackish water draining away from the healthy trees and collecting in the swampy barrier. Giant black mushrooms poked their vile, drippy heads out of the slime. Occasionally, one of them would burst, sending a cloud of noxious spores into the air.

"To the tree people, it is known as Membrane," Trianna said matter of factly. "It surrounds the Glades like a protective shield. Life-giving water from the Font flows out to nourish all. When all nutrients are absorbed, impurities are expelled into Membrane."

"Impurities?" asked Orchid.

Trianna once again did the head tilt thing.

"Boughs of joy and boles of peace,
Cast off your woeful bracken,
Decay of acumen. Blight of judgment.
Retain wisdom gained."

Orchid thought for a few beats.

"Is it impure chemicals that are being filtered out?"

Trianna said nothing. She waited until Orchid fully understood.

"Surely you're not saying that it's negative thoughts and intentions that are being cast off?"

"Such is the way of the Glades," answered Trianna.

Orchid still didn't quite understand. She shook her head slightly and peered back out at the desert again. Directly across the morass, a cleft in the sandy ridge allowed a small river to drain from the mucky swamp and pass into the desert beyond.

"I think that's where my friends and I came out of the desert. We were following a poisoned river and I sort of remember sliding down that embankment."

"'Twas there that you and Octavia were judged worthy."

"Worthy? Worthy of what?"

"You are now of the trees, Orchid." Trianna seemed very perplexed, as though she couldn't understand Orchid's ignorance.

Orchid was on the verge of asking another of the zillion questions within her when a movement caught her eye. She focused on some activity atop the desert ridge.

"We need to get to my friends now!"

CHAPTER 24

Today – On the outskirts of The Glades

General Prixus Scapulus personally supervised the barges' descent of the ridge.

"General," said Barria, his aide and old friend, "I have to admit I was skeptical when you described how the floaters could move over non-level terrain."

"They were given to me by none other than His Imperial Majesty, Merak Himself."

"Of course, General," said Barria. She knew his moods well enough retain military discipline. "They are working fine even with those heavy siege barges . . . Sir!"

When Scapulus was in a mood, he had a full range of grunts with shades of meaning to every one. The one he chose for a reply to Barria was *I told you so! I know what I'm doing! Now piss off!*

Barria accurately read the grunt and wisely pissed off. While the General was busy playing with his new toy, she saw to the troops and made sure everyone had their deployment instructions straight. The Guardian placement would be crucial with all those cavalry units and siege support troops.

They should be able to bring the last of the barges down the steep grade by nightfall. Just enough time to set up a camp and prepare for the invasion at dawn.

Today – The Glades

Orchid and Trianna had gone hours ago, leaving Foxx, Tresado, and Serena alone in the glade with eight monkeys, who ignored them for the most part. They went about their business, grooming each other, leaning back on their tails, snacking on fruit, but always keeping an eye on the intruders.

Serena singled out the one monkey with the white stripe who threw the melon at her. She jabbed a finger in his direction.

"You, you, you. Don't think I forgot about you. Cross me again and I'll be all over you like ugly on an ape."

For an answer, Serena was treated to a cheeky tail-up display of monkey butthole with an accompanying *ooh, ooh, ooh.*

"Was he mocking me? That hairball was mocking me!"

"Forget him," said Foxx. "Anybody got a plan?"

Serena flashed the monkey an *I'm watching you gesture*, then got back on track. "Before we start planning, we gotta know what our goal is."

"Ever practical Serena," said Foxx, tipping his forest-supplied cap to her. "So what *is* our goal?"

"Getting out of this forest, away from the Treskans, and finding our way to someplace with a good restaurant," offered Tresado.

"All of us?" asked Serena.

"Meaning?" asked Foxx.

"Well, the lumba in the longhouse is Orchid," she answered. "You heard what Creepy Tree Dame said. She seemed to think this is Orchid's home now, and I wouldn't be surprised if she'd try to force the issue if Orchid doesn't agree."

"Trianna use force?" said Foxx. "She probably only weighs about eight stone."

"You've seen what she can do with these monster trees," replied Serena. "If she asked it to, this forest could squash us like bloodflies."

"She's right," said Tresado. "We've got to get Orchid out of this place."

"But what does Orchid think?" asked Foxx. "She seems very taken with this forest. The question is, is this something she really wants, or is she being influenced or coerced?"

"Can't you tell? I thought you always know what your opponent is thinking so you can cheat them," jibed the Northlands Warrior.

"I guess I need to work on my public image," said Foxx. "But, to answer your question, no, I can't detect any kind of manipulation or control, but that doesn't mean there isn't any."

"All I know is that I owe her," said Serena with conviction. "She saved my ass back there in Stadium. I owe her."

"I know how you feel," replied Foxx. "She did the same for me in Abakaar."

"Besides," Serena added, "you can't have a bunch of unpaid owed lives hanging around your neck when you go to see Crodan. He deducts points for stuff like that."

"So, you'd save Orchid to gain points? You sound like Merak and that game of his," said Foxx, who made sure he said it with a smile.

Serena threw a dirt clod at Foxx, but stopped there. A year ago, she would have broken a nose for someone saying such a thing.

"Okay, we're in agreement," said Tresado. "Here we are, trapped in this giant jail cell with unbreachable walls and monkey prison guards. So, what do we do?"

They thought and planned, proposed and rejected, threatened and yielded, for the better part of the aftermidday until finally a firm plan was in place.

"Okay," said Foxx. "First we need to dig that pit."

"I can do that Magically," said Tresado. "No sweat."

"I'll weave some bark together to make the cord," added Serena. "What did you say, two and a half reaches?"

"Two and two-thirds reaches, exactly," answered Tresado.

Foxx picked up a melon and some large nuts from the forest floor. "And I'll get to work carving the little figures."

"Are you sure this scheme is going to work?" asked Serena. "I still think my idea was better."

"Except that we don't have access to a bunch of bedsheets," reminded Foxx.

"We could use leaves!"

"The big ones are too high up," said Tresado.

"You could floatitate yourself up there to get them," said Serena, still insistent.

"You're forgetting the monkeys," said Tresado. "You saw how easily they move around in the trees. I bet they would try to stop me."

"I might be able to convince them not to," said Foxx.

"Yeah, and while you're hypnotizing the monkeys and Tresado is getting the leaves," said Serena, "I will start marking out the grid squares."

"But you're forgetting that we don't have any red paint," reminded Tresado.

"Oh, hell. That's right," said a frustrated Serena.

“I think we should stick to the original plan,” said Foxx.

“Fine, but you’ll need plenty of wood to shore up the tunnel walls, at least . . .” Serena counted on her fingers, “twenty-two square reaches.”

Not too far above their contentious heads, two women peered down from the sheltering branches of a giant cedar and listened to the conversation.

“You’ll have to forgive them, Trianna,” said Orchid. “They are frustrated and worried about me.”

Trianna tilted her head. “The Glades do not know what help these non-tree folk can be. Their souls are no different from those of the green menace.”

“I would argue that they are no different from most anybody on Lurra, including myself, Trianna.” Orchid was a bit annoyed at that last remark.

“But you are now a woman of the trees. What are these beings to you?”

Orchid looked down at Foxx the thief and conman, Serena the trained killer, and Tresado the practitioner of obscene Absolute Magic.

“They’re . . . they are my friends.”

* * *

Soldiers of the Imperium, On this eve of battle, I salute you. Your service and dedication have won you the approbation of Imperator Merak Himself. He magnanimously offers His grace and confidence of victory in the job to come. Along with that, you have the best training and the best equipment. You have your experience, your rank, and the unwavering support of your brothers and sisters in the Legion. But remember, all that does not make you a good soldier. Following orders does.

- General Prixus Scapulus, Commander of the Treskan 12th Legion

Today – The Glades

"Wait a beat, wait a beat," said Tresado. "Are you saying now that we *shouldn't* try to trap a lumba?"

"We don't even know if there are any lumbas in this forest," replied Foxx.

"Well, it doesn't matter," said Tresado. "As long as we can find something as loud as a lumba."

"If it's a loud distraction you want, why not make some Magical boom?" suggested Serena.

Tresado was getting frustrated. "That would be recognized. What we need is something indigenous to this forest, something the monkeys will rush to rescue."

"You know, the monkeys are going to witness all these preparations," said Foxx. "They'll know what we're doing."

"They're just monkeys!" yelled Serena.

"They may be smarter than you think," said Foxx.

"But the question is, are *you* as smart as you think?"

Tresado turned at the voice behind him. He was ready to fire back a sharp rebuke, but it stuck in his open mouth. Orchid stood there, leaning on her staff, looking amused. Trianna held back in the trees with a pinched expression, not looking happy.

"Nature Girl!" exclaimed Serena. "We thought . . ."

"Thought what?"

"Well, we weren't sure," stammered Tresado.

"We assumed you wanted to stay here," said Foxx.

"Yeah, and we wanted to make sure you would be happy here," added Tresado.

"By trapping a lumba?" Orchid was greatly enjoying this.

Tresado turned Eryndi red. "It was just a contingency plan in case . . . you know . . . we thought maybe you were being coerced into staying or something."

Trianna cleared her tiny throat in a kind of *I told you so way.*

"This forest is wondrous and happy," said Orchid. "Just my kind of place, but that doesn't mean I want to stay here forever."

"You wouldn't?" asked Foxx. "Why not?

"Because of friendship, you grasshead." Orchid turned to the woman of the trees. "And because I'm not worthy to. They have good intentions, Trianna, although sometimes their wisdom could stand some tweaking."

Tresado, Serena, and Foxx glanced at each other in an embarrassed sort of way.

"I'm not sure if we've been insulted or not," said Foxx.

"I'm sure," said Serena. "Still, it's good to see you again."

"Yeah, same here," said Orchid, "but now you need to come with us. There's something we need to show you. Trianna, could you . . . Wait, never mind. I can do it myself."

Orchid concentrated, not to cast a spell, but just to ask for a lift. There was motion high up among the branches. A few beats later, two empty shell boats were delivered to the floor of the glade. Orchid winked at Trianna, who appeared proud of her protégé.

Orchid beamed. "The trees are here to help. Get in."

The two shell boats, moved by the ever-accommodating

trees, whisked the now-intact Group Six along with Trianna up through the highest branches, accompanied as usual by monkeys. They were soon gazing out onto the same vista that Orchid had observed. A lot more was going on now. Serena pulled out her looker and zoomed in on the scene.

"Hmm, that's not good. Oh, what's this now? Crodan's Balls, there's a lot of 'em!"

"Could we have a look?" asked Tresado of Serena.

"No."

Serena looked over at the rest of Group Six, who were asking her a bunch of questions with just their eyebrows.

"Okay, fine," snorted Serena, who turned back to her looker. "It's a Treskan army, all right. They're trying to lead the cavalry horses down the slope. The sand isn't making it easy. Oh, there he goes! HA! One of the horses just went down and landed on a guy. They're both tumbling down the hill. There goes another one!"

"What are those big barge things?" asked Tresado.

"They're barges, numb nads. There's a green glow underneath each one. It looks like they're floating maybe a reach above the ground. I can see something that looks like folding siege towers on a couple of the biggest ones. They move so smoothly. They're not even kicking up any dust. I also count about seven or eight of those Guardian wagons like we saw in Breeos. Five of them are already at the base of the hill and seem to be deploying to the right and left."

"They generate those green protection fields," said Foxx. "They must be expecting resistance or counter-attacks."

"From whom?" asked Orchid. "The Glades doesn't have an army or any kind of defenses."

"Wait, what's this?" said Serena. "There's a kind of fog

rolling up out of the swamp." She licked her finger and tested the wind. "It's moving against the breeze! The fog is heading for that grouping on the right," she continued. "I can see several of the soldiers and the horses going down. What is that, poison? If so, this forest fights dirty."

"Sacred shade shall defend as always," said Trianna calmly. "There is naught to concern us."

Before any more soldiers were affected, a green glow emanated from the nearest Guardian. It expanded and covered the entire left flank of the Treskan cavalry. Other Guardians activated in turn, shielding the rest of the army. As the final barge reached the edge of the swamp, the last shell went up. The fog rolled over the short domes, seemingly not getting through. Once the fields stabilized, they lost their green and became transparent. The fog was still trying to penetrate to no avail. It was getting difficult to see in the fading daylight, but Serena could tell that, except for a handful of initial casualties, the invading Treskan army appeared intact and ready for action.

CHAPTER 25

And then there was the time when we played Sky Plains for a week. Windiest place you ever did see. Even the mighty colossus trees bowed before the God of Weather. We were performing to a packed house one night and were right in the middle of the grand finale. 'Twas then the fingers of Blustos Himself reached down from the elements and plucked the main tent's stakes out of their moorings. By Dorgo, that was a performance that brought the house down!

- Professor Abadiah Generax, 21862

Today – The Glades

It had been a moonless night, but Group Six's view from the treetops was illuminated by the Magical lights glowing in the interiors of the Treskan Guardian domes. Soldiers, horses, and equipment could be seen moving about within.

Orchid tried to commune with the trees again, but was having limited success. It was as though their plant minds were on something else. Tresado and Foxx were proposing and rejecting various plans, while Serena maintained a watch through her looker.

"It's less than an hour before Senrise," said Tresado. "What in hell are we going to do?"

"If the Treskans can cross that swamp, and I assume they can," said Orchid, "they will lay waste to everything. They'll use some kind of horrid Magic to get through the trees. We've all seen what Merak is capable of."

"There is something very strange about his Magic," said Tresado. "His and Rastaban's both. It's so powerful and . . ."

"Different," supplied Foxx. "Almost like it . . . doesn't belong, somehow. Think about that doodad that Rastaban shot me with and killed so many of the Queen's guards. It went through the soldiers' steel armor like it wasn't even there. Imagine what it could do to the trees!"

Orchid remembered well the fight with Rastaban in the tower of Queen Minore's Zantaryne Castle. She had watched that evil man slice through thick stone walls with ridiculous ease, turning them into rubble. The thought of that happening to this marvelous forest was too much to bear. Orchid's fists were clenching with rage.

"If the Treskans do that, it will be the most heinous crime ever!"

"Perfect night for a crime," Serena muttered. "Daeria isn't looking."

The strange fog that had emanated from the morass still hung in the air above the domes, irrespective of the breeze, which should have dispersed it. Occasionally, an appendage would reach out and test the integrity of the shells, but could never find a chink in their armor. The shells briefly flickered green when touched, as though they were laughing at the attempts.

Group Six still sat in their treetop shell boats, watching the army go about its business only a league away. The big barges containing the folded-up siege ladders were the center of much activity. Soldiers swarmed over the machines, performing some kind of maintenance on them.

Foxx had managed to talk Serena out of her looker for a few minutes while she snacked on pine nuts the size of her thumb.

"From what I can tell, it looks like they're preparing for a dawn attack," he said grimly. "That's typical Treskan tactics."

"It's everybody's tactics," said Serena.

Trianna had said little all night. Her big doe eyes were moist with as yet-unshed tears. A small whimper escaped her lips.

"Trianna, are you all right?" asked Orchid gently.

"I must sleep!" The tree woman suddenly jumped out of the shell boat and nimbly disappeared into the darkness.

"Whoa!" shouted Foxx. "Did she just . . .?"

"She didn't fall," said Orchid. "I think she is headed for her flower bed."

"She didn't seem sleepy to me," remarked Serena. "More like scared shitless."

"Trianna reflects the mood of the Glades," said Orchid, clutching her staff. She looked out at the deadly army on their doorstep. "Right now," She paused and closed her eyes, "they're still not talking, but I do know that the trees are scared, and so am I."

"They'll start their invasion at first light," said Serena. She was running battle plans through her head, but not coming up with a scenario that didn't involve everyone dying. "As I see it, we only have two choices."

“Fight or flight?” asked Tresado.

“Exactly.” Serena’s lapis eyes hardened. “I think you know which option I’ll choose, but the rest of you need to get the hell out of here.”

“I’ve got no place to go,” said Orchid.

“Me either,” replied Tresado and Foxx in perfect harmony.

“It’ll be a fight those Treskans won’t forget.” Tresado cracked his knuckles.

Orchid beamed with pride at the loyalty of her friends. “We can’t let the army get to the trees. Somehow we need to take the fight to them.”

A thought occurred to Orchid, but it didn’t belong to her. It was actually more like a tickle in the back of her skull. Something made her reach for Dementus’s journal. She opened it to the last blank page. It just sat there, looking like parchment. Now that Orchid semi-knew what to look for, her mind reached into the pages.

“Octavia, are you there?” Orchid asked aloud. The tickle in her mind itched again and the book responded.

Always

“Do you know what is happening?”

Treskans

The lettering that appeared was big and bold with a fierceness to the handwriting.

“What should we do?” Orchid queried.

Nothing

Orchid suddenly became aware of an intensifying of the floral minds around her.

“What is happening?”

What must

The air felt heavy. Foxx and Tresado both detected a great deal of Worldly Magic being gathered, but that not being their field, they didn't quite understand it. Orchid, however, knew exactly what was going on. Energy from all forms of life within the Glades was being gathered and channeled into the book in Orchid's hands. Everything contributed, however minutely, from the tiniest insect to the massive trees themselves. She felt and experienced every beat of the process. The book began to vibrate with a deep, almost inaudible hum. Orchid knew. The Glades were as one.

"NO! You cannot ask Precious One to do that!"

Group Six turned at the sound and beheld Trianna. Her usual gentle countenance had been transformed into a steely-eyed agent of vengeance. Bioenergy radiated from her slight form. She did not stand on a branch or even a shell boat, but rather hovered before them among the upper branches, an illuminated vision of power and awe.

"We are not asking anyone to do anything," said Serena, shielding her eyes against Trianna's radiance.

"She is talking to the trees," said Orchid quietly. "They are the ones asking."

"Please, I am begging you! Do not do this!" Trianna sobbed. Her tiny hands reached out and gently took Dementus's journal out of Orchid's hands and clutched it to her chest. The forest woman slowly lifted above the treetops and floated off in the direction of the encamped army, sobbing all the way.

Behind their backs, Sensang was heralding Her appearance with a faint lightening over the Glades. This morning's featured color scheme was a widening stampede of dark purple pursued by a narrow band of orange, intent on capture.

Serena put her looker to her eye again and followed Trianna's progress. To the others, she was a tiny glowing dot against the still-dark sky. The dot was heading directly for the cleft in the dunes where the deadly Noxus River had carved its course, fed by the Glades' negative discharge into the morass.

The activity in the domes increased. Troops were falling in, hover fields appeared under the barges, and whistles sounded. The lead barge, equipped with a Guardian, began slowly moving forward. The green shell it generated moved with it. Serena lowered her looker and turned to her friends.

"It's begun."

For just a beat, a tiny flash of light appeared above the river. A couple of beats later, a dull boom sounded in the Glades. The leaves and branches vibrated in response. A moment later, no one needed a looker to see the result. A directed burst of concussive energy radiated out from both sides of the river. The sandy ridge rippled as the pressure wave expanded through it. A huge crack appeared at the top of the ridge as the overhang separated from the dune. The massive landslide fled down the dune, immediately covering the shells with a zillion stone of sandy debris, trapping barges, horses, and soldiers beneath. A minute after the initial flash, nothing remained of the Treskan army but several low hills of sand and rock, no different from the rest of the landscape.

Group Six looked on in horror, stupefied by the enormity of what just happened. They had been watching what they thought would be the destruction of the Glades and everything in it. Now as the dust settled, the rays of early morning Senshine blessed the land with a promise of another beautiful day.

Meanwhile, back in Tresk

Imperator Merak exited his private sanctum with a scowl on his face. He gave one more look back at a certain console where a large clumping of green lights had suddenly gone dark. In his fury, he flung the porcelain goblet he had been drinking from back into the chamber. It passed through the ephemeral glowing sphere that dominated the center of the room before shattering on the offending console. Everything had gone wrong for him the last couple of weeks. Even the pleasure of slamming the door was denied him by the mechanism designed to close it smoothly and silently.

"A whole legion! All that equipment and horses! Over nine thousand troops! NINE THOUSAND PARAKI TROOPS! And no word of that KABINT Group Six!"

Merak stomped his feet, tore at his robes, and spat out words that no Lurran had ever heard before, let alone could understand. He made for the door with the intent of tearing a new one on the first poor soul he encountered. His hand stopped just shy of the handle. He was still furious, but his intelligence won out.

"Later," he mumbled to himself, trying to calm down. "Damage control now, Imperial wrath later."

Straightening his robes, and grabbing a bowlful of boiled booger bird eggs and a salt shaker, Merak, Imperator of the Treskan Imperium, re-entered his forbidden chamber.

Today – The Glades

It had been two days since the Treskan 12th Legion disappeared beneath the giant avalanche. The energy of the Glades, concentrated and transferred into Dementus's journal, allowed Octavia to render a terrible act of judgment and vengeance against Merak at the cost of what remaining life she had. Presumably, the Treskans under the still-operating shells were alive and functioning, but there was no outward sign of activity at all. A constant watch was maintained upon the dome-shaped hills of sand in the fear that some powerful spell or weapon would break them free. No such threat emerged, however. Orchid ferried her friends up and down in the shell boats with the helpful aid of the trees. She was the only one who could talk them into doing it. To Serena, Foxx, and Tresado, they were still just trees.

Trianna had returned to the Glades immediately after her mission to drop the book into the river canyon. She was gaunt and drained of the gathered energy that had allowed her to levitate across the morass. In her grief, she retreated deep into the forest to mourn.

The dawn of the third day found Foxx taking his turn at the treetop observation post. He passed the time with a little One-Handed Solitaire while he watched until suddenly two other shell boats joined him, carrying Serena and Tresado in one and Orchid and Trianna in the other.

"What's the deal?" he asked his friends. "I'm not due for relief for another hour."

"The trees asked us up here. We're not sure why just yet," replied Orchid.

"Hello, Trianna," said Foxx in a soothing voice. "Are you feeling better?"

There was no response from the tree woman. She clutched the edges of a big soft leaf that she had draped over her shoulders and sat up straight in the shell boat.

"The Green Menace has chosen."

Group Six looked out across the morass and saw no change in the altered landscape.

"If they were able to escape, I'd think they would have done it by now," said Foxx.

"I can't imagine what's going on under those domes," said Tresado. "They must be close to panicking with no way out."

"They're good soldiers. They won't panic," said Serena.

"If nothing else, they have to be running out of air," said Orchid. "Thousands of horses and soldiers who all want to breathe."

At that moment the landscape across the swamp once more changed dramatically. The sand and rock covering the shells suddenly dropped by several reaches. The dull sound rolled across the swamp like a massive death rattle.

"They've shut down the Guardian shells!" cried Orchid.

"Taking the coward's way out," said Tresado.

"No," offered Foxx. "The Treskan way."

CHAPTER 26

Drops of rain, grains of sand,
Zephyrs of travel,
Wing and paw,
The Lurra's Library sups well . . .

- Trianna of Sylvas, Poetess to the Glades

Today – The Glades

"Goodbye, Trianna. I shall miss you and the Glades."

Orchid and the tree woman clinched in a hug that lasted several beats. Each set of green eyes locked on the other.

"The Glades will always welcome you, Orchid the Traveler," Trianna said. "Would that I could convince you to stay."

"The road beckons, Trianna," said Orchid. A crazy thought struck her. "I don't suppose I could convince you to come with us."

"Lurra's pulse is known to the trees, gathered from every breeze, every drop of rainwater; every animal and plant that thinks and feels tells their own tale. Many thousands of rings of knowledge reside in the Glades. All I need know is here.

You must learn all yourself, and to learn of yourself, to grow, to heal. Perhaps traveling with these nobelongs will help." Trianna said that last bit with a joking smile.

"You're right, of course." The sound of arguing reached Orchid's ears, which made her smile. "Magic is everywhere here, Trianna, in the trees, the soil, and especially the water. I don't just mean the way Magic already is everywhere, it's . . . it's the most natural and pure Magic I've ever felt. All the plants, the animals, and people, they all truly belong here. You belong here, Trianna. I am not yet pure enough for this place. Perhaps . . ."

"Someday," Trianna answered for her.

"Someday," repeated Orchid.

The two tree women shared a final hug. Orchid picked up her staff and joined the rest of Group Six, who were busy loading their supplies onto two shell boats. They had spent all of yesterday in the hamlet of Shurzy. The friendly inhabitants were only too happy to prepare packets of road food for these strange foreigners, although they were still shy among the non-tree people. The rations consisted of carefully prepared meat and fruit concentrates baked together with Sustenade and pressed into wafers. They would have everything they needed for a long journey.

At Orchid's request, the ever-helpful trees picked up the two giant nutshells and whisked Group Six away through the forest. Orchid had seen much of this, but the incredible animal and plant life was mostly new to Foxx, Tresado, and Serena. A brilliantly-colored butterfly with a full-reach wingspan gracefully glided out of their way. There were mammals of every sort that lived exclusively in the trees, never touching the ground their entire lives. Some were as tiny as a thumbnail, while perfectly-adapted canines the size of ponies loped through the middle terraces in packs of dozens. A swarm of crabblers, such as they had seen in the first glade, were busy dismantling the remains of a huge tree that had been attacked by fire mites. Orchid explained how the scrap would be salvaged for any useful biologic material and the rest relegated to the morass that surrounded the Glades.

An escort of four Trimmies accompanied them, including White Stripe, the one that hit Serena with the melon. Finally, they arrived at the far southeastern border of the Glades. The trees lifted them up and over the barrier wall and set them down as gently as always, and Group Six piled out. The countryside beyond was rocky and arid, but not like the Zinji Desert had been. There were scrub brush and normal-sized trees beyond. Far off in the distance they could actually see tall mountains with snow-covered caps.

"I'm gonna miss this place," said Orchid, "but I'm ready to get back to my baby-sitting job again."

"Baby-sitting?" asked a puzzled Tresado, walking right into her trap. "Since when do you do that?" A look down her nose and a lift of her eyebrow gave everyone their answer. "Okay, I get it. Very funny." He glanced over at the Trimmies, who were preparing to build a floating log bridge for them to get across the morass. "Tell your furry friends to never mind. I can levitate us across."

Orchid laughed and said her goodbyes to the Trimmies. She received big, hairy hugs all around. Tresado was preparing his levitation spell when Serena spoke up.

"Wait just a beat, there's something I gotta do."

Serena calmly walked over to White Stripe and put out her right hand.

"So long, beetle breath. No hard feelings?"

The Trimmie looked her in the eye for a beat, then extended his prehensile tail to Serena. She shook his member and rejoined Group Six. As soon as the monkey's back was turned, Serena reached into her backpack for an overripe rockfruit that she had been saving and nailed him in the back of the head. White Stripe turned, bared his fangs, and roared in anger. Serena kept her sword sheathed, extended her arms, and roared back with her Northlands Warrior battle cry. A beat passed . . . then two . . . then both Macai and Trimmie laughed uproariously.

"Ready now?" asked an amused Tresado, looking at his friends.

"Let's go," said all three simultaneously.

Tresado formed his invisible harnesses, lifted all four of them, and floated them across the black morass containing everything negative and harmful that the Glades had excreted. He set them down on the other side of the deadly moat. They turned to wave bye-bye to the Trimmies, but they had already taken to the trees and were back in the Glades. Soon Group Six picked up a well-used game trail and were on their way to whatever the gods had in store for them.

"Wow, what a forest!" opined Tresado as they walked along. "I don't understand how such a place came to be."

"I assume it originated from the Font geyser," said Orchid. She then told them all about her brief visit there and the Magical nature of the water. "It has amazing properties. The way it filters out anything harmful and sends the waste into the leach field. According to Trianna, that includes attitudes and emotions, whether animal or vegetable."

"Oh, I doubt that. I've never known a carrot with a bad attitude," scoffed Serena.

"She also implied that, because of the water, the trees have developed a collective consciousness of sorts, as well as a memory," said Orchid. "Supposedly, they pick up on signals and impressions from all over the world, many thousands of years' worth of events."

"Now that is an intriguing thought," said Foxx. "Imagine the knowledge that is stored in those trees. Conceivably, there could be 50,000 years of history just waiting for someone to tap into it. The possibilities are endless."

"And way too dangerous for a conman like you to get his greedy paws on," stated Serena.

"That's about the wisest thing I've ever heard you say," joked Orchid, although she agreed totally with the statement. "That's probably what the Treskans were after, the memories, the water, the resources, all of it. If that kind of knowledge fell into Merak's hands, just imagine the trouble he could cause. The trees are very defensive when it comes to intruders and deal with them. In fact, they even seem to have some kind of precognitive abilities. I think the Glades knew about the Treskans and their plans. Now this is a stretch, but I think they also knew about Octavia coming to save them. Trianna first thought that I was their savior, but she just misinterpreted what the Glades were telling her."

This was far too out there for Serena. "Yeah? Then if the trees are so smart and know everything, how come they didn't just mulch us all when we arrived? Why would Trianna send the monkeys to bring us in and fix us up if the trees thought we were trouble?"

"Because if they had, there would've been a different outcome," offered Foxx. "Dementus's journal would have been lost and the Treskans wouldn't have been destroyed. Maybe they saw that."

Tresado glanced back over his shoulder, sadly thinking about Feelia. "Well, whatever the outcome, at least we're away from the Treskan Imperium."

"This is horrifying to think of," said Foxx, "but it could be said that, because of us, an entire Treskan legion was wiped out."

"Yeah, but on the other hand," beamed Orchid, "because of us that forest was saved from destruction! Not bad for a bunch of nobelongs."

"Nobo-what?" asked Serena.

"Forget it, it's not important," said Orchid. "Tresado's right. We're free and I will drink to that!" She grabbed the canteen off her belt and raised it. "To Group Six!"

"I'm afraid all we have to toast with is Font water," said Serena.

Orchid's eyes went wide for a beat, but she turned it into a smile. "Oh . . . well, that's okay."

Clink, clink, clink, clink.

"That's another country we can't go back to," said Foxx. "We seem to use up places at an alarming rate. We're running out of destinations."

"Twigs," said Orchid. "Lurra's plenty big enough. There are countries enough and Magic enough for everyone."

EPILOGUE

207,809 years from today

The scrounger picked his way among the rocks and bushes, looking for anything edible. A lizard, a bird, a withered bush, anything. Even water was hard to come by. Life existed in these high mountains, but was scarce. The scrounger had no name that he could remember. He thought it might be something like Kern or Dern, but there is no need for a name when there is no one else to call him anything. He had not seen another of his kind since his father died long ago. He did not remember his mother or any Macai other than his father. He had never seen a female.

The lowlands were fertile, but had grown far too dangerous, as evidenced by the pursuers that had followed him up from the fields. He thought that he had lost them, but when he looked back down toward the valley, he saw a group of mounted riders on his trail. The search for food would have to wait. The riders were coming fast. His only escape was up, to the ledge far above him. If he could only reach that, the riders would be forced to take the long way up. It was a difficult climb, but he had no choice if he wanted to live. He struggled up the rugged cliffside, nearly losing his footing several times, but at last managed to pull himself up and over the jutting ledge.

He had done it! Coming up this way gained him some distance from his pursuers. He looked about at the rough terrain. Great slabs of rock jutted out of the ground at all angles, creating natural caves and deep crevasses. There were plenty of places to hide, if only they didn't sniff him out.

Kern was considering which hiding place was best when he was distracted by a faint sound. It was a kind of intermittent whistling barely even discernible. Out of habit, Kern looked back to make sure his pursuers hadn't caught up with him yet. His eyes saw movement in the sky just for a moment; then it was gone. There it was again! Several objects fell from the sky and disappeared into the ground. The things had a flickering, unreal quality to them. Sometimes they disappeared from the sky before they reached the ground. The whistling stopped.

Now Kern could hear yelling, vague and fluctuating. Suddenly, Kern beheld something his eyes had never seen. Many, many creatures that looked like his father and himself were rushing toward him, yelling wildly. Their appearance flickered and faded. Another sound from all around him! More creatures were approaching from above him on all sides. They were as ants in their nest.

The sheer numbers panicked Kern and he started to run. The hordes were approaching rapidly. As he maneuvered around a large boulder, Kern came suddenly upon one of the creatures directly in front of him. It appeared like himself, but the being had strange, cone-shaped ears and its chin came to a sharp point. The thing was lying on the ground, grasping its head in pain. Another creature flickered into existence and crawled over toward the first one, but disappeared again, leaving only the one on the ground. The thing turned its head and seemed to look right at Kern. The tortured look on its face unnerved the man and he stumbled backward, catching the heel of his bare foot on a sharp rock. The scrounger tumbled into a crevasse and landed hard, shattering the vertebrae in his neck, paralyzing him instantly. The strange creature, who still called itself Onderast, continued for a few more beats, until finally, mercifully, it vanished for all of eternity, with a strange smile of relief on its face.

Kern lay on his back, unable to move, his breath coming harder and harder. A shadow passed over his face. The last thing his eyes beheld was the silhouettes of two large faces peering down on him from the top of the crevasse. Primal fear gripped the man, but his lungs could no longer draw a breath to scream. Kern, the last Macai, died in silence.

His two pursuers stood up and moved away from the dangerous crevasse. They leaned back onto their powerful tails to relax after their rigorous chase. The taller of the two pulled a gourd from the small pack wrapped around his loins, popped the lid, and took a swig.

"Well, Cheenie, we finally got rid of that pest, whatever it was," said Orpen, the male.

"It's too bad the stupid thing managed to kill itself," replied the female. "I was hoping for a shot at it." Cheenie folded up her powerful slingshot and stowed it away in her own pack.

"It won't be tearing up the harvest anymore. That's the important thing." Orpen glanced up at the sun. "Let's get back to the others. We can still make it home before dark."

The two Trimmans quickly descended the cliff face that their prey had climbed, their agile limbs unerringly grasping every hand, foot, and tailhold.

Their four companions waited below, holding their mounts, a pair of thoroughbred hurdlebirds of impressive lineage. Orpen and Cheenie leapt up onto the saddles.

One of the others, a Trimman named Klupee, said something, but Cheenie didn't understand.

"What did she say?"

"She wants to know if you got the bastard," replied Bolu, who translated. Klupee was from Endon, where they spoke a different language.

"He got himself," answered Orpen. "Fell into a hole."

The troop laughed raucously at that and turned back toward town. This had been a fun day's outing, but it was time to head home again. The kids needed supper and a good night's sleep, so as to be fresh for school in the morning.

* * *

And thus, after a quarter of a million years, a mere grain of the hourglass of Her life, planet Lurra ended Her flirtation with Eryndi, with Macai, and with Magic. It was time to write a new chapter.

TRESKAN GODS TO SWEAR BY:

Dyhendra – Great creation bird who laid the egg of Lurra.

Quiseron – God of Water.

Shalaki – God of Soil and Agriculture.

Dajari – Goddess of the Forest.

Vistaria – Goddess of Travel.

Heitus – God of Mountains.

Veratu – Goddess of Food.

Jeruma – Goddess of the Dead. She is not the devil, but rather a caretaker of those who've passed.

Dramin and Kermin – Goddess and God of Love – a mated couple who oversee procreation and love in all its forms. People pray in their temple to find love, become pregnant, etc. In past times, love for a Macai was considered in bad taste, if not taboo. A common saying concerning this is, "Dramin and Kermin can't make a sandwich."

Krinol – God of Waste and Lost Causes.

Parakline – God of Knowledge.

Comatus – God of Wine.

Ayendea – Goddess of Ocean.

Rookus – God of Corruption and Vice.

LEXICON

ABAKAAR ('ă-bə-kär)
A country in central Aris.

ABSOLUTE MAGIC
A powerful form of magic mostly practiced by Macai. Alters and recombines, controls and directs.

AMORAN SEA ('ă-mor-ən)
A mostly landlocked sea in northwestern Aris.

ARIS
Second largest, but most heavily populated continent of Lurra.

BEAT
An indefinite span of time approximately equal to a single heartbeat.

BERGALO
A large, buffalo-like creature.

BOINGBALL
Eryndi sport.

BREEOS
A country of Aris, recently conquered by the Treskan Imperium.

CLEE-AT

A horrid, bipedal rat-like predator that lived in ancient times.

COLOSSUS TREE

An enormous conifer of northern climes.

CONVEYOR

A Magical and mechanical train in the Treskan Imperium

CRODAN

War god of the Northlands.

CRODAN'S KEEP

The afterlife where valiant Northlanders aspire to go.

CRYSTAL PALACE

A fabulous gambling casino/resort in the crater lake of Mount Boronay.

DAERIA – (dä-'ēr-ē-ə)

Queen of the Northlanders' gods. Wife to Crodan.

DAURIC

A common gold coin used throughout central Aris.

DIRKFISH

A predator of the Serin Sea. It is highly dangerous, but also highly valued for its meat and eggs.

DIRKOVA

The eggs of a dirkfish, considered an expensive delicacy.

DRAGON

A huge, reptilian flying predator.

ERIM RIVER

A swift-flowing river running through the City of Tresk.

ERNIE

A racial epithet for Eryndi.

ERYNDI (ə-'rĭn-dē)

Race of people on Lurra.

FINGER

A unit of measurement equal to 1/100th of a reach. It is approximately the width of a man's finger (about ¾ inch.)

FIRE WOLF

A large, canine predator that hunts in packs.

FLICKEN

A common, domesticated food bird.

FONT

A geyser of hot, mineral water, considered to be the most sacred place in the Glades.

FOUR-CARD BLITZKRIEG

A popular card game.

GENDRIN

A common copper coin.

GLADES

A Magical, forested area known to the Treskans as Sylvas.

GRANNUGH

A town on the western coast of The Northlands. Birthplace of Serena.

GRILK

A hippo-sized wild mountain sheep inhabiting northern climes.

HAUNTED MOUNTAINS
A rugged area of Aris, part of the Perlan frontier.

HEROIC HARE
A popular children's story character.

HOBO CLAM
A small shellfish found in ocean shallows, considered a delicacy.

HROLVAD THE BERSERKER
('rōl-väd) A legendary hero and founder of Northlands culture.

HURDLEBIRD
A large, flightless bird known for its ground speed.

JAMBA
A plant-based narcotic used, among other things, as an aid to Magical concentration.

LEAGUE
A unit of measurement equal to 1000 reaches (about 6000 feet.)

LUMBA
A huge, slow-moving herbivore inhabiting temperate forests.

LURRA ('lə-rə)
Name of the world.

MACAI (mä-'kī)
Race of people on Lurra.

MAKARA ('mä-kə-rä)
A tart citrus fruit.

MAGIC

A form of metaphysical energy that permeates Lurra.

MELOSIAN ACADEMY OF WORLDLY ARTS

Orchid's alma mater.

MEMBRANE

A poisonous marsh that surrounds the Glades.

MERAK (mə-'răk)

Imperator of the Treskan Imperium.

MINORE ('mĭn-or-ē)

Queen of Abakaar.

MONKEYWOOD

A strong, light wood that takes well to Magical manipulation.

MOUNT BORONAY

An inland extinct volcano, location of the Crystal Palace.

NORTHLANDS

A cold, mountainous country on the northwestern tip of Aris, inhabited by tribes of fierce Macai warriors.

NOXUS RIVER

A poisonous and corrosive river running into the Serin Sea.

NYHA ('nī-yə)

Large moon in the skies over Lurra; also known as The Orb.

OSTICA ('ä̩s-tĭk-ə)

A large port city on the Talus River. Capital of Jasperia.

PALEEN ('pā-lēn)

A common silver coin worth ten copper gendrins.

PARROTOID

Species of colorful bird in the Glades.

PRAKIN'S PASS

A legendary passage through the Haunted Mountains.

REACH

A unit of measurement equal to about six feet (an average man's fingertip to fingertip span.)

RIPPER WHALE

A large, ferocious aquatic mammal of the northern seas.

ROCKFRUIT

A hardy fruit that flourishes in all mineral-rich climes.

SAKOLA BERRIES

An intoxicating fruit.

SCARLET PANTHER

A large feline predator.

SENSANG

The Sun, also called Sen.

SERIN SEA

A large, freshwater sea in the Treskan Imperium.

SHURZY

A hamlet in the Glades.

SLEEPER BUSH

Actually a creeping vine, whose thorns are coated with a powerful anesthetic. The vines slowly entwine the sedated victim, who is then broken down into plant food.

STADIUM
A huge sports arena in Tresk.

STINK RAT
An odiferous mammal with a fowl-smelling scent gland weapon.

STONE
A unit of weight equaling approximately eleven pounds.

SURRANA
Port city on the Serin Sea.

TORMAC
A common gold coin worth twenty silver paleens.

TRESKAN IMPERIUM
A large empire of western Aris consisting of dozens of conquered lands. It has been ruled by Imperator Merak for the last hundred years.

TRIMMIE
A large, tree-dwelling primate.

VORENNIUM
A meteoritic substance capable of producing great power.

WITCHHEART CRATER
A huge impact crater near Abakaar. It is surrounded by a dangerous zone of chaotic Magic and bizarre monsters.

WORLDLY MAGIC
A nature-based, conservative form of Magic mostly practiced by Eryndi.

YESSUA
An ancient mountain kingdom.

ZINJI DESERT

A lifeless desert along the Noxus River.

THE LURRAN YEAR

10 MONTHS OF 40 DAYS EACH

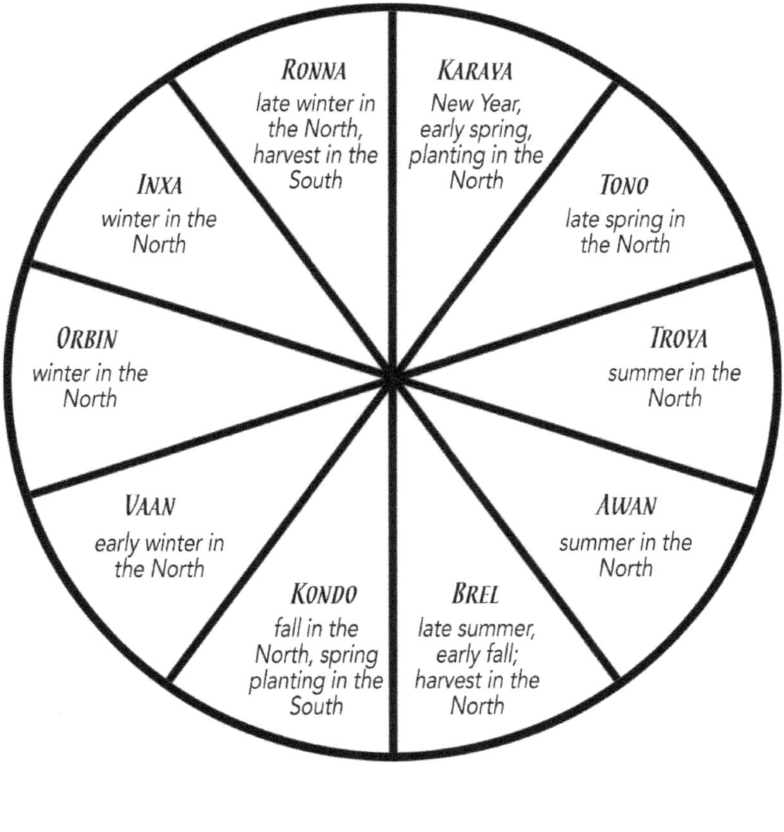
Karaya
New Year, early spring, planting in the North
Tono
late spring in the North
Troya
summer in the North
Awan
summer in the North
Brel
late summer, early fall; harvest in the North
Kondo
fall in the North, spring planting in the South
Vaan
early winter in the North
Orbin
winter in the North
Inxa
winter in the North
Ronna
late winter in the North, harvest in the South

Each month consists of five 8-day weeks. Days 4 and 8 of each week, called Honor Days, are treated like weekends; everyone honors who or what they want, such as a god or ancestors or Magic itself. The numbering of days is the same in each month (i.e., Dindays are always the 1st, 9th, 17th, 25th, and 33rd). Each day is 20 hours long.

Dinday	Gleeday	Teerday	Midweek Honor	Malday	Kevoday	Vinday	Weekend Honor
1	2	3	4	5	6	7	8
9	10	11	12	13	14	15	16
17	18	19	20	21	22	23	24
25	26	27	28	29	30	31	32
33	34	35	36	37	38	39	40

In Group Six and the Imperium, "today" is the year 21876.

Dates are expressed as "month day-year (last 2 digits)" – so Karaya 6-76 is the sixth day of Karaya in 21876.

ACKNOWLEDGMENTS

Many thanks to Giules for their talented artwork. The painting of Lurra/Nyah graces our bedroom wall. Also to my beloved Wyoming for inspiring the lands of Lurra, to Suz, my publisher, whose helpful and supportive ways earned her a namesake in this book; and, ever and always, to the Rigamaroller!

ABOUT THE AUTHOR

Ron Richard spent much of his life painting double yellow lines for the City of Casper. He is a Wyoming native, stage actor, woodworker, cat owner, and has written several plays and readers' theatre scripts designed for a planetarium setting. He also portrayed the bad guy in Crime Stoppers commercials.

Milton Keynes UK
Ingram Content Group UK Ltd.
UKHW011823140624
444031UK00015B/182/J

9 781945 146565